VIVA ANAYA

D0059159

VIVA *BLESS ME, ULTIMA*

VIVA *ALBURQUERQUE*

THE ANAYA READER

RUDOLFO ANAYA

WARNER BOOKS

A Time Warner Company

Warner Books, Inc., 1271 Avenue of the Americas, New York, NY 10020

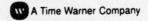 A Time Warner Company

Printed in the United States of America
First Printing: April 1995
10 9 8 7 6 5 4 3 2 1

Library of Congress Cataloging-in-Publication Data

Anaya, Rudolfo A.
    The Anaya reader / Rudolfo Anaya.
        p.   cm.
    ISBN 0-446-67077-4 (trade paper)
    1. Mexican Americans—Social life and customs—Fiction.
2. Mexican Americans—Civilization.   I. Title.
PS3551.N27A6   1995
813'.54—dc20   94-42735
                                                                                        CIP

Cover design by Diane Lugar
Cover illustration by Bernadette Vigil
Book design by Giorgetta Bell McRee

This book is dedicated to Patricia,
my constant companion and confidante
during the long years of birthing these collected pieces,
and to a new generation of readers.

Acknowledgments

My short stories and essays have been reprinted in many magazines, papers, textbooks, and anthologies. Sometimes I lose track of the homes these *children* have found. What I attempt to do here is to acknowledge, as far as I am able, the place of first publication. Some of my essays have their genesis as lectures, which I later refine into essays.

Short Stories

"B. Traven Is Alive and Well in Cuernavaca," *Escolios*, Volume IV, Numbers 1–2, Mayo–Nov., 1979, pp. 1–12. (Chicano Studies, California State, Los Angeles).

"The Apple Orchard," *Hispanics in the United States: An Anthology of Creative Literature*, Eds. Gary D. Keller and Francisco Jimenez, Bilingual Review Press, Ypsalanti, 1980.

"The Silence of the Llano," *The Silence of the Llano*, short story collection, Tonatiuh-Quinto Sol, Berkeley, 1982.

"The Gift," *2Plus2, A Collection of International Writing,* Ed. James Gill, Mylabris Press, Lausanne, Switzerland, 1986, p. 38.

"In Search of Epifano," *Voces: An Anthology of Nuevo Mexicano Writers,* Ed. Rudolfo Anaya. University of New Mexico Press, Alburquerque, 1987.

"Children of the Desert" was published as "Figli del Deserto" in *L'umana Avventura,* Primavera-Estate '89, Editoriale Jaca Book, Milano, Italy. In this country in *The Seattle Review,* Kathleen Alcala, guest editor. Vol. XII, No. 1, Spring/Summer 1990.

"The Man Who Found a Pistol," *Mirrors Beneath the Earth,* Ed. Ray Gonzalez, Curbstone Press, Willimantic, CT, 1992.

"Devil Deer" first appeared in *arellano,* P.O. Box 96, Embudo, NM, 1992.

"Message From the Inca," *RSA Journal, Rivista di Studi Nord-Americani,* No. 4, October, 1994, Mario Materassi, Ed. Via San Gallo 10, 50129 Firenze, Italy. (The publisher is "Il Sedicesimo," Firenze, Italy.)

Essays

"Requiem for a Lowrider," a commencement address to the Albuquerque High School class of 1978. *La Confluencia: A Magazine for the Southwest,* Vol. 2, Numbers 2–3, October, 1978, Alburquerque, NM.

"The Magic of Words" originally appeared as "In Commemoration: One Million Volumes" in *A Million Stars: The Millionth Acquisition for the University of New Mexico General Library,* Ed. Connie Capers Thorson, UNM General Library, 1981. Reprinted in *The Magic of Words,* Ed. Paul Vassallo, University of New Mexico Press, 1982.

"A New Mexico Christmas," *Los Angeles Times*, 1982, reprinted in *New Mexico Magazine*, Volume 60, Number 12, December, 1982, Santa Fe, NM.

"An American Chicano in King Arthur's Court," a talk. Tucson, Arizona, October, 1984, the writers of the Purple Sage project series. *Old Southwest/New Southwest: Essays on a Region and Its Literature*, Ed. Judy Nolte Lensink, The Tucson Public Library, 1987.

"At a Crossroads," 1912–1986 statehood anniversary issue, *New Mexico Magazine*, October, 1986.

"Mythical Dimensions/Political Reality" appeared as "The Myth of Quetzalcóatl in a Contemporary Setting: Mythical Dimensions/Political Reality," *Western American Literature*, Vol. XXIII, No. 3, November, 1988.

"The New World Man," a lecture presented at the Third International Conference on Hispanic Cultures of the United States in Barcelona and at La Fundación Xavier de Salas in Trujíllo. Published in the *Before Columbus Review*, Fall/Winter, 1989, Volume 1, Numbers 2 and 3.

"Aztlán," published as "Aztlán: A Homeland Without Boundaries" in *Aztlán: Essays on the Chicano Homeland*, Eds. Rudolfo A. Anaya and Francisco Lomeli, El Norte Publications/Academia, 1989. Albuquerque, NM. Delivered as the Annual Research Lecture at the University of New Mexico, 1989.

"Take the Tortillas out of Your Poetry," *Censored Books: Critical Viewpoints*, Eds. Nicholas J. Karolides, Lee Burress, and John M. Kean. Scarecrow Press, May 1993, Metuchen, NJ.

"On the Education of Hispanic Children" appeared May 12, 1991, in the *Albuquerque Journal*, p. B3 on the Op-Ed page.

"The Censorship of Neglect," presented at the Secondary

Section of the National Council of Teachers of English annual convention in Seattle, Washington, November 23, 1991. The talk was titled "Free to Learn, Free to Teach." Copyright 1992 by the National Council of Teachers of English. Reprinted with permission. *English Journal*, Vol. 81, No. 5, September, 1992.

"La Llorona, El Kookoóee, and Sexuality," *Bilingual Review/Revista Bilingue*, Vol. XVII, Number 1, January–April, 1992, Bilingual Review Press, Tempe, AZ.

"Bendíceme, América," *Bendíceme, América: Latino Writers of the United States*, Editors Harold Augenbraum, Terry Quinn and Ilan Stavans, a publication of The Mercantile Library of New York, 1993.

Plays and Poems

Who Killed Don José? appears in *New Mexico Plays*, David Richard Jones, Ed. University of New Mexico Press, 1989, Alburquerque, NM.

The "Billy the Kid Meets Lew Wallace" scene was published in the *Before Columbus Review*, *A Quarterly Review of Multicultural Literature*, Spring/Summer, 1993, Vol. 4, Number 1, p. 16. (Before Columbus Foundation, Oakland, CA.)

"Walt Whitman Strides the Llano of New Mexico" has been previously published in *Aloud*, an anthology edited by Miguel Algarin and Bob Holman, Henry Holt, 1994.

Contents

ESSAYS

PLAYS AND POEMS

Foreword

After the arrival of Europeans in the New World, the first literature written in North America, in what would later become the United States, was written in Spanish—before the *Mayflower* (1620) and before Jamestown (1607). In presenting us with *The Anaya Reader*, written by a descendent of those Hispanos, Warner Books has, therefore, created a historic presentation. Not only is it an important acknowledgment of and an awakening to the belated inclusiveness and expansion of the base of our North American literature, but it is also the first collection of writings by a major publishing company wholly focused on a single Chicano writer.

This remarkable collection of mixed genre writing—novel, short story, essay, drama and poem—by premier novelist Rudolfo A. Anaya, comes to us from his home state of New Mexico, where the earliest Spanish/Mestizo settlements in the Southwest were founded by the expedition of Juan de Oñate in 1598.

Anaya is truly *un hijo del pueblo*, a son of New Mexico, where he still lives with his wife Patricia. He was born in

the village of Pasturas, which is south of the small town
of Santa Rosa, where the family moved to when he was a
small boy. Later they moved to Albuquerque. In his sopho-
more year of high school he sustained a serious spinal injury
in a swimming accident. Out of the pain and powerful
spirit of those places and critical times, he would forge
some of the themes and questions of his writing. In time,
he would earn Masters degrees in both literature and coun-
seling, and go on to teach in high school and at the University of New Mexico, where he is now Professor Emeritus.
However, it was in 1971, when his novel *Bless Me, Ultima*
was awarded the Premio Quinto Sol national Chicano literary award, that his brilliance as a writer was publicly revealed.

You will find Anaya to be modest, a man of the people.
He has a warm, ready smile, and he listens. He is a writer's
writer, a teacher's teacher, a mentor and an advocate. He
sits on many prestigious editorial boards, and continues
to edit collections and to encourage new writers. On the
national scene, he advocates for liberation through writing
before such influential groups as the National Endowment
for the Arts and others.

The writing, spirit, and vision of Anaya have earned him
international recognition as a writer. He is acknowledged
as the *padrino*, the godfather, of the rapidly developing
canon of Chicano letters. He is a major voice in exploring
the meeting of cultures in the New World persons of Chicanos and Chicanas, and in our evolving self-definition
through our writings. Anaya is, moreover, a leading figure
in the field of Latino letters in this country. *The Anaya
Reader* shows us why.

"We are split by ethnic boundaries," he says, "we are a
border people, half in love with Mexico and half suspicious,
half in love with the United States and half wondering if
we belong." We have been rejected by our Spanish father,
forgotten by our Indian mother, and feel unwanted by our
American stepmother who passes English-only laws, lights

up the border, and proposes laws denying education and health care principally to the children of our Mexican people who come here seeking work.

Anaya urges us to say who we are. "We must tell who we are and define ourselves as a people, define our humanity," he urges again and again; "otherwise, someone else will do it and get it all wrong." Our writing must be inspired by the spirit of the place and people we call our home, our *tierra*.

As a writer, he has a keen sense of the great importance of the *spiritus loci*, the spirit of the place of the writer. This is central to Anaya's understanding of the power of the storyteller and the significance of the writer. Writers do not create the physical and human spirit of a place; that spirit, rather, must inspire and guide them. Whether it be the spirit of one of Walker Percy's Southern towns or the spirit of Anaya's own tiny village of Pasturas in the New Mexican *llanos*—the plains of *Bless Me, Ultima*—the writer must capture it and tell us about the singular spirit of that place, and explore as deeply as possible the tragedy and glory of the people there. The fire of a writer's vision will reveal to us and to the world something of the secrets of our hearts. Anaya reminds us that, despite the violence of nature and of people, "there are original archetypes of order and harmony."

The remarks of Luis Leal, the founder of Chicano literary criticism, about the future of Chicano literature, gives us the key to the abiding depth of Anaya's work. "The Chicano has to create a new synthesis out of history, tradition, and his everyday confrontation with the ever-changing culture in which he lives. But he cannot do so unless he creates mythical images." And that is what Anaya has been doing from the beginning. At the heart of his writing, we find his intriguing vision of the meeting of our everyday ritual world with the eternal. Literature and myth, he tells us, have to do with people remembering themselves, telling who they are so that they will not be forgotten, and about the values that will always matter to all people. Through his fascination with the power of the earth, tradition, and archetype, Anaya tells us about these things that matter. But, if he cherishes the old ways, he also concerns himself with the future, and with contemporary issues.

As we have noted, this country is still treating many of its immigrant groups as stepchildren. There are academics, publishers, and those who see multiculturalism as a threat. We must not allow ourselves to be censored, Anaya says in his essay "Take the Tortillas out of Your Poetry," nor must we censor ourselves in order to be accepted. "If we leave out our tortillas," he says, "we take the language, history, cultural values and themes out of our literature—the very culture we're portraying will die." He also addresses his concern with the continuing racism and politics of exclusion of this country, in his powerful quincentennial essay "Bendíceme, América." To the point, he cites from Eduardo Galeano's *The Book of Embraces*: "Until lions have their own historians, histories of the hunt will glorify the hunter."

Several of his other essays, including "An American Chicano in King Arthur's Court," address teachers about these matters. Teachers must cultivate a respectful awareness of the cultural reality and heritage of all of their students. Nurturing students on the mythology of King Arthur's Court alone can be a limiting and destructive experience for student and teacher alike. Anaya's cameo "A New Mexico Christmas," echoing Dylan Thomas's "A Christmas in Wales," is an example of how we all win by opening our hearts to one another's ways.

But it is in his novels and short fiction that we find the classic Anaya. The opening selections of *The Anaya Reader* are from *Bless Me, Ultima*. They reveal a writer who challenges, and a writer who perpetually hopes—a refreshing respite from the despair of postmodernism. Despite the demons of destruction within us, Anaya insists that the human spirit and truth and life will endure.

Ultima is a richly textured novel of awakening, written in the early '60s. Anaya was an original, a part of our country's ferment in a way that few doctrinaire insiders understood, but to which the world has responded. At that time—he notes in his essay "Mythical Dimensions/Political Reality"—he was "still tied to the people and the earth of the Pecos River Valley, the small town of Santa Rosa, [and] the villages of Puerto de Luna and Pastura." He tells us more about the physical and moral environment in which *Ultima* was written in his intriguing essay "La Llorona, El Kookoóee, and Sexuality."

The novel unfolds at the end of World War II, with the world on the cusp of change. The boy, Antonio Márez, finds himself in the beauty and austerity of a traditional New Mexican setting, colored by Native American and Catholic traditions. Through his confrontations with death and his relationship with Ultima, a *curandera*, a healer with the power of the ancestors, he comes to question his traditional beliefs. Like Job, he questions even God. In questioning, he arrives at a moment when he is ready to risk the search for alternatives. He is poised to exercise his freedom. He may get lost in the process of seeking answers, even from his mediator and guide, who at the end empowers him with her ultimate blessing. This is what the reader will discover.

Tortuga, Anaya's third novel, again addresses a perplexing question. In a sanitorium for children, we meet a boy with a serious back injury, nicknamed Tortuga—whom we have met as Benji in the preceding novel, *Heart of Aztlán*—because of his turtle-like cast that profiles a nearby volcanic mountain with the same name. Rising magically to the east, the mountain seems "to hold the heavens and the earth together." Confronting evil and death, Tortuga faces the archetypal temptation, the sin against the Holy Spirit—to believe that love is not possible.

Solomon, a child so totally paralyzed that he is practically a disembodied spirit, is one of the mediating shamans of

the protagonist of the tale. Tortuga is also informed by
Solomon through dreams. Solomon tells of an initiation
rite gone awry. A turtle that he decapitated escaped into
the water. The order of nature was violated. Because he
did not follow the rite correctly, he is at odds with nature.
Something that should have been returned was profaned.
"Since that day," he says, "I have been a storyteller, forced
by the order of my destiny to reveal my story."

Anaya himself, as we have seen, sustained a serious back
injury in 1954, as a teenager in high school. Readers will
find his tales charged, throughout, with an intriguing con-
fluence of biography, history, and a care for preserving
cultural traditions. "Everyone has their own mission," he
tells us. His mission is to tell stories.

Critic Juan Bruce-Novoa describes the center of Anaya's
prophetic stance. Anaya, Bruce-Novoa says, will not give
chaos the last word. His heroes will "lead the community
into a higher realm of existence, one in which the essential,
transcendent order of being can be recognized and followed
in daily life."

Selections from two of Anaya's most recent novels reflect
his sustained interest with transcendent concerns, as he
moves toward a more popular voice. *Alburquerque*, the
first novel of his new quartet, the title of which restores
the original spelling of the city's name, crackles with action
and intrigue. The characters reflect the tension as old and
new ways clash in the development of the new Southwest.
In search of his father, a young boxer, Abrán, is the coyote
offspring of a Chicano father and an Anglo American
mother—Benji and Cindy from *Heart of Aztlán*. Cindy,
his mother, is dying as the novel opens. The excerpt from
Alburquerque tunes us into Anaya's humorous account of
what happens when the city boys of corporate computerized America return to their village for a traditional *matanza*, the killing of a pig.

Always ready to experiment with a new form, Anaya
presents us, in the selection from *Zia Summer*, with a chap-

ter from his new mystery novel. Rich with the history of New Mexico, played against the background of the dusty trail, which would become now Old Route 66, the chapter mixes a bit of bawdiness with an intriguing scene between a healer and Sonny Baca, a private investigator whom we met briefly in *Alburquerque*.

In his pioneering critical article on Anaya's short fiction, Luis Leal remarks that his stories are "in the tradition of the *cuentero* [the storyteller] who transcends the anecdotal . . . and who sees reality as it has been seen from the people whose culture he has inherited." As Anaya tells us in his essay "The Magic of Words," he was "fortunate to have those old and wise *viejitos* as guides (shamans) into the world of nature and knowledge. They taught me," he continues, "with their stories; they taught me with the magic of their words."

Anaya, the storyteller, is the quintessential human seeker. In his story "B. Traven Is Alive and Well in Cuernavaca," he presents us with a wonder-filled variant on the mystery of B. Traven [Hal Croves], author of *The Treasure of the Sierra Madre*. A writer in search of the germ of a tale meets Justino, "a rogue with class," who tells him about el Pozo de Mendoza, a hole in the earth, full of treasure. Openings in the earth are classically seen as sacred places, the womb where the transcendent past and future meet the contingent present. Readers will be entertained and delighted to learn more about why "a writer's job is to find and follow people like Justino." The story returns us to Anaya's insistence that we must listen to the people and to the spirit of a place. "Listening," he says, "is the catching of dreams, the catching of stories."

Through his stories, Anaya continues to surprise and engage us as he creates characters exploring the human condition. We see what can happen in the absence of a storyteller, in his re-creation of a traditional tale of incest in "The Silence of the Llano."

"The Apple Orchard" is a story about a young boy eager

to learn about his sexuality. A teacher, the ultimate mentor in this case, guides him toward a personal epiphany. In an important moment of insight, he realizes that sexuality is not bad, nor evil. He is only beginning his awareness of his sexual self. He experiences the beginning of wisdom. Woman becomes a metaphor of beauty [or goodness, or truth, or unity]; "the mystery would always be there, and [he] would be exploring its form forever."

Anaya's stories not infrequently search into human sexuality and love, as when he takes us into the loneliness of the desert. "Children of the Desert" and "In Search of Epifano" speak of our human inquisition for that divine beauty "ever ancient, ever new" in one another. Anaya considers the infinite in the feminine search for human plenitude, and the deafness of men to the voice of the anima within them.

A monstrous mutant "Devil Deer" fenced in by the Los Alamos Atomic Laboratory returns us to the theme of the consequences of our loss of oneness with and our destruction of the earth. In his entire canon he demonstrates a unique vision of a will to life empowered not by ego, but by his classic sense of the earth, *la tierra*, and his place, his *tierra*, and people. He calls this a "taking off point," where unity of "place, imagination and memory" nurture his work.

In his plays, Anaya continues his "determined effort to stretch himself as an artist," as David Richard Jones puts it. These works further demonstrate his concern with contemporary issues and with the future. Through the humor and whodunit format of the play *Who Killed Don José?*, Anaya deals with serious issues facing our community. The sheep rancher, Don José, like Anaya, cherishes the ways of the ancestors, but is ready to lead his community into the high-tech future. He recognizes that information is power. "If we don't change now," he warns, "we get left behind" again.

Through the historical character of *Billy the Kid*, Anaya

portrays the Mexican influence in the Southwest. Billy learns to speak Spanish; and, rightly or wrongly, Anaya says, he is seen as a person who stood up for Mexicans. Billy's battle with tuberculosis, and Billy's struggle to get out of a gang, parallel our concerns today with AIDS, gangs, and racism. The play experiments with extensive use of bilingual dialogue and explores the theme of *el destino*, a concern also found in the eerie story of "The Man Who Found a Pistol."

Even as *The Anaya Reader* engages, entertains, and educates us, it calls us as individuals, in our communities, to recover the lost, to accept the excluded, to mend the broken within us. This is also the sense of the seemingly spontaneous poem "Walt Whitman Strides the Llano of New Mexico" that provides the celebratory closing frame of this collection. It captures the pain of Whitman's sense of the human figure as immigrant. Anaya, too, would speak with the voice of the dead, and of the living to come.

The Anaya Reader, then, invites us to refresh and recreate ourselves at the deepest well of human remembering and to reach into Ultima's vision. There we will find the origins of the community of all human aspirations. Through his narrative and discourse, Anaya calls for an end to historical exclusion, for the acceptance of traditions, and for the remembrance of tales and values in danger of being forgotten. Through this *Reader*, Anaya continues to fulfill his *destino*, his mission as a writer, to tell the truth, to center, to heal. He becomes a shaman for a world audience.

César A. González-T.
San Diego Mesa College

THE ANAYA
READER

NOVEL
EXCERPTS

Bless Me, Ultima

Chapter 1

Ultima came to stay with us the summer I was almost seven. When she came the beauty of the llano unfolded before my eyes, and the gurgling waters of the river sang to the hum of the turning earth. The magical time of childhood stood still, and the pulse of the living earth pressed its mystery into my living blood. She took my hand, and the silent, magic powers she possessed made beauty from the raw, sun-baked llano, the green river valley, and the blue bowl which was the white sun's home. My bare feet felt the throbbing earth and my body trembled with excitement. Time stood still, and it shared with me all that had been, and all that was to come . . .

Let me begin at the beginning. I do not mean the beginning that was in my dreams and the stories they whispered to me about my birth, and the people of my father and mother, and my three brothers—but the beginning that came with Ultima.

The attic of our home was partitioned into two small rooms. My sisters, Deborah and Theresa, slept in one and I slept in the small cubicle by the door. The wooden steps creaked down into a small hallway that led into the kitchen. From the top of the stairs I had a vantage point into the heart of our home, my mother's kitchen. From there I was to see the terrified face of Chávez when he brought the terrible news of the murder of the sheriff; I was to see the rebellion of my brothers against my father; and many times late at night I was to see Ultima returning from the llano where she gathered the herbs that can be harvested only in the light of the full moon by the careful hands of a curandera.

That night I lay very quietly in my bed, and I heard my father and mother speak of Ultima.

"Está sola," my father said, "ya no queda gente en el pueblito de Las Pasturas—"

He spoke in Spanish, and the village he mentioned was his home. My father had been a vaquero all his life, a calling as ancient as the coming of the Spaniard to Nuevo México. Even after the big rancheros and the tejanos came and fenced the beautiful llano, he and those like him continued to work there, I guess because only in that wide expanse of land and sky could they feel the freedom their spirits needed.

"Qué lástima," my mother answered, and I knew her nimble fingers worked the pattern on the doily she crocheted for the big chair in the sala.

I heard her sigh, and she must have shuddered too when she thought of Ultima living alone in the loneliness of the wide llano. My mother was not a woman of the llano, she was the daughter of a farmer. She could not see beauty in the llano and she could not understand the coarse men who lived half their lifetimes on horseback. After I was born in Las Pasturas she persuaded my father to leave the llano and bring her family to the town of Guadalupe where she said there would be opportunity and school for us. The move lowered my father in the esteem of his compadres, the other vaqueros of the llano who clung tenaciously to their way of life and freedom. There was no room to keep animals in town so my father had to sell his small herd, but he would not sell his horse so he gave it to a good friend, Benito Campos. But Campos could not keep the animal penned up because somehow the horse was very close to the spirit of the man, and so the horse was allowed to roam free and no vaquero on that llano would throw a lazo on that horse. It was as if someone had died, and they turned their gaze from the spirit that walked the earth.

It hurt my father's pride. He saw less and less of his old compadres. He went to work on the highway and on Saturdays after they collected their pay he drank with his crew at the Longhorn, but he was never close to the men of the town. Some weekends the llaneros would come into town for supplies and old amigos like Bonney or Campos or the Gonzales brothers would come by to visit. Then my father's eyes lit up as they drank and talked of the old days and told the old stories. But when the western sun touched the clouds with orange and gold the vaqueros got in their trucks and headed home, and my father was left to drink alone in the long night. Sunday morning he would get up very crudo and complain about having to go to early mass.

"—She served the people all her life, and now the people are scattered, driven like tumbleweeds by the winds of war. The war sucks everything dry," my father said solemnly, "it takes the young boys overseas, and their families move to California where there is work—"

"Ave María Purísima," my mother made the sign of the cross for my three brothers who were away at war. "Gabriel," she said to my father, "it is not right that la Grande be alone in her old age—"

"No," my father agreed.

"When I married you and went to the llano to live with you and raise your family, I could not have survived without la Grande's help. Oh, those were hard years—"

"Those were good years," my father countered. But my mother would not argue.

"There isn't a family she did not help," she continued,

"no road was too long for her to walk to its end to snatch somebody from the jaws of death, and not even the blizzards of the llano could keep her from the appointed place where a baby was to be delivered—"

"Es verdad," my father nodded.

"She tended me at the birth of my sons—" And then I knew her eyes glanced briefly at my father. "Gabriel, we cannot let her live her last days in loneliness—"

"No," my father agreed, "it is not the way of our people."

"It would be a great honor to provide a home for la Grande," my mother murmured. My mother called Ultima la Grande out of respect. It meant the woman was old and wise.

"I have already sent word with Campos that Ultima is to come and live with us," my father said with some satisfaction. He knew it would please my mother.

"I am grateful," my mother said tenderly, "perhaps we can repay a little of the kindness la Grande has given to so many."

"And the children?" my father asked. I knew why he expressed concern for me and my sisters. It was because Ultima was a curandera, a woman who knew the herbs and remedies of the ancients, a miracle worker who could heal the sick. And I had heard that Ultima could lift the curses laid by brujas, that she could exorcise the evil the witches planted in people to make them sick. And because a curandera had this power she was misunderstood and often suspected of practicing witchcraft herself.

I shuddered and my heart turned cold at the thought. The cuentos of the people were full of the tales of evil done by brujas.

"She helped bring them into the world, she cannot be but good for the children," my mother answered.

"Está bien," my father yawned, "I will go for her in the morning."

So it was decided that Ultima should come and live with us. I knew that my father and mother did good by providing a home for Ultima. It was the custom to provide for the old and the sick. There was always room in the safety and warmth of la familia for one more person, be that person stranger or friend.

It was warm in the attic, and as I lay quietly listening to the sounds of the house, falling asleep and repeating a Hail Mary over and over in my thoughts, I drifted into the time of dreams. Once I had told my mother about my dreams, and she said they were visions from God and she was happy, because her own dream was that I should grow up and become a priest. After that I did not tell her about my dreams, and they remained in me forever and ever . . .

In my dream I flew over the rolling hills of the llano. My soul wandered over the dark plain until it came to a cluster of adobe huts. I recognized the village of Las Pasturas and my heart grew happy. One mud hut had a lighted window, and the vision of my dream swept me towards it to be witness at the birth of a baby.

I could not make out the face of the mother who rested from the pains of birth, but I could see the old woman in black who tended the just-arrived, steaming baby. She nimbly tied a knot on the cord that had connected the baby to its mother's blood, then quickly she bent and with her teeth she bit off the loose end. She wrapped the squirming baby and laid it at the mother's side, then she returned to cleaning the bed. All linen was swept aside to be washed, but she carefully wrapped the useless cord and the afterbirth and laid the package at the feet of the Virgin on the small altar. I sensed that these things were yet to be delivered to someone.

Now the people who had waited patiently in the dark were allowed to come in and speak to the mother and deliver their gifts to the baby. I recognized my mother's brothers, my uncles from El Puerto de los Lunas. They entered ceremoniously. A patient hope stirred in their dark, brooding eyes.

This one will be a Luna, the old man said, he will be a farmer and keep our customs and traditions. Perhaps God will bless our family and make the baby a priest.

And to show their hope they rubbed the dark earth of the river valley on the baby's forehead, and they surrounded the bed with the fruits of their harvest so the small room smelled of fresh green chile and corn, ripe apples and peaches, pumpkins and green beans.

Then the silence was shattered with the thunder of hoofbeats; vaqueros surrounded the small house with shouts and gunshots, and when they entered the room they were laughing and singing and drinking.

Gabriel, they shouted, you have a fine son! He will make a fine vaquero! And they smashed the fruits and vegetables that surrounded the bed and replaced them with a saddle, horse blankets, bottles of whiskey, a new rope, bridles, chapas, and an old guitar. And they rubbed the stain of earth from the baby's forehead because man was not to be tied to the earth but free upon it.

These were the people of my father, the vaqueros of the llano. They were an exuberant, restless people, wandering across the ocean of the plain.

We must return to our valley, the old man who led the farmers spoke. We must take with us the blood that comes after the birth. We will bury it in our fields to renew their fertility and to assure that the baby will follow our ways. He nodded for the old woman to deliver the package at the altar.

No! the llaneros protested, it will stay here! We will burn it and let the winds of the llano scatter the ashes.

It is blasphemy to scatter a man's blood on unholy ground, the farmers chanted. The new son must fulfill his mother's dream. He must come to El Puerto and rule over the Lunas of the valley. The blood of the Lunas is strong in him.

He is a Márez, the vaqueros shouted. His forefathers were conquistadores, men as restless as the seas they sailed and as free as the land they conquered. He is his father's blood!

Curses and threats filled the air, pistols were drawn, and the opposing sides made ready for battle. But the clash was stopped by the old woman who delivered the baby.

Cease! she cried, and the men were quiet. I pulled this baby into the light of life, so I will bury the afterbirth and the cord that once linked him to eternity. Only I will know his destiny.

The dream began to dissolve. When I opened my eyes I heard my father cranking the truck outside. I wanted to go with him, I wanted to see Las Pasturas, I wanted to see Ultima. I dressed hurriedly, but I was too late. The truck was bouncing down the goat path that led to the bridge and the highway.

I turned, as I always did, and looked down the slope of our hill to the green of the river, and I raised my eyes and saw the town of Guadalupe. Towering above the housetops and the trees of the town was the church tower. I made the sign of the cross on my lips. The only other building that rose above the housetops to compete with the church tower was the yellow top of the schoolhouse. This fall I would be going to school.

My heart sank. When I thought of leaving my mother and going to school a warm, sick feeling came to my stomach. To get rid of it I ran to the pens we kept by the molino to feed the animals. I had fed the rabbits that night and they still had alfalfa and so I only changed their water. I scattered some grain for the hungry chickens and watched their mad scramble as the rooster called them to peck. I milked the cow and turned her loose. During the day she would forage along the highway where the grass was thick and green, then she would return at nightfall. She was a good cow and there were very few times when I had to run and bring her back in the evening. Then I dreaded it, because she might wander into the hills where the bats flew at dusk and there was only the sound of my heart beating as I ran and it made me sad and frightened to be alone.

I collected three eggs in the chicken house and returned for breakfast.

"Antonio," my mother smiled and took the eggs and milk, "come and eat your breakfast."

I sat across the table from Deborah and Theresa and ate my atole and the hot tortilla with butter. I said very little. I usually spoke very little to my two sisters. They were older than I and they were very close. They usually spent the entire day in the attic, playing dolls and giggling. I did not concern myself with those things.

"Your father has gone to Las Pasturas," my mother chattered, "he has gone to bring la Grande." Her hands were white with the flour of the dough. I watched carefully. "—And when he returns, I want you children to show your manners. You must not shame your father or your mother—"

"Isn't her real name Ultima?" Deborah asked. She was like that, always asking grown-up questions.

"You will address her as la Grande," my mother said flatly. I looked at her and wondered if this woman with the black hair and laughing eyes was the woman who gave birth in my dream.

"Grande," Theresa repeated.

"Is it true she is a witch?" Deborah asked. Oh, she was in for it. I saw my mother whirl then pause and control herself.

"No!" she scolded. "You must not speak of such things! Oh, I don't know where you learn such ways—" Her eyes flooded with tears. She always cried when she thought we were learning the ways of my father, the ways of the Márez. "She is a woman of learning," she went on, and I knew she didn't have time to stop and cry, "she has worked hard for all the people of the village. Oh, I would never have survived those hard years if it had not been for her—so show her respect. We are honored that she comes to live with us, understand?"

"Sí, mamá," Deborah said half willingly.

"Sí, mamá," Theresa repeated.

"Now run and sweep the room at the end of the hall. Eugene's room—" I heard her voice choke. She breathed a prayer and crossed her forehead. The flour left white stains on her, the four points of the cross. I knew it was because my three brothers were at war that she was sad, and Eugene was the youngest.

"Mamá." I wanted to speak to her. I wanted to know who the old woman was who cut the baby's cord.

"Sí." She turned and looked at me.

"Was Ultima at my birth?" I asked.

"¡Ay Dios mío!" my mother cried. She came to where I sat and ran her hand through my hair. She smelled warm, like bread. "Where do you get such questions, my son? Yes," she smiled, "la Grande was there to help me. She was there to help at the birth of all of my children—"

"And my uncles from El Puerto were there?"

"Of course," she answered, "my brothers have always been at my side when I needed them. They have always prayed that I would bless them with a—"

I did not hear what she said because I was hearing the sounds of the dream, and I was seeing the dream again. The warm cereal in my stomach made me feel sick.

"And my father's brother was there, the Márez and their friends, the vaqueros—"

"¡Ay!" she cried out. "Don't speak to me of those worthless Márez and their friends!"

"There was a fight?" I asked.

"No," she said, "a silly argument. They wanted to start a fight with my brothers—that is all they are good for. Vaqueros, they call themselves, they are worthless drunks! Thieves! Always on the move, like gypsies, always dragging their families around the country like vagabonds—"

As long as I could remember she always raged about the Márez family and their friends. She called the village of Las Pasturas beautiful; she had gotten used to the loneliness, but she had never accepted its people. She was the daughter of farmers.

But the dream was true. It was as I had seen it. Ultima knew.

"But you will not be like them." She caught her breath and stopped. She kissed my forehead. "You will be like my brothers. You will be a Luna, Antonio. You will be a man of the people, and perhaps a priest." She smiled.

A priest, I thought, that was her dream. I was to hold mass on Sundays like Father Byrnes did in the church in town. I was to hear the confessions of the silent people of the valley, and I was to administer the holy Sacrament to them.

"Perhaps," I said.

"Yes," my mother smiled. She held me tenderly. The fragrance of her body was sweet.

"But then," I whispered, "who will hear my confession?"

"What?"

"Nothing," I answered. I felt a cool sweat on my forehead and I knew I had to run, I had to clear my mind of the dream. "I am going to Jasón's house," I said hurriedly, and slid past my mother. I ran out the kitchen door, past the animal pens, towards Jasón's house. The white sun and the fresh air cleansed me.

On this side of the river there were only three houses. The slope of the hill rose gradually into the hills of juniper and mesquite and cedar clumps. Jasón's house was farther away from the river than our house. On the path that led to the bridge lived huge, fat Fío and his beautiful wife. Fío and my father worked together on the highway. They were good drinking friends.

"¡Jasón!" I called at the kitchen door. I had run hard and was panting. His mother appeared at the door.

"Jasón no está aquí," she said. All of the older people

spoke only in Spanish, and I myself understood only Spanish. It was only after one went to school that one learned English.

"¿Dónde está?" I asked.

She pointed towards the river, northwest, past the railroad tracks to the dark hills. The river came through those hills and there were old Indian grounds there, holy burial grounds Jasón told me. There in an old cave lived his Indian. At least everybody called him Jasón's Indian. He was the only Indian of the town, and he talked only to Jasón. Jasón's father had forbidden Jasón to talk to the Indian, he had beaten him, he had tried in every way to keep Jasón from the Indian.

But Jasón persisted. Jasón was not a bad boy, he was just Jasón. He was quiet and moody, and sometimes for no reason at all, wild, loud sounds came exploding from his throat and lungs. Sometimes I felt like Jasón, like I wanted to shout and cry, but I never did.

I looked at his mother's eyes and I saw they were sad. "Thank you," I said, and returned home. While I waited for my father to return with Ultima I worked in the garden. Every day I had to work in the garden. Every day I reclaimed from the rocky soil of the hill a few more feet of earth to cultivate. The land of the llano was not good for farming, the good land was along the river. But my mother wanted a garden and I worked to make her happy. Already we had a few chile and tomato plants growing. It was hard work. My fingers bled from scraping out the rocks and it seemed that a square yard of ground produced a wheelbarrow full of rocks which I had to push down to the retaining wall.

The sun was white in the bright blue sky. The shade of the clouds would not come until the afternoon. The sweat was sticky on my brown body. I heard the truck and turned to see it chugging up the dusty goat path. My father was returning with Ultima.

"¡Mamá!" I called. My mother came running out, Deborah and Theresa trailed after her.

"I'm afraid," I heard Theresa whimper.

"There's nothing to be afraid of," Deborah said confidently. My mother said there was too much Márez blood in Deborah. Her eyes and hair were very dark, and she was always running. She had been to school two years and she spoke only English. She was teaching Theresa and half the time I didn't understand what they were saying.

"Madre de Dios, but mind your manners!" my mother scolded. The truck stopped and she ran to greet Ultima. "Buenos días le de Dios, Grande," my mother cried. She smiled and hugged and kissed the old woman.

"Ay, María Luna," Ultima smiled, "buenos días te de Dios, a ti y a tu familia." She wrapped the black shawl around her hair and shoulders. Her face was brown and very wrinkled. When she smiled her teeth were brown. I remembered the dream.

"Come, come!" my mother urged us forward. It was the custom to greet the old. "Deborah!" my mother urged. Deborah stepped forward and took Ultima's withered hand.

"Buenos días, Grande," she smiled. She even bowed slightly. Then she pulled Theresa forward and told her to greet la Grande. My mother beamed. Deborah's good manners surprised her, but they made her happy, because a family was judged by its manners.

"What beautiful daughters you have raised," Ultima nodded to my mother. Nothing could have pleased my mother more. She looked proudly at my father, who stood leaning against the truck, watching and judging the introductions.

"Antonio," he said simply. I stepped forward and took Ultima's hand. I looked up into her clear brown eyes and shivered. Her face was old and wrinkled, but her eyes were clear and sparkling, like the eyes of a young child.

"Antonio," she smiled. She took my hand, and I felt the power of a whirlwind sweep around me. Her eyes swept the surrounding hills and through them I saw for the first time the wild beauty of our hills and the magic of the green river. My nostrils quivered as I felt the song of the mockingbirds and the drone of the grasshoppers mingle with the pulse of the earth. The four directions of the llano met in me, and the white sun shone on my soul. The granules of sand at my feet and the sun and sky above me seemed to dissolve into one strange, complete being.

A cry came to my throat, and I wanted to shout it and run in the beauty I had found.

"Antonio." I felt my mother prod me. Deborah giggled because she had made the right greeting, and I who was to be my mother's hope and joy stood voiceless.

"Buenos días le de Dios, Ultima," I muttered. I saw in her eyes my dream. I saw the old woman who had delivered me from my mother's womb. I knew she held the secret of my destiny.

"Antonio!" My mother was shocked I had used her name instead of calling her Grande. But Ultima held up her hand.

"Let it be," she smiled. "This was the last child I pulled from your womb, María. I knew there would be something between us."

My mother, who had started to mumble apologies, was quiet. "As you wish, Grande," she nodded.

"I have come to spend the last days of my life here, Antonio," Ultima said to me.

"You will never die, Ultima," I answered. "I will take care of you—" She let go of my hand and laughed. Then my father said, "Pase, Grande, pase. Nuestra casa es su casa. It is too hot to stand and visit in the sun—"

"Sí, sí," my mother urged. I watched them go in. My father carried on his shoulders the large blue-tin trunk which later I learned contained all of Ultima's earthly possessions, the black dresses and shawls she wore, and the magic of her sweet-smelling herbs.

As Ultima walked past me I smelled for the first time a trace of the sweet fragrance of herbs that always lingered in her wake. Many years later, long after Ultima was gone and I had grown to be a man, I would awaken sometimes at night and think I caught a scent of her fragrance in the cool-night breeze.

And with Ultima came the owl. I heard it that night for the first time in the juniper tree outside of Ultima's window. I knew it was her owl because the other owls of the llano did not come that near the house. At first it disturbed me, and Deborah and Theresa too. I heard them whispering through the partition. I heard Deborah reassuring Theresa that she would take care of her, and then she took Theresa in her arms and rocked her until they were both asleep.

I waited. I was sure my father would get up and shoot the owl with the old rifle he kept on the kitchen wall. But he didn't, and I accepted his understanding. In many cuentos I had heard the owl was one of the disguises a bruja took, and so it struck a chord of fear in the heart to hear them hooting at night. But not Ultima's owl. Its soft hooting was like a song, and as it grew rhythmic it calmed the moonlit hills and lulled us to sleep. Its song seemed to say that it had come to watch over us.

I dreamed about the owl that night, and my dream was good. La Virgen de Guadalupe was the patron saint of our town. The town was named after her. In my dream I saw Ultima's owl lift la Virgen on her wide wings and fly her to heaven. Then the owl returned and gathered up all the babes of Limbo and flew them up to the clouds of heaven.

The Virgin smiled at the goodness of the owl.

Chapter 2

Ultima slipped easily into the routine of our daily life. The first day, she put on her apron and helped my mother with breakfast, later she swept the house and then helped my mother wash our clothes in the old washing machine they pulled outside where it was cooler under the shade of the young elm trees. It was as if she had always been here. My mother was very happy because now she had someone to talk to and she didn't have to wait until Sunday when her women friends from the town came up the dusty path to sit in the sala and visit.

Deborah and Theresa were happy because Ultima did many of the household chores they normally did, and they had more time to spend in the attic and cut out an interminable train of paper dolls which they dressed, gave names to, and most miraculously, made talk.

My father was also pleased. Now he had one more person to tell his dream to. My father's dream was to gather his sons around him and move westward to the land of the setting sun, to the vineyards of California. But the war had taken his three sons and it had made him bitter. He often got drunk on Saturday afternoons and then he would rave against old age. He would rage against the town on the opposite side of the river which drained a man of his freedom, and he would cry because the war had ruined his dream. It was very sad to see my father cry, but I understood it, because sometimes a man has to cry. Even if he is a man.

And I was happy with Ultima. We walked together in the llano and along the riverbanks to gather herbs and roots for her medicines. She taught me the names of plants and flowers, of trees and bushes, of birds and animals; but most important, I learned from her that there was a beauty in the time of day and in the time of night, and that there was peace in the river and in the hills. She taught me to listen to the mystery of the groaning earth and to feel complete in the fulfillment of its time. My soul grew under her careful guidance.

I had been afraid of the awful *presence* of the river, which was the soul of the river, but through her I learned that my spirit shared in the spirit of all things. But the innocence which our isolation sheltered could not last forever, and the affairs of the town began to reach across our bridge and enter my life. Ultima's owl gave the warning that the time of peace on our hill was drawing to an end.

It was Saturday night. My mother had laid out our clean clothes for Sunday mass, and we had gone to bed early because we always went to early mass. The house was quiet, and I was in the mist of some dream when I heard the owl cry its warning. I was up instantly, looking through the small window at the dark figure that ran madly towards the house. He hurled himself at the door and began pounding.

"¡Márez!" he shouted. "¡Márez! ¡Andale, hombre!"

I was frightened, but I recognized the voice. It was Jasón's father.

"¡Un momento!" I heard my father call. He fumbled with the farol.

"¡Andale, hombre, andale!" Chávez cried pitifully. "Mataron a mi hermano—"

"Ya vengo—" My father opened the door and the frightened man burst in. In the kitchen I heard my mother moan, "Ave María Purísima, mis hijos—" She had not heard Chávez' last words, and so she assumed the aviso was one that brought bad news about her sons.

"Chávez, ¿qué pasa?" My father held the trembling man.

"¡Mi hermano, mi hermano!" Chávez sobbed. "He has killed my brother!"

"¿Pero qué dices, hombre?" my father exclaimed. He pulled Chávez into the hall and held up the farol. The light cast by the farol revealed the wild, frightened eyes of Chávez.

"¡Gabriel!" my mother cried, and came forward, but my father pushed her back. He did not want her to see the monstrous mask of fear on the man's face.

"It is not our sons, it is something in town—get him some water."

"Lo mató, lo mató—" Chávez repeated.

"Get hold of yourself, hombre, tell me what has happened!" My father shook Chávez and the man's sobbing subsided. He took the glass of water and drank, then he could talk.

"Reynaldo has just brought the news, my brother is dead," he sighed and slumped against the wall. Chávez' brother was the sheriff of the town. The man would have fallen if my father had not held him up.

"¡Madre de Dios! Who? How?"

"¡Lupito!" Chávez cried out. His face corded with thick veins. For the first time his left arm came up and I saw the rifle he held.

"Jesús, María y José," my mother prayed.

My father groaned and slumped against the wall. "Ay que Lupito," he shook his head, "the war made him crazy—"

Chávez regained part of his composure. "Get your rifle, we must go to the bridge—"

"The bridge?"

"Reynaldo said to meet him there—the crazy bastard has taken to the river—"

My father nodded silently. He went to the bedroom and returned with his coat. While he loaded his rifle in the kitchen Chávez related what he knew.

"My brother had just finished his rounds," he gasped, "he was at the bus depot cafe, having coffee, sitting without a care in the world—and the bastard came up to where he sat and without warning shot him in the head—" His body shook as he retold the story.

"Perhaps it is better if you wait here, hombre," my father said with consolation.

"No!" Chávez shouted. "I must go. He was my brother!"

My father nodded. I saw him stand beside Chávez and put his arm around his shoulders. Now he too was armed. I had only seen him shoot the rifle when we slaughtered pigs in the fall. Now they were going armed for a man.

"Gabriel, be careful," my mother called as my father and Chávez slipped out into the dark.

"Sí," I heard him answer, then the screen door banged. "Keep the doors locked—" My mother went to the door and shut the latch. We never locked our doors, but tonight there was something strange and fearful in the air.

Perhaps this is what drew me out into the night to follow my father and Chávez down to the bridge, or perhaps it was some concern I had for my father. I do not know. I waited until my mother was in the sala then I dressed and slipped downstairs. I glanced down the hall and saw candlelight flickering from the sala. That room was never entered unless there were Sunday visitors, or unless my mother took us in to pray novenas and rosaries for my brothers at war. I knew she was kneeling at her altar now, praying. I knew she would pray until my father returned.

I slipped out the kitchen door and into the night. It was cool. I sniffed the air; there was a tinge of autumn in it. I ran up the goat path until I caught sight of two dark shadows ahead of me. Chávez and my father.

We passed Fío's dark house and then the tall juniper tree that stood where the hill sloped down to the bridge. Even from this distance I could hear the commotion on the bridge. As we neared the bridge I was afraid of being discovered as I had no reason for being there. My father would be very angry. To escape detection I cut to the right and was swallowed up by the dark brush of the river. I pushed through the dense bosque until I came to the bank of the river. From where I stood I could look up into the flooding beams of light that were pointed down by the excited men. I could hear them giving frenzied, shouted instructions. I looked to my left where the bridge started and saw my father and Chávez running towards the excitement at the center of the bridge.

My eyes were now accustomed to the dark, but it was a glint of light that made me turn and look at a clump of bullrushes in the sweeping water of the river just a few yards away. What I saw made my blood run cold. Crouched in the reeds and half submerged in the muddy waters lay the figure of Lupito, the man who had killed the sheriff. The glint of light was from the pistol he held in his hand.

It was frightening enough to come upon him so suddenly, but as I dropped to my knees in fright I must have uttered a cry because he turned and looked directly at me. At that same moment a beam of light found him and illuminated a face twisted with madness. I do not know if he saw me, or if the light cut off his vision, but I saw his bitter, contorted grin. As long as I live I will never forget those wild eyes, like the eyes of a trapped, savage animal.

At the same time someone shouted from the bridge. "There!" Then all the lights found the crouched figure. He jumped and I saw him as clear as if it were daylight.

"Ayeeeeee!" He screamed a bloodcurdling cry that echoed down the river. The men on the bridge didn't know what to do. They stood transfixed, looking down at the mad man waving the pistol in the air. "Ayeeeeeeee!" he cried again. It was a cry of rage and pain, and it made my soul sick. The cry of a tormented man had come to the peaceful green mystery of my river, and the great *presence* of the river watched from the shadows and deep recesses, as I watched from where I crouched at the bank.

"Japanese sol'jer, Japanese sol'jer!" he cried. "I am wounded. Come help me—" he called to the men on the bridge. The rising mist of the river swirled in the beams of spotlights. It was like a horrible nightmare.

Suddenly he leaped up and ran splashing through the water towards me. The lights followed him. He grew bigger, I heard his panting, the water his feet kicked up splashed on my face, and I thought he would run over me. Then as quickly as he had sprinted in my direction he turned and disappeared again into the dark clumps of reeds in the river. The lights moved in all directions, but they couldn't find him. Some of the lights swept over me and I trembled with fear that I would be found out, or worse, that I would be mistaken for Lupito and shot.

"The crazy bastard got away!" someone shouted on the bridge.

"Ayeeeeee!" the scream sounded again. It was a cry that I did not understand, and I am sure the men on the bridge did not either. The man they hunted had slipped away from human understanding; he had become a wild animal, and they were afraid.

"Damn!" I heard them cursing themselves. Then a car with a siren and flashing red light came on the bridge. It was Vigil, the state policeman who patrolled our town.

"Chávez is dead!" I heard him shout. "He never had a chance. His brains blown out—" There was silence.

"We have to kill him!" Jasón's father shouted. His voice was full of anger, rage and desperation.

"I have to deputize you—" Vigil started to say.

"The hell with deputizing!" Chávez shouted. "He killed my brother! ¡Está loco!" The men agreed with their silence.

"Have you spotted him?" Vigil asked.

"Just now we saw him, but we lost him—"

"He's down there," someone added.

"He is an animal! He has to be shot!" Chávez cried out.

"¡Sí!" the men agreed.

"Now wait a moment—" It was my father who spoke. I do not know what he said because of the shouting. In the meantime I searched the dark of the river for Lupito. I finally saw him. He was about forty feet away, crouched in the reeds as before. The muddy waters of the river lapped and gurgled savagely around him. Before, the night had been only cool, now it turned cold and I shivered. I was torn between a fear that made my body tremble and a desire to help the poor man. But I could not move, I could only watch like a chained spectator.

"Márez is right!" I heard a booming voice on the bridge. In the lights I could make out the figure of Narciso. There was only one man that big and with that voice in town. I knew that Narciso was one of the old people from Las Pasturas, and that he was a good friend to my father. I knew they often drank together on Saturdays, and once or twice he had been to our house.

"¡Por Dios, hombres!" he shouted. "Let us act like men! That is not an animal down there, that is a man. Lupito. You all know Lupito. You know that the war made him sick—" But the men would not listen to Narciso. I guess it was because he was the town drunk, and they said he never did anything useful.

"Go back to your drinking and leave this job to men," one of them jeered at him.

"He killed the sheriff in cold blood," another added. I knew that the sheriff had been greatly admired.

"I am not drinking," Narciso persisted, "it is you men who are drunk for blood. You have lost your reason—"

"Reason!" Chávez countered. "What reason did he have for killing my brother. You know," he addressed the men, "my brother did no one harm. Tonight a mad animal crawled behind him and took his life. You call that reason! That animal has to be destroyed!"

"¡Sí! ¡Sí!" the men shouted in unison.

"At least let us try to talk to him," Narciso begged. I knew that it was hard for a man of the llano to beg.

"Yes," Vigil added, "perhaps he will give himself up—"

"Do you think he'll listen to talk!" Chávez jumped forward. "He's down there, and he still has the pistol that killed my brother! Go down and talk to him!" I could see Chávez shouting in Vigil's face, and Vigil said nothing. Chávez laughed. "This is the only talk he will understand—" He turned and fired over the railing of the bridge. His shots roared then whined away down the river. I could hear the bullets make splashing noises in the water.

"Wait!" Narciso shouted. He took Chávez' rifle and with one hand held it up. Chávez struggled against him but Narciso was too big and strong. "I will talk to him," Narciso said. He pushed Chávez back. "I understand your sorrow, Chávez," he said, "but one killing is enough for tonight—" The men must have been impressed by his sincerity because they stood back and waited.

Narciso leaned over the concrete railing and shouted down into the darkness. "Hey, Lupito! It is me, Narciso. It is me, hombre, your compadre. Listen, my friend, a very bad business has happened tonight, but if we act like men we can settle it— Let me come down and talk to you, Lupito. Let me help you—"

I looked at Lupito. He had been watching the action on the bridge, but now as Narciso talked to him I saw his head slump on his chest. He seemed to be thinking. I prayed that he would listen to Narciso and that the angry and frustrated men on the bridge would not commit mortal sin. The night was very quiet. The men on the bridge awaited an answer. Only the lapping water of the river made a sound.

"¡Amigo!" Narciso shouted. "You know I am your friend, I want to help you, hombre—" He laughed softly. "Hey, Lupito, you remember just a few years ago, before you went to the war, you remember the first time you came into the Eight Ball to gamble a little. Remember how I taught you how Juan Botas marked the aces with a little tobacco juice, and he thought you were green, but you beat him!" He laughed again. "Those were good times, Lupito, before the war came. Now we have this bad business to settle. But we are friends who will help you—"

I saw Lupito's tense body shake. A low, sad, mournful cry tore itself from his throat and mixed into the lapping sound of the waters of the river. His head shook slowly, and I guess he must have been thinking and fighting between surrendering and remaining free, and hunted. Then like a coiled spring he jumped up, his pistol aimed straight up. There was a flash of fire and the loud report of the pistol. But he had not fired at Narciso or at any of the men on the bridge! The spotlights found him.

"There's your answer!" Chávez shouted.

"He's firing! He's firing!" another voice shouted. "He's crazy!"

Lupito's pistol sounded again. Still he was not aiming at the men on the bridge. He was shooting to draw their fire!

"Shoot! Shoot!" someone on the bridge called.

"No, no," I whispered through clenched lips. But it was too late for anything. The frightened men responded by aiming their rifles over the side of the bridge. One single shot sounded then a barrage followed it like the roar of a cannon, like the rumble of thunder in a summer thunderstorm.

Many shots found their mark. I saw Lupito lifted off his feet and hurled backward by the bullets. But he got up and ran limping and crying towards the bank where I lay.

"Bless me—" I thought he cried, and the second volley of shots from the bridge sounded, but this time they sounded like a great whirling of wings, like pigeons swirling to roost on the church top. He fell forward then clawed and crawled out of the holy water of the river onto the bank in front of me. I wanted to reach out and help him, but I was frozen by my fear. He looked up at me and his face was bathed in water and flowing, hot blood, but it was also dark and peaceful as it slumped into the sand of the riverbank. He made a strange gurgling sound in his throat, then he was still. Up on the bridge a great shout went up. The men were already running to the end of the bridge to come down and claim the man whose dead hands dug into the soft, wet sand in front of me.

I turned and ran. The dark shadows of the river enveloped me as I raced for the safety of home. Branches whipped at my face and cut it, and vines and tree trunks caught at my feet and tripped me. In my headlong rush I disturbed sleeping birds and their shrill cries and slapping wings hit at my face. The horror of darkness had never been so complete as it was for me that night.

I had started praying to myself from the moment I heard the first shot, and I never stopped praying until I reached home. Over and over through my mind ran the words of the Act of Contrition. I had not yet been to catechism, nor had I made my first holy communion, but my mother had taught me the Act of Contrition. It was to be said after one made his confession to the priest, and as the last prayer before death.

Did God listen? Would he hear? Had he seen my father on the bridge? And where was Lupito's soul winging to, or was it washing down the river to the fertile valley of my uncles' farms?

A priest could have saved Lupito. Oh, why did my mother dream for me to be a priest! How would I ever wash away the stain of blood from the sweet waters of my river! I think at that time I began to cry because as I left the river brush and headed up the hills I heard my sobs for the first time.

It was also then that I heard the owl. Between my gasps for air and my sobs I stopped and listened for its song. My heart was pounding and my lungs hurt, but a calmness had come over the moonlit night when I heard the hooting of Ultima's owl. I stood still for a long time. I realized that the owl had been with me throughout the night. It had watched over all that had happened on the bridge. Suddenly the terrible, dark fear that had possessed me was gone.

I looked at the house that my father and my brothers had built on the juniper-patched hill; it was quiet and peaceful in the blue night. The sky sparkled with a million stars and the Virgin's horned moon, the moon of my mother's people, the moon of the Lunas. My mother would be praying for the soul of Lupito.

Again the owl sang; Ultima's spirit bathed me with its strong resolution. I turned and looked across the river. Some lights shone in the town. In the moonlight I could make out the tower of the church, the schoolhouse top, and way beyond the glistening of the town's water tank. I heard the soft wail of a siren, and I knew the men would be pulling Lupito from the river.

The river's brown waters would be stained with blood, forever and ever and ever . . .

In the autumn I would have to go to the school in the town, and in a few years I would go to catechism lessons in the church. I shivered. My body began to hurt from the beating it had taken from the brush of the river. But what hurt more was that I had witnessed for the first time the death of a man.

My father did not like the town or its way. When we had first moved from Las Pasturas we had lived in a rented house in the town. But every evening after work he had looked across the river to these barren, empty hills, and finally he had bought a couple of acres and began building our house. Everyone told him he was crazy, that the rocky, wild hill could sustain no life, and my mother was more than upset. She wanted to buy along the river where the land was fertile and there was water for the plants and trees. But my father won the fight to be close to his llano, because truthfully our hill was the beginning of the llano, from here it stretched away as far as the eye could see, to Las Pasturas and beyond.

The men of the town had murdered Lupito. But he had murdered the sheriff. They said the war had made him crazy. The prayers for Lupito mixed into prayers for my brothers. So many different thoughts raced through my mind that I felt dizzy, and very weary and sick. I ran the last of the way and slipped quietly into the house. I groped for the stair railing in the dark and felt a warm hand take mine. Startled, I looked up into Ultima's brown, wrinkled face.

"You knew!" I whispered. I understood that she did not want my mother to hear.

"Sí," she replied.

"And the owl—" I gasped. My mind searched for answers, but my body was so tired that my knees buckled and I fell forward. As small and thin as Ultima was she had the strength to lift me in her arms and carry me into her room. She placed me on her bed and then by the light of a small, flickering candle she mixed one of her herbs in a tin cup, held it over the flame to warm, then gave it to me to drink.

"They killed Lupito," I said as I gulped the medicine.

"I know," she nodded. She prepared a new potion and with this she washed the cuts on my face and feet.

"Will he go to hell?" I asked.

"That is not for us to say, Antonio. The war-sickness was not taken out of him, he did not know what he was doing—"

"And the men on the bridge, my father!"

"Men will do what they must do," she answered. She sat on the bed by my side. Her voice was soothing, and the drink she had given me made me sleepy. The wild, frightening excitement in my body began to die.

"The ways of men are strange, and hard to learn," I heard her say.

"Will I learn them?" I asked. I felt the weight on my eyelids.

"You will learn much, you will see much," I heard her faraway voice. I felt a blanket cover me. I felt safe in the warm sweetness of the room. Outside the owl sang its dark questioning to the night, and I slept.

But even into my deep sleep my dreams came. In my dream I saw my three brothers. I saw them as I remembered them before they went away to war, which seemed so very long ago. They stood by the house that we rented in town, and they looked across the river at the hills of the llano.

Father says that the town steals our freedom; he says that we must build a castle across the river, on the lonely hill of the mockingbirds. I think it was León who spoke first, he was the eldest, and his voice always had a sad note to it. But in the dark mist of the dream I could not be sure.

His heart had been heavy since we came to the town, the second figure spoke, his forefathers were men of the sea, the Márez people, they were conquistadors, men whose freedom was unbounded.

It was Andrew who said that! It was Andrew! I was sure because his voice was husky like his thick and sturdy body.

Father says the freedom of the wild horse is in the Márez blood, and his gaze is always westward. His fathers before him were vaqueros, and so he expects us to be men of the llano. I was sure the third voice belonged to Eugene.

I longed to touch them. I was hungry for their company. Instead I spoke.

We must all gather around our father, I heard myself

say. His dream is to ride westward in search of new adventure. He builds highways that stretch into the sun, and we must travel that road with him.

My brothers frowned. You are a Luna, they chanted in unison, you are to be a farmer-priest for Mother!

The doves came to drink in the still pools of the river and their cry was mournful in the darkness of my dream.

My brothers laughed. You are but a baby, Tony, you are our mother's dream. Stay and sleep to the doves' *courou* while we cross the mighty River of the Carp to build our father's castle in the hills.

I must go! I cried to the three dark figures. I must lift the muddy waters of the river in blessing to our new home!

Along the river the tormented cry of a lonely goddess filled the valley. The winding wail made the blood of men run cold.

It is La Llorona, my brothers cried in fear, the old witch who cries along the riverbanks and seeks the blood of boys and men to drink!

La Llorona seeks the soul of Antonioooooooooo . . .

It is the soul of Lupito, they cried in fear, doomed to wander the river at night because the waters washed his soul away!

Lupito seeks his blessingggggggggg . . .

It is neither! I shouted. I swung the dark robe of the priest over my shoulders then lifted my hands in the air. The mist swirled around me and sparks flew when I spoke. It is the presence of the river!

Save us, my brothers cried and cowered at my words.

I spoke to the presence of the river and it allowed my brothers to cross with their carpenter tools to build our castle on the hill.

Behind us I heard my mother moan and cry because with each turning of the sun her son was growing old . . .

Tortuga

Chapter 1

I awoke from a restless sleep. For a moment I couldn't remember where I was, then I heard Filomón and Clepo talking up front and I felt the wind sway the old ambulance. I tried to turn my body, but it was impossible. Upon waking it was always the same; I tried to move but the paralysis held me firmly in its grip.

I could not turn my head and look out the small window. The cold winter rain was still falling. It had been only a gray drizzle when we left the hospital, but the farther south we went into the desert the sheets of icy rain became more intense. For a great part of the trip we had been surrounded by darkness. Only the flashes of lightning which tore through the sky illuminated the desolate landscape.

I had slept most of the way; the rain drumming against the ambulance and the rumble of the distant thunder lulled me to sleep. Now I blinked my eyes and remembered that we had left at daybreak, and Filomón had said that it would be mid-afternoon before we arrived at the new hospital.

Your new home, he had said.

Home. Up north, at home, it would be snowing, but here it was only the dark, dismal rain which swept across the wide desert and covered us with its darkness. I tried to turn again, but the paralysis compounded by the bone-chilling cold held me. I cursed silently.

"It's never been this dark before," I heard Clepo whisper.

"Don't worry," Filomón answered, "it'll get better before it gets worse. You have to know the desert to know rain don't last. It can be raining one minute and blowing dust devils the next. But the clouds are beginning to break, see, to the west."

I turned my head and looked out the window. In the distance I could see the bare outline of a mountain range. Around us the desert was alkaline and white. Only the most tenacious shrubs and brittle grasses seemed to grow, clinging to the harsh land like tufts of mouldy hair. Over-head, the sun struggled to break through the clouds. To the east, a diffused, distorted rainbow stretched across the vast, gray sky.

I remembered the rainbows of my childhood, beautifully sculptured arches reaching from north to south, shafts of light so pure their harmony seemed to wed the sky and earth. My mother had taught me to look at rainbows, the mantle of the Blessed Virgin Mary she called them. When a summer thunderstorm passed she would take me out and we would stand in the thin drops which followed the storm. We would turn our faces up to the sky, and the large, glistening drops of rain would pelt our faces. She would open her mouth and hold out her tongue to receive the large, golden drops. She would stir the muddy ponds and pick up the little frogs which came with the rain. "They are like you," she told me, "blessed by the rain, children of the water." When I was hurt she would take me in her arms and sing . . .

> *Sana, sana*
> *colita de rana*

Si no sanas hoy
sanarás manñana . . .

And her touch could drive away the worst of pains. But then the paralysis had come, and suddenly her prayers and her touch were not enough. Her face grew pale and thin, her eyes grew dark. "It is God's will," she had said.

"It's clearing now," Filomón said, "see, the sun is beginning to break through!"

"Yes, the sun!" Clepo shouted. He was Filomón's assistant, a small impish man with hunched shoulders. I noticed he limped when they loaded me on the ambulance.

"I think I see the top of the mountain!" Filomón cried cheerfully.

I was fully awake. The last images of the dreams faded as the darkness of the rain moved over us and eastward. Only occasional peals of thunder rumbled across the sky. Beneath us the ambulance rocked like a ship. Memories of my life moved in and out of my troubled consciousness. My mother's face appeared again and again. She had cried when they loaded me on the ambulance, but she knew it was necessary. The doctors there had helped as much as they could. Now, they insisted, they had to move me to this new hospital in the south where they specialized in taking care of crippled children. If there was any hope of regaining the use of my stiff limbs, it was there. So early in the morning they wheeled me on a gurney to the outpatient area, loaded me onto Filomón's ambulance and the journey began.

"There!" Filomón shouted again. "There's the mountain!"

I tried to turn my head to see, but I couldn't. "What mountain?" I asked.

"Tortuga Mountain," he said, and looked back, "it's right by the hospital. Don't worry, I'll stop so you can see it." He sounded happy, revived, after the long, monotonous drive across the desert. I felt a sense of urgency as he pulled the ambulance onto the shoulder of the road. We bounced along until he found the right spot, then he stopped the ambulance and turned off the motor. He climbed over the seat to where I lay strapped on the small cot.

"Ah, Filo," Clepo grumbled, "you've stopped here every time we bring a new kid. Don't you ever get tired of showing them that damned mountain?"

"It's always a new kid," Filomón smiled as he loosened the straps that held me, "and each kid deserves to see the mountain from here. I want the boy to see it."

Filomón was an old man with a deep wrinkled face and rough, callused hands, but he moved like a younger man as he lifted me tenderly so I could look out the window and see the mountain.

"There it is," he nodded, "that's Tortuga." His eyes sparkled as he looked at the volcanic mountain that loomed over the otherwise empty desert. It rose so magically into the gray sky that it seemed to hold the heavens and the earth together. It lay just east of the river valley, and the afternoon sun shining on it after the rain covered it with a sheen of silver.

"It's a magic mountain," Filomón whispered, and I felt his heart beating against me as he held me. "See!" he whispered, "see!" I tried to see beyond the volcanic slabs and granite boulders which formed the outline of a turtle, I tried to sense the steady rhythm of his pulse which seemed to be draining into the giant mountain, but I couldn't. I was too tired, and my faith in magic had drained out the night the paralysis came and in the ensuing nights and days which I spent without movement on the hospital bed.

I shook my head.

"That's okay," he smiled, "it comes slowly sometimes. But now at least you know it's there—" He seemed very tired. It had been a long trip for him too. He had had to keep the ambulance on course through one of the worst storms I could remember. But now we were almost there.

"Where's the hospital?" I asked.

"It's on this side of the river, you can't see it from here. See the smoke rising in the valley? That's Agua Bendita. It's a small town, but people come from all over to bathe in the mineral waters from the springs which drain from the mountain—"

"It's a town full of old arthritics," Clepo giggled, "old people who think they can escape the pains of old age by dipping themselves in the mountain's water, but they can't run fast enough from death!" He slapped his thigh and laughed.

Filomón didn't answer. He sat beside the cot and looked out the window into the desert. "Even as terrible as the storm was for us, it will be good for the plants in the spring. After a good, wet winter the desert blooms like a garden," he nodded and rolled a cigarette. There was something about the way he spoke, the strength of his face, that reminded me of someone I had known—my grandfather perhaps, but I hadn't thought of him in years.

"These old villages cling to the river like the beads of a rosary," he continued, thinking aloud.

"Whoever crosses this desert has a lot of praying to do," Clepo agreed, "it's a journey of death."

"No, a journey of life. Our forefathers have wandered up and down this river valley for a long, long time. First the Indians roamed up and down this river, then others came, but they all stopped here at this same place: the springs of Tortuga, the place of the healing water—"

He talked and smoked. The dull sun shone through the window and played on the swirling smoke. I was fully awake now, but I felt feverish, and I couldn't help wondering what a strange day it had been to ride all this way with the old man and his assistant. I shivered, but not from the cold. The inside of the ambulance was now stifling. It glowed with white smoke and golden light which poured through the window. Filomón's eyes shone.

"How long have you been bringing kids to the hospital?" I asked.

"As long as I can remember," Filomón answered. "I bought this old hearse in a junk yard and I fixed it up like an ambulance. I've been transporting kids ever since."

"We get thirty dollars a kid, dead or alive," Clepo laughed. "And we get to hear a lot of interesting stories. We've taken every kind of diseased body there is to the hospital. Why, Filo and I could become doctors if we wanted to, couldn't we, Filo? But we don't know anything about you. You slept most of the way." He leaned over the seat and peered at me.

"He's tired," Filomón said.

"Yeah, but he's awake now," Clepo grinned. "So how did he get crippled? I know it ain't polio, I know polio. And how come his left hand is bandaged, huh? There's quite a story there, but he hasn't said a word!"

He seemed put out that I had slept most of the way and had not told the story of my past. But since the paralysis the past didn't matter. It was as if everything had died, except the dreams and the memories which kept haunting me. And even those were useless against the terrible weight which had fallen over me and which I cursed until I could curse no more.

"Do you take the kids back?" I asked.

"No, we don't!" Clepo said. "That's against the rules!"

"I picked you up," Filomón reminded him.

"I was hitch-hiking," Clepo said smartly, "somebody would have picked me up."

"You were lost. I found you in the middle of a sandstorm, crying. Lucky for you I came along."

"I wasn't crying, I had sand in my eyes," Clepo insisted.

Filomón smiled. "It doesn't matter, you've been a good assistant." That seemed to satisfy Clepo, he grunted and sat back down. Filomón drew close and looked at me. "We can't take anybody back, that's not our job. But when you get better you can make the trip back home by yourself. Just wait till spring, and you'll be better. I know it looks bad now, but in the spring the river comes alive and the desert dresses like a young bride. The lizards come out to play in the warm sun, and even the mountain moves—" He touched my forehead with his fingers, then he leaned close to me and I felt his forehead touch mine. Perhaps he was just leaning to retrieve one of the straps to tie me up again, but I felt his forehead brush mine, and I felt a relief from the paralysis which I hadn't felt since it came. Then he tied the strap and climbed back into the driver's seat.

"Filomón says you gotta keep your eyes on the mountain," Clepo said to fill in the silence.

"Well, it's helped us," Filomón answered, "it's been our faith in this wasteland . . . and it's helped a lot of kids. There's a strong power there."

He started the ambulance and let it coast down the long slope of the hill into the valley. I knew he was still looking at the mountain, still feeling the strange power that resided there for him.

"The water from the mountain springs is holy," he mused aloud, "long ago the place was used as a winter ceremonial ground by the Indians. They came to purify themselves by bathing in the warm waters . . . the waters of the turtle . . . Later, when the Spaniards came, they called the springs Los Ojos de la Tortuga, and when they discovered the waters could cure many illnesses they called the village Agua Bendita . . ."

"Who lives here?" I asked. We had entered the edge of the small town. Through the window I could see the tops of run-down gas stations, motels and cafes. There was a dilapidated movie house, a brownstone hotel, and many signs which creaked in the wind as they advertised the hot mineral baths.

"Mostly old people who come for the baths, people who work at the hospital, and a few of the old people who try to make a living from the small farms along the river—"

Filomón turned the ambulance and I caught a glimpse of a weathered sign that read *Crippled Children and Orphans Hospital*. The arrow pointed up the hill, so from the highway which ran through the small town we had to turn up the hill again towards the washed-out buildings which huddled together at the top. I struggled to turn to see more, instinctively, as I had so many times before, but it was useless, I couldn't move. I could only turn my head and watch the mountain across the valley. An air of hopelessness brooded over the dull mountain as the remaining winter clouds huddled at its peak. It seemed lost and out of place in the immense desert which surrounded it, and I wondered what secret rested in its core. Whatever it was, it was something that made Filomón's voice ring with hope and made his eyes sparkle even after the fatigue of the long journey.

"The doctors here can work miracles," Filomón was saying, "they've got ways now of straightening out bones and sewing together nerves and flesh—"

"Yeah, but they didn't fix my limp," Clepo said. "And they sure as hell don't believe in all this mumbo jumbo you've been giving the kid."

"Don't mind Clepo," Filomón laughed, "he just likes to act tough, but deep down inside he knows—"

But what is there to know, I wondered, as the huge bulk of the mountain held me hypnotized. The shape of the old volcano was obvious. Its hump curved down like a bow to a reptilian head. Huge, volcanic slabs of dark lava formed the massive plates of the shell. Near the bottom, jagged hills and the shadows of deep ravines created the illusion of webbed, leathery feet. Even the glaze of rain glistening on its back reminded me of the way the back of a snake or a toad will shine with oily rainbow colors. The more I gazed at it the more alive it grew, until I thought I was actually looking at a giant turtle which had paused to rest for the night. But where was its magic? Nothing seemed to grow on its sides; it was bare and dark and gloomy.

"Listen carefully and you'll hear the underground river which flows from Tortuga," Filomón was saying. "There are huge caverns beneath the mountain, and through them run powerful rivers, rivers of turtle pee. Yes, that old mountain is alive . . . a real sea turtle which wandered north when the oceans dried and became deserts. But it's alive, just waiting for another earth change to come along and free it from its prison. And it will happen. The old people told the stories that everything comes in cycles, even time itself . . . so the oceans will return and cover everything as they once did. Then Tortuga will be free—"

"You're crazy, Filo," Clepo laughed.

"And is that its secret," I asked bitterly, "to wait until the ocean returns? I don't want to wait that long! I want to move, now!" I cursed and struggled against the paralysis which held me as tight as the earth held Filomón's turtle.

"It takes time," Filomón said.

"Yeah, time," Clepo agreed.

"How much time?" I asked aloud. "How much time?" I agreed with Clepo, Filomón was crazy. The sea would never return. The earth was drying up and dying. Even the rain which pelted us during the trip fell hot and boiling on the empty desert. I had no faith left to believe his crazy story. Already the paralysis seemed to have gripped me forever.

"Here's the hospital," Filomón said. He had turned into a graveled driveway bordered by bare trees. I looked out the window and caught sight of the gray buildings. Winter-burned juniper bushes pressed against the wind-scoured hospital walls.

"It was a long trip," Clepo stretched and yawned, then he added, "I'm glad I'm not at this damned place anymore. Gives me the shivers—"

"It's always a long trip," Filomón said as he turned the ambulance and backed it up to the door, "and just the beginning for him—" I knew he meant me.

Clepo jumped out and opened the door. The cold air made me shiver. Overhead the wind drove the thin, icy clouds towards the mountain.

"Looks like snow," I heard someone say. "This the new kid?"

"It ain't Goldilocks," Clepo chattered. The voice belonged to the attendant who had brought a gurney. Together they slid out the cot and lifting me gently onto the gurney, covered me with a blanket, then pushed me through the open door and into the darkness of an enormous room.

"Filomón!" I called.

"Right here," he answered.

"Are you going back now?"

"As soon as the doctor signs the papers—"

"As soon as they sign the papers we're no longer responsible for you," Clepo added.

"Where are we?" I asked. The size of the room, its gloom and staleness were disturbing. I turned my head and peered into the darkness. I saw people lining the walls of the room, mostly women. They were dressed in dark clothes. Some held small children in their arms. All seemed to be crippled. Some wore braces, some crutches, others sat quietly in wheelchairs. Above them, on the high walls, hung huge portraits of solemn-looking men.

"This is the receiving room," Filomón explained. "Everybody that comes to the hospital gets admitted here. All the doctors' offices are up here, behind them is the surgery ward. Don't worry, as soon as the doctor checks you in you'll get sent to a ward in the back."

"How many wards are there?" I asked.

"Too many," Clepo answered. "I'm going to buy a Coke," he said, and wandered off.

"It must be visiting day," Filomón continued, "the parents who live close by can come and visit their children." Then he added as if in warning, "Your folks are way up north, and it's hard to make that long trip across the desert . . . don't expect too many visits."

"I know," I nodded. How well I knew the poverty and misery which surrounded us and suffocated us and held us

enslaved as the paralysis held me now. There would be no
money, no way for my mother to come, and perhaps it
would be better if she didn't come. What could she do for
me now, sit and look at me as the women who lined the
walls sat and looked at their crippled children? No, that I
didn't want. Better to write her and tell her not to worry,
or to send a message with Filomón and tell them that I
understood how hard times were and that whatever happened to me here at the hospital it was better if I worked
it out alone. Pity could not help me, and I had long ago
lost the faith in my mother's gods.

"Tell them not to come, if you see them," I said to
Filomón.

"I will," he nodded. At the same time a young girl appeared by the side of the gurney and Filomón's eyes lit up.
"Ah, Ismelda," he smiled. "What are you doing here?"

The girl smiled. "I'm helping the nurses bring the kids
from the wards for their visits . . . it's been a busy day, in
spite of the cold. Is this the new boy?" she asked, and
looked at me. She had a warm smile. Her dark eyes and
long hair set off the most beautiful oval face I had ever
seen. She was about my age, maybe a little older, but dressed
in the white uniform of a nurse's aide.

"Yeah, we just brought him in," Filomón nodded.

"Paralysis," she murmured as she touched my forehead
and brushed back my hair. Her touch sent a tingle running
down my back and arms. Her eyes bore into mine with
the same intensity I had felt in Filomón's eyes. She rubbed
my forehead gently and looked at Filomón.

"He busted his back," Filomón said, and added, "he's
from up north."

"I can tell that from his dark, curly hair," she smiled.
"And he's thirsty." She disappeared. How she knew I was
thirsty I didn't know, but I was. My throat felt parched
and I felt a fever building up deep in my guts.

"What does she do here?" I asked Filomón.

"She lives with Josefa in the valley, just on the outskirts of the town. They both work here. They do beds, sweep floors, help in any way they can—"

She returned and held a straw to my lips. I sucked greedily and felt the cold water wash down my throat. It was the first drink I had had all day and it instantly refreshed me.

"Good," I said when I had finished, "tastes strong."

"The water of the mountain is strong," she nodded, "that's because it's full of good medicine."

I didn't know if it was the water which had refreshed me or her touch, but I felt better. When I looked from her to Filomón I had the strange feeling that they knew each other very well. They had greeted each other like old friends and the sense of ease that passed between them helped to dispel the dread which had filled me the moment I entered the room.

"I have to go," she said, and touched my hand. "Visiting hours are almost over and we have to return the kids to their rooms. But I'll come and see you." She squeezed my hand and I felt the pressure. Instinctively I squeezed back and felt my fingers respond, lock in hers for a moment, felt a surge of energy pass through our hands, then she was gone. Someone stuck a thermometer in my mouth before I could call her name.

"You'll dream about that girl," Filomón smiled, "she's very strong . . . knows the mountain."

Clepo reappeared. He had poured salted peanuts into his Coke bottle and when he held it up to drink his red tongue reached into the bottle in search of the illusive, floating peanuts.

"Want some?" he asked me. I shook my head.

The nurse pulled out the thermometer, glanced at it and motioned for an orderly. "Get this kid over to Steel's receiving room," she snapped. "That's it, Filomón," she said as she signed the paper on his clipboard, then she walked away.

"Hey, you're getting Steel for a doctor," Filomón whispered, "he's the best."

"The kids like him," Clepo nodded, "he used to be my doctor."

The orderly began to push the gurney. Filomón stopped him for a moment, leaned over and whispered, "Remember, keep your eye on the mountain, that's the secret. Watch this girl Ismelda, she and Josefa know a lot of strong medicine . . ." Then the orderly began to push the gurney again and I saw Filomón and Clepo wave goodbye.

"Wait till spring!" Filomón called, and Clepo repeated, "Yeah, wait till spring!"

Somewhere in the enormous room a harsh voice called, "Visiting hours are over!" The people rose and began to leave, some of the children cried. I turned my head to call to Filomón, because the dread of the hospital had returned and I didn't want to be alone, but I couldn't see him.

"See you in the spring!" I thought I heard him shout above the noise of departure. "Just wait till spring!" Then the orderly pushed me out of the room and into a long quiet hall. He pushed the gurney into a brightly lighted room and left. The glare from the overhead lamp hurt my eyes, so I closed them and waited. In my mind I could see Filomón and Clepo waving goodbye. I tried to recall the desert we had crossed, but it was so wide and lifeless that I couldn't remember its features. The sun seemed to burn it lifeless. Whirlwinds rose like snakes into the sky. Then the rain came and pounded us and made me sleep.

Now here I was, somewhere in the middle of that desert, but I really didn't know where. My last contact with home had been Filomón and Clepo, now they were gone. But the girl, Ismelda, was here. I could still feel her touch, and I could remember her face clearly.

A nurse interrupted my thoughts. She took my temperature again, felt the pulse at my wrist and asked me if I had had a BM. I laughed. It was such a crazy question. She smiled and went on to ask me other questions. She recorded the answers on a chart. When she was done she said the doctor would be in shortly and left. I closed my eyes again and lay listening to the sounds of the hospital.

I could hear the sound of kids yelling; sometimes they seemed to pass by outside. I listened very closely and thought I heard the sound of water gurgling far beneath the earth. I floated in and out of light sleep and dreamed of my mother, and she said that all was the will of God and could not be questioned . . . and then my father appeared, and he said that each man was forced to live by his destiny and there was no escaping it . . . and I was about to curse both views which sought in vain to explain my paralysis when someone touched my shoulder.

"Sleeping?" the doctor said. He held my wrist and felt my pulse. His eyes were slate blue, piercing. He smiled. "It was a long trip, wasn't it?" I nodded. He placed his stethoscope to my chest and listened. "Any pain?"

"I think the bedsores on my ass and feet are burning again," I said. The first week I was in the hospital they had kept me in traction and on my back so the bed had burned sores which bled into my buttocks and my heels. Now Steel looked at them and shook his head.

"Bad burns," he said. "The trip didn't help any. I'll have the nurse clean them and put something on to relieve the burning and itch." He gave me a long examination, jabbing a pin up and down my arms, trying to find a live spot, asking me to try to move different muscles in my legs which seemed completely dead. When he finished he said, "We're going to do some X rays and have a look at the back—" and he gave instructions to the nurse and she and the orderly wheeled me into the X-ray room. They slid me onto the hard, shiny surface of the table, the technician straightened me out and from somewhere behind a screen told me to hold my breath. I looked up and saw the metallic shutter wink, felt something like a warm liquid pass through my bones, then the whirring sound died. The technician repeated the procedure, propping me on my side to get side views, and took over a dozen pictures. It was uncomfortable and painful. The more he worked over me, the more I felt the fever returning inside my stomach. Finally I closed my eyes and tried not to think about the clicking and the buzzing of the machine and the "Hold your breath," "Just one more" of the pale, thin technician. I thought of Filomón riding across the empty desert in his remodeled hearse, and I laughed bitterly to myself. Maybe I had really died and the whole idea of the hospital was just a dream to keep from facing that reality . . . and I suddenly thought about how much Filomón reminded me of my grandfather. He used to come riding across the wide plain in a mule-pulled wagon, the most beautiful cream-colored mules in the entire country . . . lashing the air with his whip . . . coming to visit us . . .

"Just one more fuckin' time!" the technician swore beneath his breath. Sweat poured from his forehead. "That Steel is a sonofabitch. If it's not just right he'll send it back—"

But Steel didn't reject any of the X rays. When they were dry and hanging on the illuminated glass he looked at each one carefully, made some notes, then he turned around.

"Okay," he said, "looks good. How long were you in traction?" he asked.

I didn't remember. I only remembered the long, agonizing nights, the suffocation, the heat, the sweat which wet the sheets, and how I tried not to sleep because I thought if I did I would die.

"It doesn't matter," he said, "they did a good job. You don't need surgery. I think the best thing for you would be a nice sturdy body cast, from the belly button to the top of your head. That way we can start you on physical therapy as soon as possible. You need that if we're going to try to save the legs. Do you understand?"

I nodded.

"Good. If there's anything left in those legs I'm going

to find it, and we'll go as far as we can. But you've got to help. I don't want you to give up." His voice was firm, but it was sincere. He wanted to help. "You have to keep working at it all the time," he said. He placed two fingers in my hand and said "Squeeze," and I squeezed. "That hand is strong, so's the arm—"

It was strange, but I couldn't remember squeezing anything with my hand up to the time Ismelda held my hand. Now my body seemed to want to come alive. It was a new sensation, especially sharp because of the dread I had lived with since the night of the paralysis.

"I do want to walk," I said eagerly. I did want to walk and run free again!

"Good," he nodded, "then you and I are in business. Let's get with it. First the barber. He's going to cut your hair, shave it. It'll be more comfortable and easier to work with when the cast goes around your head," he explained as a short, pudgy man entered the room. "Okay, Cano, make him bald."

"Yes sir," Cano said, and snapped open a cloth which he threw around me. "How you doin', kid," he smiled and began cutting. He talked continuously while he cut, and when he smiled, his thin, penciled mustache turned up at the edges. "You got good hair, dark and wavy, the kind girls like," he winked and rolled his eyes, ooh-la-la. "My poor mother, she used to say hair like this should be burned so the witches don't get hold of it . . . they like to build nests in it. Just like a woman, huh, build a nest in your hair!" He roared with laughter and swept aside the hair he had cut. "My mother believed in witches . . . see?" he held up his hand. He had only four fingers. "She says I got this 'cause a curse was put on her when I was in her belly. Who knows. Dr. Steel, he wanted to make me a new finger, and I bet he could, these doctors can do anything nowadays, they're getting too much power, like God, but I said, 'No thanks, Doc, if I can clip hair with four fingers then I'm happy. Don't go tampering with God's ways,' I said to him . . ."

He finished cutting, lathered the top of my head with thick, warm soap, slapped his razor on a leather strap and began shaving.

"So how old are you, kid?" he asked.

"Sixteen," I answered.

"You're lucky, you still got lots of time in life. You'll like it here. They got everything for you, a swimming pool, school, church, good food, TV, games, everything. For some of the kids it's better than home . . . some don't wanna leave after a while . . ."

I felt cold as the razor shaved swathes across the top of my head.

"So what happened to you?" he asked as he wiped his razor on a cloth on my chest.

"Accident—"

"Ah, life is full of accidents. Too many kids get hurt nowadays. Polio, epilepsy, everything . . . sometimes I get sad when I see it all. Wonder why God would do a thing like that. One day I asked Filo. You came with Filo, right? Well, he's a smart man. Must be over a hundred years old and still carting the kids around. Anyway, you know what he said? He said it's just a way station on the journey of life. I don' know what he meant. Do you?"

I shook my head. He wiped my bald head with a wet cloth then dried it. "No, I don' know what he meant. 'This is like a station,' he said, so that means there are more. And here they sew you kids back together. They can take a piece of bone from the tail and put it in your arm. They can take bones broken in ten places and put them together with steel pins. They can make crooked feet straight. Kids you think are dead, they bring to life . . . damn, one of these days they are going to put a motor in you and make you walk whether you want to or not!" He laughed uneasily. His mood had grown serious. "So that's it, kid," he

smiled and held up a hand mirror. I looked at my shiny
bald head. My arched nose and dark eyes seemed more
pronounced without the hair.

"Don' worry," he said, "it will grow back. Better than
my finger, which never grew. You know, they say hair
grows even on people who are dead—" He gathered up
his tools and went out waving and saying, "Don' worry,
kid, it will grow back . . ."

I closed my eyes and thought, but if it grows equally on
the dead and the living, how can one tell if he is alive or
dead? And this Dr. Steel, I thought, the miracle worker
according to Cano, what in the hell is he going to do with
me? How in the hell is this cast going to help me walk?
What do I have to find inside this broken body to make it
move again? I strained and pushed my legs, but felt nothing.
Damn, I cursed, damn!

Then I lay quietly and listened to the hospital sounds. I
thought I heard a group of girls calling to each other.
Clepo had said something about a girls' ward. Somewhere
someone strummed on a guitar and sang softly . . .

> It's been a blue, blue day
> I feel like running away
> I feel like running away from it all . . .

Dr. Steel reappeared with two other doctors. "These are
the plasterers," he said as he inspected my head. "Cano
did a good job, not a scratch." He ran his hand over my
bald head.

"Looks as bald as the mountain," one of them joked.

"Well, let's give him a shell, then. You ready?" Dr. Steel
asked. I nodded and they went to work. They worked
quietly and efficiently. One of them mixed the gypsum with
water and a smell of fresh, wet earth filled the room. Dr.
Steel and the other man covered me with cotton bandages
and a thick gauze. They wet the bandages in the mixture
and covered me with them, winding the bandages around

and around. The cast grew quickly, covering me from my hips to the top of my head with a hole left for my face and ears. I closed my eyes as the shell grew. With Dr. Steel directing the operation I felt in safe hands. He was a cold, methodical person, but he knew what he was doing. So I lost interest in the process and retreated into my thoughts, and there I saw the image of the mountain, imprisoned like me, until, as Filomón said, an earth change would come and free it. Did he mean that I would have to learn to be patient like the mountain, to sleep in my shell until the blood clotted and I was barely alive . . . just waiting for the spring . . .

"But why the spring?" I wondered aloud.

"Yeah, almost through," the doctor answered.

The shell tightened around me, from my navel to the top of my head, with holes for my arms so I could drag myself around like Tortuga, when the sea swept over the desert again . . . white and pure as the plaster my mother's saints were made of . . . Outside the winter wind moaned and I wondered what time it was. Someone sang

Who'ca took'ca my soda cracker
Does your mama chew tobaccer . . .

"Damn kids," the doctor laughed. He leaned back and lit a cigarette. They were done. Only Steel continued pulling and tugging at the cast, trying to get it perfect.

"Good enough to dry," one of them said. They looked at Steel. Finally he nodded. "Yes, good enough to dry. It's going to set straight as a ramrod."

So I was safe, safe in my new shell, safe as the mountain, shouldering a new burden which was already tightening on me.

"You'll feel it tighten a bit," Steel said, "but that's normal. We'll give it a little while to dry and then we'll X-ray to make sure it's set straight. Then you're on your way," he patted my arm and they went out of the room, closing the door behind them.

Safe as hell, I thought. Safe in my new shell. Safe as the mountain. With the door shut the room grew hot and stifling. I drifted in and out of troubled sleep. Once I thought I heard someone open the door.

"Hey, there's somebody in here."

"One of Steel's new ones . . . drying out, looks like."

"Let's use another room."

"Whatever you say, nurse . . ."

They went out and so did the lights. The dark grew more oppressive. The cast tightened like a vise around my chest, its sharp edges dug into my stomach. I called out a couple of times, but no one heard me. With the door shut I couldn't hear any of the sounds in the hall, but if I lay very quietly I could hear the sound of water running somewhere. I listened to the rushing sound for a long time, then no longer able to hold my own water I wet the gurney mattress and the sheet that covered me. I cursed, tried to turn my head and discovered that I no longer had even that freedom. I cursed again and tried to sleep, but I couldn't with the cast tightening in on me and the heat of the room suffocating me. The nurse had cleaned my bedsores and powdered them with something, but they were hurting again, burning and sending stabs of pain up my back. I was about to call again when I heard the door open, saw the shaft of light on the ceiling, then heard it close.

"Doctor!" I called out. "Nurse!" But there wasn't anybody there. Someone had just looked in and I had missed my chance. Then I felt a presence in the room. Someone had come in and was standing by the door! I held my breath and listened and I heard someone moving very softly towards me.

"Who's there?" I asked. There was no answer, but someone was in the room. "Who's there?" I called again.

"I been watching you since you got here," a voice answered.

"Who are you?"

"Never mind who I am! But I know who you are," the voice answered. There was a threat in the sharp answer.

"Call the doctor," I said.

"No!"

"Then I'll call him myself—" I started to shout but a thin, withered hand clamped my mouth shut. I gagged at the rancid fishy smell on the hand. I spit and tried to shout but the dirty, scaly hand held tight.

"The doctors are all on a coffee break," he taunted, "and by the time they get back it will be too late, turtle!" He laughed and drew closer and I could smell his bad breath and see his yellow eyes shining in the dark. "Don't shout!" he hissed. "Don't shout and I'll let you loose—" Slowly he removed his dry, twisted hand from my mouth.

I gasped for air. "Who are you? What do you want?"

"I heard you were here . . . you came today with Filomón. Did he tell you his crazy stories about the mountain?"

"I don't know what you're talking about," I answered. He sounded crazy.

"Oh yes you do, Tortuga!" he snapped. "Don't get smart with me! I saw Filomón bring you in! I know Cano cut your hair! Now they put you in this turtle shell, trying to make you like a turtle! So Filomón says every time the mountain moves, somebody in here moves! That's his story. And he thinks you can beat the paralysis that keeps you on your back like an overturned turtle. Well, I think that's a bunch of bullshit! You hear me, Tortuga? Bullshit! Go ahead! Try moving! Try it!" His voice rose, shrill and insane.

"You're crazy," I said.

"Crazy, huh," he sneered. "See this hand?" He held up his withered hand for me to see. "It's been drying up like this for a year, and nobody can do anything about it! I used to believe in Filomón's crazy stories, but that didn't do any good either!"

He was shouting and panting. His spittle fell on my face, and his eyes opened wide and glowed in the dim light.

"So you're supposed to be the new Tortuga, huh! They gave you a large shell, just like the mountain, huh! Well I'm going to find out if Filomón's story is true or not! Let's see if you can move!"

He struck a match. The light flared in the dark and filled the air with the sharp smell of sulphur. In the light I could see his face, twisted and angry, and his withered hand which was brown and wrinkled.

"I'm going to find out if you're Tortuga!" he shouted, and brought the match close to my eyes.

"Tortuga!" I shouted. "You're crazy!" I tried to turn my face from the hot flame but I couldn't.

"Move!" he shouted. "Move, mountain! Come and cure my hand! Move, Tortuga!"

"No!" I cried. "I can't!" I closed my eyes and smelled my singed eyelashes.

"Move, Tortuga!" he shouted insanely. "Move! Show us the secret!"

Just as the hot flame seared my eyes I heard the door open and somebody shouted, "Danny! What the hell are you doing in here!"

Lights flooded the room. The hot flame quickly disappeared.

"Nah-nothing," the boy named Danny whimpered, and drew away. I opened my eyes and saw him move around the gurney. "I was just visiting, Mike, I, I was just visiting with Tortuga—"

"The hell you were!" Mike shouted at him. "You're up to no good again! Get the fuck outta here or I'll break your goddamned arm!"

I heard Danny run out of the room, then the squeak of a wheelchair as Mike approached me.

"You okay?" he asked.

"You came just in time," I answered. "I don't know why he did it, but he was holding a match up to my face—"

"He's crazy," Mike swore, "he does crazy things. Once

I lay the law on him he behaves pretty well—Hey, you're
the new kid the ward is talking about. Just got in with
Filo, huh? I'm Mike. I heard Danny call you Tortuga, like
the mountain, fits now that you got that body cast . . . you
kinda look like a turtle, you know." He tapped the cast.
"They did a beautiful job on it, bet Steel did it."

"Someone taking my name in vain," Dr. Steel said as he
entered the room.

"Hey, Doc, how you doing? I was just talking to Tortuga
here, praising your work . . ."

"Tortuga," Dr. Steel murmured as he tapped the cast
and felt its dryness, "so Mike's given you a nickname already—"

"Fits, don't it?" Mike smiled. "Besides, Danny beat me
to the punch. Danny gave him the name."

Dr. Steel smiled. "Yeah, Tortuga fits just right. How
does the cast feel?"

"A little tight."

"You'll get used to it," he nodded.

"Cuts around the stomach, shoulders—"

"That's no problem. We trim that and tape it. Feel up
to an X ray?"

"Sure."

"Okay, let's see how it set—" He pushed the gurney out
of the room while Mike asked him if I could stay with
them when I got back to the ward.

"He's from my part of the country," Mike said.

"We'll see," Dr. Steel nodded and pushed me into the
X-ray room. The X-raying didn't take long, a couple of
shots and Dr. Steel was satisfied that the cast had set right.
"You're ready for some rest, and some supper." He
trimmed the edges of the cast with a small electrical saw,
then quickly taped them. It felt better, though the weight
of the cast was still strange to me. "It's been a long day,"
he said as he finished the taping, "we had visiting day and
surgery at the same time, that's why there's been so much

confusion in the halls. It'll be more quiet in the ward. I'll prescribe something for you to sleep tonight, then I'll see you in the morning, okay?" He called for an orderly and a slick, gum-popping man jumped forward and saluted.

"At your orders, Doc."

Chapter 2

"My name's Waldo," he said, "but everybody calls me Speed-o. Jack-of-all trades, orderly, driver, I can get you anything, I mean anything you want from town. And I take care of a few of the nurse's aides around here." He leaned over me and winked as he pushed the squeaking gurney down the deserted hall. I could smell the sweet smell of pomade on his hair and the Dentyne gum he chewed. "What's your name, kid?"

I thought awhile then answered, "Tortuga."

"Tortuga! Hey, that's all right, daddy-o! I like that!" Then he burst out singing.

> Hey, watch out!
> Turtle man coming down the road
> And he's carrying a heavy load
> Just looking for a place to sleep tonight!

"Like that, huh?" he snapped his fingers. "I'm a real swinger, just a real cool swinger!" He stopped suddenly and pushed the gurney into a dark corner. "Hey, Tortuga, you don't mind if we slide in here for a minute, right. There's a new nurse in this ward that is bad. I mean really bad! but she likes you know what. Every time I pass by we slip into the linen closet for a quickie." He giggled crazily. "Whad'ya say?"

I was about to answer, but he was already gone. I just wanted to get somewhere and rest, I wanted to put everything in perspective and get a sense of where I was. But why did the girl Ismelda keep popping in and out of my thoughts? I had only been here a few hours and already met some crazy characters . . . what would the future hold for me? How soon would the doctor start the therapy? And how much movement could I recover from my legs?

I closed my eyes and listened to the sounds of the hospital. Somewhere dishes clanged and kids shouted to each other. From far away I thought I heard the whimper of babies crying. Along the wall the steam radiators pinged and groaned as they swelled with steam. Overhead the cold wind moaned . . . and if I listened very carefully far beneath the frozen earth I could hear the sound of water, Tortuga's warm pee cutting new channels through the frozen wasteland . . .

Follow the river, Filomón had said, and yet even he seemed lost in the storms which racked us as we crossed the barren desert.

Wait till spring . . .

Pray to God, God's will be done . . .

I prayed, a million times I prayed, why the paralysis? Why me? What did I do to deserve this punishment? Why? Why? Why?

I awoke in a sweat. "Where am I?" I asked, and in the darkness I heard an answer, I heard someone moving around the gurney and for a moment I thought Danny had returned.

"Is this Tortuga?" the voice asked.

"Yes, he has come to live with us."

"Filomón brought him."

"Is he an orphan, like us?"

"Will he go to live with Salomón?" the voices whispered.

"Pray he doesn't, sister, but Salomón knows he's here."

I thought I was dreaming. Dark figures shuffled around the gurney, wheelchairs squeaked. "Who's there?" I asked.

"Are you awake, Tortuga?"

"Who is it?" I asked.

"Your brothers and sisters," came the answer.

Someone tapped on the cast, but because the gurney was high I couldn't see anyone. Then I felt a tug as an arm wrapped itself around my cast and pulled. At first I thought they were pulling me down and when the face of the girl appeared suddenly over me I realized she had pulled herself up. I gasped with fear. Her twisted face was gray and wrinkled, the face of an old woman. She drew closer and I saw the hump on her back. She was a small, deformed creature. She had clawed her way to the top of the gurney, now she smiled at me.

"Who are you?" I cried. Around me the others also squirmed their way up the side of the gurney, giggling and calling out, "Is that Tortuga?" "Does he look like Tortuga?" "Lemme see—"

"Yes, it is Tortuga," the hunched-back girl smiled. Her eyes were pale green in the dark. Her breath was sweet on my face, but her face was twisted and deformed.

"Who are you?" I cried again.

"Cynthia," she whispered.

"Is he going to stay in our ward?" another one asked.

"Salomón will say," she answered, studying me closely, curiously, and drawing closer and closer as if to kiss me.

"No!" I finally screamed as loud as I could. "Get away! Get away!"

"Shhh—" she tried to quiet me by placing her thin fingers over my mouth. "It's okay . . . we know . . ."

I gagged with panic, heaved and shouted again. "Get away! Get away! Don't touch me!"

They were swarming over me now, pulling themselves

over the side of the gurney, their twisted gnome faces loom-ing over me, whispering, giggling, poking at the cast, calling it a turtle shell, celebrating my arrival, vying for my friendship, then suddenly scattering as I shouted and cursed at them. They disappeared quickly, dropping off the gurney and scrambling away. I was still shouting when I felt Speed-o's hand clamp over my mouth.

"Shh—hold it! What the hell's the matter with you, kid? You wanna wake the dead?"

"Freaks," I gasped, "freaks—"

"Oh, that group," he said, and shook his head as he lit a cigarette. "That's Cynthia's group . . . they prowl the halls at night . . . know everything that goes on in this hospital . . . but they don't come out during the day . . . bad cases . . . but if you ask me the whole place is crawling with freaks . . ."

He pulled the gurney out of the corner and pushed it down the hall. Somewhere the sun was about to set because the pale ochre light which touched the high windows which faced the patio created a haze in the dim hallway. At the end of the hall he stopped at the nurses' station and rang the bell on the counter. He paced nervously back and forth, muttering, "I wonder where in the hell everyone is? I'm asked to deliver a body and there's no one waiting at the gate! This is your ward . . . but I wanna get back to that quickie I didn't finish. Nooooorse! New boy!"

"They're gone," someone whispered.

"Where?" Speed-o asked.

"Supper."

"And the nurse?"

"Chasing Danny."

"What'd he do now?"

"Started throwing spaghetti in the dining room. Big fight. Lots of fun."

"For cryin' out loud," Speed-o groaned. "I can't stand around and babysit this turtle man . . . he's gotta get to bed and I gotta get back to my beaver . . . Any empty rooms around here?" he asked the kid.

"Maybe up the hall, some—"

"Well let's go," Speed-o said, and pushed me hurriedly down the long, empty hallway. "We'll find you a room, ole buddy, we'll find you a nice and private place—"

We went deeper into the ward until he found a room without a name tag on the door. There he turned the gurney in and swung it alongside the only bed in the otherwise empty room.

"This will do fine," he nodded. He grunted and pushed and managed to slide me off the gurney onto the bed. "Just fine, just fine," he smiled and covered me with a sheet. "The nurse will be here in no time," he smiled and smoothed back his slick hair. "I'll see you in the funny papers, Tortuga," he winked and went out singing

> *If all little girls*
> *Were like bells in a tower!*
> *And I was the preacher*
> *I'd bang them each hour!*

Then the door clicked shut and I could only hear the echo of his song in the hallway.

The room was dark and silent. Through the window I could see the top of the mountain, glowing magenta as the winter clouds lifted long enough to let the setting sun shine on its back. The gigantic mass of boulders seemed to breathe with life as the color grew a soft watermelon pink then salmon orange. The light glowed from within the mountain as Tortuga seemed to lift his head into the setting sun . . . he turned to look at me, another crippled turtle come to live at his feet. The rheumy eyes draped with wrinkled flaps of skin bore into my soul and touched me with their kindness. For a moment the mountain was alive. It called to me, and I lay quietly in my dark room, hypnotized by the sight. Now I knew what Filomón had meant. There was a secret in the mountain, and it was calling me, unfolding with movement and power as the dying rays of the sun infused the earth with light.

Then a gray wash fell over the desert and the golden light was gone. The cold wind rattled the roof of the hospital. Brittle tumbleweeds rolled across the frozen waste. The fatigue of the journey settled over me and I fell into a troubled, restless sleep. In my dream I saw myself crawling across the desert like a crippled turtle. I made my way slowly towards the mountain, and when I was there I found the secret ponds and springs at the foot of the mountain. A ring of young girls danced around the water . . . they sang and danced like the group of first communion girls who had shared my holy communion so many years ago . . . when I was only a child. Then one of them, a dark-haired girl with flashing eyes, broke loose from the dance and ran towards me, calling my name as she ran. Tortuga! Oh, we're so glad you've come. Come and swim in the holy waters of the mountain! Come and hear Salomón tell his stories! I recognized Ismelda, dressed in flowing white and singing a song of joy . . . She took my hand and together we tumbled into the warm, bubbling waters. I'll drown! I cried, I'll drown! No, she cried, you will not drown in the mountain's waters. And holding me tight she taught me how to move my turtle flippers until I too could swim in the rushing water. Around me golden fish swam as effortlessly as birds float and glide in the air on a still day. See! she shouted with joy as she led me deeper and deeper into the mountain's heart, see the blood of the mountain. I looked and saw the rivers which fed the springs, one molten and red with burning lava and the other blue with cold water . . . and where the two rivers met, the water hissed and became a golden liquid, apricot scented. This is where the waters meet, she whispered to me as we swam towards the shore, this is the place of power. Look! I looked and

there on the bank sat a small, thin boy surrounded by
cripples. He smiled and waved to us. This is Salomón,
Ismelda said, and you have come to hear his story. Salomón
knows the magic of the mountain . . . he is the mountain.
Listen to his story. I listened as the frail, angelic boy opened
his lips to speak. Then in the deep night and in the dream
there was only silence as Salomón began his story . . .

Before I came here I was a hunter, but that was long
ago . . . Still, it was in the pursuit of the hunt that I came
face-to-face with my destiny, so I will tell my story and
you will know.

We called ourselves a tribe and we spent our time hunting
and fishing along the river. For young boys that was a great
adventure, so each morning I stole away from my father's
home to meet my fellow hunters by the river. My father
was a farmer who planted corn on the hills along the river.
He was a good man. He kept the ritual of the seasons,
marked the path of the sun and the moon across the sky,
and he prayed each day that the order of things not be
disturbed.

He did his duty and tried to teach me the order in the
weather and the seasons, but a wild urge in my blood drove
me from him. I went to join the tribe along the river. At
first I went willingly, the call of the hunt was exciting, the
slaughter of the animals and the smell of blood drove us
deeper and deeper into the dark river until I found that I
was enslaved by the tribe and I forgot the fields of my father.
We hunted birds with our crude weapons and battered to
death stray raccoons and rabbits. Then we cooked the meat
and filled the air with the smoke of roasting meat. The
tribe was pleased with me and welcomed me as a hunter.
They prepared for my initiation.

I, Salomón, tell you this so that you may know the meaning of life and death. How well I know it now, how clear
the events are of the day I killed the giant river turtle. I tell

you this because since that day I have been a storyteller, forced by the order of my destiny to reveal my story. So I speak to you to tell you how the killing became a horror.

The silence of the river was heavier than usual that day. The heat stuck to our sweating skin like sticky syrup and the insects sucked our blood. Our half-naked bodies moved like shadows in the brush. Those ahead and behind me whispered from time to time, complained that we were lost, suggested that we turn back. I said nothing, it was the day of my initiation, I could not speak. There had been a fight at camp the night before and the bad feelings still lingered. But we hunted anyway, there was nothing else to do. I was just beginning to realize that we were compelled to hunt in the dark shadows of the river. Some days the spirit for the hunt was not good, fellow hunters quarreled over small things, and still we had to start early at daybreak to begin the long day's journey which would not bring us out of the shadows until sunset.

In the branches above us the bird cries were sharp and frightful, and more than once the leader lifted his arm and the line froze, ready for action. The humid air was tense. Somewhere to my left I heard the river murmur as it swept south, and for the first time, the dissatisfaction which had been building within me surfaced, and I cursed the oppressive darkness and wished I was free of it. I thought of my father walking in the sunlight of his green fields, and I wished I were with him. But I could not; I owed the tribe a debt. Today I would become a full member. I would kill the first animal we encountered.

We moved farther than usual into unknown territory. We cursed as we hacked away at the thick underbrush; behind me I heard murmurs of dissension. Some wanted to turn back, others wanted to rest on the warm sandbars of the river, still others wanted to finish the argument which had started the night before. My father had given me an amulet to wear and he had instructed me on the hunt, and this made the leader jealous. So there had been those who argued that I could wear the amulet and those who said no. In the end the jealous leader tore it from my neck and said that I would have to face my initiation alone.

I was thinking about how poorly prepared I was and how my father had tried to help when the leader raised his arm and sounded the alarm. A friend behind me whispered that if we were in luck there would be a deer drinking at the river. No one had ever killed a deer in the memory of our tribe. We held our breath and waited, until the leader motioned and I moved forward to see. There in the middle of the narrow path lay the biggest tortoise any of us had ever seen. It was a huge monster which had crawled out of the dark river to lay its eggs in the warm sand. I felt a shiver when I saw it, and when I breathed I smelled the spoor of the sea. The taste of copper drained in my mouth and settled in my queasy stomach.

The giant turtle lifted its huge head and looked at us with dull, glintless eyes. The tribe drew back. Only I remained facing the monster from the water. Its slimy head dripped with bright green algae. It hissed a warning, asking me to move. It had come out of the water to lay its eggs, now it had to return to the river. Wet, leathery eggs fresh from the laying clung to its webbed feet, and as it moved forward it crushed them into the sand. Its gray shell was dry, dulled by the sun, encrusted with dead parasites and green growth; it needed the water.

Kill it, the leader cried, and at the same time the hunting horn sounded its *tooooo-ouuu* and echoed down the valley. Ah, its call was so sad and mournful I can hear it today as I tell my story . . . Listen, Tortuga, for it is now I know that at that time I could have forsaken my initiation and denounced the darkness and the insanity that urged us to the never-ending hunt. Now I remember that the words my father taught me were not in my heart. The time was not right.

The knife, the leader called, and the knife of the tribe was passed then slipped into my hand. The huge turtle lumbered forward. I could not speak to it, and in fear I raised the knife and brought it down with all my might. Oh, I prayed to no gods then, but how I have wished that I could undo what I did . . . One blow severed the giant turtle's head. One clean blow and the head rolled in the sand as the reptilian body reared back, gushing green slime as it died. The tribe cheered and pressed forward. They were as surprised as I that the kill had been so swift and clean. We had hunted smaller tortoises before and we knew that once they retreated into their shells it took hours to kill them. Then knives and spears had to be poked into the holes and the turtle had to be turned on its back so the tedious task of cutting the softer underside could begin. But now I had beheaded the giant turtle with one blow!

There will be enough meat for the entire tribe, one of the boys cried, and he speared the reptilian head and held it aloft for everyone to see. I could only look at the dead turtle that lay quivering on the sand, its death urine and green blood staining the damp earth.

He has passed his test, the leader shouted, he did not need the amulet of his father! We will clean the shell and it will be his shield! And he shall now be called the man who slew the turtle!

The tribe cheered, and for a moment I bathed in my glory. The fear left me, and so did the desire to be with my father on the harsh hills where he cultivated his fields of corn. He had been wrong; I could trust the tribe and its magic. Then someone cried and we turned to see the turtle struggling toward us. It reared up, exposing the gaping hole where the head had been, then it charged, surprisingly swift for its huge size. Even without its head it headed for the river. The tribe fell back in panic.

Kill it, the leader shouted. Kill it before it reaches the water! If it escapes into the water it will grow two heads and return to haunt us!

I understood what he meant. If the creature reached the safety of the water it would live again, and it would become one more of the ghosts of the bush that lurked along our never-ending path. Now there was nothing I could do but stand my ground and finish the killing. I struck at it until the knife broke on its hard shell, and still the turtle rumbled towards me, pushing me back. Terror and fear made me fall on the sand and grab it with my bare hands. Grunting and gasping for breath I dug my bare feet into the sand and tried to stop its mad rush for the water. I slipped one hand into the dark, bleeding hole where the head had been and with the other I grabbed its huge foot. I struggled to turn it on its back and rob it of its strength, but I couldn't. Its dark instinct for the water and the pull of death were stronger than my fear and desperation. I grunted and cursed it as its claws cut my arms and legs. The brush shook with our violent thrashing as we rolled down the bank towards the river. Even mortally wounded it was too strong for me. Finally, at the edge of the river, it broke free from me and plunged into the water, and trailing frothy blood and bile it disappeared into the gurgling waters.

Covered with the turtle's blood, I stood numb and trembling from the encounter, and as I watched it disappear into the dark waters of the river, I knew I had done a wrong. Instead of conquering my fear, I had created another shadow which would return to haunt us. I turned and looked at my companions; they trembled with fright. You have failed us, the leader whispered, and you have angered the river gods. He raised his talisman, a stick on which hung chicken feathers, dried juniper berries and the rattler of a snake we had killed in the spring, and he waved it in front of me to ward off the curse. Then they withdrew in silence and vanished into the dark brush, leaving me alone on that stygian bank.

Oh, I wish I could tell you how lonely I felt. I cried for the turtle to return so that I could finish the kill, or return its life, but the force of my destiny was already set and that was not to be. I understand that now. That is why I tell my story. And so I left the river, free of the tribe, but

unclean and smelling of death . . . That night the bad
dreams came, and then the paralysis . . .

I awoke sobbing and gasping for breath. I reached out
in the dark to touch Salomón . . . I called Ismelda's name.
I knew I had been there with them, listening to his sad
story, sitting by the warm water which gurgled from the
spring.

My arms and legs shook uncontrollably. Searing jolts of
electricity surged through my body as the water bathed my
tired body. The hot energy tore through my guts, gathered
in my balls and erupted out of my wet, warm tool, spewing
the marrow of blood and streams of hot pee on the cold
bed. Ismelda's tongue flickered in my mouth, she smiled
and sang, a song like the crescendo of water which kept
slapping against me . . . a song burning into every dead
nerve and fiber in my arms and legs.

"I'm alive!" I shouted. "Hey! Come and see! I hurt! Oh
I hurt! Come and see!"

I opened my eyes, the room was dark, my cry echoed
against the walls then died down, as the fire died down. I
was panting and gasping for breath. The cotton lining of
my cast felt moist with sweat.

"Water!" I cried. "I'm burning up! Help me!"

I jerked spasmodically on the wet bed. Then the newly
wired nerves rested and the pain subsided, but I knew
something had happened in the magic of my dream to help
me tear loose from the paralysis. I felt the bedsores burning
on my ass and my feet and still I felt like laughing. I
squirmed and felt the ripple of a quiver run down my legs
and tickle my toes. I looked, but it was too dark to see,
still I was sure something had moved. I cried again.

"Hey! Dr. Steel! Nurse! Anyone! Come and see! Get me
out of here!"

I thought I heard footsteps and listened quietly in the
dark, but no one appeared. Somewhere an owl called then
flew across the river towards the mountain. The storm

howled again, but now in the distance, farther south. I reached and touched the cast with my trembling right hand, felt the texture of the plaster which had become my shell, touched my face which was soaked with sweat. Good, I thought, good. I closed my eyes and slept again, smiling with joy, covered with sweat and stink, but glad to be quivering with the pain of the nerves and muscles which were coming alive. By the mountain, by the side of the spring, Ismelda waited.

Chapter 8

Peeeeeeeeee-Teeeeeeeeeeeeee.

Ready for PT?

What's PT?

PT PT PT, you mean you don' know!

Oh my.

PT is prick teaser, get it?

PT is PT boat—

PT is the end of the line, or the beginning.

PT is physical therapy, that's when they start pulling your legs and arms apart and making them move. And KC is going to be your PT!

Oh, KC will rub you sooooo close, ooooooh soooo close. She'll put her big fat boobs all over you, she's a teaser, a real teaser. She makes your wand feel soooo good—

Then she asks you, you wanna little?

And if you can climb on she'll let you have it!

She'll do anything to get you to move. She'll torture you, threaten you, tease you, play with you, rub her boobs on your face, but she gets you to movin'—

I like the way she smells. Sweet sweat. She sweats with you while she's working you over.

Oh my—

Who's KC?

She's the physical therapist, the wonder woman of exercise who makes you wish you never got paralyzed! She makes you move even if you don't want to—she's kinda like Jesus, she pulls you out of the dead—who was the guy Jesus pulled out of the dead?

Laz-rus.

Yeah, Laz-rus. Laz-rus was dead, dead and buried, paralyzed cold, and Jesus said, Laz-rus, come out of the dead! I command you, come out of the dead! And poor ole Laz-rus had to do what the Lord commanded, but can you imagine how painful it was?

Oh mmmmy—

Yeah, I mean those nerves and bones were cold, and he had to move them again! And the heart started to pump again, and the blood shot into his dry veins and pounded in his head, and the juices started flowing into his empty stomach and burning everything, and the nerves started jangling like live telephone wires, shooting sparks and messages to the brain and the balls and everywhere! Can you imagine ole Laz-rus shouting, Stop, dear Jesus, stop! Oooooh, stop this friggin' pain! Oh God he was hurtin', and he probably thought he was better off dead, 'cause there ain't no pain like the pain of coming back to life!

Jesus is the patron saint of all the PT's.

Yeah.

They love to bring people outta the dead.

Yeah.

Especially KC. You can be burning with pain like Laz-rus, and all she says is come on, baby, give it to me, sweet baby—

It's worse than being born.

Yeah, except when you're born you want it. Salomón

said we can't help wanting to swim in the electric-acid of life. It takes only a while to suck air and feel its force in your lungs, and only a while till the acid burns you, then you're safe and warm sucking at your momma's breast. But PT is like coming back from the dead, and who in the hell wants to come back from the dead, huh?

Maybe we did come back from the dead, ever think of that? I mean, this place is like a dumping station between life and death. Our twisted bodies were dumped somewhere and Filomón picked them up to bring them to Dr. Steel to straighten them out . . . and where do we go from here?

Back to where we came from—

Or back to the dead.

Oh my—

I remember the pain. Oh God, I never want to feel pain like that again! Never. I'd rather stay dead! There's nothing to compare it to, unless it's Laz-rus. He knows what it's like to be born again, and I bet you all my comic books that if he had known he'd ah said no thanks Jesus, leave me alone, find somebody else to bring back from the dead. I'm happy here, it's quiet and peaceful, just watching the worms do their business, I don't wanna be an experiment, no suh. And he should've been left alone, right? Because what does the guy get for coming back? A pat on the shoulder, then everybody turns to the miracle worker and Laz-rus is left out in the cold, alone, to wander in his crumbling, stinking body forever, worse than a leper, a man no one will touch, they throw rocks at him, the dogs tear at his mouldy flesh, there are no friends left, who wants to have anything to do with a man who came back from the dead?

What about us? We will be born again in Jesus Christ. The preacher said we will be born again!

Listen, if it's going to be that painful then you can have it. I don't want anything to do with that being born again business. It's too painful. If St. Peter met me at the pearly gates and said before you come in I've got to work you over so you'll fit in heaven, I'd say screw it. I wanna be just as I am, even if I am a lopsided freak. Send me where I don't have to face another PT in my life, ever—

What about Tortuga?

It's his time, man, he has to decide.

You know damn well KC's not gonna sit around and twiddle her fingers while he decides. When she comes in she's ready for work. She grabs ahold of an arm or leg and starts pulling. She's so mean she'll break open that friggin' cast if she has to! She's a mean, mean momma.

But she's good, don't forget that. She may be a bitch, but she does it for your own good! I mean she will beat the hell outta you to get you goin', but she does it for you. She pushes you to the end, I mean the goddamn living end!

This is the living end, har, har, har, our ward is the living end!

And when she asks you if you've had enough and you can't stand the pain anymore just say, give me more! Give it to me!

Why?

'Cause if you give up, she gives up. If you get your it-hurts-too-much feeling into her, then she can't do her work, and you'll be the loser. Look at Sadsack. He cried and begged 'cause he couldn't stand the pain, and pretty soon she felt sorry for him and she began to lay back and so he never came all the way back from paralysis—

PT is like life . . .

Hey, watch it! A philosopher loose among the cripples!

It is, man, you gotta commit yourself to it, and once you do there's no turning back and no excuses. You're either for it or not, right?

Raaaaght!

KC gets you hot but she stays cool. I mean, she knows what she's doing. When she did it to me she spread herself all over me. She spread her big, sweet boobs over my face and my little wand was waving like mad. She grabbed it and laughed. This is the cure, she laughed, as long as this pecker keeps tickling you've got the stuff to make it! I couldn't move an inch when I first got here, except my flagpole was sticking straight up for somebody to hang a flag on it, and the minute KC touched it it exploded. And now look at me, here I am running around! I swear she can do anything.

Yeah, and the first thing she's going to ask you is: Are you a turtle?

And the answer is: You bet your sweet ass I'm a turtle!

They all laughed, and their laughter was like the roar of a hurricane in the enormous white room.

"Hey," the dark woman laughed, "you look like a turtle! Are you a turtle?"

I looked at her and said, "You bet your sweet ass I am."

She laughed a deep, throaty laugh, and her big breasts shook. She leaned back and slapped her big hips. She had bright red lips and flashing eyes.

When she stopped laughing she looked at me and asked, "Hey, you're a smart one. Now tell me, sweet child, you wanna walk like a man . . . or you wanna stay a turtle?"

"I want to walk like a man," I answered, "I want to get up and get the hell out of here."

She smiled, then she nodded. "Good. We got a lot of work to do, honey—"

She pulled off the sheet that covered me, felt my arms and legs, told me to push and pull, feeling each muscle for its strength, jotting down her findings on a chart. She pulled harder than Dr. Steel had ever pulled and when I felt the first stabs of pain my legs drew back, like a turtle draws into its shell at danger. But she drew them out, slowly at first, warming up the muscles, cooing, "Push, baby, push, now don't that feel good . . ."

She pulled and the feeling was a fire that went screaming down broken nerves and dead muscles. I screamed at first. Like a wounded animal in pain I heard my pitiful cry echo in the room, I saw Jerry turn momentarily, his eyes cold to the cry he hadn't expected, then he turned back to his work and I learned to hold the pain in check. KC paused, pulled again, waited for my response, and when I clenched my teeth she smiled and pressed her body closer to mine and whispered, "Give it to me, baby, give it to your momma—" And I gave it to her, one more inch of bending joints and muscles full of searing pain, one more grunt which popped the sweat at my forehead, then the relaxing and the massage of KC's hands as the rhythm rested, then the pull again, like two people making love, pushing against each other, learning to work together. She took as much of the pain as she could into her arms and body, but she couldn't take it all. I thought the exercises I had been doing on my own were painful, but that was nothing compared to the forced movement. The added pressure shot pain through the bones and blood and left me exhausted, sweating, gasping for air. White light exploded in my brain, exploded in each muscle that moved for the first time as the tentacles of pain reached out and suffocated me. Soon there was nothing but pain. I ceased to exist. I couldn't feel KC's hands on me. I felt swept away into the blinding, white light which kept exploding to the throb of the veins on my temples.

It ain't easy, Tortuga, it ain't easy, Salomón said to me. Nobody promised the electric-acid wouldn't burn you, and that's the beauty of it, that's the beauty of life—no eternal rose gardens, no repetitive sweet melodies, instead a search for the fragile flowers of the desert and a floundering to find our own voice to sing our own songs . . . It ain't easy, Tortuga, but being born ain't easy. In the spring there's a blind-green force that pushes to renew itself in dormant limbs, and as it forces itself to life it burns the tender marrow of the shoots with its acid . . . ah, pity the sleeping plant which awakens one day throbbing with the wet electric juice of life, Tortuga, pity it for the pain it feels—but celebrate its dance . . .

Long after KC left I could still feel the piercing pain in my newly awakened, trembling muscles and tendons. I lay trembling and shivering, like a rabbit which has been mauled by a dog, gasping for breath. I felt limp and weak, but I felt exhilarated. The pain meant the muscles weren't dead.

"It takes time," Jerry said.

I smiled. He had shared the half hour of therapy with me. He had tried to weave as much of the pain as he could into the patterns of clouds and sky and thunder in the beads. "It takes time," I agreed.

At noon Mike and Ronco and Sadsack returned from swimming and we shared Ismelda's lunch. We were all hungry from our morning's work, and the flat, round tortilla bread was the only thing we had tasted of home in a long time.

"First time Ismelda's ever brought anyone a gift," Mike winked.

"She sure likes Tortuga," Ronco said.

"Better be careful with her, Tortuga, she's a witch—"

She is a witch, I thought, through the power in her fingertips she started to draw me from my paralysis. Now there was the new strength of KC. I wanted to shout. I wanted to kick my legs like a young foal to show the world it could not keep me down. Instead I smiled and tasted Ismelda's fragrance in her warm tortilla bread.

That night when lights were out Mike and Ronco celebrated my first therapy session with a party. Ronco mixed aftershave lotion, rubbing alcohol and orange juice, a drink he called the Ronco Lift and which he swore was stronger than bird farts. They had a little marijuana which Ronco had bought from Speed-o, so they rolled some and smoked and drank. Franco, in one of his rare times when he left his room, came by and played his guitar for us and smoked with us. I think he came because he was glad for me and because in the dark room we could see each other only as shadows. Outside, a storm whipped down from the north and rattled the hospital like an old tin shack, but inside, the time was mellow and lazy in the heavy, sweet drift of smoke.

You scored a big one today, Tortuga . . . I bet KC's gonna bring you through . . .

I feel high on pain, like I'm floating out there, somewhere . . .

That's the way it is. I cried the first session I had with her, Ronco said.

I wanted her soooo bad, my pecker was aching, but I couldn't take the friggin' pain, Sadsack cursed, and spit in the dark.

I never got my turn, Franco said sadly.

> *I tried, oh yes I tried*
> *To satisfy, her wandering way . . .*

Ah, screw it! he mumbled, and pushed his chair out of the room.

We were silent for a long time then Mike said, Pain is a high, and we try to replace that high with songs or women or booze. We never learned to live with pain, or we knew how once then we forgot. It's as natural as being born . . .

Or gettin' laid . . .

Yeah. But we're always running away from it. There's a whole ward over on the other side full of glue sniffers. Kids that ran away from all that pain out in the world. You pass by there and the place smells like a glue factory, and to come down they smoke some of this dope. Burned brains.

How many wards are there?

Lots . . . but let's not talk about that now, why man, we're celebrating!

Wheeeeeeeeeee—

I'm sure getting sleepy, Sadsack mumbled.

The talk drifted slowly back and forth, soft words riding softly on the dark velvet of the night. Nobody got wild or loud. We talked about the memories of good times, and we made up stories about the things we wanted to do when we got out of the hospital. Silence crept into the long space between words as the rest of the kids got sleepy and wandered off to their own rooms. Somewhere Franco crooned,

> *A little love*
> *That slowly grows and grows*
> *Not one that comes and goes*
> *That's all I want from you . . .*

The rusty sand of sleep and the mellow memories of bygone times covered our eyes and we slept. I remember Mike getting up to throw a blanket over Ronco, who had fallen asleep in his chair.

That little evil smoke gets him every time, he mumbled in the dark, then he tumbled into his bed and was instantly asleep.

The room was warm and peaceful and quiet, but outside I heard the screech of great warring owls as they swept across the valley; the feathers of their warfare swirled in the wind and turned the earth white. The wind howled as the storm worked its way back and forth across the empty desert. I tried to sleep, but the air was too charged with electricity, too full of strange sounds which cried like lost ghosts in the raging storm. It wasn't just the marijuana or Ronco's drink . . . it was something else . . . Something or someone seemed lost in the storm, working its way towards the hospital in search of one of us. But who? I wondered in my restless sleep . . . and suddenly my nightmare is alive with La Llorona, the old and demented woman of childhood stories who searches the river for her drowned sons . . . sons she herself has cut into pieces and fed to the fish . . . Now I see her again, as I saw her that day of my first communion . . . But where? On the trash heap of the

town, along the highest cliff which dropped from the edge
of the town towards the river below, there where the people
of the town dumped their garbage, trash which burned
perpetually as the coals crept beneath the rubbish and
erupted in small fires and evil-smelling columns of smoke.
There on the narrow path which ran along the steep cliff
... I walked, feeling my loss of innocence in the face of
the first communion girls who had danced their spring
dance for me while our parents picnicked down by the
river. She appeared unexpectedly, dressed in rags, eyes
streaked red from crying, fingers raw from tearing at her
hair ... You, my son! she cried as we met on the narrow
path. She reached out to grab me, mistaking me for her
murdered son, scratching at my face and eyes with long,
black fingernails, crying like a wild witch ... and I fighting
back, driven by terror ... No, no, I am not your son, I
am my mother's son, I live, I believe in the Holy Trinity
which I now call to dissolve you, to make you disappear!
But she is too strong, she has cried too many times at night
along the river, and I have sat awake and listened ... and
she has filled my soul with the dread of her stories. You
are the son I butchered for love, she cries, you are the son
I lost at war, the babe forced into my womb by the power
of your father, abandoned child. She reaches out and her
long fingernails cut through my flesh as I struggle and cry
for help in the smouldering darkness of the ash heap. Do
not fear me, she cries, I am your mother, your sister, your
beloved ... I suckled you at my breasts, sang lullabies for
you, wrapped you in rags torn from my skirts ... I am all
the women you have violated ...

No, no, I cry, and fight, pounding at her, stepping back
and feeling the fires that burn beneath me and threaten to
cave in and swallow us both. No, I am not your son. I am
not your son. I step off the narrow path, totter at its edge,
see the bright green of the river below, catch sight of the
clean lines of cornfields which line the other bank, then I
leap ... tear loose of her grasp and leap off the cliff

and fall and tumble into the air . . . fall until I can fall no more . . .

Then I awaken with a start, gasping for breath. My body is soaked with sweat. Only a dream, I tell myself, only a bad dream. The room is dark, outside the storm has let up. The small radio on Mike's nightstand buzzes with static. I lie back and catch my breath. In the silence I create I hear the room breathing. In the hallway all is quiet, but here in the room a strange presence breathes. My hair tingles, for a moment I believe that La Llorona has followed me out of the dream and into my room.

Who's there? I whisper in the darkness. There is no answer, but the cold night is heavy with a presence which is in the room or just outside the room. I cannot see in the darkness. I lie very quietly, listening for sounds which will explain the presence, waiting for a movement of shadows. I lie like that for a long time . . . and I think of Ismelda, is she safe, sleeping in her house by the river, does the wailing woman visit her dreams or is it we who are men the only ones tormented by that witch? Who visits Ismelda's dreams? Do giant snowmen awaken from the drifts of snow and move to her window to admire her beauty? Is her soft, smooth skin smothered in warm goose down . . . her heart beating in the middle of the tempest which covers the desert as heavy as the paralysis which infuses each of us . . . Her eyes are closed in peace, the long dark lashes undisturbed by the shadows of nightmares, her lips slightly parted, as if in a smile . . . Is she dreaming of me? Am I the man in the white turtle shell who swims nightly in the liquid of her dreams . . . hungry for her love and the touch which can melt the cold away . . .

Who's there, I call again . . . and wonder if Ismelda is sister to La Llorona . . . daughter of the same womb . . . companion to those young girls which shared the altar with me the last day of my childhood and who return to haunt every dream which seeks to tell me that in my innocence lies the answer to the question I seek now. Why me? Who was I then? Who am I now?

Where am I? I call . . . and thinking of the vegetables sleeping in their cold iron lungs . . . and Salomón, reading long into the night . . . dreaming what all of us will come to be . . . Salomón, I say, can you hear me? Tell me what will become of all of this.

Someone moves in the dark. A bed squeaks. Who's there? Who moves in the dark? Ghost . . . or man . . . or both?

I listen closely and hear a sound which is unmistakable . . . It is the same sound my grandfather's mules made as they thundered across the llano as he came swooping down on us, calling out his hello, slashing his whip and making it pop over the heads of the gray mules . . . Grandfather, I say.

I hold my breath and tremble. I hear the blue hooves chop into the frozen earth and turn the clods, then the rider pulls up outside, a rider with a remuda of horses, sliding to a stop, pawing at the ground, lathered hot with spume and froth, jerking at their halters . . . thick woven blankets of earth colors beneath the saddles . . . the air is sweet with their lather and urine smell . . . Grandfather, I say again, I had not expected you . . .

I hear my cry mix into the heavy silence of the night, then a shadow moves to the window and opens it. Cold air bellows up in the room, icy snow explodes like a cloud, the horses whinny to be away, and overhead the owls are screeching . . . their blood and feathers fall softly on the white earth. The rider waits motionlessly. He has called, but in another tongue. It is not the llano Spanish of my grandfather, it is not his cry of vámooooooo-nos! Away!

Who? I ask in the dark, and it's then I hear the sharp hiss of the well-thrown lariat as it snakes swift and deadly around the hump of the mountain. The rider on the red stallion has cast his lasso on the mountain, and now he is tugging at the huge hump, softly pulling the massive weight aside, slowly letting the streaks of light clothe the pre-dawn sky. I hear a song. Jerry sings at the window. It is his morning song.

Jerry, I whisper.

Jerry turns and stands like a warrior over my bed. He is dressed in buckskin now, rich and tanned buckskin which fills the room with its sweetness.

It is my turn, Tortuga, he whispers, my grandfather has found me. I leave this place forever. His voice is full of joy. His breath is warm as he speaks. His words are like yellow tendrils of light which reach out all around me to lift the dark rock of night.

A drum beats. He sings

> I walk in the path of the sun
> My grandfather commands
> I walk in the path of the sun
> He calls me to walk in his path
> As he once called the turtles from the sea . . .

Yes, Tortuga, long before his word was flesh the sea covered the earth, and men and turtles were brothers in the sea. Together they ruled the world of the fish . . . But the world was dark and so our grandfather called them forth from the sea. He opened a hole in the waters and for the first time man and turtle saw the bright sun and the clear sky. Man stood upon the back of the turtle and climbed into this world of light. Immediately he was blinded by the sun, he lost his golden scales and his skin turned dark and hard. But he was determined to walk upon the earth and to explore this new land of the sun. He called his new life "walking the path of the sun" and he sang its praises. He wanted to share the new beauty with his brother the turtle, so he reached back to pull him through the hole in the dark water. But the turtle was afraid. Only a few came upon the land, and they were so frightened by the sun and the cold winds that they grew thick shells to protect

themselves . . . and when frightened, they always retreat to
the safety of the water. We cannot retreat into the darkness,
Tortuga, we cannot build shells like the turtle . . . our
commandment is to live in the light of the sun . . . to walk
in the light of the sun . . .

"Jerry," I called.

"Goodbye, Tortuga," he whispered, "perhaps we will meet again, on the path of the sun . . ." He placed his open hand on my cast and with a black crayon he traced its outline on my shell. Then he turned and walked quickly to the window.

"Jerry!" I cried, fully awake, desperately, suddenly knowing that he was determined to go home. Outside I thought I heard the uneasy snorting and pawing of horses.

"On the path of the sun," he smiled and stepped out the open window. He disappeared into the morning shadows. I held my breath and listened for a long time. I heard the sound of horses riding away, shaggy horses crunching the thick snow, moving towards the river where they would turn to the west, towards the lost tribe.

The words of the morning chant echoed in the room, and hung like an incantation which raised the sun, because instantly the sun was a red, glorious stallion leaping over Tortuga's shell, and the rider was an old warrior dressed in brilliant headdress which sparkled and changed the pale pearl color of dawn into a fiery rainbow. He shouted his war cry and cast his burning spear which melted away the darkness and the ice.

I listened as long as I could, listened to the sound of horses breaking snow. The war cry was a cry which echoed all over the desert, far beyond its reaches, far beyond the serpentine Gila range, and into the last nook of every iron lung which provided the precious air for Salomón's vegetables. The cry and the light penetrated everything, even Ismelda's room, where she turned and moaned in her sleep . . .

"Mike!" I shouted. "Mike! Get up!" I suddenly knew Jerry would have to climb the mountain, and the passes would be covered and packed with snow.

Ronco stirred in his chair. Mike yawned and shivered. He sat up and looked at the window. "Who in the hell left the window open?" he asked and turned to look at me.

"Jerry," I said, "Jerry's gone!"

"Gone? What the hell—" Mike jumped into his chair and rushed to the window. I knew he was looking at the tracks which led from the window down the hill. He turned and looked at me and I wanted to tell him what had happened, but he already knew. He turned and raced his chair out of the room and I knew he was going for Dr. Steel.

Alburquerque

Chapter 8

I'm going to fight," he told Sara the following Sunday.

He had been nervous all day about telling her, and as he stood next to her while she prepared a salad he suddenly blurted out the news.

She paused and looked at him. "You're going to box?"

"Yes. In a few weeks."

"But why?"

He told her about Dominic's offer. She listened, but in the end shook her head. "I feel like Lucinda," she said, "I just don't like it. Isn't there another way? Maybe I could go to Mr. Johnson—"

"No, Mamá! I don't want you to have to beg from that man. If he knows, he won't say anything. Look, it's just one fight."

She knew how much he had suffered when Junior died, and how hard it was for him to go back into the ring, and it was natural for him to want to know his father. But she didn't like his being mixed up with the attorney who was so rich and always in the papers. Being mixed up with the rich could only bring trouble. She didn't like it, but for her son she would bear it without complaint.

"Go and get Lucinda, I'll finish here," she said calmly. He handed her the vegetables he had cut, and washed his hands.

"It's going to be all right, jefita. It's something I have to do." He kissed her.

"I know, I know," she answered. "Go on, the enchiladas will be ready when you return."

He drove to Lucinda's. She was radiant in a white summer dress. She kissed him and whispered, "Tú eres tú. You're all I want."

Sara had prepared red chile enchiladas, beans, and tortillas. For dessert she served sopa, a sweet bread pudding topped with melted cheese. It felt good to have Lucinda in her home. This was what Abrán needed, not the boxing and not the running around and making deals with the big-shot lawyer.

Time was the most valuable ingredient in life, and for Sara it was to be enjoyed with family and friends. She sipped wine and enjoyed the warmth of their company as they ate. Lucinda talked about her life in the mountain village of Córdova. Sara had asked her about her family. ¿Quién es tu familia? was one of the first questions that was always asked. One was known by one's family.

Lucinda told about her father and how he came to be a santero, and she told them about her mother and many of the old customs in the isolated villages of the Sangre de Cristo. She wanted Abrán to visit her family, she said with a glance at Sara. "That would be good for Abrán," Sara agreed. "He's a city boy. He needs to see the villages."

"How about the training?" Lucinda asked.

"I can jog up and down the mountain," Abrán said. "We'll go on Good Friday, come back after Easter. The doctor gave me a physical, said I'm in great shape."

"I knew that," Lucinda teased him.

"He is in good shape," Sara said as she cleaned up the dishes. "He runs every day, he doesn't smoke, but he drinks beer," she said with a mock frown. "Bueno, let's go in the living room. Lucinda, help me get the coffee and sopa. Then I want Abrán to read the beautiful story Cynthia wrote. She was not only an artist, she could write like a poet."

They gathered in the front room for dessert. Abrán flipped through Cynthia's diary. "This is an old entry, and it's as close as she comes to describing my father. They went to a matanza in the South Valley, near Los Padillas. It was the day they discovered the bower where we buried her ashes. She never mentions his name. She refers to him only as 'mi árabe.' "

"So he is dark," Sara said. A dark and handsome Mexicano was her son's father, an indio like Ramiro, a dark, curly-haired árabe. She looked at her son and admired him. Yes, he would find his father, it was best to believe that. He had been bound by destiny long enough, now he had to break those old ropes and create his own future.

Abrán smiled at his mother. "Yes. Bueno, aquí 'stá."

He read Cynthia's "la matanza," the entry that described the killing of the hogs for winter meat:

It was in the fiestas of the people that I discovered the essence of my people, the Mexican heritage of my mother. Other painters had concentrated on the Indians; I went to the small, out-of-the-way family fiestas of the Mexicanos. There is a chronicle of life in the fiestas, beginning with baptism. La fiesta de bautismo. I painted the padrinos at church as they held the baby over the font for the priest to bless el niño with holy water. In the faces of the padrino and madrina I saw and understood the godparents' role. The padrinos would become the child's second parents, and the familial kinship in the village or in the barrio would be extended. La familia would grow. I painted a scene where the baby was returned from church by the padrinos, the joy of the parents, the song of entriego, the return of the child, the food and drink, the hopeful, gay faces of family and neighbors.

And I painted wedding scenes. Gloria has my favorite. She has the painting that captures the moment when two of the groom's friends grab the bride and stand ready to spirit her away. The bridegroom is caught off guard, someone is pouring him a glass of champagne. The fiddler is leaning low, playing away, his eyes laughing. The other músicos join in the polka, drawing attention away from the traditional "stealing of the bride."

Fiestas, I loved the fiestas. There is a series: "Spring Planting," "Cleaning the Acequias," "Misa del Gallo," "Los Matachines." I did the Bernalillo Matachines, although my favorite was the Jémez Pueblo Matachines. I painted los hermanos penitentes on Good Friday, the holy communion of Easter Sunday, the little-known dances of Los Abuelos and Los Comanches. I painted a triptych of Los Pastores at the Trampas church one Christmas. And the Christmas Posadas. All the fiestas of life that might die as the viejitos die.

I painted the fiestas of the Rio Grande, the fiestas of your people, mi amor, the fiestas my mother used to tell me about when I was a child, because if life had not been so cruel, we would have shared these fiestas.

Do you remember la Matanza in Los Padillas, mi árabe moreno? We were invited by your friend Isidro. His family was having a matanza. We had fallen in love that summer, and suddenly it was October, a more brilliant October I never saw again. The entire river was golden, the álamos had turned the color of fire. Long strings of geese flew south and filled the valley with their call, and we, too, drove south along Isleta. Farmers lined the road, their trucks filled with bushels of green chile, red chile ristras, corn and pumpkins, apples. It was autumn, and the fiesta of the harvest drew people together.

It was my first trip into the South Valley. I was a gringita from the Country Club; I had been protected from the world. But the valley was to become my valley. I would visit the villages of the Rio Grande again and again, until the old residents got to know well the sunburned gringa who trampled around with easel, paint, and brushes. I earned their respect. They invited me into their homes, and later they invited me to their fiestas. Their acceptance kept me alive.

The night had been cold, and the thin ice of morning cracked like a fresh apple bitten. The sun rising over Tijeras Canyon melted the frost. Gloria helped, as usual. She picked me up. I told my parents I was spending the day with her. Without her help we could never have had time together. Why did she marry F? What a pity.

The colors of autumn were like a bright colcha, a warm and timeless beauty covering the earth. The sounds carried in the morning air, and all was vibrant with life before the cold of winter. Oh, if we had only known that the wrath of parents can kill!

The matanza was beginning when we arrived. Cars and trucks filled the gravel driveway. Family, friends, and neighbors filled the backyard of the old adobe home. Isidro greeted us.

"Just in time," he said, and we followed him to the back where the women were serving breakfast. They had set a board over barrels to use as a table, and on it rested the steaming plates of eggs, bacon, potatoes, chile stew, hot tortillas, and coffee. The men were stuffing down the food. Somebody had already called for the first pig to be brought out of the pen. Whiskey bottles were passed around; those who had gotten up early to help the women start the fires and heat the huge vats of lye-water had been drinking for hours.

A very handsome, but very troubled, young man held a rifle in one hand and a bottle of whiskey in the other. Remember Marcos? I will never forget him; he learned a lesson that day. We all did. At the pigpen the frightened sow was being roped and wrestled out.

The women watched; they goaded the men. My mother was a woman of great strength, I always knew, and I saw that same strength in those women of the valley.

"Ya no pueden," they teased the men wrestling with the sow. The worst thing to tell a macho, especially when he's drinking and doing the "bringing the meat home" business. But it was a fiesta, and the teasing was part of it.

"¡Andale! ¡Con ganas!"

"¡Qué ganas, con huevos!"

They laughed; the men cursed and grunted as they lassoed the pig.

"Don't shoot yourself, Marcos!"

"Don't stab yourself, Jerry!" they said to the young man who held the knife.

Isidro told us that Marcos was an attorney in town and Jerry was a computer man at Sandia Labs. Like other young men who had left the valley for a middle-class life in the city, they only returned once in a while to visit the parents and grandparents. Or they returned for the fiestas. They had almost forgotten the old ways, and so the older aunts teased them.

Who remembered the old ways? The old men standing along the adobe wall warming themselves in the morning sun. With them stood don Pedro, Isidro's grandfather, the old patriarch of the clan. These were the vecinos, the neighbors who had worked together all their lives. Men from Los Padillas and Pajarito and Isleta Pueblo. Now they were too old to kill the pigs, so they had handed over the task to their grandsons. They warmed their bones in the morning sun and watched as the young men drank and strutted about in their new shirts and Levi's. Those old men knew the old ways. Maybe it was that day that I vowed to paint them, to preserve their faces and their way of life for posterity. They would all die soon.

"Hispano Gothic," I called the painting I did of those old men. The last patriarchs of the valley. And their women, las viejitas, las jefitas of the large families, stood next to their men and watched. These old men and women remembered the proper way of the fiestas, and so they watched with great patience as their uprooted grandsons struggled to prove their manhood. What a chorus of wisdom and strength shone in their eyes. What will happen to our people when those viejitos are gone? Will our ceremonies disappear from the face of the earth? Is that what drives me to paint them with such urgency?

Time has been like a wind swirling around me, my love, since I last touched you. Time will scatter my paintings, but the seed planted that autumn day will survive. Our seed will grow, but we were not destined to nourish it.

The children were always present at the fiestas, and they were there that day. They laughed and played tag, chased each other, the boys shot baskets through a hoop, a baby nursed at his mother's breast. As the squealing, struggling pig was pulled out of the pen, the children paused to watch. Here was the link between past and future generations, this is how the young would learn the old ways.

Near the fire a large, wood plank was set over two barrels. The dead pig would be hoisted up onto the rough table to be gutted and cleaned. A huge cauldron sat over the hot fire that had been lighted before the sun was up. Boiling water laced with lye let off wisps of steam; a thin scum clouded the surface. When the dead pig was raised onto the plank, it would be covered with gunnysacks and the hot water poured over the sacks. The bristle would be softened and easy to scrape off with knives.

The shouts of the men grew agitated, the sow was big and nervous. The men pulled with ropes, others poked and pushed from behind. "¡Nalgona!" one cursed. The women laughed. "That's the way you like them, Freddie!"

Don Pedro and his compadres watched patiently.

"¡Sonamagon! ¡Pinche! ¡Muevete!" the young men cursed the pig.

"Come on!" Marcos shouted. "A little closer!" He aimed the rifle. He was drunk.

Marcos' wife stood in the circle of people around the pig. She was a Northeast Heights gringa, and she didn't like what they were doing. She wished they hadn't come. Marcos was making a fool of himself, she thought, and he was going to muddy the new boots and Levi's she bought him for the State Fair. Too much pagan ritual in the air for her taste.

"Hold him still," Marcos shouted.

They had frightened the pig, made it nervous, now they couldn't hold the struggling animal that pulled from side to side.

"Watch out, Marcos!"

"He's going to shoot someone!"

"Ramona. Take the gun away," someone said to the oldest aunt. She was in charge of the fire and the cleaning, and tough enough to keep the men in line.

"Marcos?" she called.

"I'm okay," he answered angrily. He threw the empty bottle aside and cocked the rifle.

"No tiene huevos," somebody shouted. Marcos heard. He turned and glared at his cousins, those who had not left the valley.

"Sonofabitches!" he spat. They'd been razzing him all morning, now they came out and said he didn't have the balls to do the job. He was a drugstore cowboy playing at being a macho man. He'd show them.

Then his wife whined. "Marcos, let somebody else do it. You're ruining your boots."

His face grew livid. I painted anger in his eyes, for it was there. Bitch, he wanted to scream, I'll show you.

"Grandpa," Ramona said, and for a moment everyone glanced at don Pedro. Would he stop the charade before someone got hurt? The old man looked at Marcos' father. The father shrugged; it was up to don Pedro to decide.

The old man nodded. Continue. He held up a finger. Make a clean kill with one shot, he said.

"You damn right, daddy-o," Marcos grinned. Somebody handed him a just-opened bottle of Jim Beam and he took a big swig.

"Don't give him any more to drink, he's going to shoot somebody." The women were worried, they had known of matanzas that turned deadly.

The men heaved and pushed the pig in front of Marcos. He aimed, the rifle wavering.

"¡Cuidao!" one man shouted, and jumped aside.

"Behind the ear! Behind the ear!"

"Between the eyes!"

"Watch out!"

"He's drunk!"

"Get back!"

The men jumped away from the pig and a deafening explosion filled the air. The baby cried, the children screamed, the cows in the giant cottonwoods by the ditch rose cawing into the air. Dogs barked, and the air echoed with the report of the rifle. The smell of gunpowder filled the clean morning air.

The pig gave a shrill cry and reared up. The bullet had only grazed it. Marcos fired again, wildly, and the second bullet entered above the left shoulder. The sow hit the ground, turning round and round in the dirt, crying shrilly as blood spurted from its wound.

"You missed, cabrón!"

"Shoot!"

"No! The knife!"

The men pulled at the ropes around the pig's feet and held it. But Marcos would not take the knife. The pig's hot blood made him turn away and vomit, the stuff splattering his new boots.

Tío Mateo took the knife and pounced on the screaming

sow. He grabbed an ear for leverage then plunged the knife into the throat as hard and deep as he could. The wounded sow thrashed and turned.

"Hol'im! Goddammit hold him!"

The men held, dirtying themselves with mud and blood as the knife found an artery and the blood rushed out. Then the pig grew still. The men got up slowly, covered with filth and blood, wiped their hands on their Levi's and cursed Marcos. They spit out the bitter taste in their mouths and reached for a drink.

Against the wall the old men stood quietly. They shook their heads; it was not good. The frightened children had turned to the women, hiding in folds of skirts. This is not how it should be.

"Pinche marrano," Marcos cursed, and kicked the dead pig at his feet. "You sonofbitches didn't hold it," he blamed the men.

"Fuck you," one of the men answered, "you're a lousy shot!"

They faced each other, angry that it had not gone right. They blamed Marcos, he blamed them. None looked at the old men along the wall.

"Bring the other one! I'll show you who's a good shot!" Marcos bragged, and wiped the vomit from his mouth. He cocked the rifle.

"Put the gun away, Marcos, you're drunk," tía Ramona said. She was angry, too. She remembered matanzas that were done right, not crazy and dirty like the one she had just seen. She looked at the children; they shouldn't be frightened, they should be learning to value this old custom.

"Stay out of this, tía!" Marcos insisted. "Bring the other pig!" he shouted, waving the rifle. "I'm gonna blow his brains out!"

"No!" a stern voice broke the tension in the air. We turned to see don Pedro step forward, bent with age but resolute. He had stayed out of the argument as long as he

could, but now he had to set things right. I think it was
the frightened children who compelled him to stop the
debacle.

He walked right up to Marcos and looked squarely at
his grandson. "Ya no valen ni para matar un marrano,"
he said.

Marcos and the other men stiffened. It was an insult,
and if any other man had said that, there would have been
a fight, but this was their grandfather so they swallowed
their pride.

Don Pedro, still sinewy and tough, was the patriarch of
the family, and respect for elders was still a value in the
family. He took the rifle from Marcos.

"You call yourselves men," he said firmly, "and look at
this mess. You can't even kill a pig."

His words stung. His sons and grandsons looked at their
dirtied clothes and the mess of blood on the ground and
knew he was right.

"Ah, come on, Grandpa," one of his grandsons said,
"don't take it so serious. We're just killing a pig, it's no
big deal, ese."

"It is a big deal," the old man retorted. "It has to be
done right."

Marcos' eyes narrowed, but he tried to make amends.
"Come on, Grandpa, have a drink . . ."

"I don't drink with boys," don Pedro answered, a hard-
ness in his voice. He stood unwavering, strong as an old
tree of the river.

The silence was deadly. Marcos clenched his jaws in
anger.

They were young men full of booze, and the smell of
blood had made their own blood boil. I felt something
terrible was about to happen.

So did don Pedro's wife, because she stepped forward
and put her hand on his arm, trying to coax him back. The
arena of blood and drunk young men was no place for an

old man. Better to stand with his compadres at the wall and warm his bones in safety. But don Pedro wouldn't budge.

"Okay, Grandpa," Marcos spit out the bile in his mouth. "If you're such a man, why don't you do it."

It was the grandfather's turn to be stung. He looked around and saw the men nod. Yes, if you're such a man, you show us how it's done.

"Grandpa likes to talk," Marcos continued, "but he's too old to cut the mustard."

The young men smiled.

"¿Qué pasa, Grandpa?" a grandson said, and slapped the old man on the back.

"No puede," Marcos snickered. They stood facing each other, Marcos and don Pedro, the young and the old. Their veins bulged with tension, their eyes glared.

The old woman whispered, "Anda, Pedro, vente." Come away, leave this to the young men. The old man straightened his shoulders, looked at her and smiled. Then he turned to the old compadres who stood along the wall.

"Secundino," he said softly, "el martillo."

The old man Secundino thought he hadn't heard, then he smiled and nodded. It was the call to the matanza, an old calling, something they knew in their blood, something they had done surely and swiftly all their lives. The right way. He hobbled to the shed and returned with a ten-pound, short-handled sledgehammer.

"Procopio, ponle filo a la navaja," the old man said as he rolled up his sleeves.

"Con mucho gusto," Procopio spat a quick stream of chewing tobacco through yellow-stained teeth and smiled. He took the long knife and began sharpening it on a small whetstone. "Lana sube, lana baja," he whispered as the blade swished back and forth on the stone.

"Compadres," don Pedro whispered, "la marrana." The old men ambled silently but quickly toward the pen.

"Wait, Grandpa," Marcos said, "you don't have to—"

But it was too late, the old man's eyes were fixed on the huge sow that the men moved out of the pen by softly clicking their tongues. They needed no ropes to move the pig. Secundino slipped the big hammer into don Pedro's hand. Then Procopio handed don Pedro the sharpened knife, so now the old man balanced the hammer in one hand and the knife in the other.

The young men had only heard these stories, that long ago when rifles and bullets were scarce, the matanza was done like this. Like a bullfighter meeting a bull with just a cape, the old man met the two-hundred-pound pig with just a blade and hammer.

Don Pedro moved in a circle, keeping his eye on the pig as it came closer and closer to him. There was no noise, no ropes, no fast motions to spook the pig, just the circle of men getting smaller.

The compadres smiled and remembered all the years of their lives when they had done this. It was a ceremony, the taking of the animal's life to provide meat for the family. The young men needed to be reminded that it was not sport, it was a tradition as old as the first Hispanos who settled along the river.

This is how we have lived along the river, the viejos said. We have raised generations on this earth along the Rio Grande, and we have done it with pride and honor. Each new generation must accept the custom and likewise pass it on.

The air grew still, we stood transfixed. The circle closed in, until the animal was only an arm's length away.

Crows called from the cottonwoods of the river, a dog whined, the wood embers popped, the wisps of steam hissed and rose from the lye-water in the cauldron.

When don Pedro had come face-to-face with the pig, he raised his hammer, and with the speed of a matador, there was a brief glint in the sunlight, the arc of his arm, a dull thud, and the pig jerked back and stiffened. The kill was complete and clean.

It had taken all the old man's strength to make the kill, but he had done it with grace. There was no loud thunder of the rifle, no crying children or barking dogs, just a clean kill. We stood hypnotized as don Pedro dropped to his knees in front of the quivering pig. Two of the men held the pig by the ears as don Pedro plunged the knife into the pig's heart. The blood flowed swiftly.

Tía Ramona stepped forward with a pan to save the hot, gushing blood. Not a drop was wasted. She would mix it with water in a bowl, then slowly stir it with her hand until the thick coagulants were removed and only the pure blood remained. This she would fry with onion and pieces of liver as a blood pudding, a delicacy for the guests.

When don Pedro withdrew the knife it seemed to come out spotless, unbloodied, and his hands were clean. Then the old man stood, and a shudder of fatigue passed through his frail body. He took a deep breath, and then sipped from the tin cup of water his wife handed him. He smiled at her, and when he looked at us, there was a serene beauty in his face. A noble look on the faces of the old men of the clan.

His compadres nodded, slapped him gently on the back. That's the way we used to do it, their nods said.

"Chingao," one of the grandsons exclaimed, breaking the silence.

"Did you see that?"

"Damn, Grandpa."

They moved forward to touch the old man. One handed him a bottle so he could drink. They were filled with admiration. Even Marcos reached out to touch the grandfather, as if to share in the old man's valor.

"You're too old to be killing pigs," his wife scolded. She took his arm, and together they walked back to the safety of the warm adobe wall.

"A man's never too old," he winked, willing to withdraw. Let the young men lift the hog and begin the gutting and cleaning, he would sit with his old vecinos and watch. They had done their duty, they had shown the young people the right way to perform the ceremony.

The pig was gutted and the liver was thrown on the hot coals. When it was baked, the first slice was served on hot tortillas with green chile and offered to don Pedro, a tribute to the old warrior. Then he and the rest of the men ate, drank wine, and talked about the old days when the people of the valley lived in harmony with the earth and their neighbors.

"We will die and all this will pass away," I remember don Pedro saying.

That is why I had to paint. I wanted to preserve the beauty of those moments. That was the gift and the commitment which came to rest in my soul that day. The life and love of the old people opened my eyes, and I wanted to share that gift.

Love filled that entire space of time, the people and the golden colors of the river. Love consumed us, and we thought time would never change. We drove south and walked along the river bosque. There we found our bower. Do you remember, mi amor? The warmth of the brilliant October sun, the love we shared? The beauty of your bronze body was so new and pure that I couldn't get enough of you. That bower became our place of love, it will always be my home. I return there to be with you.

Abrán finished reading and placed the diary on his lap. Sara sighed, and Lucinda's eyes were filled with tears.

"It's beautiful."

"Yes, it is."

"Such a gifted woman," Sara whispered. She looked at Abrán. So this was her son, the child of that woman. Ah well, life is passed on like that, not to own and possess, but to nurture for a while. The woman had given him the gift of life, but she had given Abrán love all these years. Each had offered what she could, and at that instant Sara felt very satisfied and content.

Zia Summer

Chapter 18

Sonny hurried back to his apartment, afraid tears might well in his eyes. He showered and dressed then drove to Garcia's Kitchen for breakfast. Garcia's served some of the best huevos rancheros and green chile in town. Sonny liked to sit at a window booth and look out on the traffic which moved up and down Central as he ate. Old-timers from la Plaza Vieja frequented Garcia's, sat around, drank coffee, gossiped.

The gathering of the old men was an old custom. When the villages were small along the Río Grande, the center of the community was la Plaza de Armas and the church. There the old Mexicanos gathered to discuss the affairs of state. Warming their bones against southern adobe walls in winter and cooling off under the shade of the álamos in summer, the discourse of the old men was an essential part of the politics which ran the village.

Now the villages from Isleta to Bernalillo were swallowed up by the expanding city, but the men still found a place to gather to talk. In the mornings it was Garcia's, or Duran's Pharmacy or the Village Inn Pancake House; in the afternoon they sat under the shade trees of the Old Town Plaza and discussed the events of their community and of the world as they watched the tourists.

"Hi, Sonny," Rosa greeted him.

"Rosa, mi amor, when are you going to give me a chance," he smiled, took the menu from her as he sat. Rosa was vivacious, an attractive woman, short and stocky with big breasts and a big smile. Sonny could tease her, and she teased back.

"Soon as my old man's out of town," she smiled and poured his coffee. "The usual?"

Sonny nodded. For breakfast he always had huevos rancheros.

"What's the usual?" the woman in the booth next to him asked.

Sonny turned to look into a pair of bright blue eyes that smiled invitingly. She sat alone, her blond hair teased up, her complexion white and smooth, in her thirties and dressed in a bright blue summer dress.

An adventuresome tourist, Sonny assumed, and very lovely. Her kind didn't often stop for breakfast at Garcia's. They usually stayed at the Sheraton where they felt "safe." This lady was obviously out for a real taste of Albukirk.

"Huevos rancheros," Sonny smiled.

"That's what I'll have," the blonde said to Rosa, "a rancheroo with huevos."

Rosa bit her lip to keep from laughing. "Yes, ma'am," she smiled, glancing at Sonny. "You want him over easy or scrambled?" she asked, and the blonde said over easy as Rosa hurried away to the kitchen, where Sonny knew she would burst out laughing and tell the cooks that the blonde had just ordered a rancher with balls.

"New in town?" Sonny asked, also trying to keep from laughing.

"We visit every summer. My husband sells kitchen equipment. We're at the Hyatt, but that's not real, you know what I mean?"

From the kitchen Sonny heard a roar of laughter. Rosa had just told her story.

"I know what you mean."

"I love Old Town. I'm going to look around. Any suggestions?" Her blue eyes were direct, inviting. She crossed her long legs, waited.

Sonny looked at her, felt the tug of the flesh. She was lovely, special. And alone. She wanted suggestions.

"Hmmmm . . ." he thought.

She waited, the crossed leg swinging softly.

"Well?"

Sonny cleared his throat. "Oh, there's a lot to see. Lots of shops, jewelry . . ." he stammered.

"Yes, thank you," the woman in blue nodded, "I intend to do the shops." She broke off the conversation, sensing Sonny's reluctance, and turned back to her newspaper.

From where he sat Sonny could smell her perfume. Her lips were painted candy red. A very nice-looking woman, attractive, and obviously in the mood. But not today, he thought, and tried not to kick himself too hard for turning her down. He consoled himself by looking out the window at Central Avenue and concentrating on anything but the woman in blue.

Central was the original Highway 66 which ran east to west through the city. Before the interstate was built, old 66 had cut through Tijeras Canyon and entered the city. It ran through town before it crossed the Rio Grande and climbed up the long slope of Ten Mile Hill. There it dipped into the Río Puerco Valley, crossed the continental divide somewhere around Gallup, crossed the deserts of Arizona and ended on the California coast.

California, the land of dreams. The highway, too, was a road of dreams.

A ranchero with huevos, Sonny mused, and glanced at the woman in blue. She glanced at him, smiled. He smiled, sipped his coffee, and returned his gaze to the slow traffic moving outside.

Route 66, a road of dreams, generations of dreams crossing the nation on the mother road. Fleeing the Dust Bowl,
the Okies moved west, and Elfego Baca had stood somewhere near this very spot and watched the migration. The
story was handed down the generations, how the Bisabuelo
had helped an Okie family change a tire, paid for the repair
and given the man a few dollars for gas. Enough to get to
Gallup.

The people here felt sorry for the dislocated, Sonny's
father had told him. They often fed them, gave them food
before they moved on to the dream of California.

A few stayed. Cars broke down and some were forced
to plant their dream in the Río Grande Valley. Lean men
and women with bony bodies and faces, trudging west to
California, cars and trucks packed with all their worldly
possessions, piled high, canvas water bags cooling as they
hung over rearview mirrors or over the front of the radiator
grille, broke and without a dime, those who had no strength
to continue on to the land of milk and honey laid down
their load and learned to eat beans, chile, tortillas.

As they became learned in the cultural ways, some moved
into the barrios, lost their prejudices against the Mexicans,
started businesses in the booming downtown area, and now
their grandkids were third-generation Albuquerqueans, as
proud of the city as any Nuevo Mexicano.

Blacks who worked on the railroad, the cooks and wait-
ers of the Super Chief, had brought their families and settled
along Broadway, and their community thrived. Indians
from the Pueblos and Navajos from the Diné Nation moved
in and out of the city, creating a cultural cloth of many
colors. Newer immigrants arrived, Japanese and Southeast
Asians, more Mexicans and those who fled the wars in
Central America, each lending a new color and texture of
fabric to the cloth, the woof and warp took on the earth
tones of a Chimayo blanket.

The city was the blanket, each color representing different heritages, traditions, languages, folkways, and each

struggling to remain distinct, full of pride, history, honor, family roots, clannish, protective, often prejudiced and bigoted. Yes, the city was full of growing pains, bound to old political oaths and allegiances, lustful, violent, murderous when the moon was wild, drunk on lost loves, and at the center—struggling for identity.

What will bind? What will bring us together?

"What?" Sonny asked.

"What you ordered," Rosa replied, sliding the plate full of eggs, beans and green chile in front of him. In a small dish came the just-baked corn tortillas. "Just like you like them, hot," she smiled.

"And here's your ranchero with huevos," she said to the woman in blue, served her and rushed back to the kitchen.

Rosa was devilish. Sonny smiled and looked at the blonde.

"Looks delicious," she said.

"The best in town," Sonny replied.

"I'm glad I took a chance," she smiled again.

"Provecho."

"Provecho?"

"It means, enjoy."

"Oh, I intend to," she said, and ate. Sonny saw her eyes go full of tears as the first bite of hot chile burned her mouth. He expected a cry, a protest, but she only sniffed, touched her napkin to her nose and said, "Excellent."

She had spunk. She intended to enjoy. Sonny dug into his huevos rancheros.

Sonny cut two smaller pieces from his tortillas, making little spoons with which to pick up the eggs, potatoes, beans and chile. He glanced at the blonde and saw her cut gingerly with a fork into the food.

"Like this," Sonny wanted to tell her. "Here in New Mexico we are so rich that we use a new spoon for each bite we take. A piece of tortilla with which we scoop up the food." But he said nothing. Let it be, he said to himself.

He looked out the window. Across the way was Old

Town, la Plaza Vieja. From this spot, or one close to it, the Mexicanos of Old Town had seen the Okies and other displaced people of the Dust Bowl era travel west to the promise of California. Elfego Baca, too, sat here with his amigos and watched the poor on their westward migration. Watched displaced farmers, factory workers, those who built railroads and highways, women with families to feed, all colors and all kinds of workers, leaving the old to create the new in California.

Elfego Baca had also been witness to the migration west after World War II. The greatest boom the country ever experienced, the greatest change for New Mexico. The city was a migration point on the east-west road across the southern belly of the country, the oasis where travelers paused to fill their water bags and bellies.

Change came, new colors, new sounds, new threads, and the blanket extended itself to the foothills of the Sandias to cover the houses of gringos, south into the valley to cover the homes of the old Atrisco land grant settlers, north into the valley where the new estates of the ricos were being built. The cloth was the new society, a green oasis with cottonwoods fed by Río Grande water.

Sonny sniffed, blew his nose, smacked his lips and felt the sting of the hot green chile, wiped the tears from his eyes. Great! The duende spirit of the Río Grande lived in the green chile. And in the red. Comida sin chile no es comida, his father always said.

Heat waves danced on the hot asphalt of Central Avenue. Across the road lay Duran's Pharmacy, which also served a hot chile verde stew with homemade tortillas. Next to it a summer-silent Manzano Day School brooded in the morning heat.

In the Old Town Plaza the summer tourists were already arriving to gawk and and buy turquoise jewelry, paintings, arts and crafts, baskets, perfumes, candles, cards to send home, every imaginable item of Nuevo México available.

They would go to the nearby restaurants to eat New Mexican food, and write home about the hot chile that "blew them out." They would walk under the portal on the east side of the plaza and look at the handmade jewelry the vendors displayed, escaping the June heat for a moment in the shade.

They would enter the San Felipe de Neri Church, the church of the parishioners of Old Town, take pictures in the courtyard, take pictures in the kiosk of the plaza, pictures to return home with, to rekindle the memory when memory failed. Old Town was a tourist museum. Although many of the old families still lived in the community, it was a thriving tourist museum which catered to the visitors, sold bits and pieces of the many-colored cloth, trinkets for those who browsed through on a hot, summer day.

Frank Dominic wanted to change all this by building canals from downtown to Old Town. Sonny couldn't picture Venetian boats rowing up Central to Old Town. Venetian boats loaded with mariachi groups sernading the tourists who came shopping? Ah, the developers had gotten out of hand.

He looked out into the bright glare outside, and the traffic moving as if in a dream. He blew his nose again.

"Good chile," he said to the woman in blue. She was perspiring.

"I love hot chili," she smiled. "Really hot."

I bet, Sonny nodded, touched his napkin to his eyes. He didn't know what was gnawing at him. Why couldn't he tell this well-dressed and looking-for-excitement-in-funky-Alburquerque woman sitting across from him that he'd love to show her Old Town, the nooks and crannies the tourists didn't know. Nooks and crannies, yeah.

Because I have to see Lorenza. I promised Rita, he thought, and rose. "Enjoy yourself," he said in goodbye to the blonde.

"I'll try," she whispered, blotting her lips. "Hot chili."

"Yeah," he said, moved to the cash register to pay his bill.

"What's the matter? Don't you like blondes?" Rosa whispered as she rang up the register and gave him change.

"I'm not the right ranchero," Sonny said lamely.

"Pendejo," Rosa chastised him.

He glanced one more time at the woman. That's life, he thought, and borrowed the phone to call Lorenza. Yes, she was home and she was free. He could come by for coffee.

He drove north on Rio Grande, across the new Alameda bridge and to Corrales. Once an agricultural community like the North Valley, the village was now a bedroom community for professionals who worked in the city. A few continued farming, there were fine apple orchards left, but more and more the place was becoming gentrified by those who could afford the prices of expensive real estate and custom-built adobe homes.

Lorenza Villa lived in a modest adobe home at the edge of the river bosque. Sonny knew she had been married, had two kids, both grown, but he didn't know much more. She did her thing, healing people, and kept much to herself. It had been a year, Sonny guessed, since he had last seen her. He and Rita ran into her at the Kimo theatre at a play.

The thing Sonny always remembered about her was her eyes. They were dark, intense, no doubt the eyes of a woman who could see into other realities, but each eye seemed to belong to a different person. It wasn't a disfigurement, she wasn't cross-eyed, just a nuance of difference from one to the other.

When she opened the door, she smiled and stepped out to greet him, taking his hand in hers. Her grip was firm, warm.

"Sonny, I'm glad to see you. Come in."

She turned and led him into a small living area brightly done in Mexican prints and paintings. She was dressed in a white, cotton gown, the edges embroidered with bright flower designs. Oaxaca, Sonny guessed. She was barefoot.

"Sientate," she said, pointing to a comfortable easy chair. "¿Café?"

"Gracias," Sonny nodded. He watched her move to the kitchen counter, her walk graceful. She was a handsome woman, dark like Rita, long, raven-black hair falling over her shoulders, the high Indian cheekbones, full lips, full-bodied. Not slim like the woman in blue. A trickster woman, Sonny figured, and a very good-looking one. Dark and lovely as a Río Grande Nefertiti. There was Moorish blood lapping at the banks of the river.

"How's Rita?"

"Good. Saw her last night. She suggested—"

"She called me," Lorenza smiled as she returned with coffee. "She's concerned . . ."

"Right," Sonny relaxed. "So here I am," he smiled at her, letting his eyes take in her beauty. What a woman, Sonny thought. How can she help me if I feel so attracted? Try to get the cabrón out of you! he chided himself.

"What are you thinking?" Lorenza asked.

He shook his head. "Nada," he lied.

"Sometimes talking helps," Lorenza said, and sipped her coffee.

"Yeah. Sure. Well, to tell the truth, Rita thinks I have susto. From Gloria . . ."

"You saw her body?"

"Yes."

"Ah," Lorenza whispered, and Sonny felt the thing with the eyes was there. She was looking at him as if two persons were looking at him. Then she rose and walked to the window.

"The morning is beautiful. I was up to see the sunrise," she said. In the brush of the river bosque she caught sight of a shadow. The movement became a form, a river coyote. Two more appeared, pausing to look toward the house.

Poised by the window, Sonny thought she might disappear into the shining sunlight, her white dress radiating light, her long, black hair glistening with light, and he wondered if she knew about don Eliseo's Señores and Señoras de la Luz. Was she becoming one? Was that the secret of the curandera?

"The coyotes watch over you," she whispered.

He was puzzled.

"Your animal spirit," she said, "watches over you."

He got up and went to stand beside her. The sun coming through the window was dazzling, but he followed her gaze and saw the coyotes.

"River coyotes," he said.

"When the animal spirit appears, it means they come to help," she said, turning to look at him, her eyes fixing him with a stare which held him immobile. "It implies danger . . ."

She brushed past him and he caught a scent of her perfume, deep, like chamisa after a rainstorm, other pleasant herbs, perhaps manzanilla . . . The scent of light, the warm comforting aroma of sunlight on her body.

Watching the coyotes, he remembered a story his father told. The man had been haunted by a coyote which came at night to prowl around the house. For months the man was allowed no sleep, and the man's rifle was useless against the ghostly coyote. Finally he etched a cross on a bullet. He went to the priest and had it blessed. That night he shot the coyote, and in the morning he found the spot of blood. He called his neighbors and they followed the trail of blood to the house of an old woman who lived in the hills. They found her dead from a bullet wound.

Legends. Cuentos de la gente. The brujo could take the form of the animal, an owl or coyote. If the stories told of such occurrences, there was something to it.

Sonny sighed and went to Lorenza. He sat across from her and she took his hands in hers. She closed her eyes, and for a long time she just sat there, holding his hands. When she opened her eyes she asked, "Do you know what a limpieza is?"

Don Eliseo had told Sonny about the cleansing ceremony.

"To cleanse . . ."

"A spirit has gotten into your soul. It has to be cleaned away . . ."

"Spirit?" Sonny said. The stories of souls moving around were cuentos the old people told. Stories to scare the children on late winter nights. To pass the time. Did Lorenza believe?

"Gloria's alma. The limpieza would clean it away."

"If her soul is in me," he questioned, "why would I want it cleansed away?"

"You loved her."

"She was the first woman I loved."

"No matter how much we love the person, when they die the soul must move on. The soul is on a journey, seeking its own light, its own clarity . . ."

Ah, she did know don Eliseo's philosophy, or something close to it. The soul had to leave, to become a Señora de la Luz. But for some reason Gloria's soul didn't want to continue on its natural journey. It had fastened to him.

"Does she want revenge?" Sonny asked.

Lorenza nodded. "The soul has a reason for refusing to move on. It's in you, and that's what's troubling you. It could get worse . . ."

Why would Gloria diminish him? She had taught him love; she had been his lover, the first woman he ever knew. He would give anything to have her alive. But something had sapped his strength last night, creating a sense of growing depression, fatigue, not thinking straight. He wanted to find Gloria's murderers, and he had nothing to go on. A sense of hopelessness haunted him.

And he hadn't been able to get it up with Rita. How could it get worse? Complete impotence? Damn, he was only thirty, so he was screwed up because of Gloria's death, he wasn't an impotent old man yet.

"Maybe I should do this limpieza," he said, and stood.

"It's up to you," she replied. "It takes a few hours."

Did he doubt her? Is that why he was hesitating?

"You decide," she said. "The old curanderas and soba-doras knew how to release the susto, release the souls of the dead. I've studied their ways, I can help you."

Sonny was still hesitating when Lorenza spoke again. "There is a strong animal spirit acting against you," she sighed. "In the old teachings, the nagual is the animal energy of a person. We all have it. Someone is using their animal energy against you."

"How do you know?"

"I can see it," she whispered. The light oozing from Sonny was so clear she wondered that he didn't see it. He was being cut into, drained, and only because he had his own strength within was he able to keep going. He was a brujo within, a powerful but kind shaman, but one without training. He had not yet recognized his own power.

Raven, Sonny thought. That's the animal Lorenza is seeing. Or the animals had killed Gloria. Human animals.

"Soon as I have time, I'll make an appointment," he said.

She walked him to the door. The sunlight revealed the curves of her body. He was drawn to her, a magnetic pull, and he wondered if she was feeling the attraction. He felt an urge to say something, but he thought it would be banal.

"Thanks for the café."

"De nada," she replied. "Before you go, come with me." She took his hand and walked toward the bosque where they had seen the coyotes.

She walked softly, so silently she didn't stir the dry grasses of the path. Where the coyotes had stood, she pointed. On the soft sand lay the faint outline of the coyotes' prints. They followed the tracks into a densely shaded Russian-olive grove. She stopped and searched carefully until she spied what she was after: the fine strands of coyote fur caught on a thorn.

She gathered the few hairs and held them up for Sonny to see, then turned to inspect the path again, looking for coyote nails or a tooth an old coyote might have lost on the river trail. No, today she was not to be as lucky, but the coyotes had left strands of their hair for Sonny.

Above the canopy of shade the sunlight was bright, warm. A drone of cicadas filled the green bosque, otherwise the place was silent. She took a small leather pouch tied at her belt, put the coyote hairs in it and handed it to Sonny.

"Keep it safe," she said.

Sonny took it, nodded, slipped the bag into his shirt pocket.

He followed her back to her house, feeling for the first time that he was being watched. But they were alone except for a crow calling from the top of a cottonwood tree.

A giant crow perched at the top of a dry branch of the gnarled tree. A raven.

"Go away, diablo!" Lorenza cried out. "We're not afraid of you!"

The big bird lifted from the branch, crying angrily as it did, circling the clearing then disappearing over the treetops.

Sonny remembered the large crow rising from the pine tree at Raven's compound. He looked at Lorenza but she had already turned up the path toward the house. "Be careful," she said in parting, and disappeared into the house.

Yeah, Sonny thought as he got into his truck. He had left the window rolled down, but it was still stifling. He felt the pouch in his shirt pocket, resting over his heart. Ravens and coyotes and a woman who reads my thoughts. Where in the hell is all this going to end?

SHORT
STORIES

B. Traven
Is Alive and Well
in Cuernavaca

I didn't go to Mexico to find B. Traven. Why should I? I have enough to do writing my own fiction, so I go to Mexico to write, not to search out writers. B. Traven? you ask. Don't you remember *The Treasure of the Sierra Madre*? A real classic. They made a movie from the novel. I remember seeing it when I was a kid. It was set in Mexico, and it had all the elements of a real adventure story. B. Traven was an adventurous man, traveled all over the world, then disappeared into Mexico and cut himself off from society. He gave no interviews and allowed few photographs. While he lived he remained unapproachable, anonymous to his public, a writer shrouded in mystery.

He's dead now, or they say he's dead. I think he's alive and well. At any rate, he has become something of an institution in Mexico, a man honored for his work. The cantineros and taxi drivers in Mexico City know about him as well as the cantineros of Spain knew Hemingway, or they claim to. I never mention I'm a writer when I'm in a cantina, because inevitably some aficionado will ask, "Do you know the work of B. Traven?" And from some dusty niche will appear a yellowed, thumb-worn novel by Traven. Then if the cantinero knows his business, and they all do in Mexico, he is apt to say, "Did you know that B. Traven used to drink here?" If you show the slightest interest, he will follow with, "Sure, he used to sit right over here. In this corner . . ." And if you don't leave right then you will wind up hearing many stories about the mysterious B. Traven while buying many drinks for the local patrons.

Everybody reads his novels, on the buses, on street corners, and if you look closely you'll spot one of his titles. One turned up for me, and that's how this story started. I was sitting in the train station in Juárez, waiting for the train to Cuernavaca, which would be an exciting title for this story except that there is no train to Cuernavaca. I was drinking beer to kill time, the erotic and sensitive Mexican time which is so different from the clean-packaged, well-kept time of the Americanos. Time in Mexico is at times cruel and punishing, but it is never indifferent. It permeates everything, it changes reality. Einstein would have loved Mexico because there time and space are one. I stare more often into empty space when I'm in Mexico. The past seems to infuse the present, and in the brown, wrinkled faces of the old people one sees the presence of the past. In Mexico I like to walk the narrow streets of the cities and the smaller pueblos, wandering aimlessly, feeling the sunlight which is so distinctively Mexican, listening to the voices which call in the streets, peering into the dark eyes which are so secretive and so proud. The Mexican people guard a secret. But in the end, one is never really lost in Mexico. All streets lead to a good cantina. All good stories start in a cantina.

At the train station, after I let the kids who hustle the tourists know that I didn't want chewing gum or cigarettes, and I didn't want my shoes shined, and I didn't want a woman at the moment, I was left alone to drink my beer. Luke-cold Dos Equis. I don't remember how long I had been there or how many Dos Equis I had finished when I glanced at the seat next to me and saw a book which turned out to be a B. Traven novel, old and used and obviously much read, but a novel nevertheless. What's so strange about finding a B. Traven novel in that dingy little corner of a bar in the Juárez train station? Nothing, unless you know that in Mexico one never finds anything. It is a country that doesn't waste anything, everything is recycled. Chevrolets run with patched-up Ford engines and Chrysler transmissions, buses are kept together, and kept running, with baling wire and homemade parts, yesterday's Traven novel is the pulp on which tomorrow's Fuentes story will appear. Time recycles in Mexico. Time returns to the past, and the Christian finds himself dreaming of ancient Aztec rituals. He who does not believe that Quetzalcóatl will return to save Mexico has little faith.

So the novel was the first clue. Later there was Justino. "Who is Justino?" you want to know. Justino was the jardinero who cared for the garden of my friend, the friend who had invited me to stay at his home in Cuernavaca while I continued to write. The day after I arrived I was sitting in the sun, letting the fatigue of the long journey ooze away, thinking nothing, when Justino appeared on the scene. He had finished cleaning the swimming pool and was taking his morning break, so he sat in the shade of the orange tree and introduced himself. Right away I could tell that he would rather be a movie actor or an adventurer, a real free spirit. But things didn't work out for him. He got married, children appeared, he took a couple of mistresses, more children appeared, so he had to work to support his family. "A man is like a rooster," he said after we talked awhile, "the more chickens he has the happier he is." Then he asked me what I was going to do about a woman while I was there, and I told him I hadn't thought that far ahead, that I would be happy if I could just get a damned story going.

This puzzled Justino, and I think for a few days it worried him. So on Saturday night he took me out for a few drinks and we wound up in some of the bordellos of Cuernavaca in the company of some of the most beautiful women in the world. Justino knew them all. They loved him, and he loved them.

I learned something more of the nature of this jardinero a few nights later when the heat and an irritating mosquito wouldn't let me sleep. I heard music from a radio, so I put on my pants and walked out into the Cuernavacan night, an oppressive, warm night heavy with the sweet perfume of the dama de la noche bushes which lined the wall of my friend's villa. From time to time I heard a dog cry in the distance, and I remembered that in Mexico many people die of rabies. Perhaps that is why the walls of the wealthy are always so high and the locks always secure. Or maybe it was because of the occasional gunshots which explode in the night. The news media tells us that Mexico is the most stable country in Latin America, and with the recent oil finds the bankers and the oil men want to keep it that way. I sense, and many know, that in the dark the revolution does not sleep. It is a spirit kept at bay by the high fences and the locked gates, yet it prowls the heart of every man. "Oil will create a new revolution," Justino had told me, "but it's going to be for our people. Mexicans are tired of building gas stations for the gringos from Gringolandia." I understood what he meant: there is much hunger in the country.

I lit a cigarette and walked towards my friend's car which was parked in the driveway near the swimming pool. I approached quietly and peered in. On the back seat with his legs propped on the front seat-back and smoking a cigar sat Justino. Two big, luscious women sat on either side of him, running their fingers through his hair and whispering in his ears. The doors were open to allow a breeze. He looked content. Sitting there he was that famous artist on his way to an afternoon reception in Mexico City, or he was a movie star on his way to the premiere of his most recent movie. Or perhaps it was Sunday and he was taking a Sunday drive in the country, towards Tepoztlán. And why shouldn't his two friends accompany him? I had to smile. Unnoticed I backed away and returned to my room. So there was quite a bit more than met the eye to this short, dark Indian from Ocosingo.

In the morning I asked my friend, "What do you know about Justino?"

"Justino? You mean Vitorino."

"Is that his real name?"

"Sometimes he calls himself Trinidad."

"Maybe his name is Justino Vitorino Trinidad," I suggested.

"I don't know and I don't care," my friend answered. "He told me he used to be a guide in the jungle. Who knows? The Mexican Indian has an incredible imagination. Really gifted people. He's a good jardinero, and that's what matters to me. It's difficult to get good jardineros, so I don't ask questions."

"Is he reliable?" I wondered aloud.

"As reliable as a ripe mango," my friend nodded.

I wondered how much he knew, so I pushed a little further. "And the radio at night?"

"Oh, that. I hope it doesn't bother you. Robberies and break-ins are increasing here in the colonia. Something we never used to have. Vitorino said that if he keeps the radio on low the sound keeps thieves away. A very good idea, don't you think?"

I nodded. A very good idea.

"And I sleep very soundly," my friend concluded, "so I never hear it."

The following night when I awakened and heard the soft sound of the music from the radio and heard the splashing of water, I had only to look from my window to see Justino and his friends in the pool, swimming nude in the moonlight. They were joking and laughing softly as they splashed each other, being quiet so as not to awaken my friend, the patrón who slept so soundly. The women were beautiful.

Brown skinned and glistening with water in the moonlight they reminded me of ancient Aztec maidens, swimming around Chac, their god of rain. They teased Justino, and he smiled as he floated on a rubber mattress in the middle of the pool, smoking his cigar, happy because they were happy. When he smiled the gold fleck of a filling glinted in the moonlight.

"¡Qué cabrón!" I laughed and closed my window.

Justino said a Mexican never lies. I believed him. If a Mexican says he will meet you at a certain time and place, he means he will meet you sometime at some place. Americans who retire in Mexico often complain of maids who swear they will come to work on a designated day, then don't show up. They did not lie, they knew they couldn't be at work, but they knew to tell the señora otherwise would make her sad or displease her, so they agree on a date so everyone would remain happy. What a beautiful aspect of character. It's a real virtue which Norteamericanos interpret as a fault in their character, because we are used to asserting ourselves on time and people. We feel secure and comfortable only when everything is neatly packaged in its proper time and place. We don't like the disorder of a free-flowing life.

Someday, I thought to myself, Justino will give a grand party in the sala of his patrón's home. His three wives, or his wife and two mistresses, and his dozens of children will be there. So will the women from the bordellos. He will preside over the feast, smoke his cigars, request his favorite beer-drinking songs from the mariachis, smile, tell stories and make sure everyone has a grand time. He will be dressed in a tuxedo, borrowed from the patrón's closet, of course, and he will act gallant and show everyone that a man who has just come into sudden wealth should share it with his friends. And in the morning he will report to the patrón that something has to be done about the poor mice that are coming in out of the streets and eating everything in the house.

"I'll buy some poison," the patrón will suggest.

"No, no," Justino will shake his head, "a little music from the radio and a candle burning in the sala will do."

And he will be right.

I liked Justino. He was a rogue with class. We talked about the weather, the lateness of the rainy season, women, the role of oil in Mexican politics. Like other workers, he believed nothing was going to filter down to the campesinos. "We could all be real Mexican greasers with all that oil," he said, "but the politicians will keep it all."

"What about the United States?" I asked.

"Oh, I have traveled in the estados unidos to the north. It's a country that's going to the dogs in a worse way than Mexico. The thing I liked the most was your cornflakes."

"Cornflakes?"

"Sí. You can make really good cornflakes."

"And women?"

"Ah, you better keep your eyes open, my friend. Those gringas are going to change the world just like the Suecas changed Spain."

"For better or for worse?"

"Spain used to be a nice country," he winked.

We talked, we argued, we drifted from subject to subject. I learned from him. I had been there a week when he told me the story which eventually led me to B. Traven. One day I was sitting under the orange tree reading the B. Traven novel I had found in the Juárez train station, keeping one eye on the ripe oranges which fell from time to time, my mind wandering as it worked to focus on a story so I could begin to write. After all, that's why I had come to Cuernavaca, to get some writing done, but nothing was coming, nothing. Justino wandered by and asked what I was reading and I replied it was an adventure story, a story of a man's search for the illusive pot of gold at the end of a make-believe rainbow. He nodded, thought awhile and gazed towards Popo, Popocatépetl, the towering volcano which lay to the south, shrouded in mist, waiting for the rains as we waited for the rains, sleeping, gazing at his female counterpart, Itza, who lay sleeping and guarding the valley of Cholula, there, where over four hundred years ago Cortés showed his wrath and executed thousands of Cholulans.

"I am going on an adventure," he finally said, and paused. "I think you might like to go with me."

I said nothing, but I put my book down and listened.

"I have been thinking about it for a long time, and now is the time to go. You see, it's like this. I grew up on the hacienda of Don Francisco Jiménez, it's to the south, just a day's drive on the carretera. In my village nobody likes Don Francisco, they fear and hate him. He has killed many men and he has taken their fortunes and buried them. He is a very rich man, muy rico. Many men have tried to kill him, but Don Francisco is like the devil, he kills them first."

I listened as I always listen, because one never knows when a word or a phrase or an idea will be the seed from which a story sprouts, but at first there was nothing interesting. It sounded like the typical patrón-peón story I had heard so many times before. A man, the patrón, keeps the workers enslaved, in serfdom, and because he wields so much power, soon stories are told about him and he begins to acquire super-human powers. He acquires a mystique, just like the divine right of old. The patrón wields a mean machete, like old King Arthur swung Excalibur. He chops off heads of dissenters and sits on top of the bones-and-skulls pyramid, the king of the mountain, the top macho.

"One day I was sent to look for lost cattle," Justino continued. "I rode back into the hills where I had never been. At the foot of a hill, near a ravine, I saw something move in the bush. I dismounted and moved forward quietly. I was afraid it might be bandidos who steal cattle, and if they saw me they would kill me. When I came near the place I heard a strange sound. Somebody was crying. My back shivered, just like a dog when he sniffs the devil at night. I thought I was going to see witches, brujas who like to go to those deserted places to dance for the devil, or La Llorona."

"La Llorona," I said aloud. My interest grew. I had been hearing Llorona stories since I was a kid, and I was always ready for one more. La Llorona was that archetypal woman of ancient legends who murdered her children, then repentant and demented she has spent the rest of eternity searching for them.

"Sí, La Llorona. You know that poor woman used to drink a lot. She played around with men, and when she had babies she got rid of them by throwing them into la barranca. One day she realized what she had done and went crazy. She started crying and pulling her hair and running up and down the sides of cliffs of the river looking for her children. It's a very sad story."

A new version, I thought, and yes, a sad story. And what of the men who made love to the woman who became La Llorona? Did they ever cry for their children? It doesn't seem fair to have only her suffer, only her crying and doing penance. Perhaps a man should run with her, and in our legends we would call him "El Mero Chingón," he who screwed up everything. Then maybe the tale of love and passion and the insanity it can bring will be complete. Yes, I think someday I will write that story.

"What did you see?" I asked Justino.

"Something worse than La Llorona," he whispered.

To the south a wind mourned and moved the clouds off Popo's crown. The bald, snow-covered mountain thrust its power into the blue Mexican sky. The light glowed like liquid gold around the god's head. Popo was a god, an ancient god. Somewhere at his feet Justino's story had taken place.

"I moved closer, and when I parted the bushes I saw don Francisco. He was sitting on a rock, and he was crying. From time to time he looked at the ravine in front of him, the hole seemed to slant into the earth. That pozo is called el Pozo de Mendoza. I had heard stories about it before, but I had never seen it. I looked into the pozo, and you wouldn't believe what I saw."

He waited, so I asked, "What?"

"Money! Huge piles of gold and silver coins! Necklaces and bracelets and crowns of gold, all loaded with all kinds of precious stones! Jewels! Diamonds! All sparkling in the sunlight that entered the hole. More money than I have ever seen! A fortune, my friend, a fortune which is still there, just waiting for two adventurers like us to take it!"

"Us? But what about don Francisco? It's his land, his fortune."

"Ah," Justino smiled, "that's the strange thing about this fortune. Don Francisco can't touch it, that's why he was crying. You see, I stayed there, and I watched him closely. Every time he stood up and started to walk into the pozo the money disappeared. He stretched out his hand to grab the gold, and poof, it was gone! That's why he was crying! He murdered all those people and hid their wealth in the pozo, but now he can't touch it. He is cursed."

"El Pozo de Mendoza," I said aloud. Something began to click in my mind. I smelled a story.

"Who was Mendoza?" I asked.

"He was a very rich man. Don Francisco killed him in a quarrel they had over some cattle. But Mendoza must have put a curse on don Francisco before he died, because now don Francisco can't get to the money."

"So Mendoza's ghost haunts old Don Francisco."

"Many ghosts haunt him," Justino answered. "He has killed many men."

"And the fortune, the money . . ."

He looked at me and his eyes were dark and piercing. "It's still there. Waiting for us!"

"But it disappears as one approaches it, you said so yourself. Perhaps it's only an hallucination."

Justino shook his head. "No, it's real gold and silver, not hallucination money. It disappears for don Francisco because the curse is on him, but the curse is not on us."

He smiled. He knew he had drawn me into his plot. "We didn't steal the money, so it won't disappear for us. And you are not connected with the place. You are innocent. I've thought very carefully about it, and now is the time to go. I can lower you into the pozo with a rope, in a few hours we can bring out the entire fortune. All we need is a car. You can borrow the patrón's car, he is your friend. But he must not know where we're going. We can be there and back in one day, one night." He nodded as if to assure me, then he turned and looked at the sky. "It will not rain today. It will not rain for a week. Now is the time to go."

He winked and returned to watering the grass and flowers of the jardín, a wild Pan among the bougainvillea and the roses, a man possessed by a dream. The gold was not for him, he told me the next day, it was for his women, he would buy them all gifts, bright dresses, and he would take them on a vacation to the United States, he would educate his children, send them to the best colleges. I listened and the germ of a story cluttered my thoughts as I sat beneath the orange tree in the mornings. I couldn't write, nothing was coming, but I knew that there were elements for a good story in Justino's tale. In dreams I saw the lonely hacienda to the south. I saw the pathetic, tormented figure of don Francisco as he cried over the fortune he couldn't touch. I saw the ghosts of the men he had killed, the lonely women who mourned over them and cursed the evil don Francisco. In one dream I saw a man I took to be B. Traven, a gray-haired, distinguished-looking gentleman who looked at me and nodded approvingly.

"Yes, there's a story there, follow it, follow it . . ."

In the meantime, other small and seemingly insignificant details came my way. During a luncheon at the home of my friend, a woman I did not know leaned towards me and asked if I would like to meet the widow of B. Traven. The woman's hair was tinged orange, her complexion was ashen gray. I didn't know who she was or why she would mention B. Traven to me. How did she know Traven had come to haunt my thoughts? Was she a clue which would help unravel the mystery?

I didn't know, but I nodded. Yes, I would like to meet her. I had heard that Traven's widow, Rosa Elena, lived in Mexico City. But what would I ask her? What did I want to know? Would she know Traven's secret? Somehow he had learned that to keep his magic intact he had to keep away from the public.

Like the fortune in the pozo, the magic feel for the story might disappear if unclean hands reached for it. I turned to look at the woman, but she was gone. I wandered to the terrace to finish my beer. Justino sat beneath the orange tree. He yawned. I knew the literary talk bored him. He was eager to be on the way to el Pozo de Mendoza.

I was nervous, too, but I didn't know why. The tension for the story was there, but something was missing. Or perhaps it was just Justino's insistence that I decide whether I was going or not that drove me out of the house in the mornings. Time usually devoted to writing found me in a small cafe in the center of town. From there I could watch the shops open, watch the people cross the zócalo, the main square. I drank lots of coffee, I smoked a lot, I daydreamed, I wondered about the significance of the pozo, the fortune, Justino, the story I wanted to write and B. Traven. In one of these moods I saw a friend from whom I hadn't heard in years. Suddenly he was there, trekking across the square, dressed like an old rabbi, moss and green algae for a beard, and followed by a troop of very dignified Lacandones, Mayan Indians from Chiapas.

"Victor," I gasped, unsure if he was real or a part of the shadows which the sun created as it flooded the square with its light.

"I have no time to talk," he said as he stopped to munch on my pan dulce and sip my coffee. "I only want you to know, for purposes of your story, that I was in a Lacandonian village last month, and a Hollywood film crew descended from the sky. They came in helicopters. They set up tents near the village, and big-bosomed, bikinied actresses emerged from them, tossed themselves on the cut trees which are the atrocity of the giant American lumber companies, and they cried while the director shot his film. Then they produced a gray-haired old man from one of the tents and took shots of him posing with the Indians. Herr Traven, the director called him."

He finished my coffee, nodded to his friends and they began to walk away.

"B. Traven?" I asked.

He turned. "No, an imposter, an actor. Be careful for imposters. Remember, even Traven used many disguises, many names!"

"Then he's alive and well?" I shouted. People around me turned to stare.

"His spirit is with us," were the last words I heard as they moved across the zócalo, a strange troop of near naked Lacandon Mayans and my friend the Guatemalan Jew, returning to the rain forest, returning to the primal innocent land.

I slumped in my chair and looked at my empty cup. What did it mean? As their trees fall the Lacandones die. Betrayed as B. Traven was betrayed. Does each one of us also die as the trees fall in the dark depths of the Chiapas jungle? Far to the north, in Aztlán, it is the same where the earth is ripped open to expose and mine the yellow uranium. A few poets sing songs and stand in the way as the giant machines of the corporations rumble over the land and grind everything into dust. New holes are made in the earth, pozos full of curses, pozos with fortunes we cannot touch, should not touch. Oil, coal, uranium, from holes in the earth through which we suck the blood of the earth.

There were other incidents. A telephone call late one night, a voice with a German accent called my name, and when I answered the line went dead. A letter addressed to B. Traven came in the mail. It was dated March 26, 1969.

My friend returned it to the post office. Justino grew more and more morose. He sat under the orange tree and stared into space, my friend complained about the garden drying up. Justino looked at me and scowled. He did a little work, then went back to daydreaming. Without the rains the garden withered. His heart was set on the adventure which lay at el pozo.

Finally I said "Yes, dammit, why not, let's go, neither one of us is getting anything done here," and Justino, cheering like a child, ran to prepare for the trip. But when I asked my friend for the weekend loan of the car he reminded me that we were invited to a tertulia, an afternoon reception, at the home of Señora Ana R. Many writers and artists would be there. It was in my honor, so I could meet the literati of Cuernavaca. I had to tell Justino I couldn't go.

Now it was I who grew morose. The story growing within would not let me sleep. I awakened in the night and looked out the window, hoping to see Justino and women bathing in the pool, enjoying themselves. But all was quiet. No radio played. The still night was warm and heavy. From time to time gunshots sounded in the dark, dogs barked, and the presence of a Mexico which never sleeps closed in on me.

Saturday morning dawned with a strange overcast. Perhaps the rains will come, I thought. In the afternoon I reluctantly accompanied my friend to the reception. I had not seen Justino all day, but I saw him at the gate as we drove out. He looked tired, as if he, too, had not slept. He wore the white shirt and baggy pants of a campesino. His straw hat cast a shadow over his eyes. I wondered if he had decided to go to the pozo alone. He didn't speak as we drove through the gate, he only nodded. When I looked back I saw him standing by the gate, looking after the car, and I had a vague, uneasy feeling that I had lost an opportunity.

The afternoon gathering was a pleasant affair, attended

by a number of affectionate artists, critics and writers who enjoyed the refreshing drinks which quenched the thirst.

But my mood drove me away from the crowd. I wandered around the terrace and found a foyer surrounded by green plants, huge fronds and ferns and flowering bougainvillea. I pushed the green aside and entered a quiet, very private alcove. The light was dim, the air was cool, a perfect place for contemplation.

At first I thought I was alone, then I saw the man sitting in one of the wicker chairs next to a small wrought-iron table. He was an elderly white-haired gentleman. His face showed he had lived a full life, yet he was still very distinguished in his manner and posture. His eyes shone brightly.

"Perdón," I apologized, and turned to leave. I did not want to intrude.

"No, no, please," he motioned to the empty chair, "I've been waiting for you." He spoke English with a slight German accent. Or perhaps it was Norwegian, I couldn't tell the difference. "I can't take the literary gossip. I prefer the quiet."

I nodded and sat. He smiled and I felt at ease. I took the cigar he offered and we lit up. He began to talk and I listened. He was a writer also, but I had the good manners not to ask his titles. He talked about the changing Mexico, the change the new oil would bring, the lateness of the rains and how they affected the people and the land, and he talked about how important a woman was in a writer's life. He wanted to know about me, about the Chicanos, of Aztlán, about our work. It was the workers, he said, who would change society. The artist learned from the worker. I talked, and sometime during the conversation I told him the name of the friend with whom I was staying. He laughed and wanted to know if Vitorino was still working for him.

"Do you know Justino?" I asked.

"Oh, yes, I know that old guide. I met him many years

ago, when I first came to Mexico," he answered. "Justino knows the campesino very well. He and I traveled many places together, he in search of adventure, I in search of stories."

I thought the coincidence strange, so I gathered the courage and asked, "Did he ever tell you the story of the fortune at el Pozo de Mendoza?"

"Tell me?" the old man smiled. "I went there."

"With Justino?"

"Yes, I went with him. What a rogue he was in those days, but a good man. If I remember correctly I even wrote a story based on that adventure. Not a very good story. Never came to anything. But we had a grand time. People like Justino are the writer's source. We met interesting people and saw fabulous places, enough to last me a lifetime. We were supposed to be gone for one day, but we were gone nearly three years. You see, I wasn't interested in the pots of gold he kept saying were just over the next hill. I went because there was a story to write."

"Yes, that's what interested me," I agreed.

"A writer has to follow a story if it leads him to hell itself. That's our curse. Ay, and each one of us knows our own private hell."

I nodded. I felt relieved. I sat back to smoke the cigar and sip from my drink. Somewhere to the west the sun bronzed the evening sky. On a clear afternoon, Popo's crown would glow like fire.

"Yes," the old man continued, "a writer's job is to find and follow people like Justino. They're the source of life. The ones you have to keep away from are the dilettantes like the ones in there." He motioned in the general direction of the noise of the party. "I stay with people like Justino. They may be illiterate, but they understand our descent into the pozo of hell, and they understand us because they're willing to share the adventure with us. You seek fame and notoriety and you're dead as a writer."

I sat upright. I understood now what the pozo meant,

why Justino had come into my life to tell me the story. It was clear. I rose quickly and shook the old man's hand. I turned and parted the palm leaves of the alcove. There, across the way, in one of the streets that led out of the maze of the town towards the south, I saw Justino. He was walking in the direction of Popo, and he was followed by women and children, a rag-tail army of adventurers, all happy, all singing. He looked up to where I stood on the terrace, and he smiled as he waved. He paused to light the stub of a cigar. The women turned, and the children turned, and all waved to me. Then they continued their walk, south, towards the foot of the volcano. They were going to the Pozo de Mendoza, to the place where the story originated.

I wanted to run after them, to join them in the glorious light which bathed the Cuernavaca valley and the majestic snow-covered head of Popo. The light was everywhere, a magnetic element which flowed from the clouds. I waved as Justino and his followers disappeared in the light. Then I turned to say something to the old man, but he was gone. I was alone in the alcove. Somewhere in the background I heard the tinkling of glasses and the laughter which came from the party, but that was not for me.

I left the terrace and crossed the lawn, found the gate and walked down the street. The sounds of Mexico filled the air. I felt light and happy. I wandered aimlessly through the curving, narrow streets, then I quickened my pace because suddenly the story was overflowing and I needed to write. I needed to get to my quiet room and write the story about B. Traven being alive and well in Cuernavaca.

The Apple Orchard

It was the last week of school and we were restless. Pico and Chueco ditched every chance they got, and when they came to school it was only to bother the girls and upset the teachers, otherwise they played hookey in Duran's apple orchard, the large orchard which lay between the school and our small neighborhood. They smoked cigarettes and looked at *Playboy* magazines which they stole from their older brothers.

I stayed with them once, but my father found out about it and was very angry. "It costs money to send you to school," he said. "So go! Go and learn to get ahead in this world! Don't play hookey with those tontos, they will never amount to anything."

I dragged myself to school which, in spite of the warm spring weather, had one consolation: Miss Brighton. She was the young substitute teacher who had come to replace Mr. Portales after his nervous breakdown. She was my teacher for first period English and last period study hall. The day she arrived I helped her move her supplies and

books, so we became friends. I think I fell in love with her,
I looked forward to her class, and I was sad when she told
me she would be with us only until the end of school. She
had a regular job in Santa Fe for the following year. For
a few weeks my fascination with Miss Brighton grew and
I was happy. During study hall I would pretend to read,
but most often I would sit and stare over my book at her.
When she happened to glance up she would smile at me,
and sometimes she came to my desk and asked me what I
was reading. She loaned me a few books, and after I read
them I told her what I had found in them. Her lips curled
in a smile which almost laughed and her bright eyes shone
with light. I began to memorize her features, and at night
I began to dream of her.

On the last day of school Pico and Chueco came up with
their crazy idea. It didn't interest me at first, but actually
I was also filled with curiosity. Reluctantly, I gave in.

"It's the only way to become a man," Pico said, as if he
really knew what he was talking about.

"Yeah," Chueco agreed, "we've seen it in pictures, but
you gotta see the real thing to know what it's like."

"Okay, okay," I said finally, "I'll do it."

That night I stole into my parents' bedroom. I had never
done that before. Their bedroom was a place where they
would go for privacy, and I was never to interrupt them
there. My father had only told me that once. We were
washing his car when unexpectedly he turned to me and
said, "When your mother and me are in the bedroom you
should never disturb us, understand?" I nodded. I knew
that part of their life was shut off to me, and it was to
remain a mystery.

Now I felt like a thief as I stood in the dark and saw
their dark forms on the bed. My father's arm rested over
my mother's hip. I heard his low, peaceful snore and I was
relieved that he was asleep. I hurried to her bureau and
opened her vanity case. The small mirror we needed for
our purpose lay among the bottles of perfume and nail

polish. My hands trembled when I found it. I slipped it into my pocket and left the room quickly.

"Did you get it?" Pico asked the next morning.

We met in the apple orchard where we always met on the way to school. The flowering trees buzzed with honey bees which swarmed over the thick clusters of white petals. The fragrance reminded me of my mother's vanity case, and for a moment I wondered if I should surrender the mirror to Pico. I had never stolen anything from her before. But it was too late to back out. I took the mirror from my pocket and held it out. For a moment it reflected the light which filtered through the canopy of apple blossoms, then Pico howled and we ran to school.

We decided to steal the glue from Miss Brighton's room. "She likes you," Pico said. "You keep her busy, I'll steal the glue." So we pushed our way past the mob which filled the hallway and slipped into her room.

"Isador," she smiled when she saw me at the door, "what are you doing at school so early?" She looked at Pico and Chueco and a slight frown crossed her face.

"I came for the book," I reminded her. She was dressed in a bright spring yellow, and the light which shone through the windows glistened on her dress and her soft hair.

"Of course . . . I have it ready . . ." I walked with her to the desk and she handed me the book. I glanced at the title, *The Arabian Nights*. I shivered because out of the corner of my eye I saw Pico grab a bottle of glue and stick it under his shirt.

"Thank you," I mumbled.

We turned and raced to the bathroom. A couple of eighth graders stood by the windows, looking out and smoking cigarettes. They usually paid little attention to us seventh graders so we slipped unnoticed into one of the stalls. Pico closed the door. Even in the early morning the stall was already warm and the odor bad.

"Okay, break the mirror," Pico whispered.

"Seven years' bad luck," Chueco reminded me.

"Don't pay attention to him, break it!" Pico commanded.

I took the mirror from my pocket, recalled for a moment the warm, sweet fragrance which filled my parents' bedroom, the aroma of the vanity case, the sweet scent of the orchard, like Miss Brighton's cologne, and then I looked at Pico and Chueco's sweating faces and smelled the bad odor of the crowded stall. My hands broke out in a sweat.

"Break it!" Pico said sharply.

I looked at the mirror, briefly I saw my face in it, saw my eyes which I knew would give everything away if we were caught, and I thought of the disgrace I would bring my father if he knew what I was about to do.

I can't, I said, but there was no sound, there was only the rancid odor which rose from the toilet stool. All of our eyes were glued to the mirror as I opened my hand and let it fall. It fell slowly, as if in slow motion, reflecting us, changing our sense of time, which had moved so fast that morning, into a time which moved so slowly I thought the mirror would never hit the floor and break. But it did. The sound exploded, the mirror broke and splintered, and each piece seemed to bounce up to reflect our dark, sweating faces.

"Shhhhhhhhh," Pico whispered, finger to lips.

We held our breath and waited. Nobody moved outside the stall. No one had heard the breaking of the mirror which for me had been like the sound of thunder.

Then Pico reached down to pick up three well-shaped pieces, about the size of silver dollars. "Just right!" He grinned and handed each of us a piece. He put his right foot on the toilet seat, opened the bottle of glue and smeared the white, sticky glue on the tip of his shoe. He placed the piece of mirror on the glue, looked down and saw his sharp, weasel face reflected in it and smiled. "Fits just right!"

We followed suit, first Chueco, then me.

"This is going to be fun!" Chueco giggled.

"Hot bloomers! Hot bloomers!" Pico slapped my back. "Now what?"

"Wait for it to dry. . . ."

We stood with our feet on the toilet seat, pant legs up, waiting for the glue to dry.

"Whose panties are you going to see first?" Chueco asked Pico.

"Concha Panocha's," Pico leered, "she's got the biggest boobs!"

"If they have big boobs does that mean they have it big downstairs?" Chueco asked.

"Damn right!"

"Zow-ee!" Chueco exclaimed, and spit all over me.

"Shhhh!" Pico whispered. Someone had come in. They talked while they used the urinals, then they left.

"Ninth graders," Pico said.

"Those guys know everything," Chueco added.

"Sure, but after today we'll know too," Pico grinned.

"Yeah," Chueco smiled.

I turned away to escape another shower and his bad breath. The wall of the bathroom stall was covered with drawings of naked men and women. Old Placido, the janitor, worked hard to keep the walls clean, but the minute he finished scrubbing off the drawings in one stall others appeared next door. The drawings were crude, hastily done outlines. The ninth graders drew them because they knew everything. But after today, Pico had assured us, we would all know, and we would be real men.

Last year the girls didn't seem to matter to us, we played freely with them, but the summer seemed to change everything. When we came back to school the girls had changed. They were bigger, some of them began to wear lipstick and nail polish. They carried their bodies differently, and I couldn't help but notice for the first time their small, swollen breasts. Pico explained about brassieres to me. An air of mystery began to surround the girls we had once known so well.

I began to listen closely to the stories ninth grade boys told about girls. They gathered in the bathroom to smoke before class and during lunch break, and they either talked about cars or sports or girls. Some of them already dated girls, and a few bragged about girls they had seen naked. They always talked about the girls who were "easy" or girls they had "made," and they laughed at us, chasing us away when we asked questions.

Their stories were incomplete, half whispered, and the crude drawings only aroused more curiosity. The more I thought about the change which was coming over us, the more troubled I became, and at night my sweaty dreams were filled with images of women, phantasmal creatures who danced in a mist and removed their veils as they swirled around me. But always I awoke before the last veil was removed. I knew nothing. That's why I gave in to Pico's idea. I wanted to know.

He had said that if we glued a small piece of mirror to our shoes we could push our feet between the girls' legs when they weren't watching, then we could see everything.

"And they don't wear panties in the spring," he said. "Everybody knows that. So you can see everything!"

"Eehola!" Chueco whistled.

"And sometimes there's a little cherry there. . . ."

"Really?" Chueco exclaimed. "Like a cherry from a cherry tree?"

"Sure," Pico said, "watch for it, it's good luck." He reached down and tested the mirror on his shoe. "Hey, it's dry! Let's go!"

We piled out of the dirty stall and followed Pico towards the water fountain at the end of the hall. That's where the girls usually gathered because it was outside their bathroom.

"Watch me," he said daringly, then he worked his way carefully behind Concha Panocha who stood talking to her friends. She wore a very loose skirt, perfect for Pico's plan. She was a big girl, and she wasn't very pretty, but Pico liked her. Now we watched as he slowly worked his foot between her feet until the mirror was in position. Then he looked down and we saw his eyes light up. He turned and looked at us with a grin. He had seen everything!

"Perfect! Perfect!" he shouted when he came back to us. "I could see everything! Panties! Nalgas! The spot!"

"Eee-heee-heeee," Chueco laughed. "Now it's my turn!"

They ran off to try Concha again, and I followed them. I felt the blood pounding in my head and a strange excitement ran through my body. If Pico could see everything, then I could, too! I could solve the terrible mystery which had pulled me back and forth all year long. I slipped up behind a girl, not even knowing who she was, and with my heart pounding madly I carefully pushed my foot between her feet. I worked cautiously, afraid to get caught, afraid of what I was about to see. Then I peered into the mirror, saw in a flash my guilty eyes, moved my foot to see more, but all I could see was darkness. I leaned closer to her, looked closely into the mirror, but there was nothing except the brief glimpse of her white panties and then the darkness.

I moved closer, accidentally bumped her, and she turned, looking puzzled. I said excuse me, pulled back and ran away. There was nothing to see; Pico had lied. I felt disappointed. So was Chueco when we met again at the bathroom.

"They all wear panties, you liar!" Chueco accused Pico. "I couldn't see anything. One girl caught me looking at her and she hit me with her purse," he complained. His left eye was red. "What do we do now?" Chueco asked.

"Let's forget the whole thing," I suggested. The excitement was gone, there was nothing to discover. The mystery which was changing the girls into women would remain unexplained. And not being responsible for the answer was even a relief. I reached down to pull the mirror from my foot. My leg was stiff from holding it between the girl's legs.

"No!" Pico exclaimed, and grabbed my arm. "Let's try one more thing!"

"What?"

He looked at me and grinned. "Let's look at one of the teachers."

"What? You're crazy!"

"No, I'm not! The teachers are more grown up than the girls! They're really women!"

"Bah, they're old hags," Chueco frowned.

"Not Miss Brighton!" Pico smiled.

"Yeah." Chueco's eyes lit up and he wiped the white spittle that gathered at the edges of his mouth. "She reminds me of Wonder Woman!" he laughed and made a big curve with his hands.

"And she doesn't wear a bra, I know, I've seen her," Pico added.

"No," I shook my head. No, it was crazy. It would be as bad as looking at my mother. Again I reached down to tear the mirror from my shoe and again Pico stopped me.

"You can't back out now!" he hissed.

"Yeah," Chueco agreed, "we're in this together."

"If you back out now you're out of the gang," Pico warned. He held my arm tightly, hard enough for it to hurt. Chueco nodded. I looked from one to the other, and I knew they meant it. I had grown up with them, knew them even before we started school, we were a gang. Friends.

"This summer we'll be the kings of the apple orchard, and you won't be able to come in," Pico added to his threat.

"But I don't want to do it," I insisted.

"Who, then?" Chueco asked, and looked at Pico. "We can't all do it, she'd know."

"So let's draw," Pico said, and drew three toothpicks out of his pocket. He always carried toothpicks and usually had one hanging from his lips. "Short man does it. Fair?"

Chueco nodded. "Fair." They looked at me. I nodded. Pico broke one toothpick in half, then he put one half with two whole ones in his hand, made a fist and held it out for us to draw. I lost.

"Eho, Isador, you're lucky," Chueco said.

"I, I can't," I mumbled.

"You have to!" Pico said. "That was the deal!"

"Yeah, and we never break our deals," Chueco reminded me, "as long as we've been playing together we never broke a deal."

"If you back out now, that's the end . . . no more gang," Pico said seriously. Then he added, "Look, I'll help you. It's the last day of school, right? So there's going to be a lot of noise during last period. I'll call her to my desk and when she bends over it'll be easy! She won't know!" He slapped my back.

"Yeah, she won't know!" Chueco repeated. I finally nodded. Why argue with them, I thought, I'll just put my foot out and fake it, and later I'll make up a big story to tell them in the apple orchard. I'll tell them I saw everything. I'll say it was like the drawing in the bathroom. But it wasn't that easy. The rest of the day my thoughts crashed into each other like the goats Mr. Duran sometimes lets out in his orchard. Fake it, one side said; look and solve the mystery, the other whispered. Now's your chance!

By the time I got to last period study hall I was very nervous. I slipped into my seat across the aisle from Pico and buried my head in the book Miss Brighton had lent me. I sat with my feet drawn in beneath my desk so the mirror wouldn't show. After a while my foot grew numb in its cramped position. I flipped through the pages and tried to read, but it was no use, my thoughts were on Miss Brighton. Was she the woman who danced in my dreams? Why did I always blush when I looked in her clear, blue eyes, those eyes that even now seemed to be daring me to learn their secret.

"Ready," Pico whispered, and raised his hand. I felt my throat tighten and go dry. My hands broke out in a sweat.

I slipped lower into my desk, trying to hide as I heard her walk towards Pico's desk.

"I want to know this word," Pico pointed.

"Contradictory," she said, "con-tra-dic-to-ry."

"Cunt-try-dick-tory," Pico repeated.

I turned and looked at her. Beyond her, through the window, I could see the apple orchard. The buzz of the bees swarming over the blossoms filled my ears.

"It means to contradict . . . like if one thing is true then the other is false," I heard her say.

I would have to confess, I thought . . . forgive me, Father, but I have contradicted you. I stole from my mother. I looked in the mirror and saw the secret of the woman. And why shouldn't you, something screamed in my head. You have to know! It's the only way to become a man! Look now! See! Learn everything you can!

I took a deep breath and slipped my foot from beneath my desk. I looked down, saw my eyes reflected in the small mirror. I slid it quietly between her feet. I could almost touch her skirt, smell her perfume. Behind her the light of the window and the glow from the orchard were blinding. I will pull back now, won't go all the way, I thought.

"Con-tra . . ." she repeated.

"Cunt-ra . . ." Pico stuttered.

Then I looked, saw in a flash her long, tanned legs, leaned to get a better image, saw the white frill, then nothing. Nothing. The swirl of darkness and the secret. The mystery remained hidden in darkness.

I gasped as she turned. She saw me pull my leg back, caught my eyes before I could bury myself in the book again, and in that brief instant I knew she had seen me. A frown crossed her face. She started to say something, then she stood very straight.

"Get your books ready, the bell's about to ring," was all she said. Then she walked quickly to her desk and sat down.

"Did you see?" Pico whispered. I said nothing, but stared

at a page of the book which was a blur. The last few minutes of the class passed very slowly. I thought I could even hear the clock ticking.

Then seconds before the bell rang I heard her say, "Isador, I want you to stay after school."

My heart sank. She knew my crime. I felt sick in the pit of my stomach. I cursed Pico and Chueco for talking me into the awful thing. Better to have let everything remain as it was. Let them keep their secret, whatever it was, it wasn't worth the love I knew would end between me and Miss Brighton. She would tell my parents, everyone would know. I wished that I could reach down and rip the cursed mirror from my shoe, undo everything and set it right again.

But I couldn't. The bell rang. The room was quickly emptied. I remained sitting at my desk. Long after the noise had cleared in the school ground she called me to her desk. I got up slowly, my legs weak and trembling, and I went to her. The room felt very big and empty, bigger than I could ever remember it. And it was very quiet.

She stood and came around her desk. Then she reached down, grabbed the small mirror on my shoe and jerked it. It splintered when she pulled and cut her thumb, but she didn't cry out, she was trembling with anger. She let the pieces drop on the floor; I saw the blood as it smeared her skirt and formed red balls on the tip of her thumb.

"Why did you do it?" she asked. Her voice was angry. "I know that Pico and Chueco would do things like that, but not you, Isador, not you!"

I shook my head. "I wanted to know," I heard myself say, "I wanted to know. . . ."

"To know what?" she asked.

"About women. . . ."

"But what's there to know? You saw the film the coach showed you . . . and later we talked in class when the nurse came. She showed you the diagrams, pictures!"

I could only shake my head. "It's not the same. I wanted to know how women are . . . why different? How?"

She stopped trembling. Her breathing became regular. She took my chin in her hand and made me look at her. Her eyes were clear, not angry, and the frown had left her face. I felt her blood wet my chin.

"There's stories . . . and drawings, everywhere . . . and at night I dream, but I still don't know, I don't know anything," I cried.

She looked at me while my frustrations came pouring out, then she drew me close and put her arms around me and smoothed my hair. "I understand," she said, "I understand . . . but you don't need to hide and see through the mirror. That makes it dirty. There's no secret to hide . . . nothing to hide. . . ."

She held me tight, I could feel her heart pounding, and I heard her sigh, as if she too was troubled by the same questions which hounded me. Then she let me go and went to the windows where she pulled shut all of the venetian blinds. Except for a ray of light streaming through the top, the room grew dark. She went to the door and locked it, turned and looked at me, smiled with a look I had never seen before, then she walked gracefully to the small elevated platform in the back of the room.

She stood in the center and very slowly and carefully she unbuttoned her blouse. She let it drop to her feet, then she undid her bra and let it fall. I held my breath and felt my heart pounding wildly. Never had I seen such beauty as I saw then in the pale light which bathed her naked shoulders and her small breasts. She unfastened her skirt and let it drop, then she lowered her panties and stepped out of them. When she was completely naked, she called me.

"Come and see what a woman is like," she smiled.

I walked very slowly to the platform. My legs trembled, and I heard a buzzing sound, the kind bees make when they are swarming around the new blossoms of the apple trees. I stood looking at her for a long time, and she stood very still, like a statue. Then I began to walk around the platform, still looking at her, noting every feature and every curve of her long, firm legs, her flat stomach with its dot of a navel, the small round behind that curved down between her legs, then rose along her spine to her hair which fell over her shoulders. I walked around and began to feel a swirling, pleasant sensation, as if I was getting drunk. I continued to hear the humming sound, perhaps she was singing, or it was the sound of the bees in the orchard, I didn't know. She was smiling, a distant, pleasant smile.

The glowing light of the afternoon slipped through the top of the blinds and rested on her hair. It was the color of honey, spun so fine I wanted to reach out and touch it, but I was content to look at her beauty. Once I had gone hunting with my uncles and I had seen a golden aspen forest which had entranced me, but even that was not as beautiful as this. Not even the summer nights, when I slept outside and watched the swirl of the Milky Way in the dark sky, could compare with the soft curves of her body. Not even the brilliant sunsets of the summer, when the light seemed painted on the glowing clouds, could be as full of wonder as the light which fell on her naked body. I looked until I thought I had memorized every curve, every nook and every shadow of her body. I breathed in deep, to inhale her aroma, then when I could no longer stand the beauty of the mystery unraveling itself before my eyes, I turned and ran.

I ran out the door into the bright setting sun, a cry of joy exploding from my lips. I ran as hard as I could, and I felt I was turning and leaping in the air like one of the goats in the apple orchard.

"Now I know!" I shouted to myself. "Now I know the secret and I'll keep it forever!"

I ran through the orchard, laughing with joy. All around me the bright white blossoms of the trees shimmered in the spring light. I heard music in the radiance which exploded around me; I felt I was dreaming.

I ran around the trees and then stopped to caress them, the smooth trunks and branches reminding me of her body.

Each curve developed a slope and shadow of its own, each twist was rich with the secret we now shared. The flowers smelled like her hair and reminded me of her smile. Gasping for breath and still trembling with excitement, I fell exhausted on the ground.

It's a dream, I thought, and I'll soon wake up. No, it had happened! For a few brief moments I had shared the secret of her body, her mystery. But even now, as I tried to remember how she looked, her image was fading like a dream fades. I sat up straight, looked towards the school, and tried to picture the room and the light which had fallen on her bare shoulders, but the image was fuzzy. Her smile, her golden hair and the soft curves of her body were already fading into the sunset light, dissolving into the graceful curves of the trees. The image of her body, which just a short time ago had been so vivid, was working itself into the apple orchard, becoming the shape of trunks and branches . . . and her sweet fragrance blended into the damp earth-smell of the orchard with its nettles and wild alfalfa.

For a moment I tried to keep her image from fading away. Then I realized that she would fade and grow softer in my memory, and that was the real beauty! That's why she told me to look! It was like the mystery of the apple orchard, changing before my eyes even as the sun set. All the curves and shadows, and the sounds and smells, were changing form! In a few days the flowers would wilt and drop, then I would have to wait until next spring to see them again, but the memory would linger, parts of it would keep turning in my mind . . . then next spring I would come back to the apple orchard to see the blossoms again. I would always keep coming back, to rediscover, to feel the smoothness of flesh and bark, to smell hair and flower, to linger as I bathed in beauty. The mystery would always be there, and I would be exploring its form forever.

The Silence of the Llano

I

His name was Rafael, and he lived on a ranch in the lonely and desolate llano. He had no close neighbors; the nearest home was many miles away on the dirt road which led to the small village of Las Animas. Rafael went to the village only once a month for provisions, quickly buying what he needed, never stopping to talk with the other rancheros who came to the general store to buy what they needed and to swap stories.

Long ago, the friends his parents had known stopped visiting Rafael. The people whispered that the silence of the llano had taken Rafael's soul, and they respected his right to live alone. They knew the hurt he suffered. The dirt road which led from the village to his ranch was overgrown with mesquite bushes and the sparse grasses of the flat country. The dry plain was a cruel expanse broken only by gullies and mesas spotted with juniper and piñon trees.

The people of this country knew the loneliness of the

llano; they realized that sometimes the silence of the endless plain grew so heavy and oppressive it became unbearable. When a man heard voices in the wind of the llano, he knew it was time to ride to the village just to listen to the voices of other men. They knew that after many days of riding alone under the burning sun and listening only to the moaning wind, a man could begin to talk to himself. When a man heard the sound of his voice in the silence, he sensed the danger of his lonely existence. Then he would ride to his ranch, saddle a fresh horse, explain to his wife that he needed something in the village, a plug of tobacco, perhaps a new knife, or a jar of salve for deworming the cattle. It was a pretense, in his heart each man knew he went to break the hold of the silence.

Las Animas was only a mud-cluster of homes, a general store, a small church, a sparse gathering of life in the wide plain. The old men of the village sat on a bench in front of the store, shaded by the portal in summer, warmed by the southern sun in winter. They talked about the weather, the dry spells they had known as rancheros on the llano, the bad winters, the price of cattle and sheep. They sniffed the air and predicted the coming of the summer rains, and they discussed the news of the latest politics at the county seat.

The men who rode in listened attentively, nodding as they listened to the soft, full words of the old men, rocking back and forth on their boots, taking pleasure in the sounds they heard. Sometimes one of them would buy a bottle and they would drink and laugh and slap each other on the back as friends will do. Then, fortified by this simple act, each man returned home to share what he had heard with his family. Each would lie with his wife in the warm bed of night, the wind moaning softly outside, and he would tell the stories he had heard: so-and-so had died, someone they knew had married and moved away, the current price of wool and yearlings. The news of a world so far away was like a dream. The wife listened and was also fortified for the long days of loneliness. In adjoining rooms the children listened and heard the muffled sounds of the words and laughter of the father and mother. Later they would speak the words they heard as they cared for the ranch animals or helped the mother in the house, and in this way their own world grew and expanded.

Rafael knew well the silence of the llano. He was only fifteen when his father and mother died in a sudden, deadly blizzard which caught them on the road to Las Animas. Days later, when finally Rafael could break the snowdrifts for the horse, he had found them. There at La Angostura, where the road followed the edge of a deep arroyo, the horses had bolted or the wagon had slipped in the snow and ice. The wagon had overturned, pinning his father beneath the massive weight. His mother lay beside him, holding him in her arms. His father had been a strong man, he could have made a shelter, burned the wagon to survive the night, but pinned as he was he had been helpless and his wife could not lift the weight of the huge wagon. She had held him in her arms, covered both of them with her coat and blankets, but that night they had frozen. It took Rafael all day to dig graves in the frozen ground, then he buried them there, high on the slope of La Angostura where the summer rains would not wash away the graves.

That winter was cruel in other ways. Blizzards swept in from the north and piled the snowdrifts around the house. Snow and wind drove the cattle against the fences where they huddled together and suffocated as the drifts grew. Rafael worked night and day to try to save his animals, and still he lost half of the herd to the punishing storms. Only the constant work and simple words and phrases he remembered his father and mother speaking kept Rafael alive that winter.

Spring came, the land thawed, the calves were born, and the work of a new season began. But first Rafael rode to the place where he had buried his parents. He placed a cross over their common grave, then he rode to the village of Las Animas and told the priest what had happened. The people gathered and a Mass for the dead was prayed. The women cried and the men slapped Rafael on the back and offered their condolences. All grieved, they had lost good friends, but they knew that was the way of death on the llano, swift and sudden. Now the work of spring was on them. The herds had to be rebuilt after the terrible winter, fences needed mending. As the people returned to their work they forgot about Rafael.

But one woman in the village did not forget. She saw the loneliness in his face, she sensed the pain he felt at the loss of his parents. At first she felt pity when she saw him standing in the church alone, then she felt love. She knew about loneliness, she had lost her parents when she was very young and she had lived most of her life in a room at the back of the small adobe church. Her work was to keep the church clean and to take care of the old priest. It was this young woman who reached out and spoke to Rafael, and when he heard her voice he remembered the danger of the silence of the llano. He smiled and spoke to her. Thereafter, on Sundays he began to ride in to visit her. They would sit together during the Mass, and after that they would walk together to the general store where he would buy a small bag of hard sugar candy, and they would sit on the bench in front of the store, eat their candy and talk. The old people of the village as well as those who rode in from distant ranches knew Rafael was courting her, and knew it was good for both of them. The men tipped their hats as they passed by because Rafael was now a man.

Love grew between the young woman and Rafael. One day she said, "You need someone to take care of you. I will go with you." Her voice filled his heart with joy. They talked to the priest, and he married them, and after Mass there was a feast. The women set up tables in front of the church, covering them with their brightest table oilcloths, and they brought food which they served to everyone who had come to the celebration. The men drank whiskey and talked about the good grass growing high on the llano, and about the herds which would grow and multiply. One of the old men of the village brought out his violin, followed by his friend with his accordion. The two men played the old polkas and the varsilonas while the people danced on the hard-packed dirt in front of the church. The fiesta brought the people of the big and lonely llano together.

The violin and accordion music was accompanied by the clapping of hands and the stamping of feet. The dancing was lively and the people were happy. They laughed and congratulated the young couple. They brought gifts, kitchen utensils for the young bride, ranch tools for Rafael, whiskey for everyone who would drink, real whiskey bought in the general store, not the mula some of the men made in their stills. Even Rafael took a drink, his first drink with the men, and he grew flushed and happy with it. He danced every dance with his young wife and everyone could see that his love was deep and devoted. He laughed with the men when they slapped his back and whispered advice for the wedding night. Then the wind began to rise and it started to rain; the first huge drops mixed with the blowing dust. People sought cover, others hitched their wagons and headed home, all calling their goodbyes and buena suerte in the gathering wind. And so Rafael lifted his young bride onto his horse and they waved goodbye to the remaining villagers as they, too, rode away, south, deep into the empty llano, deep into the storm which came rumbling across the sky with thunder and lightning flashes, pushing the cool wind before it.

And that is how the immense silence of the land and the heavy burden of loneliness came to be lifted from Rafael's heart. His young bride had come to share his life and give it meaning and form. Sometimes late at night when the owl called from its perch on the windmill and the coyotes sang in the hills, he would lie awake and feel the presence of her young, thin body next to his. On such nights the stillness of the spring air and her fragrance intoxicated him and made him drunk with happiness; then he would feel compelled to rise and walk out into the night which was bright with the moon and the million stars which swirled overhead in the sky. He breathed the cool air of the llano night, and it was like a liquor which made his head swirl and his heart pound. He was a happy man.

In the morning she arose before him and fixed his coffee and brought it to him, and at first he insisted that it was he who should get up to start the fire in the wood stove because he was used to rising long before the sun and riding in the range while the dawn was alive with its bright colors, but she laughed and told him she would spoil him in the summer, and in the winter, when it was cold, he would be the one to rise and start the fire and bring her coffee in bed. They laughed and talked during those still-dark, early hours of the morning. He told her where he would ride that day and about the work that needed to be done. She, in turn, told him about the curtains she was sewing and the cabinet she was painting and how she would cover each drawer with oilcloth.

He had whitewashed the inside of the small adobe home for her, then plastered the outside walls with mud to keep out the dust which came with the spring winds and the cold which would come with winter. He fixed the roof and patched the leaks, and one night when it rained they didn't have to rise to catch the leaking water in pots and pans. They laughed and were happy. Just as the spring rains made the land green, so his love made her grow, and one morning she quietly whispered in his ear that by Christmas they would have a child.

Her words brought great joy to him. "A child," she had said, and excitement tightened in his throat. That day he didn't work on the range. He had promised her a garden, so he hitched up one of the old horses to his father's plow and he spent all day plowing the soft, sandy earth by the windmill. He spread manure from the corral on the soil and turned it into the earth. He fixed an old pipe leading to the windmill and showed her how to turn it to water the garden. She was pleased. She spent days planting flowers and vegetables. She watered the old, gnarled peach trees near the garden and they burst into a late bloom. She worked the earth with care and by midsummer she was already picking green vegetables to cook with the meat and potatoes. It became a part of his life to stop on the rise above the ranch when he rode in from the range, to pause and watch her working in the garden in the cool of the afternoon. There was something in that image, something which made a mark of permanence on the otherwise empty llano.

Her slender body began to grow heavier. Sometimes he heard her singing, and he knew it was not only to herself she sang or hummed. Sometimes he glanced at her when her gaze was fixed on some distant object, and he realized it was not a distant mesa or cloud she was seeing, but a distant future which was growing in her.

Time flowed past them. He thinned his herds, prepared for the approaching winter, and she gathered the last of the fruits and vegetables. But something was not right. Her excitement of the summer was gone. She began to grow pale and weak. She would rise in the mornings and fix breakfast, then she would have to return to bed and rest. By late December, as the first clouds of winter appeared and the winds from the west blew sharp and cold, she could no longer rise in the mornings. He tried to help, but there was little he could do except sit by her side and keep her silent company while she slept her troubled sleep. A few weeks later a small flow of blood began, as pains and cramps wracked her body. Something was pulling at the child she carried, but it was not the natural rhythm she had expected.

"Go for Doña Rufina," she said. "Go for help!"

He hitched the wagon and made the long drive into the village, arriving at the break of light to rouse the old partera from her sleep. For many years the old woman had delivered the babies born in the village or in the nearby ranches, and now, as he explained what had happened and the need to hurry, she nodded solemnly. She packed the things she would need, then kneeled at her altar and made the sign of the cross. She prayed to el Santo Niño for help and whispered to the Virgin Mary that she would return when her work was done. Then she turned the small statues to face the wall. Rafael helped her on the wagon, loaded her bags, then used the reins as a whip to drive the horses at a fast trot on their long journey back. They arrived at the ranch as the sun was setting. That night a child was born, a girl, pulled from the womb by the old woman's practiced hands. The old woman placed her mouth to the baby's and pushed in air. The baby gasped, sucked in air and came alive. Doña Rufina smiled as she cleaned the small, squirming body. The sound was good. The cry filled the night, shattering the silence in the room.

"A daughter," the old woman said. "A hard birth." She cleaned away the sheets, made the bed, washed the young wife who lay so pale and quiet on the bed, and when there was nothing more she could do she rolled a cigarette and sat back to smoke and wait. The baby lay quietly at her mother's side, while the breathing of the young mother grew weaker and weaker and the blood which the old woman was powerless to stop continued to flow. By morning she was dead. She had opened her eyes and looked at the small white bundle which lay at her side. She smiled and tried to speak, but there was no strength left. She sighed and closed her eyes.

"She is dead," Doña Rufina said.

"No, no," Rafael moaned. He held his wife in his arms and shook his head in disbelief. "She cannot die, she cannot die," he whispered over and over. Her body, once so warm and full of joy, was now cold and lifeless, and he cursed the forces he didn't understand but which had drawn her into that eternal silence. He would never again hear her voice, never hear her singing in her garden, never see her waving as he came over the rise from the llano. A long time later he allowed Doña Rufina's hands to draw him away. Slowly he took the shovel she handed him and dug the grave beneath the peach trees by the garden, that place of shade she had loved so much in the summer and which now appeared so deserted in the December cold. He buried her, then quickly saddled his horse and rode into the llano. He was gone for days. When he returned, he was pale and haggard from the great emptiness which filled him. Doña Rufina was there, caring for the child, nursing her as best she could with the little milk she could draw from the milk cow they kept in the corral. Although the baby was thin and sick with colic, she was alive. Rafael looked only once at the child, then he turned his back to her. In his mind the child had taken the life of his wife, and he didn't care if the baby lived or died. He didn't care if he lived or died. The joy he had known was gone, her soul had been pulled into the silence he felt around him, and his only wish was to be with her. She was out there somewhere, alone and lost on the cold and desolate plain. If he could only hear her voice he was sure he could find her. That was his only thought as he rode out every day across the plain. He rode and listened for her voice in the wind which moaned across the cold landscape, but there was no sound, only the silence. His tortured body was always cold and shivering from the snow and wind, and when the dim sun sank in the west it was his horse which trembled and turned homeward, not he. He would have been content to ride forever, to ride until the cold numbed his body and he could join her in the silence.

When he returned late in the evenings he would eat alone and in silence. He did not speak to the old woman who sat huddled near the stove, holding the baby on her lap, rocking softly back and forth and singing wisps of the old songs. The baby listened, as if she, too, already realized the strangeness of the silent world she had entered. Over them the storms of winter howled and tore at the small home where the three waited for spring in silence. But there was no promise in the spring. When the days grew longer and the earth began to thaw, Rafael threw himself into his work. He separated his herd, branded the new calves, then drove a few yearlings into the village where he sold them for the provisions he needed. But even the silence of the llano carries whispers. People asked about the child and Doña Rufina and only once did he look at them and say, "My wife is dead." Then he turned away and spoke no more. The people understood his silence and his need to live in it, alone. No more questions were ever asked. He came into the village only when the need for more provisions brought him, moving like a ghost, a haunted man, a man the silence of the llano had conquered and claimed. The old people of the village crossed their foreheads and whispered silent prayers when he rode by.

Seven years passed, unheeded in time, unmarked time, change felt only because the seasons changed. Doña Rufina died. During those years she and Rafael had not exchanged a dozen words. She had done what she could for the child, and she had come to love her as her own. Leaving the child behind was the only regret she felt the day she looked out the window and heard the creaking sound in the silence of the day. In the distance, as if in a whirlwind which swirled slowly across the llano, she saw the figure of death riding a creaking cart which moved slowly towards the ranch house. So, she thought, my comadre la muerte comes for me. It is time to leave this earth. She fed the child and put her to bed, then she wrapped herself in a warm quilt and sat by the stove, smoking her last cigarette, quietly rocking back and forth, listening to the creaking of the rocking chair, listening to the moan of the wind which swept across the land. She felt a peace. The chills she had felt the past month left her. She felt light and airy, as if she were entering a pleasant dream. She heard the voices of old friends she had known on the llano, and she saw the faces of the many babies she had delivered during her lifetime. Then she heard a knock on the door. Rafael, who sat at his bed repairing his bridle and oiling the leather, heard her say, "Enter," but he did not look up. He did not hear her last gasp for air. He did not see the dark figure of the old woman who stood at the door, beckoning to Doña Rufina.

When Rafael looked up he saw her head slump forward. He arose and filled a glass with water. He held her head up and touched the water to her lips, but it was no use. He knew she was dead. The wind had forced the door open and it banged against the wall, filling the room with a cold gust, awakening the child, who started from her bed. He moved quickly to shut the door, and the room again became dark and silent. One more death, one more burial, and again he returned to his work. Only out there, in the vast space of the llano, could he find something in which he could lose himself.

Only the weather and the seasons marked time for Rafael as he watched over his land and his herd. Summer nights he slept outside, and the galaxies swirling overhead reminded him he was alone. Out there, in that strange darkness, the soul of his wife rested. In the day, when the wind shifted direction, he sometimes thought he heard the whisper of her voice. Other times he thought he saw the outline of her face in the huge clouds which billowed up in the summer. And always he had to drive away the dream and put away the voice or the image, because the memory only increased his sadness. He learned to live alone, completely alone. The seasons changed, the rains came in July and the llano was green, then the summer sun burned it dry. Later the cold of winter came with its fury. And all these seasons he survived, moving across the desolate land, hunched over his horse. He was a man who could not allow himself to dream. He rode alone.

II

And the daughter? What of the daughter? The seasons brought growth to her, and she grew into young woman-hood. She learned to watch the man who came and went and did not speak, and so she, too, learned to live in her own world. She learned to prepare the food and to sit aside in silence while he ate, to sweep the floor and keep the small house clean, to keep alive the fire in the iron stove, and to wash the clothes with the scrub-board at the water tank by the windmill. In the summer her greatest pleasure was the cool place by the windmill where the water flowed.

The year she was sixteen, during springtime she stood and bathed in the cool water which came clean and cold out of the pipe, and as she stood under the water the numbing sensation reminded her of the first time the blood had come. She had not known what it was: it came without warning, without her knowledge. She had felt a fever in the night, and cramps in her stomach, then in the restlessness of sleep she had awakened and felt the warm flow between her legs. She was not frightened, but she did remember that for the first time she became aware of her father snoring in his sleep on the bed at the other side of the room. She arose quietly, without disturbing him, and walked out into the summer night, going to the water tank where she washed herself. The water which washed her blood splashed and ran into the garden.

That same summer she felt her breasts mature, her hips widen, and when she ran to gather her chickens into the coop for the night she felt a difference in her movement. She did not think or dwell on it, a dark part of her intuition told her that this was a natural element which belonged to the greater mystery of birth which she had seen take place on the llano around her. She had seen her hens seek secret nests to hatch their eggs, and she knew the proud, clucking noises the hens made when they appeared with the small yellow chicks trailing. There was life in the eggs.

Once when the herd was being moved and they came to the water tank to drink she had seen the great bull mount one of the cows, and she remembered the whirling of dust and the bellowing which filled the air. Later, the cow would seek a nest and there would be a calf. These things she knew.

Now she was a young woman. When she went to the water tank to bathe she sometimes paused and looked at her reflection in the water. Her face was smooth and oval, dark from the summer sun, as beautiful as the mother she had not known. When she slipped off her blouse and saw how full and firm her breasts had grown and how rosy the nipples appeared, she smiled and touched them and felt a pleasure she couldn't explain. There had been no one to ask about the changes which came into her life. Once a woman and her daughters had come. She saw the wagon coming up on the road, but instead of going out to greet them she ran and hid in the house, watching through parted curtains as the woman and her daughters came and knocked at the door. She could hear them calling in strange words, words she did not know. She huddled in the corner and kept very still until the knocking at the door had ceased, then she edged closer to the window and watched as they climbed back on the wagon, laughing and talking in a strange, exciting way. Long after they were gone she could still smell the foreign, sweet odors they had brought to her doorstep.

After that, no one came. She remembered the words of Doña Rufina and often spoke them aloud just to hear the sound they made as they exploded from her lips. "Lumbre," she said in the morning when she put kindling on the banked ashes in the stove, whispering the word so the man who slept would not hear her. "Agua," she said when she drew water at the well. "Viento de diablo," she hissed to let her chickens know a swirling dust storm was on its way, and when they did not respond she reverted to the language she had learned from them and with a clucking sound she drove them where she wanted. "Tote! Tote!" she called, and made the clicking sound for danger when she saw the gray figure of the coyote stalking close to the ranch house. The chickens understood and hurried into the safety of the coop. She learned to imitate the call of the wild doves. In the evening when they came to drink at the water tank she called to them, and they sang back. The roadrunner which came to chase lizards near the windmill learned to "cou" for her, and the wild sparrows and other birds also heard her call and grew to know her presence. They fed at her feet like chickens.

When the milk cow wandered away from the corral she learned to whistle to bring it back. She invented other sounds, other words, words for the seasons and the weather they brought, words for the birds she loved, words for the juniper and piñon and yucca and wild grass which grew on the llano, words for the light of the sun and dark of the night, words which when uttered broke the silence of the long days she spent alone, never words to be shared with the man who came to eat late in the evenings, who came enveloped in silence, his eyes cast down in a bitterness she did not understand. He ate the meals she served in silence, then he smoked a cigarette, then he slept. Their lives were unencumbered by each other's presence, they did not exist for each other, each had learned to live in a silent world.

But other presences began to appear on the llano, even at this isolated edge of the plain which lay so far beyond the village of Las Animas. Men came during the season of the yellow moon, and they carried long sticks which made thunder. In that season when the antelopes were rutting they came, and she could hear the sound of the thunder they made, even feel the panic of the antelopes which ran across the llano. "Hunters!" her father said, and he spat the word like a curse. He did not want them to enter his world, but still they came, not in the silent, horse-drawn wagons, but in an iron wagon which made noise and smoked.

The sound of these men frightened her. Life on the llano grew tense as they drew near. One day, five of the hunters drove up to the ranch house in one of their iron wagons. She moved quickly to lock the door, to hide, for she had seen the antelope they had killed hung over the front of their wagon, a beautiful tan-colored buck splattered with blood. It was tied with rope and wire, its dry tongue hanging from its mouth, its large eyes still open. The men pounded on the door and called her father's name. She held her breath and peered through the window. She saw them drink from a bottle they passed to each other. They pounded on the door again and fired their rifles into the air, filling the llano with explosions. The smell of burned powder filled the air. The house seemed to shake as they called words she did not understand. "Rafael!" they called. "A virgin daughter!" They roared with laughter as they climbed in their wagon, and the motor shrieked and roared as they drove away. All day the vibration of the noise and awful presence of the men lay over the house, and at night in nightmares she saw the faces of the men, heard their laughter and the sound of the rifle's penetrating roar as it shattered the silence of the llano. Two of them had been young men, broad-shouldered boys who looked at the buck they had killed and smiled. The faces of these strange men drifted through her dreams and she was at once afraid and attracted by them.

One night in her dreams she saw the face of the man who lived there, the man Doña Rufina had told her was to be called father, and she could not understand why he should appear in her dream. When she awoke she heard the owl cry a warning from its perch on the windmill. She hurried outside, saw the dark form of the coyote slinking toward the chicken coop. A snarl hissed in her throat as she threw a rock, and instantly the coyote faded into the night. She waited in the dark, troubled by her dream and by the appearance of the coyote, then she slipped quietly back into the house. She did not want to awaken the man, but he was awake. He, too, had heard the coyote, and had heard her slip out, but he said nothing. In the warm summer night, each lay awake, encased in their solitary silence, expecting no words, but aware of each other as animals are aware when another is close by, as she had been aware even in her sleep that the coyote was drawing near.

III

One afternoon Rafael returned home early. He had seen a cloud of dust on the road to his ranch house. It was not the movement of cattle, and it wasn't the dust of the summer dustdevils. The rising dust could only mean there was a car on the road. He cursed under his breath, remembering the signs he had posted on his fence, and the chain with a lock he had bought in the village to secure his gate. He did not want to be bothered, he would keep everyone away. For a time he continued to repair the fence, using his horse to draw the wire taut, nailing the barbed wire to the cedar posts he had set that morning. The day was warm, he sweated as he worked, but again he paused. Something made him restless, uneasy. He wiped his brow and looked towards the ranch house. Perhaps it was only his imagination, he thought, perhaps the whirlwind was only a mirage, a reflection of the strange uneasiness he felt. He looked to the west where two buzzards circled over the coyote he had shot that morning. Soon they would drop to feed. Around him the ants scurried through the dry grass, working their hills as he worked his land. There was the buzz of grasshoppers, the occasional call of prairie dogs, each sound in its turn absorbed into the hum which was the silence of the land. He continued his work but the image of the cloud of dust returned, the thought of strangers on his land filled him with anger and apprehension. The bad feeling grew until he couldn't work. He packed his tools, swung on his horse and rode homeward.

Later, as he sat on his horse at the top of the rise from where he could view his house, the uneasy feeling grew more intense. Something was wrong, someone had come. Around him a strange dark cloud gathered, shutting off the sun, stirring the wind into frenzy. He urged his horse down the slope and rode up to the front door. All was quiet. The girl usually came out to take his horse to the corral where she unsaddled and fed it, but today there was no sight of her. He turned and looked towards the windmill and the plot of ground where he had buried his wife. The pile of rocks which marked her grave was almost covered by wind-swept sand. The peach trees were almost dead. The girl had watered them from time to time, as she had watered the garden, but no one had helped or taught her and so her efforts were poorly rewarded. Only a few flowers survived in the garden, spots of color in the otherwise dry, tawny landscape.

His horse moved uneasily beneath him; he dismounted slowly. The door of the house was ajar, he pushed it open and entered. The room was dark and cool, the curtains at the window were drawn, the fire for the evening meal was not yet started. Outside, the first drops of rain fell on the tin roof as the cloud darkened the land. In the room, a fly buzzed. Perhaps the girl is not here, he thought, maybe it is just that I am tired and I have come early to rest. He turned towards the bed and saw her. She sat huddled on the bed, her knees drawn up, her arms wrapped around them. She looked at him, her eyes terrified and wild in the dim light. He started to turn away but he heard her make a sound, the soft cry of an injured animal.

"Rafael!" she moaned as she reached out for him. "Rafael. . . ."

He felt his knees grow weak. She had never used his name before.

At the same time she flung back the crumpled sheet and pointed to the stain of blood. He shook his head, gasped. Her blouse was torn off, red scratch marks scarred her white shoulders, tears glistened in her eyes as she reached out again and whispered his name. "Rafael. . . . Rafael. . . ."

Someone had come in that cloud of dust, perhaps a stray vaquero looking for work, perhaps one of the men from the village who knew she was here alone, a man had come in the whirlwind and forced himself into the house. "Oh, God . . ." he groaned as he stepped back, felt the door behind him, saw her rise from the bed, her arms out-stretched, the curves of her breasts rising and falling as she gasped for breath and called his name, "Rafael. . . . Rafael. . . ." She held out her arms, and he heard his scream echo in the small adobe room which had suddenly become a prison suffocating him. Still the girl came towards him, her eyes dark and piercing, her dark hair falling over her shoulders and throat. With great effort, he found the strength to turn and flee. Outside, he grabbed the reins of his frightened horse, mounted and dug his spurs into the sides of the poor creature. Whipping it hard he rode away from the ranch and what he had seen.

Once before he had fled, on the day he buried his wife. He had seen her face then, as he now saw the image of the girl, saw her eyes burning into him, saw the torn blouse, the bed, and most frightening of all, heard her call his name, "Rafael. . . . Rafael. . . ." It opened and broke the shell of his silence. It was a wound which brought back the ghost of his wife, the beauty of her features which he now saw again and which blurred into the image of the girl. He spurred the horse until it buckled with fatigue and sent him crashing into the earth. The impact brought a searing pain and the peace of darkness.

He didn't know how long he lay unconscious. When he awoke he touched his throbbing forehead and felt the clotted blood. The pain in his head was intense, but he could walk. Without direction he stumbled across the llano only to find that late in the afternoon when he looked around he saw his ranch house. He approached the water tank to wash the dried blood from his face, then he stumbled into the tool shed by the corral and tried to sleep. Dusk came, the bats and night hawks flew over the quiet llano, night fell and still he could not sleep. Through the chinks of the weathered boards he could see the house and the light which burned at the window. The girl was awake. All night he stared at the light burning at the window, and in his fever he saw her face again, her pleading eyes, the curve of her young breasts, her arms as she reached up and called his name. Why had she called his name? Why? Was it the devil who rode the whirlwind? Was it the devil who had come to break the silence of the llano? He groaned and shivered as the call of the owl sounded in the night. He looked into the darkness and thought he saw the figure of the girl walking to the water tank. She bathed her shoulders in the cold water, bathed her body in the moonlight. Then the owl grew still and the figure in the flowing gown disappeared as the first sign of dawn appeared in the clouds of the east.

He rose and entered the house, tremulously, unsure of what he would find. There was food on the table and hot coffee on the stove. She had prepared his breakfast as she had all those years, and now she sat by the window, withdrawn, her face pale and thin. She looked up at him, but he turned away and sat at the table with his back to her. He tried to eat but the food choked him. He drank the strong coffee, then he rose and hurried outside. He cursed as he reeled towards the corral like a drunken man, then he stopped suddenly and shuddered with a fear he had never known before. He shook his head in disbelief and raised his hand as if to ward away the figure sitting at the huge cedar block at the woodpile. It was the figure of a woman, a woman who called his name and beckoned him. And for the first time in sixteen years he called out his wife's name.

"Rita," he whispered. "Rita. . . ."

Yes, it was she, he thought, sitting there as she used to, laughing and teasing while he chopped firewood. He could see her eyes, her smile, hear her voice. He remembered how he would show off his strength with the axe, and she would compliment him in a teasing way as she gathered the chips of piñon and cedar for kindling. "Rita . . ." he whispered, and moved toward her, but now the figure sitting at the woodblock was the girl, she sat there, calling his name, smiling and coaxing him as a demon of hell would entice the sinner into the center of the whirlwind. "No!" he screamed, and grabbed the axe. Lifting it, he brought it down on the dark heart of the swirling vortex. The blow split the block in half and splintered the axe handle. He felt the pain of the vibration numb his arms. The devil is dead, he thought, opened his eyes, saw only the split block and the splintered axe in front of him. He shook his head and backed away, crying to God to exorcise the possession in his tormented soul. And even as he prayed for respite he looked up and saw the window. Behind the parted curtains he saw her face, his wife, the girl, the pale face of the woman who haunted him.

Without saddling the horse, he mounted and spurred it south. He had to leave this place, he would ride south until he could ride no more, until he disappeared into the desert. He would ride into oblivion, and when he was dead the tightness and pain in his chest and the torturous thoughts would be gone, then there would be peace. He would die and give himself to the silence, and in that element he would find rest. But, without warning, a dark whirlwind rose before him, and in the midst of the storm he saw a woman. She did not smile, she did not call his name, her horse was the dark clouds which towered over him, the cracking of her whip a fire which filled the sky. Her laughter rumbled across the sky and shook the earth, her shadow swirled around him, blocking out the sun, filling the air with choking dust, driving fear into both man and animal until they turned in a wide circle back towards the ranch house. And when he found himself once again on the small rise by his home, the whirlwind lifted and the woman disappeared. The thunder rumbled in the distance, then was gone. The air grew quiet around him. He could hear himself breathe, he could hear the pounding of his heart. Around him the sun was bright and warm.

He didn't know how long he sat there remembering other times when he had paused at that place to look down at his home. He was startled from his reverie by the slamming of a screen door. He looked and saw the girl walk towards the water tank. He watched her as she pulled the pipe clear of the tank, then she removed her dress and began to bathe. Her white skin glistened in the sunlight as the spray of water splashed over her body. Her long black hair fell over her shoulders to her waist, glistening from the water. He could hear her humming. He remembered his wife bathing there, covering herself with soap foam, and he remembered how he would sit and smoke while she bathed, and his life was full of peace and contentment. She would wrap a towel around her body and come running to sit by his side in the sun, and as she dried her hair they would talk. Her words had filled the silence of that summer. Her words were an extension of the love she had brought him.

And now? He touched his legs to the horse's sides and the horse moved, making its way down the slope towards the water tank. She turned, saw him coming, and she stepped out of the stream of the cascading water to gather a towel around her naked body. She waited quietly. He rode up to her, looked at her, looked for a long time at her face and into her eyes. Then slowly he dismounted and walked to her. She waited in silence. He moved towards her, and with a trembling hand he reached out and touched her wet hair.

"Rita," he said. "Your name is Rita."

She smiled at the sound. She remembered the name from long ago. It was a sound she remembered from Doña Rufina. It was the sound the axe made when it rang against hard cedar wood, and now, he, the man who had lived in silence all those years, he had spoken the name.

It was a good sound which brought joy to her heart. This man had come to speak this sound which she remembered. She saw him turn and point at the peach trees at the edge of the garden.

"Your mother is buried over there," he said. "This was her garden. The spring is the time for the garden. I will turn the earth for you. The seeds will grow."

The Gift

Jerónimo began his journey home to deliver his father's leg the day before el Día de los Muertos. The Cuernavaca bus station was crowded, the workers who could get a day off waited anxiously for the buses to arrive. When a bus did arrive there was a rush forward to get a good seat. All were going home to celebrate the feast of the Day of the Dead.

Jerónimo's patrona had come with him to the bus station; she bought the ticket for Jerónimo and handed him the package which contained the false leg she had bought for Jerónimo's father. Jerónimo thanked her and boarded the bus and found a seat by the window. The dusty, creaking bus was crowded, but Jerónimo knew most of the passengers would be going farther south. Only Jerónimo would be getting off at Pena Mayor.

The bus lurched forward, Jerónimo waved at his patrona. "Hasta pasando mañana!" the patrona called.

"Sí," Jerónimo answered. He was going home only for one day, only for el Día de los Muertos, then he would return to take care of the patrona's garden. A fine garden it was, Jerónimo thought with satisfaction, as fine a garden as the patrona was a good woman. Not many of the jardineros of Cuernavaca got a day off during the dry season, and fewer had as good a patrona as Jerónimo. Only a good woman like his patrona would have gone to the trouble and expense to have the false leg built so that Jerónimo's crippled father could walk.

Jerónimo thought of home as the bus headed south, climbing into the high, dry mountains. A thin, old woman dressed in black sat next to him. The fragrance around her reminded Jerónimo of the old women who burned votive candles at the church altar. He moved to make room for her, holding the package with the false leg on his lap. The old woman spoke only once, to say, "Este loco nos va'matar."

She meant the bus driver. He was driving very fast around the curves of the mountain. From time to time the driver took swigs from a bottle of tequila, then passed the bottle to his friend who stood by the front door. The friend strummed on a guitar, they sang.

They are just enjoying themselves, Jerónimo smiled. Tomorrow was the Day of the Dead, everybody was in a happy mood. Some traveled home to be with their families, others were going to mercados they knew, some went on special pilgrimages to the churches of the pueblos south of Pena Mayor. There they would visit the campo santos and make offerings to their dead; they would share the bread of the dead with those loved ones who rested in their graves.

Everyone was happy, the women talked, the men told stories of their villages, the bus driver and his friend sang, the bus swayed from one side of the road to the other. Like a giant animal drunk with the passengers it carried, it swayed back and forth and tipped dangerously on the high cliffs, catching the gravel on the shoulder of the road and spitting the small rocks to the bottom of the steep barranca.

The passengers did not appear to be apprehensive about

the wild ride and the tipsy bus driver; they were used to reckless bus drivers. He drove and sang with passion, they appreciated that. Bottles of tequila and mescal were opened, the men relaxed, the women exchanged gossip; one woman with two children, a boy and a girl, opened her bundle of food and gave her children some of the cookies she had baked for the Day of the Dead. For the boy a cookie shaped like a skull, for the girl a cookie shaped like the skeleton of death. The other women followed suit. They, too, opened their bundles and their children munched on the skeleton-shaped cookies.

Before they ate, the women and the children displayed their sweet-wares; they compared the shapes and the decoration on the cookies, the red eyes of death, the sugar bones of the skeleton, the white candy teeth. They compared prices, they talked about the best panaderías, they admired the work of the baker as art. The best-decorated cookies were passed around for all to see; the owners glowed with pride, the others grew envious.

Only Jerónimo had nothing to show. He carried the false leg for his father, but he couldn't show that; the people would only laugh. For now, he was happy to see the children eating the cookies and candy shaped in the form of death; tomorrow he would be eating the cookies his mother baked for the feast day. Tomorrow he would be resting peacefully in Pena Mayor.

Jerónimo smiled and tried to relax. He looked out the window. Far below he could see fields of corn and patches of red where roses grew. Jerónimo sighed. Something he could not understand made him uneasy. Was it the old woman falling asleep and pressing against him, or was it the wooden leg he was delivering to his father? The leg seemed to grow heavier and heavier, and he was forced to clutch it to his chest. At times the leg seemed to move in the bag, and a dread filled Jerónimo. Was the leg alive? No, it could not be. It was made only of wood and steel and leather straps.

Life was only in man, in animals, in the green plants, but if the leg felt alive maybe it had a power to help his father walk again. This is what Jerónimo was thinking when a brilliant light appeared outside the bus window. The flash was like a lightning flash which lit up the sky. It was a blinding light, with the sound of whirlwind around it. A woman screamed; others in the bus gasped as they saw the celestial light fill the bus with its brilliance.

The light lit up Jerónimo's shirt, the black-and-white-striped shirt which looked like a baseball shirt and which made him feel very self-conscious. When he had put it on that morning he was afraid his friends in the village would laugh at him. The shirt was a gift from la señora Ana Rosinski, his patrona, and to please her he had worn it. He had put the shirt on and looked in the mirror and nodded. So I will be the only person in Pena Mayor with such a shirt, he thought. Let them laugh.

The light subsided, leaving only the howling wind and the storm of dust covering the mountain.

The bus stopped. Jerónimo got off at the crossroads where a plain stone marker indicated the name of his village, Pena Mayor. He trudged up the dirt road which led to his village high on the mountain. The strong wind swept the chalky dust in great clouds and Jerónimo felt lost in the blinding dust. There was no one else on the road, no workers, no one going to or from the fields. The wind moaned and grew in force and the dust obscured the mountain and the local landmarks which were familiar to Jerónimo. Clutching the wooden leg to his chest, he lowered his head against the wind and entered the village.

One of the village dogs greeted him, growling and snarling, the dog threatened.

—Don't you know me, dog? Jerónimo spoke. This is my home. My father and mother live here, there in the house by the barranca. Don't you know me?

The dog whimpered, then turned and slunk down the dusty road.

The village appeared deserted; as clouds of white dust swept down the road Jerónimo could see only the barest outline of the stone houses which were shut tight against the wind. For a moment Jerónimo felt unsure. Had he left the bus at the right spot on the highway, had he come to the right place? Yes, he remembered the sign, Pena Mayor, the village of his birth. It was the dust which blinded him and made the surroundings unfamiliar. The white dust blew from the dry mountaintop, sifting down on the village where he had lived most of his life.

As a child he had tended goats on the mountain, following the herd, which he cared for from day to day, year to year, up the rocky cliffs. He looked up, to see if he could see the peaks where he had roamed for so many years with his goats, but the billowing dust covered everything, and the wind mourned like a lost spirit through the streets of the small village and shrieked through the cliffs and barrancas of the mountain.

In Pena Mayor life was barren. Jerónimo had left to start a new life in Cuernavaca. There he had found work as a jardinero in the gardens of the wealthy. He had made a new life among the people who seemed to have life so easy. The friends of his patrona came from many foreign places, they spoke languages he did not understand, they sat by the swimming pool, drank coffee in the morning and beer or refrescos in the afternoon; they lay in the sun, they laughed. Jerónimo listened as he trimmed the grass and the bushes, as he watered during the dry spell. Compared to the dryness and poverty of his village on the mountain, Jerónimo thought, the gardens of Cuernavaca were heaven.

And now Jerónimo was returning to his village to deliver the leg to his father, la pierna postiza, a leg made of wood, splints of steel, and straps of leather. The wood was smooth and painted a pale flesh color.

—What are you carrying? a voice asked, and startled Jerónimo.

The old woman had caught him by surprise. She had

come out of the dust, suddenly appearing close to him. A rebozo covered her head and most of her face. She was bent and old, and on her arm she carried a tin bucket covered with a threadbare towel. Jerónimo recognized her, she was the old woman who sold nopales. She went up to the mountain daily and cut the palm-shaped leaves of the cactus which she brought down to sell in the village.

Everyone said she was a witch, but they bought her nopales anyway. She was the only one who knew in which crags and cliffs the most succulent nopales grew. Jerónimo remembered that once a man had died after eating the woman's nopales. The man had laughed at the old woman and ridiculed her, then that evening at his supper he ate the nopal and died.

—The old witch poisoned me, he shouted as he ran in agony through the village. Then he collapsed and died in the dust of the street. No one laughed at the old woman after that. They bought the nopales and prepared them with goat meat for their evening meal; they enjoyed the delicacy even as they thought of death.

Jerónimo stood bewildered, looking into the dark eyes of the old woman. The wind whipped at her rebozo and ragged skirt.

—I have brought a leg for my father, a new leg for him to stand on, he said. As you know, years ago he lost his leg. Some say it was a rattlesnake which bit him and caused the leg to rot; some say he stepped on a nail. I don't know, but he lost the leg. Now he will have a new leg. Jerónimo opened the bag and showed her the false leg.

—Is it hollow? the old woman said.

—No, solid, Jerónimo answered, raising his voice to be heard above the sound of the wind. It is very heavy. Very heavy.

He did not understand why the leg should be so heavy. "It is made of good wood," the patrona had explained. "It will last forever. Now your father can wear two boots," she said, "and the boots will wear out before this leg. This leg will last forever."

Jerónimo was very grateful to his patrona for having the leg built for his father. She had heard Jerónimo speak of his father and how he could not get around on one leg, so she had the leg made in a shop in Mexico City. But when Jerónimo had taken the leg from his patrona he had felt a wave of terror. The leg felt alive, and if it was alive it could not last forever. Nothing could last forever; that is what Jerónimo had been thinking on the bus, not even the garden in Cuernavaca.

The furious wind swirling around him reminded Jerónimo that in Cuernavaca the wind did not blow. There it was always sunny, the gardens always green and in bloom.

—You are a good son, the old woman said. When you die you will go to heaven.

Then she hobbled away, disappearing into the cloud of dust. Jerónimo turned to resume his way to his father's house, but still he was unsure of his surroundings. He looked for landmarks, but in the thick dust there were none. There was only the howling wind as it swept down the rocky mountain. There on the mountainside, Jerónimo knew, were the milpas of corn, the fruit trees. In the good years the people had corn and fruit, in dry years there was hunger. Then the men tightened their belts and grimly joked when they met each other. They were robbing death of some fat, they said.

Jerónimo shivered. Something in the cry of the wind reminded him of the coyote that had come to kill his goats. He remembered again as he stood swaying in the wind, trying to get his bearings. The coyote had come near the camp late in the evening. Jerónimo had only a slingshot for protection. The coyote was big, so big it looked like a wolf. It came towards Jerónimo, looked into his eyes and seemed to laugh. Then it seized a kid from the herd and disappeared up the mountain.

After that it came every evening, filling Jerónimo with terror. It cried and howled in the crags at night, and Jerónimo shivered by the fire. He could not eat, he could only watch as he saw his herd depleted.

He remembered going to the village to the one man who owned a gun. Coyote skulls hung by his front door, and in his hut the pelts of coyotes lay on the floor. Once the old man had come to Jerónimo's camp, and Jerónimo had invited him to share his evening meal and the campfire for the night. The old man had just killed a coyote, and he put the meat in the fire to cook. He gave Jerónimo a piece of the meat when it was done.

The meat was hard and greasy. Jerónimo found he could not swallow it. The old man ate the meat of the coyote and kept his eyes on Jerónimo, but Jerónimo chewed and chewed and could not swallow the meat. Finally, the old man turned his head, and Jerónimo spit the meat into the fire. It sizzled and sputtered and strange forms rose in the smoke from the fire.

Now the evil coyote was killing his goats, so Jerónimo went to borrow the old man's rifle.

—Do not look straight at the coyote when you shoot it, the old man had said. An animal like that has the sign of the devil on its forehead. A bullet will not enter there. Shoot it only from the side, that is the only way to kill this coyote.

Jerónimo returned to his camp and waited for the coyote to appear. As darkness swept over the mountain peaks, the coyote appeared. It came straight at him, its eyes full of flame, the mark of the devil clear on its forehead. There in the dusk the young man and the coyote met, and Jerónimo was helpless. He had no strength in his arm, and his knees felt weak. His mouth became dry, then it ran with saliva as if the coyote had infected him with some strange illness. He could not kill the coyote and after that he was filled with terror.

When the last goat was taken by the coyote, Jerónimo stumbled down from the high peaks of the mountain and took the bus to Cuernavaca. He told his mother that he would never return. Now he was returning to deliver the false leg to his father.

There, Jerónimo thought, that must be the cantina. But why do I feel so disoriented, why am I thinking of these things now? I must get out of this wind; a wind like this can only carry bad spirits. The old woman who sells nopales, I should not have let her touch the leg. She may have put a spell on it.

Yes, that is the cantina, he said to himself as he moved into the sobbing wind. There was a lighted window, a blue door. Perhaps the men of the village are in there, Jerónimo thought. A long time ago, when he was still a child, he had heard someone say that his father had been stabbed in the leg in the bar. It was in a fight over a woman. They said that was how his leg was poisoned and why they had cut it off.

Jerónimo moved towards the light of the cantina, but he stopped short as he heard the song, an old childhood song he himself had once sung; now it was sung by a group of children who gathered in front of the door of the bar. They were playing and dancing.

> *La Siriaca está pegada*
> *con chicle y con caca . . .*

Jerónimo stepped back. The sight of the children dancing in the terrible sandstorm frightened him! The children were singing about death. Doña Siriaca, Siriaca, la muerte. The skeleton of death. The song said her bones were held together with chewing gum and shit. The sweet smell and the foul odor combined in death. Death was sweet, death was foul, is that what the song said? He had sung the song as a child, but he had never thought about the meaning of the words.

When one was young, one did not think of death. Nor had he thought of death that morning when he boarded the bus in Cuernavaca. No, on the contrary, he was pleased to be going to visit his parents. He had not seen them in a long time. His father would be very pleased: his son returning home to deliver his new leg.

What did it mean? Jerónimo thought, as he heard the children singing and moving away into the dust storm. He could still hear the words of the sound in the wind:

La Siriaca está pegada
con chicle y con caca . . .

He turned away from the cantina. Perhaps the men of the village were inside; perhaps they had started celebrating a day early. He was sure tomorrow was el Día de los Muertos, not today. For the first time since he had begun his journey, Jerónimo wished he had not come. He should have remained in Cuernavaca where the wind did not blow, where the gardens were green and lush and cool, where there was no death.

He shook his head in frustration. Of course death is there, he thought, death is everywhere. It is just that in the gardens of the wealthy life is so pleasant that there seems to be no death. Time is held in check by the beautiful things of the rich. The women do not seem to age, they sit by the pool, their beautiful bodies covered with oil, their sweet perfumes competing with the fragrances of the flowers, their men plump and healthy.

The large, well-polished cars came and went. Every weekend they arrived from Mexico City, cars laden with those who could afford the luxury of the Cuernavaca gardens, those who could flee to the land where there was no death, only pleasure, only the call of children as they played in the pool, only the conversation and the laughter of the sleek men and women who drank their cocktails and acted as if death were not a concern in their lives. Could money buy off death? Jerónimo had wondered.

"Hay que robarle tiempo al tiempo," his patrona had

said. Steal time from time. But could one steal time from time? Even the smartest man could not stop the ticking of the clock. Time was stronger than death, or maybe death was but a germ hidden in time. It was time that got you, put the germs of death in you and made you die. Like the germ that had gotten into his father's leg and killed it, so it had to be cut off.

Jerónimo knew the same mystery came to nestle in the flowers. The blossoms of the flowers wilted, the fruit grew rotten, decayed, gave off a bad odor. Even in the beautiful gardens of Cuernavaca, the fruit decayed. Rats from the street came to eat at the trash pile. He set traps and killed the rats. He sprayed the red ants; he set poison for the mice. He crushed the caterpillars and the snails because they ate the tender leaves. Death was in the garden, he was death. He was the jardinero, the man who kept the garden lush and trim, the man who sustained the bushes and trees and the grass, but to keep everything growing he had to kill some things. Was it that way in paradise?

He was thinking about those things now, and they frightened him. He did not like to think of such things. He was a jardinero, a worker, he did his work and did not think. That was what the patrona was for, to think. But once, a very smart man who was the guest of his patrona had told him that there was a germ which could kill even the maggots of death. Everything was slowly dying.

"Look closely," the man said, "everything is dying."

When Jerónimo looked closely, he saw there were wrinkles under the eyes of the beautiful women who came from the city. He saw their breasts sag, he saw the paunches of the businessmen. He saw that they, too, were dying, and the thought made him sad. He tried not to think about what the man had said, but it stayed with him a long time, and now the thought returned. Why had he remembered that now?

Now Jerónimo whispered to himself, Stop wind, stop so I can see my village as I knew it before I left. Am I dreaming?

Will I awaken in my room in Cuernavaca? If the patrona tells me it is time to deliver the leg to my father I will say no. I do not want to go to Pena Mayor. This is what Jerónimo thought as he closed his eyes against the wind, but when he opened them he was still there in the howling windstorm, standing in the dusty street. Far in the distance he could hear the last refrain of the children's song.

Again Jerónimo leaned into the wind, and clutching the leg tightly, he moved down the street, desperate now to find the home of his father. He felt the day had been very long and he was tired. He only wanted to rest. He had seen many windstorms on the mountain, but never one as strong as this. He felt joy when he finally recognized the door of his father's house. He blinked and looked up and suddenly it was before him, the door he knew so well. A wreath of flowers hung on the door, someone had died in his father's home. The relief Jerónimo had felt drained away.

Who had died? It had been a long time since he had communicated with his parents, and now he had come to find the wreath of death on his father's door. Jerónimo shivered, not from the gust of wind which swirled around him and battered the paper flowers of the wreath, but from the thought of death. Perhaps it is only my father's way of celebrating the Day of the Dead, Jerónimo thought. He knocked and entered.

He closed the door quickly behind him and leaned against the door and sighed a sigh of relief. How calm and peaceful the dark room felt. Here there was relief from the howling wind which had battered him since he left the bus. He blinked to grow accustomed to the dark. Outside, the dust had shut off the sun and yet the strange opaque light hurt his eyes. He had been squinting from the dust and the light, now the darkness provided respite.

—Papá, Jerónimo spoke into the dark, soy yo, Jerónimo.

He peered into the room and saw his father sitting at the table. Behind him the figure of his mother like a shadow at the stove. The sweet aroma of sugar cookies filled the room. It was as he had imagined, she was baking the cookies for the Day of the Dead.

Jerónimo moved to his father, took his father's hand and kissed it in respect. This is how he had always greeted his father. They had never exchanged the abrazo as a greeting, only this kiss of respect.

—I have brought you a new leg, Jerónimo said proudly. He held the leg out, presented it to his father. He felt relief when his father took the leg. His errand was done.—It was built in one of the finest shops in Mexico City, Jerónimo explained. My patrona had it made for you. I came to bring it to you.

He looked at his father and at the stump of the amputated leg. He watched as his father took the leg, admired it, then brought it down to the stump where it would fit.

—You are a good son, his father said, fitting the false leg to his stump, adjusting the straps and tying them.

Jerónimo moved to his mother. He took her hand and kissed it. In the daylight he thought he saw tears in her eyes.

—Why is the room so dark? Jerónimo asked.

—We are in mourning, his mother whispered. She turned and looked at the cookies she had already baked and which were spread out on a cloth on the table. She took one, a perfectly shaped skeleton of death, and handed it to Jerónimo. She poured a cup of coffee and gave it to him to drink.

Jerónimo looked at the sugar cookie. When he was a child he always liked to bite off the head first. The head of the skeleton of death. Now as he looked at the perfectly shaped skeleton, brown from the oven and shimmering from the sugar sprinkled on it, he remembered how once the family had gone on a pilgrimage to the cathedral in Mexico City. Even now he remembered that in different churches there was a wall or a niche where the people left their crutches or canes or casts once the person had been cured. It was customary to make a promise to a saint or to la Virgen, and if the saint helped the person get well then the pilgrimage was made to church and a token of the sickness was left there. The ex votos, the votive offerings, marked the promises made, the return of good health.

But what Jerónimo remembered now was the zócalo. He liked to see the vendors, he liked to wander along the back of the cathedral where people set up their stalls to sell their goods. It was there he saw a young man selling little skeletons which were no bigger than a man's hand but which danced like puppets. The young man held no strings, but the skeleton danced. Jerónimo had been fascinated, and for a long time he had wondered what made the skeletons dance. After a short time the skeleton would fall lifeless on the sidewalk, as if the magic energy the vendor commanded had suddenly run out. Those who could afford the price came to buy the tiny skeletal dolls for their children.

—This is la muerte, the skeleton of death, the young salesman had said. Long ago, when the Aztecs ruled Mexico, at this very place, two sorcerers came to do evil to the people. One was dressed as a vendor, the other dressed as a mannequin, a skeleton of death. When the people came to see the dancing figure of death the sorcerer turned on them and killed them.

The people laughed at the young man's story. Jerónimo had begged his father to buy one of the dancing skeletons, but no, there was not enough money, and so he had returned to his village without the skeleton of death.

Now as he looked at the cookie his mother had offered him he remembered that incident, but when he went to bite the cookie he found he could not. He held the cookie to his mouth to bite the head of the skeleton figure, but he could not. He turned away, so his mother would not see him.

—I thought perhaps the men were in the cantina, he said to his father. The village appears empty.

—Yes, they are in the cantina, his father answered. He

had strapped on the leg. Now he stood. He was a giant figure rising from his chair. Jerónimo knew his father was a short man, thick and squat, surely no taller than Jerónimo. But now his father rose like a giant shadow in the darkened room. It was the first time Jerónimo had ever seen his father stand on two legs; perhaps that was why he appeared so tall.

—Now I feel complete again, his father said, and he walked slowly to the window. He walked unsteadily, feeling the newness of the leg. He parted the curtains and motioned for Jerónimo to have a look out the window.

Jerónimo stepped forward and looked out the window. A line of mourners came down the street. All were dressed in black, all were bent with the hard work and the misery of life in the village, and now added to that was the burden of death. Four men carried the plain casket. The casket was open and Jerónimo found himself leaning forward to peer into the casket as it passed outside the window. He wanted to look into the casket, and yet he felt afraid. Who had died? He heard the song of the children. That is what they had been waiting for, for the funeral procession which was now leaving the cantina, the largest building in the village.

Some of the men held bottles of tequila and mescal. They drank as they stepped into the wind. The four men who held the casket on their shoulders leaned into the wind, then the procession stopped in front of the window.

Who has died? Jerónimo wondered.

His father turned to face his mother, and when he spoke, there was sadness in his voice.

—Do you remember Cruz? I don't know why I remember his death now, it was so many years ago. He fell in love with a married woman. Later she turned against Cruz and confessed everything to her husband. Then together they plotted to kill him. We found him in his orchard, and there wasn't a mark on him. It was as if he had died in his sleep, but when we went to bathe his body for the wake we saw his testicles had been crushed. There was no other mark on him. Death itself is not evil, but evil uses the disguise of death.

Jerónimo saw his father shake his head, as if to say he did not understand death and how it came in such strange ways. Then his father turned and walked back to his chair. Slowly he unbuckled the wooden leg and laid it aside. He was not yet ready to walk on the leg, he would have to do it slowly, a day at a time, with practice, as life was learned slowly, a day at a time.

His father picked up his old worn jacket, which had been neatly pressed by his wife for the funeral. He put it on, then he took his crutches and walked slowly across the room to the door, where he waited for the woman. Her baking was done, the cookies were laid on the table to cool.

Later the mourners would come to their home to eat the cookies of the feast of the dead and drink hot coffee. Some of the men would drink tequila. Perhaps one of the men would sing, a song for the dead. They would speak of the dead person, remember him for the things he had done in life. Some of the men would get drunk, and the feast of the wake would continue into the night, long after the deceased was buried, and in the morning the sun would shine and the wind would no longer be blowing in Pena Mayor. The Day of the Dead would arrive, the people would celebrate. Those who had died would be remembered.

Jerónimo watched as his mother covered the cookies with a white towel. Then she went to the door, where she took her rebozo from a hook. She drew it tightly around her shoulders, looked sadly once about the room, then followed her husband. The wind roared as they stepped outside, then died down as the door closed behind them.

Jerónimo looked out the window. He saw his father and mother join the mourners. He heard the wail of the women become the cry of the wind. He saw the men hug his father, and Jerónimo knew they were giving him their condolences. Then the line of mourners began to move towards the cemetery just outside the village. They passed under the window and disappeared into the sandstorm.

At the campo santo they would lower the plain casket into the grave with ropes. Then each person would toss paper flowers into the hole; there were no fresh flowers in Pena Mayor. The priest would pray, each person would walk by the open grave and toss in a handful of earth, the chalky earth of the mountain. The men would begin to fill the grave with shovels full of earth, the wind would rise and sweep up the dust, and the women would cry and hold Jerónimo's mother. They would huddle in their dark rebozos to ward off the cold wind. The men would stand stiffly, knowing each one owed death a visit. Life was only a handful of earth, and the earth of Pena Mayor was so poor and miserable that it was worth next to nothing.

Jerónimo sighed, a deep sigh. It had been a long day, a strange journey home. He had delivered his father's leg, for that he felt proud. Now his father could work in the fields again, and on Saturdays he could stand at the bar like the other men. He was glad of that. Jerónimo felt complete. Perhaps it was his destiny to return to Pena Mayor. After all, no one knows a man's destiny. No one knows where death comes from, how it is that each person carries it so lightly within the heart, how it turns in the most simple way to claim what is due.

Perhaps when his father returned from the burial Jerónimo could ask him some of the strange questions which had plagued his day. Yes, he would wait for his parents to return, then he would speak to his father. Man-to-man they would speak, about the weather, the crops in the field, the gardens of Cuernavaca, the simple work of farmers and jardineros.

Jerónimo looked out the window. He could see nothing but swirls of dust, and the opaque light which hurt his eyes. He turned away from the window towards the darkness of the room. He looked at his hand and saw that he still held the cookie his mother had given him. He smiled. There was no better cook than his mother. He remembered that after a long day's work in the garden of his patrona he would often lie in his room and remember his mother's cooking. That was one thing he missed in Cuernavaca.

As he thought of Cuernavaca he thought of the garden of his patrona. He thought about which bushes he had to trim, and he remembered where the grass was dry and he would have to water. He knew which flowers would be in bloom, and he knew exactly how their aroma would fill the garden in the quiet of the night. He thought of all the gardens where he had worked and how beautiful his labor had left them. Thinking about this, he felt complete.

He looked at the figure of the skeleton in the cookie. Tomorrow was el Día de los Muertos, the feast day of the dead. Today it had been his day to return to the village. He raised the cookie to his mouth and bit off the head of the figure of death. It tasted sweet. He sat down to finish the sweet bread of the dead and drink his coffee, and as he did he thought of the things he yet had to do when he returned to his garden in Cuernavaca.

In Search of Epifano

She drove into the desert of Sonora in search of Epifano. For years, when summer came and she finished her classes, she had loaded her old Jeep with supplies and gone south into Mexico.

Now she was almost eighty and, she thought, ready for death but not afraid of death. It was the pain of the bone-jarring journey which was her reality, not thoughts of death. But that did not diminish the urgency she felt as she drove south, across the desert. She was following the north rim of El Cañon de Cobre towards the land of the Tarahumaras. In the Indian villages there was always a welcome and fresh water.

The battered Jeep kicked up a cloud of chalky dust which rose into the empty and searing sky of summer. Around her, nothing moved in the heat. Dry mirages rose and shimmered, without content, without form. Her bright, clear eyes remained fixed on the rocky, rutted road in front. Around her there was only the vast and empty space of the desert. The dry heat.

The Jeep wrenched sideways, the low gear groaning and

complaining. It had broken down once, and had cost her many days' delay in Mexicali. The mechanic at the garage told her not to worry. In one day the parts would be in Calexico and she would be on her way.

But she knew the way of the Mexican, so she rented a room in a hotel nearby. Yes, she knew the Mexican. Part of her blood was Mexican, wasn't it? Her great-grandfather, Epifano, had come north to Chihuahua to ranch and mine. She knew the stories whispered about the man, how he had built a great ranch in the desert. His picture was preserved in the family album, at his side his wife, a dark-haired woman. Around them, their sons.

The dry desert air burned her nostrils. A scent of the green ocotillo reached her, reminded her of other times, other years. She knew how to live in the sun, how to travel and how to survive, and she knew how to be alone under the stars. Night was her time in the desert. She liked to lie in her bedroll and look up at the swirling dance of the stars. In the cool of evening, her pulse would quicken. The sure path of the stars was her map, drawing her south.

Sweat streaked her wrinkled skin. Sweat and dust, the scent commingling. She felt alive. "At least I'm not dry and dead," she said aloud. Sweat and pleasure, it came together.

The Jeep worried her now. A sound somewhere in the gearbox was not right. "It has trouble," the mechanic had said, wiping his oily hands on a dirty rag. What he meant was that he did not trust his work. It was best to return home, he suggested with a shrug. He had seen her musing over the old and tattered map, and he was concerned about the old woman going south. Alone. It was not good.

"We all have trouble," she mumbled. We live too long and the bones get brittle and the blood dries up. Why can't I taste the desert in my mouth? Have I grown so old? Epifano? How does it feel to become a spirit of the desert?

Her back and arms ached from driving; she was covered with the dust of the desert. Deep inside, in her liver or in her spleen, in one of those organs that the ancients called the seat of life, there was an ache, a dull, persistent pain. In her heart there was a tightness. Would she die and never reach the land of Epifano?

She slept while she waited for the Jeep to be repaired. Slept and dreamed under the shade of the laurel in the patio of the small hotel. Around her, Mexican sounds and colors permeated her dream. What did she dream? That it was too late in her life to go once again into the desert? That she was an old woman and her life was lived, and the only evidence she would leave of her existence would be her sketches and paintings? Even now, as weariness filled her, the dreams came, and she slipped in and out of past and present. In her dreams she heard the voice of the old man, Epifano.

She saw his eyes, blue and bright like hers, piercing but soft. The eyes of a kind man. He had died. Of course, he had died. He belonged to the past. But she had not forgotten him. In the family album, which she carried with her, his gaze was the one that looked out at her and drew her into the desert. She was the artist of the family. She had taken up painting. She heard voices. The voice of her great-grandfather. The rest of her family had forgotten the past, forgotten Mexico and the old man, Epifano.

The groaning of the Jeep shattered the silence of the desert. She tasted dust in her mouth, she yearned for a drink of water. She smiled. A thirst to be satisfied. Always there was one more desire to be satisfied. Her paintings were like that, a desire from within to be satisfied, a call to do one more sketch of the desert in the molten light before night came. And always the voice of Epifano drawing her to the trek into the past.

The immense solitude of the desert swallowed her. She was only a moving shadow in the burning day. Overhead, vultures circled in the sky, the heat grew intense. She was alone on a dirt road she barely remembered, taking her bearings only by instinct, roughly following the north rim of the Cañon de Cobre, drawn by the thin line of the horizon, where the dull peaks of las montañas met the dull blue of the sky. Whirlwinds danced in her eyes, memories flooded at her soul.

She had married young. She thought she was in love; he was a man of ambition. It took her years to learn that he had little desire or passion. He could not, or would not, fulfill her. What was the fulfillment she sought? It had to do with something that lay even beneath the moments of love or children carried in the womb. Of that she was sure.

She turned to painting, she took classes, she traveled alone. She came to understand that she and the man were not meant for each other.

She remembered a strange thing had happened in the chapel where the family gathered to attend her marriage. An Indian had entered and stood at the back of the room. She had turned and looked at him. Then he was gone, and later she was not sure if the appearance was real or imagined.

But she did not forget. She had looked into his eyes. He had the features of a Tarahumara. Was he Epifano's messenger? Had he brought a warning? For a moment she hesitated, then she had turned and said yes to the preacher's question. Yes to the man who could never understand the depth of her passion. She did what was expected of her there in the land of ocean and sun. She bore him a daughter and a son. But in all those years, the man never understood the desire in her, he never explored her depth of passion. She turned to her dreams, and there she heard the voice of Epifano, a resonant voice imparting seductive images of the past.

Years later she left her husband, left everything, left the dream of southern California where there was no love in the arms of the man, no sweet juices in the nights of love pretended. She left the circle of pretend. She needed a meaning, she needed desperately to understand the voices which spoke in her soul. She drove south, alone, in search of Epifano. The desert dried her by day, but replenished her at night. She learned that the mystery of the stars at night was like the mystery in her soul.

She sketched, she painted, and each year in springtime she drove farther south. On her map she marked her goal, the place where once stood Epifano's hacienda.

In the desert the voices were clear. She followed the road into Tarahumara country, she dreamed of the old man, Epifano. She was his blood, the only one who remembered him.

At the end of day she stood at the side of a pool of water, a small, desert spring surrounded by desert trees. The smell of the air was cool, wet. At her feet, tracks of deer, a desert cat. Ocelot. She stooped to drink, like a cautious animal.

"Thank the gods for this water which quenches our thirst," she said, splashing the precious water on her face, knowing there is no life in the desert without the water which flows from deep within the earth. Around her, the first stars of dusk began to appear.

She had come at last to the ranch of Epifano. There, below the spring where she stood, on the flat ground, was the hacienda. Now could be seen only the outlines of the foundation and the shape of the old corrals. From here his family had spread, northwest, up into Mexicali and finally into southern California. Seeds. Desert seeds seeking precious water. The water of desire. And only she had returned.

She sat and gazed at the desert, the peaceful, quiet mauve of the setting sun. She felt a deep sadness within. An old woman, sitting alone in the wide desert, her dream done.

A noise caused her to turn. Perhaps an animal come to drink at the spring, the same spring where Epifano had once wet his lips. She waited, and in the shadows of the palo verde and the desert willows she saw the Indian appear. She smiled.

She was dressed in white, the color of desire not consummated. Shadows moved around her. She had come home, home to the arms of Epifano. The Indian was a tall, splendid man. Silent. He wore paint, as they did in the old days when they ran the game of the pelota up and down las montañas of the Cañon de Cobre.

"Epifano," she said, "I came in search of Epifano." He understood the name. Epifano. He held his hand to his chest. His eyes were bright and blue, not Tarahumara eyes, but the eyes of Epifano. He had known she would come. Around her, other shadows moved, the women. Indian women of the desert. They moved silently around her, a circle of women, an old ceremony about to begin.

The sadness left her. She struggled to rise, and in the dying light of the sun a blinding flash filled her being. Like desire, or like an arrow from the bow of the Indian, the light filled her and she quivered.

The moan of love is like the moan of life. She was dressed in white.

Children of the Desert

He had worked the oil fields of south Texas for as long as he could remember. Abandoned as a child, he was passed from family to family until he was old enough to work. He grew up living and breathing the desert, but never trusting it. He sometimes drove into the desert alone, not looking for anything in particular, perhaps testing some inner fear he felt of the vast landscape. Sometimes he would find sunbleached bones, and he would feel compelled to take one back to his trailer.

Once he had seen the bodies of two Mexicans the sheriff had brought in. They had died of heat exposure in the desert. Their mouths were stuffed with sand, sand that in their last feverish moments they must have thought was water.

He could not forget the image of the two wetbacks, and after that he developed the habit of hiding plastic milk containers full of water along the desert trails he knew. The desert was merciless; without water a man would die of thirst.

He kept to himself, but once a year at Christmastime he went to Juárez. He took the long drive across the desert to drink and visit the brothels. It was a week in which he went crazy, drinking to excess and spending his money on the prostitutes.

When his money was gone he headed back to the oil town, his physical yearning satisfied, but the deeper communion he had sought in the women remained unfulfilled.

One Christmas he stopped to clean up and eat at a trucker's cafe on the outskirts of El Paso. The waitress at his table was a young woman, not especially pretty, but flirtatious. She wore bright red lipstick which contrasted with her white skin. She drew him into conversation.

He was self-conscious, but he smiled and told her he was going home. He talked about the oil town, the aluminum trailers clustered together in the desert. He had a job, he had a truck, and he lived alone.

"A man without water will die in that desert," he said, and held his breath. Would she understand?

"The desert's all we got," she nodded, looking out the window, beyond the trucks and cars of the gas station to the desert which stretched into Mexico. "It's both mother and father. Lover and brother." She was like him, an abandoned child of the desert. He looked at her and felt troubled. Why did she pay attention to him? What did she want?

She wanted to go with him. Would he take her? He had never shared his space with anyone. Only during the week in Juárez, and then he went crazy and could not remember what he had done. The women he slept with were a blur. After that week of debauchery he felt empty, like the unsatisfied desert.

Now a new emotion crept into his loneliness. He thought the feeling came with the sweet smell of her perfume, her red lips and blue eyes. She squinted in the bright sun as she looked at him. Her skin was white, and beneath her blouse he saw the rise and fall of her breasts. He wanted to touch her.

"I can't take you," he mumbled.

"Why not?" she asked. "I can take care of your place, wash your clothes, sew, cook. You said you ain't got a woman."

No, he didn't have a woman. Did he need one? He needed something, someone.

"Get in," he nodded.

"You won't be sorry," she said. She ran back into the cafe and returned with a small, worn suitcase. "All I got's in here," she smiled.

He had never been able to say much more than a few words to any woman, but as they drove across the desert he opened up to her. He told her about his work on the oil rigs and about the small aluminum trailer he had in the oil town. He told her how once a year he went to Juárez and became a different person, but he would give that up for her.

She had no family, so they guessed they belonged together. She was happy with the trailer, she was happy to belong.

He was happy too, now he whistled on the way to work. He gave up the old habit of hiding the containers full of water, and he began to forget where the precious water lay hidden.

The other workers joked about him. The older men said they had never seen him so happy, and it must be because he was getting it regular now. Get your young wife pregnant, they said, otherwise she might start running around. They knew the women of the oil town were lonely. There was nothing for them to do in the desert, and each woman spent a lot of time alone. Sometimes three or four of them gathered together to talk or exchange recipes or to play cards. Usually they drank, and then they cursed their life in the lonely and merciless desert.

The men didn't want their wives to form these groups. On those days dinner wasn't ready, they argued and fought. It was better to have the women stay at home, alone, not getting fancy ideas from the neighbor ladies, each man thought. In preserving that false peace each woman was driven deeper into loneliness.

He thought about a baby, but he didn't mention it to her. The child would be an extension of something that happened when they made love. That was what he felt, and it provided a small measure of contentment.

He wondered if she thought of a child. She said nothing, she seemed happy. There was no sign of pregnancy, and he grew more intense, driving deeper into her flesh to deposit his fluid of life, water he hid in her desert. But she, like the desert, was never satisfied. She took pleasure from his emptying in her, but he had nothing to show for his possession. She lay in bed when he was done, glowing with the sweat of their love.

She is the desert, he thought, she thrives on the heat and sweat.

"I love the heat," she had told him once, and what she said mystified him. The heat of the desert was death. The men with sand stuffed in their mouths, the bleached bones of those who died there.

He remembered the earrings he had found in the sand. The glitter of gold and the red rubies had caught his attention. Someone had lost her way, a woman. The sheriff found dead people out there all the time. Mexicans coming across to look for work, looking for a better life. The promised land.

He had not told her of the earrings. He felt them in his pocket. Would he give them to her someday?

"Come here," she smiled and drew him to bed to make love, her words like the cry of the doves when they came to drink water. Her movements beneath him were urgent, searching for her relief. He was still thinking of the earrings when he tasted sand in his mouth.

He felt the hair rise along his back, he drew away. She moaned and smiled, awash in the convulsion that swept over her. Sweat glistened on her breasts and stomach. She kept her eyes closed as she caressed herself, slowly running her hands between her breasts, along her flat stomach.

"Hotter than hell," he said, and lighted a cigarette.

She was still out there, in the space the orgasm created. The soft sounds she made irritated him.

"You sound like a cat," he said.

"It's just 'cause you make me feel so good," she answered. "When you're on me," she said, "a bubble forms right here, between us. I can feel it. I hold you tight so the bubble won't escape. Here. Feel."

He felt sand.

She held onto him even after he was spent. She held tight even when he was choking for air. The desert swept over him and covered his mouth with sand. At that moment he always cried out. Why did fear and pleasure come together?

"You're crazy," he said.

"I can feel it," she said.

He looked out the window at the hot, burning land. Mirages formed in the distance, green trees and the blue shimmer of water. An oasis. Hell, he knew there wasn't water out there. A mirage. Nothing. Death. Like the bubble, sucking you in.

"Crazy woman," he repeated. There she was covered with sweat and rubbing herself, in dreamland, and the trailer was hot as an oven.

"It's hotter than hell," he shouted, got up and flipped on the air conditioner.

"I like it hot," she answered.

He looked at her. She was caressing the spot where she said the bubble formed. Her nails were red against her white skin. Her breasts were full, round, crowned with pink nipples.

Sweat dripped from his armpits, ran in tricklets down his ribs. He thought of the pile of bones around the side of the trailer, bones he had collected over the years.

"What do you think about when you feel that bubble?" he asked.

"It's a secret," she smiled.

A secret, he thought. A fucking secret. The men were right, a young wife shouldn't be running around with the other women. Getting ideas. He knew she went into town with them, drove the seventy miles just to sit in the cool movie house. Hell, they probably went drinking.

"I don't want you hanging around with the women. Damn floozies."

She looked at him. "They're not floozies."

"You do what I say!" he shouted, and kicked the small table near him. The red plastic flowers crashed to the floor.

"Get rid of your crazy ideas," he said in anger, and fell down on her, to crush away the secret of the bubble. But he couldn't do it. The irritation he felt made him impotent.

"You're hurting me," she said, and struggled away.

He stood over her, trying to catch his breath, trying to understand what was happening. Her toenails were painted red. Red like the fruit of the cactus. Her lips were red, the curtains were red, the dress was red, even the plastic flowers were red. And the earrings were red. He stumbled to the sink to splash water on his face.

"You okay?" she asked.

The water was like sand. His hands trembled.

"You like it here, because of the bubble," he said.

"We both like it here," she answered. "Didn't I tell you, we're children of the desert."

He looked out the window over the sink. There was nothing. Nothing. Only heat and sand. He had forgotten where he hid the water, or where he had found the earrings. Now he had nothing. He was at the mercy of the desert.

"There is no bubble!" he shouted at her, struck out. The slap caught her flush across the mouth. Blood oozed from her lips.

"There is," she insisted, fighting back the pain. "It's here, between us. It's the most beautiful feeling on earth. There's no harm in it!"

Her cry rang in his ears long after he left the trailer. In the desert he could hear the sound of her voice, see the red of her lips. He drove deep into the desert, away from her. But now being alone frightened him. He lost his way, panic swept over him like a suffocating sandstorm.

He had never before been lost. He stopped at an arroyo he thought he knew and tore into the sand until his hands bled, but he couldn't find any of his water containers. He remembered the men with their mouths full of sand, their eyes eaten out by the vultures. In that moment of fear, his mother spoke to him, her red lips taunting him. He saw her clearly, the gold earrings dangling.

Finally, when he found his way back, he was exhausted and trembling. A terrible fear made him shiver. He drank all night and the following day.

He used her roughly in a brutal attempt to destroy the images which haunted him. "No more bubble!" he insisted when he was done. "It's gone!" he shouted triumphantly.

But what was that pocket of air he had killed? The child he had wished for? The secret she hid from him? His failure to understand? And why had he seen his mother in the desert? The questions haunted him.

She withdrew, cowering in fear. He had become a man she did not know. He used her, but now there was only the suffering. The bed became a bed of sand. The more frantic his need, the more silent and withdrawn she became.

He went across the border to Agua Arenosa, to the whorehouse. He drank and went to the prostitutes until he was exhausted. When his money was gone he argued and fought, and the cantinero threw him out in the street.

He sat in the dust, a bitter taste in his mouth. Around him the town was deserted. Dervish dust swirled down the street, the wind cried like a mourning woman.

He was lost in that wailing wind. Sand stung his eyes, he tasted it in his mouth.

He turned to an old woman who sat by the door of the

cantina. Old and wrinkled and dirty, she was called into the cantina only to test the men before they went to the whores. He reached out and grabbed her.

"¡Demonio!" she cried in terror, and struggled to pull away. "¡Deja me ir, diablo!"

"No! No! I won't hurt you!" he cried. "I won't hurt you. I only want to know! Inside! ¡Aquí!" he shouted, and pointed to his chest, the place where emptiness gnawed at his heart.

His cry was one of torment. The old woman grew calm. She had seen eyes like his before. The devil of the desert was in the man. He had seen death, or he was about to die.

"Aquí," she said. "Corazón."

Heart? His heart was dry. He had opened his heart and the desert had swept in.

"Mira, hijo," the woman said kindly. She drew a line on the dirt. She spit to one side and a ball of mud formed from the dirt and the spittle. "Hombre," she said.

She spit to the other side. "Mujer," she said.

Then she spit on the line, and a perfect ball of wet earth formed. "Semilla," she smiled.

She pushed the two balls towards the one in the middle, and the three dissolved into one.

"Amor," she said, and moved away.

The seed was love. It lay between the man and the woman. It belonged to both. It was like a child growing in the belly, or like the bubble she caressed.

Even in the sand the seed of love could grow. He reached into his pocket and found the gold earrings with the red rubies. He looked at them, feeling the great burden of the past. Whatever was out there in the desert would haunt him no more, and he threw the earrings as far as he could. For a moment they glistened in the sun then disappeared into the sand.

He drove home, careening down the road, a speck in the vast bowl of desert and sky. He drove fast, full of a new urgency to see her. Near the trailer he crossed an arroyo, the front tires caught in the sand, the truck flipped over and he was thrown out.

For some time he lay unconscious, then awoke to feel a sharp pain in his lungs. When he spit he saw the red stain of blood. But he could not rest until he saw her and told her what he had discovered.

Holding his side, he ran to the trailer, calling her name. She was not there when he arrived. The trailer was empty.

He slumped to the ground by the door. The pain was sharp in his chest, he could not breathe, but he felt a calmness. Around him the desert was a space opening and receding. Her bubble. A space to hold a seed. He looked across the silent sand and understood.

The Man Who Found
a Pistol

This was the man who found the pistol, Procopio said as he pushed the newspaper across the bar for me to read. Procopio has worked in the village cantina many years; he knows the stories of the village. He wiped the bar thoughtfully and placed my drink in front of me. When he begins a story, I listen. He doesn't embellish the story, he just tells it. If you listen, fine; if you don't, there's always another customer at the bar.

The story of the man who found the pistol reminded me of something that happened to me years ago. My wife and I were driving up in the Jemez Mountains when we came to a stream. We stopped to eat lunch and enjoy the beauty. While my wife spread our picnic lunch I walked along the bank of the stream, enjoying the beauty of the forest. I came to a place on the stream where I felt a presence.

There were no footprints, but I knew someone had been there. I looked around the clearing but there was no one. Then I looked into the water. Submerged in the water lay a handsome double-bladed axe. Someone had left it there.

Again I looked around, but there was no one in sight. Maybe one of the locals had forgotten it.

Why had he left it in the water? Perhaps he wanted the water to swell the wood so the axe head would not slip. But there was no camp nearby, and no logging in the area. There was no sign of life.

I took the axe out of the water and felt its weight. It was a well-used axe, and it fitted snugly in my hands. I admired it, for I did not have such an axe. But as I held it, a strange feeling came over me. I felt I was being watched. Around me the forest grew very quiet. The mountain stream gurgled and a few birds cried, but the forest grew still and sullen. I thought of taking the axe, but I didn't. I put it back in the cold water where I had found it, and I hurried back and told my wife we should leave that place.

When I drove away I felt I had come upon a mystery that was not for me. Many years later I still remembered the axe I found in the stream.

The man who found the pistol lived in the village of Corrales. He taught at the university, Procopio told me. In the afternoons he came to the cantina to drink a beer after his walk. He was a loner, Procopio continued, nobody in the village knew him well. He wasn't a talker. It was the man's wife who told Procopio's wife that her husband grew up in a ranch in Texas. When he was a boy her husband was hunting rabbits with his brother: there was an accident. That's all she said.

What happened? I wondered. Procopio shrugged and shook his head.

Procopio never told a story all at once, he told it piece by piece. He would be relating the events in his quiet way, then new customers would come in and he lumbered off to serve them. I had to return to the bar from time to time to listen to the story.

I learned that the man who found the pistol used to go walking along the irrigation ditch in the afternoons. Tall grass covers the banks of the ditch. The fields and orchards in that part of the village are isolated. During his walk the man could enjoy the silence of the pastoral valley. That's why he had moved to Corrales, to be away from the city where he worked.

In the fields of the valley he could be alone with his thoughts. I began to understand the man was much like me. I, too, enjoy being alone; I like the silence of mountains. One has to be alone to know oneself. I also realize that one must return to the circle of the family to stay in balance. But the way Procopio told it, the man spent most of his time alone. His wife did all the chores and taking care of the house; the man only went to teach his classes then returned to walk alone in the fields.

Hearing Procopio talk about the man who found the pistol made me curious about him. I drove by his home with the old, weathered barns. The place looked deserted and haunted in the sharp January wind. Dark curtains covered the windows, and the banging of a loose tin on the barn roof made a lonely sound. Later, when I told Procopio this he looked at me strangely. Let it go, he said.

I couldn't let it go. The story of the man who found the pistol became an obsession with me.

One day I walked along the irrigation ditch where the man had walked, and standing in the open fields, I could see what he had seen. He could look east and see the stately face of the Sandia Mountain. The mountain reminds me of a giant turtle. When I was a boy I had killed a turtle, and when I look at the mountain I am sometimes reminded of that incident. This is the way of life: remembering one incident kindles another, and one doesn't know where the stampede of thoughts may lead.

Around him he could see the fields, winter-bare now, but in the summer they were green and buzzing with life. Meadowlarks called, blackbirds flew to the horse corrals, pheasants lay their eggs in the tall grass, and an occasional roadrunner scuttled in front of him. How could a man who had so much beauty around him do what he did?

Maybe Procopio knew more than he was telling. I found excuses to ask questions of other people in the village, but no one had known the man well. They knew he was a teacher, most said he kept to himself. He was always alone. The man who dug wells for a living had dug a well for the teacher. The well digger told me something horrible had happened back in Texas. There was a hunting accident, that's all the teacher said, and he grew melancholy.

I stood in the field alone and thought about the man. Walking here, he would meet no one. Here he could be at peace with himself. In the winter he could feel the earth sleeping, in the spring he could breathe the fresh scent of apple blossoms from the orchards, and in summer he could see the green of the alfalfa fields.

Was he not happy in that silence of the valley? Had it become like the silence in his heart, a haunting silence? When one is alone the hum of the earth becomes a mantra whose vibration works its way into the soul. Maybe the man was sucked deeper and deeper into that loneliness until there was no escape.

The day he found the pistol, Procopio said, he came to the bar and he didn't order his usual beer, he drank a whiskey. His hands were trembling. I found a pistol, he told us. There was only me and Primo in the bar, and Primo's nephew, the boy with the harelip. We looked at him. What should I do? he asked. Don't give it to the sheriff, Primo said, he will only keep it for himself. The boy with the harelip said, You can shoot rabbits with it. I said, Keep the pistol, you found it, it's yours.

I have thought often of the man finding the pistol in the grass by the side of the ditch, Procopio said, maybe it belonged to a criminal who threw it there to get rid of it. Maybe he had killed someone with it. There is a curse on things you find. They can never be yours.

There it was, I thought, like a snake concealed in the grass, ready to strike, perhaps glistening in the sun. There was mud on it, perhaps the stain of blood. The man trembled when he stooped to pick it up. The hair along his neck stood on edge, he felt a shiver. It isn't every day a man finds a pistol. Should he dare to pick it up? Yes, he did, as I had picked up the axe. It fitted into his hand.

Should I take it? the man thought. He weighed it in his hand and then looked around. He was alone, the fields were quiet. A cool breeze hissed as it swept across the grass. The man shivered. Many thoughts must have gone through his mind, memories of the past, things he knew he had to resolve. Aren't we all like that, haunted by memories of the past, the sights and sounds which come to overwhelm us? Maybe he knew that, and that's why he sighed when he slipped the pistol into his pocket.

After that he came to drink every day, Procopio said. He would drink whiskey, always alone. Once he asked me if anyone had reported the pistol as lost or stolen. No one in the village had mentioned the pistol. His hand was always in his pocket, as if he was making sure the pistol was still there.

He had cleaned the pistol until it was shiny, Procopio said. He bought bullets for it, but I think he was afraid to fire it.

I listened intently. There was something in the man's story which seemed to be my story. A word, a fragrance, the time of day can transport me into that depth of memory I know so well. The man's story was doing that to me, allowing me no rest.

I began to go into the bar every day, and when Procopio had time the conversation would get around to the story of the man who found the pistol. My own work began to suffer; I was obsessed with the story. Why did this man find the pistol? Was it his destiny, his destino, as we say in Spanish? Our tragic sense of life allied so close to the emotions of memory.

No one can escape el destino, Procopio said, as if reading my thoughts. When your time comes, it comes. Karma, I said, and we argued about the meaning of words.

That night I dreamed of the axe I had found in the mountain stream. I saw it submerged in the cold water of the stream, the steel as blue as the sky. I saw myself picking it up, and a voice in the dream saying no. The next day I drove to the mountain to look for the place, but it had been years and I no longer recognized the road that led to the stream. I wondered how many times the man who found the pistol had gone to the spot where he found it. Why didn't he throw it away and break the chain of events that was his destino?

Why are you so nervous? my wife asked me. I could not answer. I needed to be alone, and so every day I drove, up to the mountains or along the back roads of the silent mesas. When I was alone I felt the presence I had felt in the forest the day I found the axe. I was sure the man had felt the same, but he had decided to take the pistol anyway. Troubled by my thoughts, I found myself returning to Procopio's cantina to listen to the story of the man who found the pistol.

Late in the summer the wife left the man, Procopio said. He had grown more moody and introverted. He didn't clean his place all summer, the weeds took over his fields. His milk cow got loose and the people of the village complained, but he paid no attention. Perhaps they grew afraid of him. Maybe his wife became afraid also, and that's why she left.

Listening to Procopio, I thought I understood the man who found the pistol. He was like me, or like any other man who wonders how the past has shaped our destiny. He was a scholar, a sensitive man who thought of these questions. All those days alone in the fields, brooding over what he could tell no one. It was bound to catch up.

He tried to get rid of the pistol, Procopio said. He was drunk one night and he tried to give it to Primo, but Primo wouldn't take it. He begged Primo to take it, saying he was afraid something bad was going to happen. By then we knew there was a curse on the man. He always kept the pistol in his pocket, perhaps he slept with it. Now there was no peace for him in the silence of the valley. Even the mountain wore a stern, gray look as winter came.

Why? I asked myself as late at night I thought of the man who found the pistol. Why did finding the pistol change the man's life? He had committed no crime. He was a good man, a teacher. Was it because he had taken the pistol, or was there a greater design, a destiny he had to fulfill? Was the pistol like the axe, something which came to sever the cord of life?

The past haunts us, and only the person who carries the sack knows how much it weighs, as the saying goes.

Do you remember the day we found the axe in the stream? I asked my wife. But she had forgotten. To me the time and place and the texture of the day and the stream were so clear I would never forget. But she had forgotten. It was that way with the man who found the pistol, he would never forget that time and place. Maybe he knew that by taking the pistol he would have to settle a score with the past.

Ghosts of the past come to haunt our lives. What ghost came to haunt this man? I felt I knew what the man thought when he sat up late at night and stared at the pistol at his bedside, or when he walked through the village with the pistol in his pocket. He knew why the people let him pass in silence.

Then they found the man dead, Procopio said softly. Shot.

Shot himself, I nodded. This is what I had assumed all along, but there was a new twist Procopio had not yet shared with me.

No, Procopio shook his head. That's what the paper said, but what do they know! I will tell you, he whispered. You remember the boy with the harelip? He used to do odd jobs around the village? I nodded.

He was staying with the man, because the man had grown fearful of living alone. The boy slept in a small room near the front door. Late one night he heard someone knocking at the door. He got up and was going to open the door, but the man told him no. It is a ghost, the man shouted. Don't open the door!

The man went to the door and listened. He shouted at the ghost to go away. The boy saw the man was terrified, and the boy too was full of fear. Both felt it was no ordinary person who came to knock at night.

For weeks they were haunted by the knocking on the door. It was the feast of the Epiphany, and the night was cold. You remember, so cold it cracked some of the apple trees. Late at night the knocking came, the man went to the door. This time he held the pistol in his hand. This time he opened the door.

Procopio paused. I waited, my hands trembling. He poured me another shot which I drank to calm myself.

What? I asked.

Procopio shrugged. This is the strange part, he said. The boy with the harelip swears that when the man opened the door he saw the man's double standing there. The man raised the pistol and fired at his image. A cold wind shook the house, and the boy with the harelip rushed forward to shut the door. The man who found the pistol was dead. The pistol was at his side. I don't know what made the boy grab the pistol and run away. Later he told me he had thrown it away. Somewhere in the fields.

Procopio wiped the glasses he was drying. He was sad, sad for the man who had found the pistol and for the boy who saw the death. What was it? I asked.

Who knows, Procopio said. A ghost from the past. Maybe just the boy's imagination.

I nodded. So he had made his peace. I shivered. There are certain stories that touch us close to the heart. We listen to the tale and secretly whisper, There but for the grace of

God go I. Procopio had told me only sketches of the man, but I felt I knew the man as if he was my brother.

I rose and walked outside. The night was cold but the feel of spring was already in the air. What is the future, I thought, but a time which comes to swallow what we make of life.

Devil Deer

At night, frost settled like glass dust on the peaks of the Jemez Mountains, but when the sun came up the cold dissolved. The falling leaves of the aspen were showers of gold coins. Deer sniffed the air and moved silently along the edges of the meadows in the high country. Clean and sharp and well defined, autumn had come to the mountain.

In the pueblo the red ristras hung against brown adobe walls, and large ears of corn filled kitchen corners. The harvest of the valley had been brought in, and the people rested. A haze of piñon smoke clung like a veil over the valley.

Late at night the men polished their rifles and told hunting stories. Neighbors on the way to work met in front of the post office or in the pueblo center to stop and talk. It was deer season, a ritual shared since immemorial time. Friends made plans to go together, to stay maybe three or four days, to plan supplies. The women kidded the men: "You better bring me a good one this time, a big buck who maybe got a lot of does pregnant in his life. Bring a good one."

Cruz heard the sound of laughter as neighbors talked.

In the night he made love to his wife with renewed energy, just as the big buck he was dreaming about. "That was good," his young wife whispered in the dark, under the covers, as she too dreamed of the buck her husband would bring. Deer meat to make jerky, to cook with red chile all winter.

These were the dreams and planning that made the pueblo happy when deer season came. The men were excited. The old men talked of hunts long ago, told stories of the deer they had seen in the high country, sometimes meeting deer with special powers, or remembering an accident that happened long ago. Maybe a friend or brother had been shot. There were many stories to tell, and the old men talked far into the night.

The young men grew eager. They didn't want stories, they wanted the first day of deer season to come quickly so they could get up there and bag a buck. Maybe they had already scouted an area, and they knew some good meadows where a herd of does came down to browse in the evening. Or maybe they had hunted there the year before, and they had seen deer signs.

Everyone knew the deer population was growing scarce. It was harder and harder to get a buck. Too many hunters, maybe. Over the years there were fewer bucks. You had to go deeper into the forest, higher, maybe find new places, maybe have strong medicine.

Cruz thought of this as he planned. This time he and his friend Joe were going up to a place they called Black Ridge. They called it Black Ridge because there the pine trees were thick and dark. Part of the ridge was fenced in by the Los Alamos Laboratory, and few hunters wandered near the chain-link fence.

The place was difficult to get to, hard to hunt, and there were rumors that the fence carried electricity. Or there were electronic sensors and if they went off maybe a helicopter would swoop down and the lab guards would arrest you.

Nobody hunted near the fence; the ridge lay silent and ominous on the side of the mountain.

All month Cruz and Joe planned, but a few days before the season started Joe was unloading lumber at work and the pile slipped and crashed down to break his leg.

"Don't go alone," Joe told Cruz. "You don't want to be up there alone. Go with your cousin, they're going up to the brown bear area . . ."

"There's no deer there," Cruz complained. "Too many hunters." He wanted to go high, up to Black Ridge where few hunters went. Something was telling him that he was going to get a big buck this year.

So on the night before the season opened he drove his truck up to Black Ridge. He found an old road that had been cut when the Los Alamos fence had been put in, and he followed it as high as it went. That night he slept in his truck, not bothering to make a fire or set up camp. He was going to get a buck early, he was sure, maybe be back at the pueblo by afternoon.

Cruz awoke from a dream and clutched the leather bag tied at his belt. The fetish of stone, a black bear, was in the bag. He had talked to the bear before he fell asleep, and the bear had come in his dreams, standing upright like a man, walking towards Cruz, words in its mouth as if it was about to speak.

Cruz stood frozen. The bear was deformed. One paw was twisted like an old tree root, the other was missing. The legs were gnarled, and the huge animal walked like an old man with arthritis. The face was deformed, the mouth dripping with saliva. Only the eyes were clear as it looked at Cruz. Go away, it said, go away from this place. Not even the medicine of your grandfathers can help you here.

What did the dream mean? Cruz wondered, and rolled down the truck window. The thick forest around him was dark. A sound came and receded from the trees, like the moaning of wind, like a restless spirit breathing, there just beyond the Tech Area fence of the laboratories. There was a blue glow in the dark forest, but it was too early for it to be the glow of dawn.

Cruz listened intently. Someone or something was dying in the forest, and breathing in agony. The breath of life was going out of the mountain; the mountain was dying. The eerie, blue glow filled the night. In the old stories, when time was new, the earth had opened and bled its red, hot blood. But that was the coming to life of the mountain; now the glow was the emanation of death. The earth was dying, and the black bear had come to warn him.

Cruz slumped against the steering wheel. His body ached; he stretched. It wasn't good to hunt alone, he thought, then instantly tried to erase the thought. He stepped out to urinate, then he turned to pray as the dawn came over the east rim of the ridge. He held the medicine bag which contained his bear. Give me strength, he thought, to take a deer to my family. Let me not be afraid.

It was the first time that he had even thought of being afraid on the mountain, and he found the thought disturbing.

He ate the beef sandwich his wife had packed for him, and drank coffee from the thermos. Then he checked his rifle and began to walk, following the old ruts of the road along the fence, looking for deer sign, looking for movement in the thick forest. When the sun came over the volcanic peaks of the Jemez, the frost disappeared. There were no clouds to the west, no sign of a storm.

Cruz had walked a short distance when a shadow in the pine trees made him stop and freeze. Something was moving off to his right. He listened intently and heard the wheezing sound he had heard earlier. The sound was a slow inhaling and exhaling of breath. It's a buck, Cruz thought, and drew up his rifle.

As he stood looking for the outline of the buck in the

trees he felt a vibration of the earth, as if the entire ridge was moving. The sound and the movement frightened him. He knew the mountain, he had hunted its peaks since he was a boy, and he had never felt anything like this. He saw movement again, and turned to see the huge rack of the deer, dark antlers moving through the trees.

The buck was inside the fence, about fifty yards away. Cruz would have to go in for the deer. The dark pines were too thick to get a clear shot. Cruz walked quietly along the fence. At any moment he expected the buck to startle and run; instead the buck seemed to follow him.

When Cruz stopped, the buck stopped, and it blended into the trees so Cruz wasn't sure if it was a deer or if he only was imagining it. He knew excitement sometimes made the hunter see things. Tree branches became antlers, and hunters sometimes fired at movement in the brush. That's how accidents happened.

Cruz moved again and the shadow of the buck moved with him, still partially hidden by the thick trees. Cruz stopped and lifted his rifle, but the form of the deer was gone. The deer was stalking him, Cruz thought. Well, this happened. A hunter would be following a deer and the buck would circle around and follow the hunter. There were lots of stories. A buck would appear between two hunting parties and the hunters would fire at each other while the buck slipped away.

Cruz sat on a log and looked into the forest. There it was, the outline of the buck in the shadows. Cruz opened his leather bag and took out the small, stone bear. What he saw made him shudder. There was a crack along the length of the bear. A crack in his medicine. He looked up and the blank eyes of the buck in the trees were staring at him.

Cruz fired from the hip, cursing the buck as he did. The report of the rifle echoed down the ridge. Nearby a black crow cried in surprise and rose into the air. The wind moaned in the treetops. The chill in the air made Cruz shiver. Why did I do that? he thought. He looked for the buck: it was still there. It had not moved.

Cruz rose and walked until he came to a place where someone had ripped a large hole in the fence. He stepped through the opening, knowing he shouldn't enter the area, but he wasn't going to lose the buck. The big bucks had been thinned out of the mountain, there weren't many left. This one had probably escaped by living inside the fenced area.

I'm going to get me a pampered Los Alamos buck, Cruz thought. Sonofabitch is not going to get away from me. The buck moved and Cruz followed. He knew that he had come a long way from the truck. If he got the buck he would have to quarter it, and it would take two days to get it back. I'll find a way, he thought, not wanting to give up the buck which led him forward. I can drive the truck up close to the fence.

But why didn't the buck spook when he fired at it? And why did he continue to hear the sound in the forest? And the vibration beneath his feet? What kind of devil machines were they running over in the labs that made the earth tremble? Accelerators. Plutonium. Atom smashers. What do I know, Cruz thought. I only know I want my brother to return to the pueblo with me. Feed my family. Venison steaks with fried potatoes and onions.

As he followed the buck, Cruz begin to feel better. They had gone up to the top of the ridge and started back down. The buck was heading back toward the truck. Good, Cruz thought.

Now the buck paused, and Cruz could clearly see the thick antlers for the first time. They were thick with velvet and lichen clinging to them. A pine branch clung to the antlers, Cruz thought, or patches of old velvet. But when he looked close he saw it was patches of hair that grew on the antlers.

"God almighty," Cruz mumbled. He had never seen anything like that. He said a prayer and fired. The buck gave a grunt, Cruz fired again. The buck fell to its knees.

"Fall, you sonofabitch!" Cruz cursed, and fired again. He knew he had placed three bullets right in the heart.

The buck toppled on its side and Cruz rushed forward to cut its throat and drain its blood. When he knelt down to lift the animal's head he stopped. The deer was deformed. The hide was torn and bleeding in places, and a green bile seeped from the holes the bullets had made. The hair on the antlers looked like mangy, human hair, and the eyes were two white stones mottled with blood. The buck was blind.

Cruz felt his stomach heave. He turned and vomited, the sandwich and coffee of the morning meal splashed at his feet. He turned and looked at the buck again. Its legs were bent and gnarled. That's why it didn't bound away. The tail was long, like a donkey tail.

Cruz stood and looked at the deer, and he looked into the dark pine forest. On the other side of the ridge lay Los Alamos, the laboratories, and nobody knew what in the hell went on there. But whatever it was, it was seeping into the earth, seeping into the animals of the forest. To live within the fence was deadly, and now there were holes in the fence.

Cruz felt no celebration in taking the life of the buck. He could not raise the buck's head and offer the breath of life to his people. He couldn't offer the cornmeal. He was afraid to touch the buck, but something told him he couldn't leave the deer on the mountainside. He had to get it back to the pueblo; he had to let the old men see it.

He gathered his resolve and began dragging the buck down the ridge towards the truck. Patches of skin caught in the branches of fallen trees and ripped away. Cruz sweated and cursed. Why did this deer come to haunt me? he thought. The bear in the dream had warned him, and he had not paid attention to the vision. It was not a good sign, but he had to get the deformed deer to the old men.

It was dark when he drove into the pueblo. When he came over the hill and saw the lighted windows, his spirits rose. This was home, a safe circle. But in his soul Cruz didn't feel well. Going into the fenced area for the deer had sapped his strength.

He turned down the dirt road to his home. Dogs came out to bark, people peered from windows. They knew his truck had come in. He parked in front of his home, but he sat in the truck. His wife came out, and sensing his mood, she said nothing. Joe appeared in the dark, a flashlight in his hand.

"What happened?" Joe asked. Cruz motioned to the back of the truck. Joe flashed the light on the buck. It was an ugly sight which made him recoil. "Oh God," he whispered. He whistled, and other shadows appeared in the dark, neighbors who had seen Cruz's truck drive in. The men looked at the buck and shook their heads.

"I got him inside the fence," Cruz said.

"Take Cruz in the house," one of the men told Joe. They would get rid of the animal.

"Come inside," Joe said. His friend had been up on the mountain all day, and he had killed this devil deer. Cruz's voice and vacant stare told the rest.

Cruz followed Joe and his wife into the house. He sat at the kitchen table and his wife poured him a cup of coffee. Cruz drank, thankful that the rich taste washed away the bitterness he felt in his mouth.

Joe said nothing. Outside the men were taking the deformed buck away. Probably burn it, he thought. How in the hell did something like that happen? We've never seen a deer like this, the old men would say later. A new story would grow up around Cruz, the man who killed the devil deer. Even his grandchildren would hear the story in the future.

And Cruz? What was to become of Cruz? He had gone into the forbidden land, into the mountain area surrounded by the laboratory fence. There where the forest glowed at night and the earth vibrated to the hum of atom smashers, lasers, and radioactivity.

The medicine men would perform a cleansing ceremony; they would pray for Cruz. But did they have enough good medicine to wash away the evil the young man had touched?

Message from the Inca

He prayed and drank the coca tea, preparing himself for the run. He concentrated only on the task ahead of him, blocking out the sound of the fire sticks which sounded outside in the streets. The city of Cuzco, the capital city of the Inca, was under siege. The barbarians, speaking a strange tongue, had come, casting fire and death from their pointed sticks.

Even now the runner could hear the cries and screams of the people, and the terrifying curses of the barbarians. These bearded socerers were too powerful to stop; they rode huge beasts which trampled the people in their path. The runner had caught a glimpse of the carnage before the priest pulled him into the secret rooms beneath the Inca's temple. But even these sacred rooms would soon be discovered, and the barbarians' wrath would destroy everything.

Through the small window cut into the stone wall he could see the glare of the holy city as it burned. The sight saddened the runner. All the Inca's warriors were powerless to stop the calamity. If Cuzco fell, the empire of the Inca would be lost.

Outside the cell, the runner heard the footsteps of the priest as he approached. The priest opened the door and looked at the young man. This young man had been taken from his parents when he was a child and trained to be a runner in the service of the Inca. He had run up and down the Mountains of the Gods, even to the seacoast. Now he was the only runner left in Cuzco. The others had been sent in all directions, carrying messages to the people. They had been sent from Cuzco, and none had returned. One, as he tried to escape from the city, was attacked by the dogs of the barbarians. He died in the arms of the priests, crying there was no way out.

This runner was the last one left, and the message he would carry to Machu Picchu would be the last message to leave Cuzco before it fell. The salvation of the people of the Inca depended on the message.

"Are you ready, my son?" the priest asked.

"Yes," the runner replied.

"Cuzco cannot be saved," the priest said. There was no fear in his voice, only finality. "Come," he said, and the runner stood and followed the priest down a dark corridor.

Outside, the runner could hear the faint reports of the fire sticks, and the cries of women. For a moment he thought of the woman he had known as a mother as a child, then he shook the thought away.

He shivered. A horrifying time had come to the land of the Inca. The priests had warned the people that the bearded barbarians would destroy everything in their search for gold, but it was worse than they could have imagined. Time itself was ending.

The young man and the priest entered the room of the Inca, the room of gold. Here the torches reflected the glitter of the precious metal. This metal used to create the art of the Inca, this gift from the Sun God used as decoration to please those one loved, was the obsession of the barbarians.

The runner bowed, low to the ground, not daring to look into the face of the Inca. Even so, he had caught a glimpse of the noble family, huddling in the shadows of the room. Only the Inca remained unperturbed. He sat on his throne like the god he was.

"My house is about to fall," the great king spoke, and again the runner shivered. He had never before heard words from the Inca.

"My time is ending," the Inca said. "I accept my destiny, but we must keep the Sun God crossing the heavens and giving warmth to the earth. Otherwise the earth will die. Send my son, the runner, to Vilcampa. Send him to the mountain of Machu Picchu, there where the virgins tie the Sun God to the post on the mountain. Let him warn them of the barbarians; let them guard our secrets."

The runner felt the eyes of the Inca upon him, and heard the words entrusting him with the last message from the Inca.

"Leave no trail, cut the bridges behind you. Here we accept death at the hands of the barbarians, but we must save Vilcampa. We have been told, even time dies, but a new time must be born. Our knowledge is also for the time which is being born," were the Inca's last words.

The priest pulled the runner away from the presence of the Inca. In the corridor he handed him an intricately knotted cord, the quipus which contained the message from the ruler.

"This is the message for the virgins of Vilcampa," the priest said. "It tells the chief priestess how long they must remain hidden from the world if they are to escape the wrath of the barbarians. The city of the virgins must be sealed; no one must pass through the portals of Machu Picchu. The city clothed in mountain mists will now be clothed in secrecy for all time. There the virgins will guard the knowledge of the Inca. Perhaps in a future time someone will read the message in the quipus and shed tears for the Inca."

Outside, the thunder of the fire sticks grew louder, the murderous shouts of the barbarians closer.

"Go now," the priest hurried the runner down the corridor and to the secret door. "Take the message to the priestess of Vilcampa. Do not fail us."

The priest opened the door, the screams and thunder grew louder. In the air floated a strange, acrid smoke. He pressed a pouch of dried coca leaves into the runner's hands. The runner would chew the leaves and they would deaden the pain during the long run to Vilcampa. Many of the tambos, the rest houses along the trails in the Mountains of the Gods, had been destroyed. Now there were no runners to help relay the message; this runner would run a full day and a full night.

He climbed out of the mountain bowl which was the Valley of Cuzco without incident. The Inca had thrown all of his warriors into one last stand against the barbarians, a distraction to allow the runner to slip out of the palace. Now as the runner stood on the edge of the cliff looking down on the burning city, a great sadness filled him.

The people of the Inca were being destroyed, there was no family left. Frightening sounds filled the air, sounds which echoed across the centuries of time. Cuzco was dying, now there was only the hope of Vilcampa in Machu Picchu.

Panting from the climb, the runner opened the pouch and took out the coca leaves. Now he would run continuously, stopping only to cut the bridges that spanned the mountain ravines. These bridges, constructed of lianas, the vines from the Amazon, were the most valued possession of the Inca. The runner's instructions were to cut all the bridges on the trail to Vilcampa. He would not take time to rest.

He touched the quipus. There at the end the priest had tied a piece of metal, perhaps a piece taken from one of the breastplates the barbarians wore. This hard and cold object was the symbol of the new age. The virgins of Vilcampa would shiver when they touched the metal.

Into the evening he ran, climbing higher and higher, following the hidden foot trail above the river valley. Behind him plumes of smoke rose into the orange sky, the fires of

Cuzco burning. In the sky the runner saw a strange omen, a silver bird flying over the mountain. Below him he saw a giant snake made of metal twisting its way along the Urubamba valley. He shivered. These were the strange omens of the new time the Inca predicted.

He entered the dusk, knowing his world had come to an end. Who would read the quipus when the children of the Inca were dead? Who would know the glory of Vilcampa and the virgins who tethered the Sun God at the Post of the Sun? Who would keep the calendars of the Inca and the memory of the people?

He ran along the plain of the Urubamba, and all around him the terraced fields of the people were deserted. The people had fled into the mountains. He had tied the quipus to his belt, and as he ran, the corded string bounced on his thigh. The piece of metal at the end of the cord beat against his leg, bruising and then cutting open his flesh.

He ascended the mountains, pausing only to cut the footbridges, sealing off the road to Vilcampa. He did not rest. The tambos on the trail were deserted, the ashes in the fireplaces cold. All runners and warriors had been called to defend the Inca. He was the only runner on the trail to Vilcampa.

He ran to the rhythm taught the runners of the Inca, and still his lungs began to burn. He chewed the coca leaves, swallowing the bitter juice. The rhythm he kept and the deadening effect of the coca produced a new rhythm, a new awareness. He sang the songs of the Inca as he ran; his heart grew happy and he knew he could run forever.

He could fly, yes, this is what the runners of the Inca could do. They had been taught by the shamans to fly. The runners are birds circling the Mountains of the Gods, the priests of the Inca said, the runners are the sons of the Inca, sons of the sun.

Below him the mighty waters of the Urubamba raged and rumbled as they surged down the mountain. The runner heard the sound of the river, and he heard another sound.

It was the sound of the iron serpent winding its way along the valley. A dark plume of smoke trailed the iron serpent.

Very well, the runner thought, I will run faster than the serpent of the barbarians. Let the new time come to the land of the Inca, I will deliver my message.

All night he ran, and visions came to him. He moved out of the time of the Inca into a new time. The old priests had taught him to run, and they had taught him that visions would come as he ran.

He spoke to his father as if he was running by his side, remembering the stories his father taught him. He moved back into the navel of time and spoke to runners of the past, runners who had run from the ocean to Cuzco, bearing fresh fish for the Inca's dinner. He moved so far back in time that he saw the first people arriving to settle the mountains, the first Inca in their thrones of gold. He saw the first stones laid to construct Vilcampa, the city guarded by Machu Picchu. Then the ultimate vision came, and he saw the virgins of Vilcampa tie the Sun God to its post. With perfect clarity he saw the golden disc tethered for a moment on the solstice day of rest, and peace filled him.

For a moment he saw the harmony, the earth and sun as one, the prayers of the virgins answered. Then visions of the future came, and he saw the devastation of his people. The people were enslaved, the old calendars of the sun were broken. The runner felt fatigue spreading in his muscles, and the visions became a clutter of people swarming around him, people from another time and place.

The light of dawn glowed around him, and still he had not stopped to rest. Into the new day he ran until there before him was the gate of Vilcampa. He had broken the stream of time to arrive with the message. He did not feel the exhaustion, even though the muscles of his legs quivered. He thanked the sun for his swiftness and safety; he had brought the message to Vilcampa.

He slowed to a walk as he passed through the stone gate. Just below, an alert sentry waved him forward. He paused to look at the city of the votaries of the sun, the virgins who cared for Vilcampa. The Urubamba River cut a wide curve around the promontory on which stood the city; the city was a fortress of the sun protected by the mountains Machu and Picchu. The barbarians could follow the river, but from below they could not see the city. And he had cut the bridges and obliterated the signs on the trail. Now Vilcampa could be sealed off and exist in its own time.

Just below the sentry hut was the entry door. There in the middle of the city was the meadow where the dances were held. To the left stood the houses of the virgins, and nearby the temple. And there was the sundial! Here was the center of the universe, the ombligo of time. He gazed upon the sundial and felt he was returning home, as others would come in future times. Vilcampa would stand for all time, and belong to all people. That is what the Inca meant, that the message was also for the time being born.

Here, it was known, the virgins could tie the Sun God to the Post of the Sun. Only for a moment, only to renew its energy. Here the sun gazed on the altar of sacrifice, the smooth monolith where prayers and penance were done. Here the sun had intercourse with the virgins, penetrating their flesh, blessing the fields they cultivated, renewing time. This was the navel of the world where time converged.

The runner stood transfixed, feeling the luminous moment. The quality of light was so pure it was as the light of the first dawn on earth. The air was clear and scintillating. The green mountains of the Urubamba rose around him, clouds drifted across the peaks, dappling Vilcampa with bright sun then shadow. An immense peace filled the runner's heart. Below him he could see the stonemasons working at the quarry, and on the terraces those who tended the maize and potatoes. It was a serene image, and he wished he could sit and rest, but he had to deliver the message from the Inca.

He descended and was met at the sentry hut by a young woman. She greeted him. They had been expecting him.

"You are hurt," she said, and looked at his thigh where the piece of metal on the metal tip of the quipus had drawn blood.

"It is nothing," he answered. "I bring a message from the Inca."

"Follow me," she said. At the gate she called to the others, and many stepped forward to help push the large stone into place. The city was now sealed.

"Our chief priestess had a vision," the young woman said as they walked towards the temple. "Strangers have come to burn Cuzco. We hear strange sounds in the valley."

She paused and looked at him.

"Behind me, everything is destroyed," he said sadly. "The time of the Inca is no more."

"And Vilcampa?" she asked.

He saw the fright in her eyes, and he wished he could say that Vilcampa was forever. But nothing was forever, only the path of the sun and the knowledge of the virgins. A weariness filled his body.

"For now, Vilcampa is safe. I will live here," he said.

He wanted to tell her that while he ran he had a vision of others trudging up the slopes of the mountain to the secret city, new generations who came seeking the knowledge of the Incas.

"The quipus carries the message," he said, "it will be passed on."

She led him through the narrow streets of the city, turning left towards the altar. There she invited him to sit. She left him for a moment and returned with water. She cleansed his wound, washing the blood away, and she washed his body. He closed his eyes while she washed him, enjoying the softness of her hands. Around him gathered other women, the virgins who kept Vilcampa, eager to know what message he brought.

"Now you may deliver your message," the young woman said, and led him towards the temple. They passed the sundial, the Post of the Sun which was carved from one piece of stone.

She led him to the temple where the chief priestess waited. She was surrounded by other women, priests of the sun and workers from the fields and the quarry.

"Welcome, runner of the Inca," the priestess spoke, and stepped forward. "Welcome to our home. We have been waiting for you."

The runner undid the quipus from the leather thong at his waist and handed it to her. She received it tremulously.

She read the message in a loud voice, and the wind of the mountain carried the sad words down the canyon of the Urubamba. She read the date the barbarians had come to destroy Cuzco, and the many warriors of the Inca who had been killed. In the words of the Inca, time had come to an end, now a new time had to be born. Vilcampa was to keep the calendars of the sun and the knowledge of the Inca.

A deep silence filled the air. Only the moan of the wind could be heard. Then she showed them the piece of metal tied to the tip of the quipus, and she told them this was the cause of all the destruction.

"Did you cut the bridges on the mountain passes?" she asked the runner.

"Yes," he answered.

"The Inca has commanded," she said to all gathered, "no one is to leave Vilcampa. No one can enter. Our fate is sealed. We are the last city of the Inca; we will praise and renew the sun as always."

All nodded in assent. The time of the Inca had died, and now Vilcampa was a capsule anchored to the mountains of Machu Picchu. How long they survived was not for them to say, for time on earth was short and the visions of the priests forever. They knew the secret of Vilcampa, and in the future others would come to know it. Of that they were sure.

The priestess returned the quipus to the runner. "It is yours," she said. "A message to be passed down through the centuries. Many people will come here seeking the knowledge of the Inca. They will want to know how we were attentive to the Sun God. They will seek knowledge of the harmony of our world. We will share that message," she smiled.

The runner nodded. The message of catastrophe and chaos had been received with courage. These women, these votaries of the sun, were all women of courage. They accepted the end of time because they knew a new time would be born. In their wombs they carried the rays of the sun, the penetrating light of the Giver of Life.

"Take the runner to the eating area," the priestess said to the young woman. "See that he is fed. See that he has a place to rest. He is one of us now. This is his home."

The young woman bowed and took the runner's hand. She led him through the open meadow, past a flock of alpacas and the houses of the workers.

"There," she said, "is the place to eat. The women will serve you. I will return for you."

He turned to look at the terrace where people were eating. They were clothed in garments he had never seen; they spoke a strange language. For a moment he was afraid. Was he too slipping away from the time of the Inca? Was there no spot of earth which was fixed forever? Had he died in Cuzco or in the mountain ravines? Was this his ghost moving across time to come to sit with the strangers?

"Do not be afraid," he heard the voice of the young woman. "You are one of us."

The runner's hand tightened on the quipus, as if holding tight to the cord he could hold onto reality. His body ached with fatigue, the effect of the coca had worn away. He felt hunger. He walked to the eating area. There was an empty chair, and the man next to it motioned the runner.

"Sit here," the man said. He spoke the language of the barbarians, but his smile was kind. "I have come a long way to listen to the memories of Vilcampa," he said. He had been writing on the notebook which lay on the table.

A woman served the runner food and drink. The drink was cold and bitter. It was served in a marvelous glass bottle. The food was cold and tasteless; he couldn't eat. A swarm of people moved around him. Who are these strangers? he wondered. What has happened to the Vilcampa I knew? He looked for the young woman, and spotted her near workers who stood by the large metal huts. Smoke poured from these cabins even as people stepped out of them.

"Too many tourists, too many buses," the man sitting by the runner whispered. He pointed to the long line of people disembarking. "We come looking for the magic, and we find only each other," he smiled.

It was a kind smile, the runner thought. This stranger from another country had dark, curly hair and a dark face, but he was not a child of the Inca. The children of the Inca were the workers who spoke Quechua as they ate their lunches by the side of the road.

The runner looked at the quipus. He understood now what had happened during his run, and that it was time to pass on the message. This man, too, was a messenger, he wrote his stories in the notebook. The runner pushed the quipus across the table to the man, and the man took it. Their eyes met for a moment, and in that instant each knew the message from the Inca would never die. It would be passed on, generation to generation.

The runner nodded and rose. He bowed, and the man responded. Then the runner walked away from the eating place to join the workers. These were his people, men of strong backs and honest, brown faces. They talked and joked in a language he could understand. They were cleaning the road that led down to the valley, but they had paused to eat their noonday meal. They accepted the runner easily into their company.

The young woman he had met when he entered the gate

of Vilcampa handed him Quechua food, and he ate. Here he felt at ease. These men had been in the Mountains of the Sun a long time. They were the new workers in the city of Vilcampa. They ate and talked in the shadow of Machu Picchu. They would be here forever, the runner thought.

He relaxed, looked at the young woman and smiled. He had delivered the message from the Inca, now it was in the hands of the man who sat at the table. He would read the secret of the quipus, record it in his language, and pass it on. Each new time had its runners, those whose work carried them into new visions of reality.

ESSAYS

Requiem for a Lowrider

I'd like to tell those of you who are graduating from high school a story about my graduation. In 1956 I stumbled up to the stage and received that piece of paper that said, You did it, you finally graduated from high school! It was a time for feeling high, and I don't mean just from the elation of receiving my diploma.

We already had a week of partying under our belts, and there were more to come on commencement night. During that final week of school we felt as if we owned the world. Very few of us were worrying about the really heavy concerns, like getting a job, planning our future, deciding on more education, or whether to get married or wait awhile . . . the same important decisions facing graduates today.

Graduating classes today and mine in 1956 are two generations apart, and yet we still have a lot in common. I have been asking myself, What is our common ground? What is it that we can talk about across this span of time? We were the generation of the fifties, of bebop, rock 'n' roll, sock hops, *Leave It to Beaver*, Marilyn Monroe and Joe DiMaggio. A decade of innocence, it has been called.

A lot of Chicanos living in the United States were poor and undereducated, but no one cared about the ethnic communities of this country then. My family couldn't afford to send me to college, but I enrolled anyway, paying for tuition and books by taking part-time jobs. In literature classes I fell in love with reading and the wealth of ideas literature presented. Around us, the beatnik poets were reforming the way we thought of poetry, drug use, being on the road to nirvana, social values and the so-called alternative cultures which would change the way we looked at things in the sixties.

I ask myself: What is the culture of high school students like today? How do the music, movies, and television which shape you express who you are? What books are you reading and what ideas are you discussing? What is the vision of your future?

What is the *one* thing that can help us communicate with each other? I keep asking myself that question, and my mind keeps coming back to Jessie. He was my friend; we started Albuquerque High School together. He was a great guy, a real easygoing vato loco, but he didn't graduate. He was one of the original lowriders, a crazy cruiser with a customized '48 Ford. He spent more time cruising around the school on Broadway and Central than in it.

He was one of the kindest and brightest persons I've ever known, and in thinking of him I think I discovered the one element we have in common. In different times, you and I are a generation of lowriders. In the fifties we spent four years in high school, cruising. The fifties developed lowriding and cruising to an art. The pachucos, the granddaddies of all the Chicano rebels, not only dressed cool, they drove cool ranflas.

And thank heaven for cruisers and lowriders! Just think how many lowriders it has taken to make this country what it is today. Christopher Columbus was one of the original lowriders! That's right, I think old Chris was just kicking back, cruising around the Atlantic, and by accident he happened to bump into the Americas. And most of us wouldn't be here today if he hadn't gone cruising that Sunday.

Yeah, just think for a moment what came out of that Columbus cruise.

But what is cruising all about?

When you say, "Hey, Dad," or "Oye, Jefito, I'm going cruising," the typical response is: "Where are you going?"

And the typical answer is: "I don't know, just cruising."

Just cruising, huh? That's the question that keeps turning in my mind when I think about Jessie.

"We have a big assignment in history," I'd say to him, "let's go hit the books at the library."

And he would smile and put his arm around my shoulder and say, "Hey, let's go cruising, man. You only live once. You take life too seriously . . . Just cool it . . ."

Cool it. In the fifties it meant kick back, take it easy. That's another thing I've discovered as I compare our generations: the words change, language fads come and go, but deep down inside we all still have to deal with the real gut issues that life presents us. Today you have to make choices. You have to think about cruising as I have.

Because what is it that we're looking for when we go cruising? Let me suggest to you that we are looking for excitement to put in our lives. We go cruising to meet a friend, we hope that that special someone we like is also out there, just cruising. We turn up streets randomly, we follow the crowd. If there's a wreck, a fight, or a party, everybody shows up, looking for the action, looking for some excitement. In short, we're all waiting for an accident to happen.

That's what Jessie was doing. I know now. He was dissatisfied. He cruised around waiting for something to happen. In a roundabout way he taught me that life requires a little more planning than goes into just cruising.

Oh, everybody loved Jessie. Ducktail, baggy pants, hair slick with pomade, swinging like a pachuco, he'd come dancing down the hall, snapping his fingers, looking the girls over. He was Mr. Cool! He acted crazy but he treated everybody with respect. Even the teachers liked him—that is, when he was in class long enough for them to get to know him.

"Hey, Rudy!" he used to say. "Let's go cruise around before class. We can smoke a few tokes and be back in time for third period."

Life was easy for him when he was cruising and smoking up, looking for that excitement he needed.

By his senior year he was beyond just drinking beer and smoking mota. I still remember the first night I saw him loaded with heroin. We were going to a dance at the Heights Center, and he came to pick me up. He was really high, and I knew it was on heavy stuff. Carga, horse, smack, call it what you want, the words change, the junk remains the same beneath.

I cried, "Hey, Jessie, what are you doing to yourself? Do you know what you're getting into?"

I don't want to sound moralistic. I had done a lot of the crazy things he had done. We were young men and we were growing up. Bumping into accidents and new excitement every day was a part of our lives. All I tried to tell him was that there was other excitement to life. I tried to tell him that sometimes I got my high from some of the books I was reading, and that, yes, even some of the ideas the teachers kicked around in class were exciting. It wasn't all sheer boredom. I didn't give him a lecture, I talked to him as a friend. I was concerned for him because I loved him as a friend, and I knew he was on the wrong road.

"Easy, Rudy, easy, daddy-o," he said. "I'm okay . . . I know what I'm doing, hey, this is a great high. I can handle it. Come on, let's go dancing!"

And he was a great dancer. The girls loved him. We all loved him. The only people who could have cared less about him were the ones he had run into while cruising, the ones who sold him the junk.

After a while his habit was daily. He dropped out of school. We drifted apart . . . went our separate ways. I stayed in school, hoping there was something there that would help me solve the complexity of my own life. Jessie began to run with a new crowd, but he was no longer the happy-go-lucky lowrider I once knew. He was running scared.

We talked once, but it didn't do any good. "You take life too serious," he told me. "It's only a slow cruise, so take it easy. Look, I'm not busting my ass on books, and I've got a car, plenty of bread, everything I need." And he smiled.

But we both knew it wasn't Jessie who had those things, it was the monkey on his back who owned everything, and the monkey was growing, sitting by Jessie as they cruised up and down the barrio streets.

The last time I saw him was graduation night. I remember it as if it was yesterday. I was graduating; he wasn't. I wanted him to be with me and share whatever this small accomplishment meant. "I wouldn't miss it for the world," he said. "I may not be getting my little piece of paper, but I'm glad you're getting yours. Hey, you keep getting those things and you're going to be a big vato someday!" We laughed.

How could any of us be mad at him? He was a lovable guy. We could only hurt for him. There was a gang of us, friends from the barrio, who had gone through high school together, and Jessie was the only one not graduating.

But he was there to wish us luck, and he came to the party afterwards. And for a few moments we were all happy and things seemed to be the way they used to be. We joked, laughed, and talked about what we were going to do now that we owned the world.

I could go on to tell you how each one of us, each member of that small gang, went on to develop his potential and live a worthwhile life. But this is not our story. It's Jessie's story.

He was really high that night, and he was desperate. He mentioned once that he needed money, that he had big debts to pay, and then the party got loud and crowded and I lost track of him for a while. Later, when I asked for him, somebody told me that some of his "new" friends had taken him outside. I ran outside, but his car was gone. Jessie had gone on his last ride.

The following morning his brother called me and told me Jessie was dead. They had dumped him down by the river that night. He had paid his debt. When I got to the mortuary his family was already there. It was a sad time. Nothing to say or do. I could only promise him that some-day I'd tell his story, that maybe it would make sense to someone. And now I'm telling it to you. This is Jessie's story, it's my requiem for a lowrider.

And why have I told you this story now, when graduation should be a time of rejoicing for you and for your families who have helped you through school? It's a time of celebration for the teachers and the counselors who have helped. Now you've made it, and it's your time. It's also a proper time to remember the help you received, the encouragement when you were down, the love when you thought things were hopeless. And because we share our lives with many brothers and sisters, it's also a time to remember that we, too, can give help. Maybe we didn't give Jessie enough help, maybe we didn't give him enough love, maybe we saw too late that he was drifting into an accident from which there was no return.

I sincerely believe that there is a time in life for drifting. There is a time for sitting back and getting in touch with yourself. Some of our most interesting illuminations and ideas will come when we take time to reflect, time to kick back and cruise awhile.

But there's also a time for planning, a time for looking into the future, a time for more active participation in life. You can't cruise forever. The gas is running out, you're older and at a new stage of life. Your lives will be very complex, and there will be many friends like Jessie who will need your help. So I ask you, engage life actively! Embrace it and love it! And help make it a fulfilling adventure, not a dead end where we have to write more requiems for friends like Jessie.

vato: a guy, a friend
vato loco: a fun-loving guy, maybe into using dope
pachuco: zoot-suiter of the fifties
ranfla: car
jefito (from *jefe*): father
mota: marijuana
carga: heroin

The Magic of Words

A million volumes.

A magic number.

A million books to read, to look at, to hold in one's hand, to learn, to dream . . .

I have always known there were at least a million stars. In the summer evenings when I was a child, we, all the children of the neighborhood, sat outside under the stars and listened to the stories of the old ones, los viejitos. The stories of the old people taught us to wonder and imagine. Their adivinanzas induced the stirring of our first questioning, our early learning.

I remember my grandfather raising his hand and pointing to the swirl of the Milky Way which swept over us. Then he would whisper his favorite riddle:

> Hay un hombre con tanto dinero
> Que no lo puede contar
> Una mujer con una sabana tan grande
> Que no la puede doblar.

There is a man with so much money
He cannot count it
A woman with a bedspread so large
She cannot fold it.

We know the million stars were the coins of the Lord, and the heavens were the bedspread of his mother, and in our minds the sky was a million miles wide. A hundred million. Infinite. Stuff for the imagination. And what was more important, the teachings of the old ones made us see that we were bound to the infinity of that cosmic dance of life that swept around us. Their teachings created in us a thirst for knowledge. Can this library with its million volumes bestow that same inspiration?

I was fortunate to have had those old and wise viejitos as guides into the world of nature and knowledge. They taught me with their stories; they taught me the magic of words. Now the words lie captured in ink, but the magic is still there, the power inherent in each volume. Now with book in hand we can participate in the wisdom of mankind.

Each person moves from innocence through rites of passage into the knowledge of the world, and so I entered the world of school in search of the magic in the words. The sounds were no longer the soft sounds of Spanish, which my grandfather spoke; the words were in English, and with each new awareness came my first steps toward a million volumes. I, who was used to reading my oraciones en español while I sat in the kitchen and answered the litany to the slap of my mother's tortillas, I now stumbled from sound to word to groups of words, head throbbing, painfully aware that each new sound took me deeper into the maze of the new language. Oh, how I clutched the hands of my new guides then!

Learn, my mother encouraged me, learn. Be as wise as your grandfather. He could speak many languages. He could speak to the birds and the animals of the field.

Yes, I remember the cuentos of my grandfather, the stories of the people. Words are a way, he said, they hold joy, and they are a deadly power if misused. I clung to each syllable that lisped from his tobacco-stained lips. That was the winter the snow came, he would say. It piled high and we lost many sheep and cattle, and the trees groaned and broke with its weight. I looked across the llano and saw the raging blizzard, the awful destruction of that winter, which was embedded in our people's mind.

And the following summer, he would say, the grass of the llano grew so high we couldn't see the top of the sheep. And I would look and see what was once clean and pure and green. I could see a million sheep and the pastores caring for them, as I now care for the million words that pasture in my mind.

But a million books? How can we see a million books? I don't mean just the books lining the shelves here at the University of New Mexico Library, not just the fine worn covers, the intriguing titles; how can we see the worlds that lie waiting in each book? A million worlds. A million million worlds. And the beauty of it is that each world is related to the next, as was taught to us by the old ones. Perhaps it is easier for a child to see. Perhaps it is easier for a child to ask: How many stars are there in the sky? How many leaves in the trees of the river? How many blades of grass in the llano? How many dreams in a night of dreams?

So I worked my way into the world of books, but here is the paradox: a book at once quenches the thirst of the imagination and ignites new fires. I learned that as I visited the library of my childhood, the Santa Rosa Library. It was only a dusty room in those days, a room sitting atop the town's fire department, which was comprised of one dilapidated fire truck used by the town's volunteers only in the direst emergencies. But in that small room I found my shelter and retreat. If there were a hundred books there, we were fortunate, but to me there were a million volumes. I trembled in awe when I first entered that library, because I realized that if the books held as much magic as the words of the old ones, then indeed this was a room full of power.

Miss Pansy, the librarian, became my new guide. She fed me books as any mother would nurture her child. She brought me book after book, and I consumed them all. Saturday afternoons disappeared as the time of day dissolved into the time of distant worlds. In a world that occupied most of my other schoolmates with games, I took the time to read. I was a librarian's dream. My tattered library card was my ticket into the same worlds my grandfather had known, worlds of magic that fed the imagination.

Late in the afternoon, when I was satiated with reading, when I could no longer hold in my soul the characters that crowded there, I heard the call of the llano, the real world of my father's ranchito, the solid, warm world of my mother's kitchen. Then to the surprise and bewilderment of Miss Pansy, I would rush out and race down the streets of our town, books tucked under my shirt, in my pockets, clutched tightly to my breast. Mad with the insanity of books, I would cross the river to get home, shouting my crazy challenge even at La Llorona, and that poor spirit of so many frightening cuentos would wither and withdraw. She was no match for me.

Those of you who have felt the same exhilaration from reading—or from love—will know about what I'm speaking. Alas, the people of the town could only shake their heads and pity my mother. At least one of her sons was a bit touched. Perhaps they were right, for few will trade a snug reality to float on words to other worlds.

And now there are a million volumes for us to read here at the University of New Mexico Library. Books on every imaginable subject, in every field, a history of the thought of the world, which we must keep free of censorship, because we treasure our freedoms. It is the word *freedom* that eventually must reflect what this collection, or the collection of any library, is all about. We know that as we preserve and use the literature of all cultures, we preserve and regenerate our own. The old ones knew and taught me this. They kept their dairies, they wrote décimas and cuentos, and they survived on their oral stories and traditions.

Another time, another library. I entered Albuquerque High School Library prepared to study, because that's where we spent our study time. For better or for worse, I received my first contracts as a writer there. It was a place where budding lovers spent most of their time writing notes to each other, and when my friends who didn't have the gift of words found out I could turn a phrase, I quickly had all the business I could do. I wrote poetic love notes for a dime apiece and thus worked my way through high school. And there were fringe benefits, because the young women knew very well who was writing the sweet words, and many a heart I was supposed to capture fell in love with me. And so, a library is also a place where love begins.

A library should be the heart of a city. With its storehouse of knowledge, it liberates, informs, teaches, and enthralls. A library indeed should be the cultural center of any city. Amidst the bustle of work and commerce, the great libraries of the world have provided a sanctuary where scholars and common man alike come to enlarge and clarify knowledge, to read and reflect in quiet solitude.

I knew a place like this. I spent many hours in the old library on Central Avenue and Edith Street. But my world was growing, and quite by accident I wandered up the hill to enroll in the University of New Mexico. And what a surprise lay in store for me. The libraries of my childhood paled in comparison to the new wealth of books housed in Zimmerman Library. Here there were stack after stack of books, and ample space and time to wander aimlessly in this labyrinth of new frontiers.

I had known the communal memory of my people through the newspapers and few books my grandfather read to me and through the rich oral tradition handed down by the old ones; now I discovered the collective memory of all mankind at my fingertips. I had only to reach for the books that laid all history bare. Here I could converse with the writers from every culture on earth, old and new, and at the same time I began my personal odyssey, which would add a few books to the collection that in 1981 would come to house a million volumes.

Those were exciting times. Around me swirled the busy world of the university, in many respects an alien world. Like many fellow undergraduates, I sought refuge in the library. My haven during those student university years was the reading room of the west wing of the old library. There I found peace. The carved vigas decorating the ceiling, the solid wooden table and chairs, and the warm adobe color of the stucco were things with which I was familiar. There I felt comfortable. With books scattered around me, I could read and doze and dream. I took my breaks in the warm sun of the portal, where I ate my tortilla sandwiches, which I carried in my brown paper bag. There, with friends, I sipped coffee as we talked of changing the world and exchanged idealistic dreams.

That is a rich and pleasant time in my memory. No matter how far across the world I find myself in the future, how deep in the creating of worlds with words, I shall keep the simple and poignant memories of those days. The sun set golden on the ocher walls, and the green pine trees and the blue spruce, sacred trees to our people, whispered in the breeze. I remembered my grandfather meeting with the old men of the village in the resolana of one of the men's homes, or against the wall of the church on Sundays, and I remembered the things they said. Later, alone, dreaming against the sun-warmed wall of the library, I continued that discourse in my mind.

Yes, the library is a place where people should gather. It is a place for research, reading, and for the quiet fomentation of ideas, but because it houses the collective memory of our race, it should also be a place where present issues are discussed and debated and researched in order for us to gain the knowledge and insight to create a better future. The library should be a warm place that reflects the needs and aspirations of the people.

The University of New Mexico Library didn't have a million volumes when I first haunted its corridors of stacks, but now these million volumes are available. The library has grown. Sometimes I get lost when I wander through it, and I cannot help but wonder if there are students around me who are also lost. Is there someone who will guide them through this storehouse of knowledge? A labyrinth can be a frightening place without a guide, and perhaps that is why I have written about some of the guides who took my hand and helped me. It is important not only to celebrate the acquisition of the millionth volume but to rededicate ourselves to the service of our community, which is an integral part of the history of this library. I am confident that the library will continue to grow and to be an example to other libraries. Service to the community is indeed our most important endeavor.

This millionth volume marks a momentous step in the process of growth of the University of New Mexico Library. This commemorative volume celebrates that step. In the wisest cultures of the world, entry into adulthood is a time of celebration, it is a time for dancing and thanksgiving. And that is what we, the staff of the library, the scholars of the university, the students, the friends, and the people from the community come to celebrate this year. We gather not only to celebrate growth but also to note the excellence of archives in many fields, to acknowledge the change that has met the demands of the present and needs of the future, and to honor the service provided to all of the people who come here to read, to dream, to re-create.

So, let us celebrate this rite of passage. It is a time to flex our muscles and be proud. We have come a long way from the first collection, and we will continue to build. I would like to list the names of all the people who have worked to bring us this moment, but since that is impossible it is the intent of this personal essay to thank those people. This reminiscence through libraries I have known and dreamed in is a thanks to those librarians whose efforts helped to establish this library. In their spirit we will offer help to each person who comes through the doors of this library in that curious but inalienable right to search for knowledge.

los viejitos: the elders
adivinanzas: riddles
cuentos: stories, also folktales
décima: a Spanish stanza consisting of ten verses of eight syllables
resolana: a sheltered place for taking the sun

A New Mexico Christmas

Christmas in New Mexico is unique. It is a time of celebration and a time of memories.

When I was a child, my mother's preparations for Christmas meant a week's work in the kitchen. Pots of posole would bubble on the stove, the plump tamales wrapped in their corn husks steamed in the pressure cooker. The aroma of these foods made from corn, the sacred food of the New World, pervaded the kitchen.

There were also desserts. Plates of empanadas made with fruit and sweetmeats were piled high. The anise and nutmeg fragrance of the biscochitos, the traditional sugar cookies, filled the house. These were just some of the Christmas foods prepared to celebrate Christ's birth.

It was my father's job to scour the countryside for a piñon tree. It was a treasure trip for me as I accompanied him in search of the green tree that would grace our simple home. It would be decorated with an old and frayed string of lights, bright streamers of cloth my mother sewed. My sisters would add the store-bought icicles and the angel hair.

On Christmas Eve we hung our stockings on the stout branches of the tree. In the morning the stockings would be stuffed with hard candy, nuts, and fruit. There were always plenty of apples and dried fruit, the bounty of the harvest from the farms of my uncles in Puerto de Luna. Oranges were a favorite, but they were expensive, available only if my father was working.

Christmas Eve meant bundling up at eleven o'clock at night to make the long trek into town to celebrate la Misa del Gallo, midnight Mass. The long walk into town was also a time for contemplation. Under the starry sky of the New Mexico llano it was the family unit that made its way to church. My mother led, we followed close behind, my father came after us.

That walk rekindles memories of my childhood. The night was cold. Over us sparkled the mystery of the universe, the stars of the Milky Way. Once, long ago, one star lighted the way to Bethlehem. I learned then that to celebrate the religious spirit one had to be attentive. Each person could renew the spirit within, but each had to make an offering. My mother's offering was her belief in the birth of Christ, el Cristo. My father offered the green tree, the symbol of life everlasting, the tree of life itself. And we offered the long, cold walk to join the community of the Mass.

It is that individual and communal offering that cannot be packaged in the modern department store.

After Mass we hurried home. At two in the morning the cold of the llano had set in. Plumes of our breath filled the blue night. We hurried home, where my mother prepared hot chocolate and biscochitos. Then it was off to blissful sleep under warm covers.

In the morning we would awaken to search in the stockings and to open gifts, gifts we usually made ourselves for each other, because there was little money for store-bought gifts. If lucky I might receive a pair of gloves—that is, if the fingers were showing in the old pair. My sisters received clothing, curlers, and prized nylons—as bobby socks gave way to young womanhood.

Then I would run out to join my friends to visit the houses of our neighbors. Our shout was, "¡Mis Crismes! ¡Mis Crismes!" We asked for and received the traditional gifts of Christmas, much as the trick-or-treaters do today on Halloween. Our flour sacks bulged with candy, nuts, and fruits when we returned home.

Later in the morning the family would start arriving, brothers from afar, aunts and uncles, and the entire potpourri of padrinos and madrinas, compadres and comadres, cousins, friends, the extended family.

For a child lost in the wonder of the celebration everyone was a welcome sight. They all brought gifts. If the piñon season had been good that fall, someone would arrive with a gunnysack full of piñones, those sweet, little nuts we would crack and eat in front of the stove as we listened to the stories. Another might bring carne seca, jerky to be cooked with red chile from the ristra hanging in the pantry.

Perhaps someone had been working in Texas, and his truck would be loaded with oranges and ruby red grapefruits, gifts from el Valle de Tejas where some went to make a living.

Then we would compare gifts, and my cousins would ask, "What did Santo Clos bring you?"

Our Santo Clos was the Santa Claus we knew at school, where we also decorated the classroom tree and acted in the annual Christmas play. Santo Clos, the stockings, and the Perry Como Christmas songs on the radio were the influence of the Anglo culture filtering into our way of life. The cultures were interacting, exchanging customs, and yet each group still retained its own ways, borrowing from each other and forming the mosaic of celebration that Christmas has come to be in New Mexico.

At the center of the celebration was the tree. For my father it was important to have it ready on December 21, the day of the winter solstice. This was indeed the tree of

life, and its importance and the importance of the day were
fixed in the religious nature of the Indians of New Mexico,
as it has been fixed since time immemorial in most of the
cultures of the world. The shortest day of the year reminds
us all that the sun has reached the end of its winter journey.
It will return northward to renew the earth, but for one
day it hangs in precarious balance.

Long ago on this day in ancient Mexico, and throughout
the Americas, sacrifices were made in honor of the sun, the
life giver. Incense was burned and sprigs of green were
gathered. Ancient man understood his relation to the cosmos. For him the race of the sun was a mystery to be
celebrated. One had to be attentive to the workings of the
planets and stars, as one had to attend to the working of
the spirit within.

I wonder how much of that awe we have lost today.

Our child's Christmas in New Mexico did not involve
expensive toys. There were no malls beckoning with sales
to distract the spirit and exhaust the mind. We gathered
together to celebrate two ways of life, the Christian and
the indigenous religious spirit that came to us through the
traditions founded in ancient Mexico. Our Christmas Day
was not intent on football games, but on listening to the
history of the families who came to visit. They brought
many stories. The kitchen was warm and filled with good
food, and after we ate we listened to the stories.

My child's Christmas was a celebration because it was
a sharing. Out of that past I have evolved the rituals that
are important for me to celebrate. I decorate with lights
the piñon tree near the entrance to my home. I make sure
it is lighted on the night of December 21. It also serves me
well for Christmas.

There are other celebrations to share in as the year draws
to a close. When it is possible I go to Jemez Pueblo on
December 12, el Día de Nuestra Señora de Guadalupe. The
Matachines dances at Jemez are among the most exquisite
I have ever witnessed. The color of the earth is red, the

hills are dotted with junipers and pines, and above the pueblo loom the dark Jemez Mountains. As one approaches, the pueblo appears serene and quiet, then one hears the violin of the fiddler. It is time to hurry to the plaza, where two brightly colored lines of dancers move to the music.

Each dancer wears an ornate, colorful corona, the headdress. The rattle of hollow gourds fills the air as the dancers move back and forth to the lively, repetitive strains of the fiddle. The drama is a mixture of a pueblo step and a polka, more Spanish than Indian. The Malinche, the little girl in white, symbolizing innocence, dances with the old Abuelo, the grandfather. Near her lurks the dancer dressed as El Toro. The presence of the bull frightens the children, for El Toro symbolizes evil.

This dance, brought by the Spaniards to the New World, is now danced both in the Hispano villages and in the Indian pueblos of New Mexico. It is a unique and enthralling way to start the season of renewal. An hour or two spent visiting with friends at Jemez and sitting in the winter sun while the dance drama unfolds can remind the most depressed of spirits that this community is still attentive to its spiritual needs.

All of the homes are open, strangers are fed. The tables are heaped high with posole, meat, chile dishes, tortillas and Indian bread from the hornos, pies, and biscochitos. Imagine what a better life this would be if all the homes in the cities and suburbs enacted this noble sense of community.

Another experience not to be missed is to be at the Taos Pueblo on Christmas Day, but it could be any one of the other pueblos, because they are all celebrating. It is the end of a season, a time of dancing and singing. But in Taos at dusk on Christmas Eve the Mass is celebrated. After Mass the people come pouring out of the church in a winding line.

I was there one Christmas Eve when my friend Cruz

pulled me into the procession to weave around the luminarias, stacks of crisscrossed piñon wood which are bonfires
lighting the way of the celebrants. And what are these
luminarias but a symbol of everlasting light. The bonfires
roaring into the night sky are a reflection on earth of the
stars that light the way, the star that guided the shepherds
to Bethlehem. The fires symbolize the renewal of the sun,
and renewal of the light within.

Those roaring fires at the pueblo rekindle the memory
of the stars I contemplated as a child. The sweet perfume
of the burning piñon rises into the dark, cold sky. So it is
with the votive candles in the church. The smoke rises with
its message for harmony and peace.

On Christmas Day the deer dance is performed, a dance
both for the Taoseños and for their guests. One has to be
attentive to brave the sharp cold of the winter morning.
Then from the direction of the blue Taos Mountain the
cry of the deer is heard, and the frozen spectators stamp
their feet and wait eagerly. The cold is numbing, but worth
the effort. The deer dancers unite the elements of earth,
sky, and community, symbolizing the deep, religious nature
of the pueblo.

In Alburquerque, my home, there are other old and last-
ing rituals to be enacted. Even in the city the barrios preserve
their traditions. *Los Pastores*, an old miracle play that
originated in Spain, is a favorite. Many of the barrios and
villages have their version of this nativity play. Each of the
shepherds in the play represents a vice, and when Bartolo,
the laziest of the group, is finally converted, the audience
rejoices.

Las Posadas is another favorite miracle play. It is one
of the oldest plays of the Western world continually reenacted in the New World. The story tells how Joseph and
Mary sought an inn, a posada. Those who play the parts
of Joseph and Mary go from home to home, seeking shelter
for the night. They knock at the first door and are refused.
The procession moves to another home, singing carols,

until finally they are admitted at a designated home and all the guests are fed. There is singing and great rejoicing.

There is something beneath the ritual that must be the real message. Even when *Las Posadas* is not enacted as a play, the idea of welcoming the stranger to the feast persists. That is why so many people met in my mother's kitchen in those Christmases of long ago.

Time changes the customs in small ways; it does not dim the memory. Now the farolitos are not the stacks of piñon wood to be lighted, they are votive candles placed in paper sacks with sand at the bottom. When we were children the brown paper bags from the grocery store were saved not only for sack lunches but so we would have enough sacks to use for the farolitos of Christmas.

The farolitos are a traditional New Mexico custom. Hundreds adorn homes, walkways, and street curbs. On a cold Christmas night even the most humble home is transformed as the candles flicker and glow in the dark.

In a city like Alburquerque, caravans of tourists fill the streets in the evenings to view the symphony of light that glows to announce that in this home there is posada. Neighborhoods become united as they gather in community effort to decorate their homes and streets. Candles and paper sacks are shared, even if today they are bought at the store. The children vie to light the candles, for the lighting of the farolitos keeps the child's sense of Christmas. More than one enterprising company is now making electric farolitos. Perhaps the important thing is that the lights continue to be lit.

In our memory we know that it is important to light the fire at the end of this season, whether the fire be the yule log or the luminarias of New Mexico. A fire shall light the way, just as the evergreen will remind us that life will renew itself.

Deep within the celebration of these customs there lies the flicker of hope. Christmas celebrates the birth of Christ, and it is also the celebration of the ending of the year, the cycle of the sun. Now the sun will return north and the days will grow longer, and those who were attentive to this mysterious spirit of renewal will be fulfilled.

posole: a hominy stew
tamale (tamal): thick masa harina (corn dough) wrapped around a spicy meat filling, enclosed in corn husks and steamed
empanadas: meat or fruit turnovers
biscochitos: Christmas cookies
llano: a wide plain or prairie
"¡Mis Crismes!": "Where's my Christmas gift!"
luminarias: bonfires usually lit at the church on Christmas Eve
farolitos: a candle in a bag, also called a luminaria

An American Chicano
in King Arthur's Court

A variety of voices comprises the literature of the Southwest. Writers from each of the cultural groups write from their particular perspective. Eventually these different perspectives will form the body of work we call Southwestern Literature. I say eventually, because as of now the contemporary writings of the Chicano and Native American communities—while they are flourishing—have not yet been widely disseminated and have not yet made their final impact on the region.

It is understood that whenever cultural groups as different as the Anglo-American, Chicano, Native American, and others exist side by side, cultural sharing takes place; but also each group will develop a set of biases or stereotypes about the other groups. This is unfortunate, but it is a substantiated historical fact. The problem is compounded, of course, when one of the groups holds social, political, and economic power over the other groups. Then prejudices will affect in an adverse manner the members of the minority groups.

How do we make the literature of the Southwest a truly

multicultural literature that informs the public about the variety of voices reflecting the cultures of the Southwest? Can our different literatures help to lessen the negative effect of cultural stereotypes?

I am an American Chicano, and I have titled my essay "An American Chicano in King Arthur's Court." For me, King Arthur's Court represents an archetypal time and experience in English memory, a memory that was brought to the American shores by English colonists. It is an archetype that is very much alive. (Remember the Kennedy administration reviving the dreams of Camelot?) King Arthur's Court represents a "foreign" archetype that is not indigenous to the Native American memory.

There is no judgmental value attached to what I have just said. King Arthur's Court has a right to exist in the communal memory of the British and the Anglo-Americans, and communal memory is a force that defines a group. The stories and legends surrounding King Arthur's Court are part of their history and identity. Camelot and King Arthur's Court are "real" forces inasmuch as they define part of the evolution of this group's eventual worldview.

In 1846 King Arthur's Court moved to what we now call the Southwest United States. During the war with Mexico the United States forcefully took and then occupied Mexico's northern territories. In so doing the United States acquired a large population of Native Americans and Mexicanos. What did it mean to the Mexicanos, those soon to be labeled Mexican-Americans, when suddenly a very different social, economic, and political system was placed over them?

Historians have written about the economic and political castastrophe that occurred. I wish to explore the occupation from another angle. What happened when a different worldview with its particular archetypes was imposed over the communal memory of the Mexicanos? In the area of artistic impulse and creation, this element of the Anglo culture would cause as many problems for the Mexicanos

as did the new language and value system with which they
now had to contend.

The Mexicanos of the Southwest had already spent centuries creating their own vision of the world by the time the
Anglo-Americans arrived. Their worldview was principally
Hispanic and Catholic, but it was also imbued with strains
of belief from the Native American cultures. The culture
was Hispanic in language, but in its soul and memory
resided Western European thought, Greek mythology, and
the Judeo-Christian mythology and religious thought; the
thought and mythology of Indian Mexico and of the Pueblos of the Rio Grande had already imbued the collective
memory. The Mexicano of the north was, with few and
isolated exceptions, a mestizo population. Therefore, its
worldview was informed by the memory of the native cultures of the Southwest United States.

Since 1848, King Arthur's Court has been the social and
legal authority in the Southwest. It has exercised its power,
not always in a fair and judicious way. My concern here
is to explore how the Anglo-American value system affected
the artistic impulse of the Mexicano. Did it impede and
stifle the creativity of the Mexicano, and if so, did it interfere
in the Mexicano's self-identity and aesthetic?

The artistic impulse is an energy most intricately bound
to the soul of the people. Art and literature reflect the
cultural group, and in reflecting the group they deal not
only with the surface reality but with that substratum of
thought that is the group memory. The entire spectrum
of history, language, soul, voice, and the symbols of the
collective memory affect the writer. A writer becomes a
prism to reflect those elements that are at the roots of the
value system. We write to analyze the past, explore the
present, and anticipate the future, and in so doing we utilize
the collective memory of the group. We seek new visions
and symbols to chart the future, and yet we are bound to
mythologies and symbols of our past.

I remember when I started writing as a young man, fresh

out of the university, my mind teeming with the great works I had read as a student. I was affected, as were most of my generation, by the poetry of Dylan Thomas, Eliot, Pound, Wallace Stevens. I had devoured the works of world authors, as well as the more contemporary Hemingway, Faulkner, Steinbeck, and Thomas Wolfe, and I felt I had learned a little about style and technique. I tried to imitate the work of those great writers, but that was not effective for the stories I had to tell. I made a simple discovery. I found I needed to write in *my* voice, of *my* characters, using *my* indigenous symbols. I needed to write about my culture, my history, and the collective experience of my cultural group. But I had not been prepared to explore *my* indigenous, American experience; all my education from first grade through a graduate degree had prepared me to understand King Arthur's Court. I discovered that the underlying worldview of King Arthur's Court could not serve to tell the stories about my communal group.

I suppose Ultima saved me. That strong, old curandera of my first novel, *Bless Me, Ultima,* came to me one night and pointed the way. Was she the anima, a woman of wisdom, the collective mothers of the past, or a reflection of the real curanderas I had seen do their work? I know she became a guide and mentor who was to lead me into the world of my native American experience. Write what you know, she said. Do not fear to explore the workings of your soul, your dreams, your memory. Dive deep into the lake of your subconsciousness, your memory! Find the symbols, unlock the secrets! Learn who you really are! You can't be a writer of any merit if you don't know who you are!

I took her kind and wise advice. I dove into the common memory, into the dark and hidden past which was a lake full of treasure. The symbols I discovered had very little to do with the symbols I knew from King Arthur's Court— they were new symbols, symbols I did not fully understand, but symbols that I was sure spoke of the indigenous American experience. The symbols and patterns I found connected me to the past, and that past was not only my Hispanic, Catholic heritage; that past was also Indian Mexico. I did what I had never been taught to do at the university. I explored myself and began to learn the workings of my soul. I was a reflection of that totality of the past which had worked for eons to produce me.

Each writer has to go through the process of liberating oneself and finding one's true stream of creative energy. For the Chicano writers of my generation it has been doubly difficult, because in our formative years we were not presented with the opportunity to study our culture, our history, our language.

My generation will receive at least some thanks from the future, if only because we dared to write from the perspective of our experience, our culture. Of course a steady stream of southwestern Hispanic writers had been producing works all along. Before and after 1846, poetry, novels, and newspapers were produced, but those works were never part of the school curriculum. The oral tradition was alive and well, and its artistic impulse was invigorating to those of us lucky enough to grow up in its bounty. But by the 1960s the Hispanic culture had reached a crisis point. Not only were the old prejudices affecting us adversely, but the very core of the culture was under threat.

The Mexican-American community needed economic and political justice in the 1960s. It also needed an artistic infusion of fresh, creative energy. We had to take a look at ourselves and understand the worldview that our ancestors had created. This is precisely what the Chicano Movement of the 1960s and '70s did. The Chicano Movement of those decades fought battles in the social, economic, and political arenas, and in the artistic camp. Taking up pen and paintbrushes, we found we could joust against King Arthur's knights and hold our own. In fact, we often did extremely well because we were on our soil, we knew the turf. Quite simply, what we were saying was that we wanted to assert our own rights, we wanted to define ourselves, we believed that our worldview was as important as any other in terms of sustaining the individual and the community.

We engaged actively in large-scale production of creative literature. We insisted that the real definition of our community was in the arts, in poetry and stories. A wealth of works was produced, which was labeled the Chicano Renaissance. This view of the writers working from within the Chicano community helped to dispel some of the old stereotypes and prejudices. We could think, we could write, we did honor parents and family, we did have a set of moral values, we were as rich and as complex a cultural group as any other group in the country, and so the old, one-dimensional stereotypes began to crumble.

We explained to the broader "mainstream" culture that we are American Chicanos; we are an inherently American, indigenous people. We are Hispanic from our European heritage, we are native American from our American heritage. We are heirs to the mythologies and religions and philosophic thought of Western civilization, but we are also heirs to the mythologies, religions, and thought of the Americas. A renewed pride in our native American heritage defined us.

Out of the Native American world flowed a rich mythology and symbology which the poets and writers began to tap and use. We confronted our mestizo heritage and proudly identified with this New World person. The idea of an original homeland, typified with the concept of Aztlán, became a prevalent idea. The homeland was indigenous, it was recorded in Native American legend. For the Chicano consciousness of the 1960s it provided a psychological and spiritual center. One of the most positive aspects of the Chicano Movement was its definition of a Chicano consciousness. Spiritually and psychologically, Chicanos had found their center; they could define their universe with a set of symbols and metaphors that were inherent to the New World. We had tapped our Native American experience and recovered the important archetypal symbols of that history.

That consciousness, which was defined in the art, poetry, and stories of the Chicano writers, continues to exist not just as a historical phenomenon that happened in the sixties and seventies; it continues to define the Chicano collective memory today. The power of literature, the power of story and legend, is great. True, the Chicano Movement has waned in social action, but the renewed consciousness born in the literature of those decades survives in art, writing, history, and in the language and the oral tradition of the people. In a broader sense, its humanistic principles of brotherhood, its desire for justice, its positive cultural identification, its definition of historic values, and its concern for the oppressed continue to be guiding principles in the thought and conduct of American Chicanos. Chicano consciousness continues to center us, instruct us, guide us, and define us.

The evolution of Chicano consciousness created a new perspective in humanistic philosophy. It took nothing away from our European and Mexican heritage, it took nothing away from other Western influences; on the contrary, it expanded the worldview of the Americas. We are still involved in the struggle to define ourselves, to define our community. New labels appear and each generation adds to the meaning of our history. Evolution is a slow process, and we should share in the process of identity, not allow the process to separate us.

Once a clear definition of Chicano consciousness has worked itself into the society, then we will not have to be so sensitive about the Edenic concept of King Arthur's Court. After all, we understand its right to exist as a mythology, we understand how it defines a particular group. The challenge for us, for the writers of the Southwest from all cultural groups, is to understand and accept those views that define groups and the individuals from all communities.

Part of our task is to keep reminding each other that each cultural community has an inherent right to its own definition, and so Aztlán defines us more accurately than Camelot. Hidalgo and Morelos and Zapata are as valuable as Washington, Jefferson, and Lincoln. The mythology of Mesoamerica is as interesting and informing as Greek mythology. Mexico's settlement of her northern colonies is as dramatic and challenging as the settlement of the thirteen United States colonies. As American Chicanos, we have a multilayered history on which to draw. To be complete individuals we must draw on all the world traditions and beliefs, and we must continue to understand and strengthen our own heritage. We seek not to exclude, but to build our base as we develop a vision of the interrelated nature of the Americas. Our eventual goal is to incorporate the world into our understanding.

But in the span of world time, the Chicano community is a young community. It is still growing, still exploring, still defining itself. Our history has already made valuable contributions to American thought and growth, and we will continue to contribute. What we seek now, in our relationship to the broader society, is to eliminate the mindless prejudices that hamper our evolution, and to encourage people of goodwill who do not fear a pluralistic society and who understand that the more a group of people define themselves in positive ways, the greater the contribution they make to humanity.

For over a century American Chicanos have been influenced by the beliefs imposed by a King Arthur's Court scenario. We have learned the language, we have learned the rules of the game. We have adopted part of the cultural trappings of Arthur's Court, but we also insist on keeping true to our culture. The American Southwest is a big land, a unique land. It has room for many communities. It should have no room for the old, negative prejudices of the past. When we, each one of us, impede the fulfillment of any person's abilities and dreams, we impede our own humanity.

Aztlán: The pre-Columbian cultures of Mesoamerica recorded in their legends that their original homeland lay somewhere north of Mexico. They called the place Aztlán. The place of origin is very important in Native American thought; after all, the gods often make a covenant with the people at that place of origin. In the 1960s Chicanos discovered the myth of Aztlán. If the land was "north of Mexico" it was the present-day Southwest. As mestizos, Chicanos living in the southwestern states were living in Aztlán, the land of their Native American ancestors.

mestizos: Chicanos generally define mestizo as the sons and daughters of Europeans (beginning with the Spaniards who entered Mexico with Cortés) and native Mexican women. Mestizos are La Raza (the new people) of the New World.

from
A Chicano in China

Introduction

In May 1984 I embarked on a journey to China, a pilgrimage that turned out to be one of the most incredible journeys I have ever taken. I had not had much time to think about or plan this trip to China. I had been so busy finishing my classes at the University of New Mexico, returning a week before from Iowa, where Marycrest College conferred an honorary Doctorate of Humane Letters on me, and returning home the week before that from a tour of the San Joaquin Valley of California. Also, I had been engrossed in a series of other lectures I had presented during the spring. Suddenly the reality of the trip to China was upon me and I had not had time to really anticipate it.

I had traveled abroad before, to Europe, into Greece and through the Mediterranean to Istanbul, to Canada and many times to Mexico. But there was something singular about going to China, something special that prompted me to keep a journal of my daily impressions. My response to China was highly personal. I felt that during my travels important answers would be revealed to me. What answers? What revelations did I seek? To be truthful, I did not know exactly what I sought. I would be a traveler in search of symbols that could speak the language of my soul. I would be a wanderer in a country that was the birthplace of the Asiatic people who thousands of years ago wandered over the Bering Strait into the Americas. What were the symbols of those people, and what did they communicate to me across the millennia?

I did not go to find exact answers in that country of a billion people; I only knew that the time was propitious for me to make my pilgrimage. The enlightenment that travel brings usually comes in the process of the journey, around the corners we turn in distant places where we come face-to-face with the epiphany, the sudden shock of recognition. That is how I have traveled, allowing the people and places to seep under my skin, to work their way into my blood, until I have become part of their secret.

Over the years my wife Patricia and I have traveled many places, and generally our way as pilgrims is to wander, to let our sense of adventure and intuition lead us into back streets, museums, mercados where the people buy and sell their goods, and especially into the ancient ruins of lost civilizations. We have always been rewarded by chancing upon ceremonies of life meaningful and poignant enough to change us forever. A pilgrim should remain open to those unexpected moments of change travel provides, which are the fulfillment of life on the road.

I call my notes A Chicano in China for specific reasons. First, because I am a native son of the Mexican community of the United States, I feel proud to identify with the community that has nurtured me in body and spirit. The Chicanos of this country are hard workers; they have helped shape the character and destiny of the southwestern United States, and yet they have not always shared in the fruits of that growth. Most do not know the luxury of travel; their recent migrations have been from south to north in search of work. I feel fortunate to be able to see some of the wonders of the world, and one way to bring my experience back to my community was to record my personal impressions of China. I am the first Chicano from the Southwest to journey to China, and I returned with these observations of that incredible country. These day-to-day notes are my communication with myself and with those back home. Communication, that's a part of the key to the journey of a humble pilgrim.

The other reason this is the journal of *A Chicano in China* is that as a Chicano I also take pride in the part of me that is a native American, that is, an indigenous person of this American continent. I always seek out the history and thought of the Americas, because by understanding that past I understand better the present me. The history and thought of the Americas is an incredible and enlightening experience in the spiritual evolution of mankind. For some time I have been seeking those simple secrets that hint at the deeper spiritual and humanistic relationship the pre-Columbian societies had with the Earth and with the deities of their cosmos. The ceremonies still exist, changed as they are by the passage of time and the onslaught of other cultures that have come to call the Americas their home. For those of us who listen to the Earth, and to the old legends and the myths of the people, the whispers of the blood draw us to our past. But often the secrets are locked away in symbols we can no longer read, in legends we no longer understand, in paintings and in ancient writings that puzzle us. There is a door which we can enter, and in passing through the door illumination fills us and we see the truth hidden in those symbols and secrets and stories of the past. This is what the pilgrim seeks: a key to turn, a door to enter, a new way to see his role in the universe.

I was fortunate in 1984 to hold a fellowship from the W. K. Kellogg Foundation. Each year the Kellogg Foundation awards a three-year fellowship to fifty scholars from around the country. The fellowships encourage the growth of the fellow in new and multidisciplinary ways. Certainly travel is one of those crucial ways in which we gain knowledge about the integrated Earth on which we live. So, sponsored by the Kellogg Foundation, with one of our fellows appointed as chief guide, nineteen of us set out for China in mid-May. In China our sponsor was the Chinese Athletic Association. Why? It seems that our group of nineteen was such a diverse mixture of scholars that only the athletic association dared to sponsor us.

Some of us took our spouses with us, and Patricia was able to travel with me. For this I was very grateful, because she too would profit from the incredible journey and from her own pilgrimage. We have been traveling together for a long time; we've learned to enjoy the same things. Besides, it's lonely to travel alone. Pilgrimages are most often communal enterprises, groups of people going to the source of their particular faith. We were a diverse group, and yet we were most compatible.

China is a country undergoing incredible changes. One feels the change in the social fabric, in the remaking of history. I grew to love the country and the people of the regions we visited. I say to people who want to know about China: "Go now! Go quickly!" In the meantime, I have only my personal revelations to offer as temptation. I was a pilgrim who went to China, I visited the holy mountains and temples, and I prayed at the ancient shrines; I also walked the polluted streets of the cities, I mixed with the people, I touched them, I pulled them into my dream. I walked in their factories, their prisons, their hospitals, and their markets, and I sat in their homes. I was a humble pilgrim who went to communicate, to commune, and these are my impressions of that communication.

All journeys begin with the first step, and if our Earth is truly to be an integrated world based on mutual respect, this is my first step toward you.

May 12, 1984
Alburquerque

A family story whispers that our grandfather, when he was a young man, visited China. Last week I asked my mother, "Did Grampa go to China?" She rapped my head.

"Mind your manners, boy. Don't speak ill about the dead. Yes, your grandfather could speak Chinese when he had a cup or two, but he never went to China."

Today I am going to China.

The sun rises over the Sandia Mountains, bathing with a crystalline light my city of Alburquerque. I have not had much time to think about or plan this trip to China; suddenly, the reality of the trip is upon me and I have not had time to really anticipate it.

This is not a trip to Europe or to Mexico. This is a trip to a very different country. China is part of the old Asiatic world that sent its migrations of people across the Bering Strait thousands of years ago; those people were the ancestors of Native America. They are the real source of the Mesoamerican populations, the Native American Indians, and all the mythology and thought which has intrigued and interested me for many years. Now I want to try to put my trip in a historical perspective.

I want to stop for a moment and understand what it means to be a Chicano in China, a man looking for ancestral signs: a leaf, a door, a symbol. In the meantime, I am a Chicano living in Alburquerque. I know I will not be the first Chicano in China; during World War II, many of the boys from Aztlán went to Japan and to China. Boys from the villages of New Mexico, Colorado, Texas, California— they fought the war in the Pacific. They have already been there—in China, in Bataan, in the Philippines—doughboys, navigators, pilots, men from my country who died there, men who went to Asia to keep the world free. They went before me, but they were Spanish-Americans, Latinos, not Chicanos. But I, a Chicano, am going to China today, and it's that reality I have to deal with.

Where do I find the thread, the beginning, the desire, for this pilgrimage, this journey? I remember my grandfather, farmer of the Puerto de Luna Valley, a landlocked Chicano in the llano of New Mexico. He never saw the sea, he never saw China. And still the memory whispers, "Yes, Grampa visited China, of that we're sure." I think of Grampa's typewriter, the old typewriter that now gathers dust in my garage. An old Royal, vintage early thirties. He never typed a word on it. He only sat and stared at it and wondered if the dreams of the imagination could be transferred through the steel keys to the ribbon to the paper. He never went to China, my mother says, and I say, of course he went. I remember his Chinese dreams, the cuentos and stories he never struck on his typewriter.

So I am going to China for Grampa, for myself, for . . . well, for the old people who knew the symbols of the East: the golden carp, the centuries of migration, the sacred resting places, the beginning. East is West—the two are one. This then will be the journal of *A Chicano in China*. A visit to the origin, that is, the origin that does not belong to Spain, but to my secret origin, the origin of those migra-

tions of people who came over the frozen Bering Strait
thousands of years ago, across frozen waste land, against
freezing wind; they came from Asia into the virgin Americas
and created a new consciousness, a new religion, a new
view of creation. They brought with them and preserved
certain signs, certain symbols of value, certain archetypal
memories of a biologic nature, links, a history—an understanding of that other half of my nature, which whispers
to me. Asia, land of the golden carp, Asia, land of beginning.
Sipapu of the Americas, timeless land, I return to you to
find myself. It's that simple. I don't go to create a market
for goods, I don't go to measure and count, I don't even
go with a strict academic purpose in mind. Asia, I go to
view myself in your waters, your mountains, your Great
Wall, your Xi'an, your people. I go in search of clues: a
fish, an owl, a door. I will look at signs, I will listen. China,
you are the door I will open. I know I will return loaded
with snapshots, tourist images of me in Xi'an, me at the
Great Wall, me at Peking. But that is only the image of the
day. I will return full of the secret, the dream, the memory
we call history.

I will announce to the world, I was a Chicano in China!
See! There the migrations to the Americas began! They
brought their soul onto the American continent and they
settled the Earth and cared for it.

A spring morning in Albuquerque, my favorite time of
the day. The air is clean, fresh, touched with dew.

"It's a nice day to be going to China," my wife says.

"Bury our dead behind us," I answer, my love choked
on the glare of the sun as it rears over the Sandia Mountains.

The Earth beneath us, and we are like birds over Ship-
rock, land of the Navajo, the latest Indian immigrants
into the Southwest. Over Canyon de Chelly, land of the
Anasazi, over Lake Powell, Mono Lake, the Sierras of California. The morning paper carries an article by a government spokesman who swears that Hispanics love to live
packed like sardines into small quarters, migrant camps.

What nonsense politicians preach! Did the slave Chinese laborers who built the railroads of the West love their packed quarters? Did the Japanese-Americans love Manzanar, camps of horror, camps where the migrations and the voice were killed? Dead spirits, for you I fly to China, to recapture your memory, to allow you rest.

We spend the day in San Francisco. All trips to China should begin in San Francisco, city of the Orient, city that gazes west into the setting sun. The Spaniards came into your bay in the sixteenth century; Chinese voices had lingered in your air centuries before. In Portsmouth's Square Park, in the morning, the old Chinese men of the neighborhood gather to take the sun (as I imagine today in some village in northern New Mexico the old men gather in the chill of a spring morning to take the sun). The Chinese gentlemen play cards, gamble, play dominos. Feisty old men. Brown like me. Wrinkled. Men who created history, men whose sperm flowed as sweet as the love of their women, now they take the sun and talk and remember. Here, on the bench of the park, I am in China. Here I am with them. When my own Grampa drank his good cup of New Mexico wine, he spoke with you. Remember?

I feel the rap of my mother's knuckles on my head. Don't blaspheme the dead. In heaven, Grampa plays checkers with old Chinese gentlemen.

Here in the heart of Chinatown, here under the shadow of the Chinese Cultural Center, a group of Chinese, touring San Francisco, pause to take a picture of me sitting on a bench at Portsmouth's Square Park. Tomorrow, I will take their pictures in some corner of China.

Day one on the road to China ends. I pause to write down my thoughts. I worry about going to a country so far away, so big, one billion people. In my room above the park, I write my notes. Below in the park a Chinese women's group sings traditional songs from China. I am in China. I have already had my first Chinese dream. Now their singing stops. The moon is only one night from being full. Full moon of spring coming over the Sandia Mountains of Alburquerque, full moon of Chinatown, San Francisco, full moon moving over China—sleep, my brethren, under its pale light a Chicano travels to China.

May 13, 1984
San Francisco

From our hotel window, Portsmouth's Square Park is deserted. Pigeons strut as they feed, a gull glides by, observes the scene and moves west toward the sea. The sun rises over Oakland, touches the tops of buildings. Last night voices called to me in my sleep—dark voices—the voices of China calling to me to be alert for my journey, my pilgrimage. The voices of old men, old women, they bid me hurry to their land, their secret. In my dream I felt I should not heed the voices, I should not go to China. Let the secrets sleep. I awoke in the night feeling if there were some excuse I would return home to tend my garden, to finish my novel, to feel and live in the world I know, the world which is safe and sure. The voices are disturbing, dark and threatening. Now in the sunshine of Sunday, there are no Chinese gentlemen in the park. Later in the morning, the park will fill with people. Jesse Jackson is scheduled to speak to the community of Chinatown today. The old men will come to listen to him. The young will shout: "Run, Jesse, run!" I will not be here. I will already be winging my way to China. Run, Rudy, run. Fly west with the Sunday sun. If Reagan can conquer China, so can you.

Strange how the world of politics intrudes on my journey of reconciliation, journey of discovery. Reagan admonished the Chinese to be good capitalists. Jesse will add a new shade, a new color to his rainbow coalition today. I must decide what it is I wish to ask the old ones of China.

"¿Para qué vas?" my mother asked me.

"Voy a conocer," I said.

Why go? Because it's there. Not exactly the answer I seek. Will the Chinese understand my Spanish? Will they understand my questions? Will I find the home of the golden carp? Is there an original meaning which I cannot find in words, a meaning in the eyes and hearts of the people, a meaning in their daily ritual, meaning in a gesture, a glance, a symbol? The dream last night is the door beginning to open. Do I dare push the door?

At the airport we snack on Glädjé ice cream. ¡Qué cosmopolitán! I think of sending my grandfather a postcard, not wanting to remember he has been dead for twenty years. A postcard to my mother who does not know the world beyond her back yard. "Be careful in China," she said, "I hear there are tornadoes there. Why do you go?"

"Did Grampa go?" I want to know, knowing well the old farmer never left the confines of his Puerto de Luna River Valley. He went many places in his dreams, my mother's silence says to me. The airport is packed. Japanese returning home, businessmen, tours, other members of my group. We are loaded with bags, cameras, munchies, small talk. Flight 1, San Francisco to Tokyo, is full. "Nine hours and forty minutes' flight time," the pilot announces.

Over the bay, and below us at Portsmouth's Square Park, the old men have gathered to play cards and checkers. Some dance to Tai Chi exercises. All wait for Jesse to arrive. On Flight 1 to Japan we settle down for a long flight on a 747 almost as big as my grandfather's dream.

Why do you go? To find something. What? Something about myself I have to discover. Couldn't that be done here at home? I think of Li Bai, the wise and ancient Chinese poet. I dream of dragons. I drink Sapporo beer to quench the thirst of my dragons, my questions.

The flight to the Orient is full of mystery. How could one fly to the Orient and not be tugged by its mystery? Somewhere west of Hawaii we cross the International Date Line. There, along this arbitrary line, our Sunday suddenly becomes the Monday of the Orient. Our May 13 becomes May 14. We move forward in time. Never backward. Nature does not allow us to move backward. I correct myself. On our return to Aztlán, we will move back in time, back to the center of my universe. But for now the curvature of the Earth calls us. I try to sleep. I feel the plane adjust to the curve of the Earth. It must adjust, for if it kept to its straight line, it would fly into space. The Earth calls to its curve, even the flight of men, even fantasy or imagination, or love. As the curve of the love of a woman calls us to its secret, its door to the universe, so death is never a straight line. In China, Confucius has died, the pragmatist! Long live Li Bai, the mystic, the romantic! I awaken and thank the gods for curved space, curved time. We fly west with the sun, the Sunday sun, now Monday. When will it sleep? When will I sleep?

How many of us were bred on the mystery of the Orient? Charlie Chan Saturday afternoon movies, the Buddha, the Tao which cannot be expressed. Around me the business-men, the straight-line boys aboard the plane, say: "Down with mystery, let's plot the graph of profit! That line can unite East and West." They do not know the mystery of curved space; they do not gaze at the beauty of the young Japanese women who watch over us, our hostesses of the Monday dawn. I drink a drink to them.

Beside me Patricia sleeps, or tries to sleep, dreams, or tries to dream. The brilliant sun we follow does not let us sleep or dream too deeply.

May 15, 1984
Narita, Japan
Beijing, China

Touchdown, 4:30 P.M. The weather is overcast. There is a cool breeze. I remember that a few weeks ago the governor of New Mexico, Toney Anaya, came to Narita to induce Japanese businessmen to take their plants to New Mexico where there is lots of land and cheap labor. He envisions a high-tech corridor from Los Alamos to Las Cruces. A high-tech corridor along the old Rio Grande. Sandia Labs of Albuquerque will be at the heart. A Japanese bullet train will whiz up and down the Rio Grande. Japanese sounds and microchips will fill the air. I dare to travel farther west than Japan, I will fly to Beijing, the old Peking of mainland China. I promise to bring a million Chinese dreams to New Mexico. I will let these dreams loose in the high mountains, in the desert, along the river valley, in the villages, everywhere. And in the future, Chicanitos will dream of Chinese umbrellas and Chinese chocolates. Dragons will flutter in the blue sky of New Mexico. Mao jackets will appear. My paisanos will dream in Chinese characters. My promise will come true, as my grandfather's admonition has come true. Forty years ago he told me, a barefooted, brown

Chicano boy standing in the mud of a field of corn in Puerto de Luna, "Go to China; learn Chinese; those people will rule the world. Do not fear to dream of China."

In the morning off Japan, Mount Fuji disappears below us and I dream of Chinese umbrellas and Chinese chocolates, and children in Mao jackets flying dragon kites.

Reagan wants to sell the Chinese nuclear plants. He wants to get the ball rolling for good old American capitalistic expansionism. Governor Anaya waits with open arms for Japanese factories. Run, Jesse, run. The politics of the world are mixed together. The dream is lost. Today no sun rose in the land of the rising sun. Still it is a superb day to be flying to China. A Chicano in China. "Can you imagine that," I tell my wife. "I can imagine that," she smiles. At the airport I mail a postcard with a haiku poem to Ana, a poem of love to San Miguelito in old Mexico.

Old temples and burial grounds dot the land around Narita airport. At the airport, security bristles. To build the airport, they took the land from farmers, and farmers are a tough breed. There is a moral to the haiku. "Never take the land from farmers." Do not take the land from the Rio Grande farmers to build factories or the dream will return to haunt you. Neither Toney Anaya nor Reagan nor Jesse Jackson sleep as well as they lead us to believe.

We touch down at the Beijing airport in the early afternoon. ¡El Tercer Mundo! He llegado, con una canción en mi corazón. Peking, land of my grandfather's dreams. I rush to embrace the Chinese. Brown brothers, Raza! Can you imagine a billion new souls for La Raza? We could rule the world. But immigration stops me. I cannot pass. La Migra has been stopping Chicanos at the border for a long time. Chinese sounds fill the air. I cannot speak my brother's language.

Quietly, I get in line, wait my turn, exchange U.S. bucks for Chinese play money I can use at the friendship stores, pass through customs.

Reality has a way of slapping dreamers in the face. No

one was waiting. No one knew a Chicano had come to China. They knew Alex Haley had come. He's here to make a movie on Chinese history, a new spectacular for U.S. television, for Chinese television. That's the politics of things.

Peking/Beijing does not surprise me. On the bus ride into the city I have a vague feeling I have been here before. I feel I am in Mexico. El Tercer Mundo. We know it well. Chicanos are El Tercer Mundo in the soul of the United States. The streets are busy with construction, a new subway. It's like Mexico City, but with less color, fewer cars, more people. We pass the shops that line Beijing University, the gates of the Summer Palace, the Empresses' Pagoda on the hill, and come to rest in northwest Beijing. Our hotel is a beautiful hotel in the foothills. The Fragrant Hill Hotel. A fitting name. There is a story that Jackie Onassis stayed here when she came to Beijing. I wonder if I will sleep in her room.

The rooms in Japan were prefabricated, sterile, without character. Here our bathroom has a marble countertop, a sliding glass door that looks down on a pond of the golden carp, grass, Chinese pine trees. There is a swimming pool where the hardy of the group go to swim before dinner. I drink Five-Star Beijing beer, make friends with the old pine trees outside my window, and sleep. At night the full moon of New Mexico peeks over the garden. My faith is renewed. In the branches of the pine tree, the moon is a lovely woman in the arms of a Chinese gentleman. Her light floods our room. The breeze through the open door is cool. The golden carp in the pool sleep.

May 16, 1984
Beijing

We awaken early. Birds sing in the hills around us. They sing in sweet Chinese characters. The morning is full of love and I imagine a billion Chinese are making love in the early light of the cool morning; then, with lunch in hand, it's off to do a day's work; renewed, refreshed, we vow to change the world. Today my work will be a tour of the city, camera in hand. We are ready to see China. We are ready to see the reality of El Tercer Mundo.

The ride into Beijing is bucolic, with a hard edge. People on the way to work fill the narrow streets. Peach orchards line the roads, fields of tomatoes, onions, vegetables, spring rice paddies. Farmers are at work everywhere. Grampa's folks. An occasional fisherman sits patiently by the side of the canal, bamboo pole over the water. Fish is an important source of protein. One man fishes with a large net. The fry will be boiled and then pressed into a fish patty. Lots of trucks on the road. Chinese trucks loaded for work, small tractors.

Today our destination is the Forbidden City, the old Imperial city of the Ming and Qing Dynasties, now a museum for the people. Gold Chinese roofs, pastel pink walls. It is Wednesday and still the crowds are thick. The Chinese do not smile. And yet, here, there is an air of gaiety. Workers, families with their children have come to see the glory of the old dynasties, the ancients who created such wealth, such opulence and glory. This is an old civilization. Perhaps the oldest on Earth. No wonder they have called outsiders barbarians. No wonder, throughout their history, they have been wary of the West. They did not embrace Western methods and technology until very recently. Modernism has just come to China.

The family feeling is strong. Each child is tended to and instructed. There are a lot of small children on the old and venerable grounds of the Forbidden City. When I can, I take their pictures. The families are proud of this. The small children wear no diapers or undershorts. Only a slit along the bottom of their pants. When the urge strikes, they squat. Instant night soil on the ground where emperors once walked. How fitting.

We eat an excellent lunch in the restaurant on the Palace grounds: fish, noodles, vegetables—all served in the middle of the table. We spear what we can with chopsticks. Eating is a ritual. Each plate prepares the palate for the next; the meal should be a gastronomical experience. We are hungry, we are Westerners, we eat like barbarians. The Chinese, kind enough not to watch, also are hearty eaters. But chopsticks in the hands of foreigners teach patience.

In the Palace grounds, the dragon abounds. The dragon is everywhere: carved into roofs, carved into bronze. The dragon is everywhere. That is why I have had dragon dreams. Now I know. Now I see. Something about the vast courtyards between the buildings reminds me of Teotihuacán in Mexico. The walls, the smell, the sprigs of grass and weeds on the grounds. The dragon is everywhere, the flaming Quetzalcóatl of Mexico. I am on the right track. The face of the fierce dragon looks out at me from walls, from gargoyles, from decorative pieces, almost exactly as the serpent head in the pyramids of Mexico. This is my first clue. This is the door I seek. In the faces of the people it is written: the migrations of the people from Asia across the Bering Strait, down into the Americas, thousands of years ago. Those Asiatic people came bringing their dragon dreams. In the face of our guide, Mrs. Wang, I see a woman from Laguna Pueblo. I take a picture of a bronze turtle, a heron; both mean long life. The dragon means supreme power, the wisdom of the emperors. Quetzalcóatl means supreme power. He was the god who brought wisdom and learning to the Toltecs of ancient Mexico. Quetzalcóatl, the savior prophet and god of the Americas. In what dream in Asia, millions of years ago, did he have his beginning?

We walked across the broad avenue to Tian'anmen Square, the biggest zócalo I have ever seen. Two million people can stand here and see parades, listen to the party leaders. In the review stands, the ghost of Mao still lurks.

The Chinese of Beijing ride on bikes. There are millions of bicycles crowded into the streets. These are the Chicano '57 Chevys; in truth, they are a big sturdy model produced in the biggest bicycle factory in the world in Shanghai. They last twenty years and they save on gas. I am reminded that it is the Chinese Year of the Rat. The rat is well liked for its witty, crafty character. To be born under its sign is propitious. Rats are also a delicacy: a home deer. There are no rats in China. Unless you want to talk revisionist politics, the rats, like the cucarachas of the Southwest, will survive. In the narrow street surrounded by a billion brown faces, lost in a rippling sea of Chinese bicyclists, I sing to my brothers, "La Cucaracha, la Cucaracha, ya no quiere caminar."

In the street, a man lies dying, his body and bike crushed beneath a truck. He got in the way of the modernization of China. He got in the way of a bad driver.

At night we watch in tired stupor as, in a small neighborhood theatre, the Beijing acrobatic troupe entertains us. They are good. I watch the people. They are intent on the magic of the magician. The kids love the clowns; the clowns speak a universal language: pantomime. Outside the dull full moon hangs over Beijing. In the alley I speak to the doctor of the acrobats. He speaks a little English. Then it's homeward, through dimly lit streets, through the rural roads which lead up to the northwest hills and the Fragrant Hill Hotel, our Shangri-la. The driver carefully buzzes around the walking figures, the bikes in the dark. China is dark—like the Mexico of the countryside. All night the people walk on the shoulders of the road, illuminated for a brief instant in the lights of our bus. Where will they rest, these campesinos of Beijing?

May 17, 1984
Beijing

A Chinese magpie lives in an old pine tree near our window. Early in the morning he awakens me with his complaints. He is a beautiful bird, large with shining black feathers and spots of white. He brings the gossip from the village below. The people do not know what to make of some of the members of our group who jog in the morning. These men with hairy legs are the barbarians of old. The women joggers: ladies of little decorum.

"Don't you know," Señor Magpie says, "Chinese women are women of decorum."

Mr. Magpie also tells other stories. Seems like Mr. Lu is to be tried by the neighborhood court; he got angry at his neighbor and kicked his bike. Here to kick a man's bike is like kicking a man's horse in the Old West. In the process, Mr. Lu stubbed his toe. It is now swollen; he cannot walk, he cannot work. Now he seeks retribution from the neighbor whom he set out to wrong by kicking his bike. Sounds like an Alburquerque lawyer will be needed if the case gets more complicated. In truth, the neighborhood unit will pass judgment and that is the end of that. Mr. Lu pays for the bent spokes. Also, there is the case of young Zhang who took his girlfriend into the park a few weeks ago. Seems he got carried away and took her decorum from her. Now the families are up in arms, ashamed. Good Chinese young men and young girls are not brought up to jeopardize their future plans over one moonlit walk in the park. They are taught the virtue of waiting. Wonder if we could reinstitute that in our country? But even in China, nature takes its course, Señor Magpie reports.

In the morning, our group tours a free market where farmers bring their excess crops to sell. It is nothing more than a good old-fashioned Mexican mercado. Patricia and I smile. We have probably been in every mercado in Mexico. The rest of the group seem culturally deprived. I buy a small print of a buck and doe from the artist. Now, even artists are allowed to make a living in China. Patricia also buys a print. Chinese themes for adobe walls in New Mexico. How clear is the paradox of life for those who look within.

Later we tour Haichain, a neighborhood on the outskirts of Beijing, a village. It is a wonderful place, quiet, clean. The mudpacked courtyards swept clean as can be, clean streets. We see people at their work, small shop owners, a woman who carries the mail on a bike, the local woman washing clothes at the neighborhood water pump. At the neighborhood kindergarten, we see the daily meal delivered by two women. The kids are hungry. If you have ever walked in a colonia in a Mexican city or a poor barrio in the Southwest, you will know what a typical neighborhood in Beijing is like. Clean-swept barrio streets, some vendors on the street, lots of people, a horse-drawn cart or two. Only the language is different.

In the afternoon, we tour the Summer Palace. The place is crowded with Chinese families. There is a lake there. I imagine the old emperors in their colorful garb walking the breezeway along the lake, escorting their concubines. Outside the masses toiled. Of such things are revolutions made. One empress, the Empress Suchi, while her army was in need of arms, spent a fortune building a marble boat. The boat still sits on the lake. A boat of stone. It goes nowhere. Tourists clamber aboard. Chinese children sit patiently while their parents take their pictures. All of us, the Chinese visitors and the tourists at the Summer Palace, have forgotten the exact dates of the war, who fought whom, who won; but there is the large marble boat reminding us of the whims of the empress. Beware of ladies who build marble boats.

During the Chicano Movement of the sixties in the United States, a few of the more radical Chicanos thought they would go to war against the U.S. to make their grievances known, to regain their lost rights. In California, a group of activists gathered to form the Royal Chicano Air Force; RCAF, as it was known. They built airplanes of adobe. With these we would attack. The rains came and washed the adobe away. The Royal Chicano Navy, when launched into the flood-swollen Chaves Ravine in Los Angeles, also sank. Adobe submarines. Let that be a lesson to you, Raza! Next time we build the fleet of marble. It, at least, lasts.

In the afternoon, we loiter in the lobby of the Beijing Hotel, drink beer. Everybody who goes to Beijing must spend one afternoon, at least, in the lobby of the Beijing Hotel, loitering. I am mistaken for an Arab, and soon some very suspicious fellows sit by me and make me a deal, an arms deal. For a fortune in guns, laundered through such-and-such a place, I will fly to Libya and deliver to Kadafy the army package. The two well-dressed Arabs are surprised when I answer them in Spanish. I am not their man. They scurry away. Revolutions used to be made in rousing the disgruntled masses, now they are made while loitering in the lobby of the Beijing Hotel on a Thursday afternoon. Patricia buys me a cashmere sweater in a shop in the lobby.

Something to keep me warm as I stand at the bow of the next adobe submarine we launch.

In the evening, we return to Fragrant Hill. By now I am familiar with the silver maple-lined street at dusk. Another day in El Tercer Mundo.

At a Crossroads

What changes have come to the Hispanic community of New Mexico since statehood in 1912?

That intriguing question reminds me of a book of short stories by a fellow writer from Texas. In the first story the writer describes the first day at school for Mexican-American children. The bell rings and the Anglo teacher lines up the new first graders to recite the pledge of allegiance to the flag and country.

The teacher speaks in English. To the kids from the barrio who have spoken Spanish all their lives, the pledge of allegiance sounds something like this:

Ai plesha lichans tu di flac, of de june aires taste off America; an tu di reepablic for huish eet estans, guan mayshon, andar got, wits liverty and yastes for oll.

Needless to say, it was a difficult first day of school for the kids who knew no English. In many ways it was a sad day. They tried to fake the sounds; they wanted to belong. Belonging is what allegiance is all about. But at what price allegiance? I wonder how many Hispanos in New Mexico knew only Spanish in 1912 when the territory became a state? How many had to fake allegiance to the new legal language because they did not know it?

When I began school in Santa Rosa in 1944, thirty-two years after statehood, I could not speak a word of English. In Spanish I could pledge allegiance to the love of my family, to my community, and to my religion, but in English my pledge came out something like the pledge of the boys in the story. "Hay plesha lichans tu di flac. . . ."

My first day at school was a sad and terrible time. I did not belong. Now I look back and ponder the winds of change that have swept over New Mexico since 1912.

I think of my grandfather Liborio Mares, a farmer in the Puerto de Luna Valley near Santa Rosa. For him life would go on much as it had before, uninterrupted except for the seasons. He held on to his land, his language, and his traditional lifestyle. It seems the great changes in his life, and ours, would come after World War II. But even before the war, perceptible changes crept into the Hispano villages. What were those changes? And just as important, what are the values that would remain constant and pass into the collective memory of the people?

I remember my grandfather riding his carro de vestias to Santa Rosa to sell produce from his farm. Our grandfathers no longer ride their horse-drawn wagons from the farm to town to sell the produce of harvest; trucks now appear along the side of the road to sell corn, chile, vegetables. Beneath the surface of change we see the needs and age-old patterns of the people continue to define their cultural context.

Memory records history, that which is once stored lives on. The folkways live on. But what would the Hispano legacy gain in seventy-five years? What would it lose?

The most important change came as the Hispanos adopted the English language. The Nuevo Mexicanos were forced to learn the culture and language of the Anglo-

American. The law of the United States became the law of the land, and one had to know some English or have a friend who spoke the language to file deeds to property, to buy a car or get an automobile license, to trade at the grocery store, to send the kids to school. These simple duties that we now take for granted required a major change in the daily lives of the Nuevo Mexicanos.

Other changes were discernible. At the soul of survival for the Hispano village was the earth and the sustenance it provides. The growing season in the northern mountains was short. Farmers had to sense changes in the weather and the earth. They irrigated with acequias, the irrigation ditch system that is a communal endeavor, engendering a faith that developed between the people and their earth. The patron saint of each village was taken out to bless the fields, and soon stories developed of saints who nightly walked in the fields, guarding and blessing the crops.

It is in those simple ceremonies of daily life that we can best view the concepts we call cultural values. The story of the saint who watches the fields at night combines the elements of faith. Daily life, raising crops, raising children, tending the sick, all of these touch on the element of faith. Could that faith rooted in centuries of tradition survive?

World War II brought a decisive change in many aspects of Nuevo Mexicano culture. During that time, Hispanos left the rural life of the village for the cities in unprecedented numbers. How did the new urban population relate to that faith that had allowed them to wed the elements of daily life with a more sacred order in the universe? We now plant gardens in our backyards, we visit the villages to get in touch with that lost element of the culture. We look for ways to reconstitute the faith of our ancestors. The fact that we became an urban community was, without doubt, the most drastic change in our lifestyle.

In the mid-sixties the sons and daughters of that mid-forties movement to the cities would look back in anger and realize they were losing many of their traditional ways.

To renew their sense of identity they created the most important artistic movement of our time, the Chicano Movement. The Chicano Movement really had its beginning in the struggle for the rights of workers and the civil rights of Chicanos everywhere, but the artistic arm of the movement has been very important in creating Chicano consciousness.

I think of the struggle of our community to exist and retain not only its cultural ways but its soul. It has not been easy.

My father, who spoke only Spanish most of his life, went to basic training during World War I. I have a picture of him in uniform, the American flag waving behind him. I wonder how he pledged allegiance to the flag, how he felt about the new state he was defending. He and some of his compadres went for basic training, some fought in Europe. They came back and returned to their old way of life. A generation later, my three older brothers went to World War II; when they came back, their way of life would never again be the same.

The paradox of change is that it brings with it positive and negative aspects. After the 1880s the railroad would service the New Mexico mines. Entire communities left farming for mining. The mines paid wages, and in the changing lifestyle the question was not how much land and cattle or sheep a man had, but how many bucks he had in his pocket. A man with his week's wages in his pocket could feel as rich as the patrón, but even the age of the patrón was coming to an end.

It has been the migrations of people, the periods of active colonization, that have affected and changed this land along the Río Grande. The ancient migrations of the Native Americans into the Río Grande were first. In the latter part of the sixteenth century came the Spaniards and Mexicans from Mexico, and most recently the Anglo-Americans. Around the mid-nineteenth century, immediately after the United States war with Mexico, the movement of people into the Río Grande area accelerated. The old, traditional cultures of the valley continued their struggle for survival.

Today marks another time of rapid migration into the state and border region. The weather, the natural beauty, and warm winters continue to attract people. From Mexico, new workers arrive daily. The new arrivals and the old cultures must live side by side, as they have in the past. But if we do not seize this moment to understand and plan for change, future generations will be haunted by many of the old prejudices that separate communities.

There is a saying in Spanish: Each change brings a little good, each change brings a little bad. Today, seventy-five years after statehood, the mines are closing, and those who became miners are again displaced. Those who left the villages are without roots. Are the problems insurmountable for the continuation of the traditional Nuevo Mexicano culture? Can it survive as a growing, viable culture?

The answer probably lies in the family unit. Older, traditional communal allegiances to the village, church, or the patrón disappear as we become an urban culture, but the family unit survives. Beset with many of the new social problems that come with urban mobility and assimilation into the Anglo lifestyles, and beset by lack of educational opportunities, it is now largely in the family unit that the ceremonies and language of the traditional culture will be passed on.

The American democracy and Anglo technology came, and all this appears beneficial on the surface, yet we see the cost of allegiance beneath the social fabric. Nothing is for free, and change is always painful.

Another tremendous change has come in communications. Radio, the telephone, and television were connections to the outside world, and the outside world spoke English. I remember the telephone party lines of childhood and cranking the handle to get the operator. Las comadres could now listen to the town's gossip, the mitote, by picking up the phone and listening to the party line; they didn't need to go visit. A facetious example, but one that illustrates that as the Nuevo Mexicanos adopted the English language and the American technology, changes in our lifestyle became very perceptible.

The slow pace of village communal life gathered momentum as cars and trucks filled the dusty streets. Neighbors no longer stopped to pass the time of day, they waved as they drove by. "Hi, how are you?" the kids called to their abuelos as they passed. I remember the first time I said "Hello" to a favorite uncle who came to visit. "¿Quién jálo?" he asked, his play on words reminding me I had changed my language when addressing him.

Respeto is a key value in our culture. Respect for the elders. We were bred on it as we are bred on tortillas and beans. It's a very important element in the family. Now we see signs of that respect and concern for the viejitos breaking down. That quality of respect for the elders in the culture is like the faith in the earth, and like honor in the family, pride in community, and awe in the beauty and mystery of the universe. It's those important ingredients in our culture the family has to safeguard.

Changes initiated by usage of the new English language and technology hastened the breakdown of the traditional interrelatedness of the Hispano village. How people and ceremonies are interrelated is of prime importance in viewing small-town culture. The old Hispano villages were interdependent. Change meant a breakdown or readjustment of those relationships of mutual help and dependency. The ceremonies, traditions, relationships, and communal mutual help that were in place in 1912 are still there in some form seventy-five years later, but lack of jobs, education, mass media and mobility, children leaving the villages and movement into the middle class, have affected the last two generations. If those values we identify as part of our history are to be retained, they must be retained within each family. When we recognize the strength of those values, they can again play a role in the community.

Mobility came first in the form of the Model T Ford, as clear and radical a product of Anglo technology as there ever was. People moved to California to seek a new way of life, new opportunity. The young went to seek adventure, jobs, money, an education. Strangely enough, as there were more wages, there seemed to be less leisure time, or less time to pay attention to the allegiance to old relationships. Concern for the communal systems began to erode, and in places, to disappear. If you worked for wages, your responsibility was done at the end of the day. Churches and acequias fell into disrepair, families had less time for each other.

One can see the transformation in the ceremonies. At one time the bartering system was an important aspect of village life. Work and tools and talents were bartered for. You help me fix my roof and I'll help you shoe your horses. Together we can plaster the church or the house of the viejitos. Helping and the exchange of labor are still elements of Nuevo Mexicano life, but working a tight eight-hour day interferes with the ceremonies. Assimilation has its price.

Selling the land of the abuelos, the village land of the ancestors, was viewed with disapproval. Woven into centuries of tradition was the unspoken rule, the land cannot be sold. It is part of the heritage of the land grants, part of the heritage gained from the Indian view of the earth. To sell the land was to cut your roots, and a man without roots lacked identity. Families without a village lost their allegiance to place. Allegiance to the land is as important as allegiance to the family and to God.

I remember when my family left the town of my childhood, Santa Rosa. Leaving that place meant also leaving our connection to the farming community of Puerto de Luna, leaving the open llano of Pastura. It was a wretched experience. Sad. Part of our honor, pride, and history, elements important to the culture, was being left behind. Torn from the land of our birth, would we survive?

The land had been sold cheaply, and leaving the land was leaving the energy force and the blood source of the culture. The Hispanos became the new Okies as they moved west to the imagined land of milk and honey, as they moved to California. Recently I asked a cousin of mine who grew into manhood in the village of Puerto de Luna and who now lives in Albuquerque if he would ever return there. No, he replied, there is nothing there for him in the village of his childhood. Still, in his own way, in the urban environment, he lives in the old lifestyle, tending his garden and raising a few sheep. But there is no return.

Thomas Wolfe reflected on his South and saw similar changes take place. He put it best when he said, "Oh, lost, and by the wind grieved. . . ."

Now as the sons and daughters of the generation of the forties join the middle class, a greater change will take place. I teach their children in my university classes and find most don't speak Spanish, most do not know the ways or the history of the traditional culture. Now we will see if the elements of that culture that took hundreds of years to evolve can survive in the middle class. Now there are more stratified groups within the Hispano community. There are the Hispano members of the middle class, living in cities, adopting more and more the way of the Anglo. There are the country cousins, those who held on to the land and still follow the folkways.

And there are the new workers from Mexico, who in future years will make their connection to the old legacy. These workers of the fields, the Mexicans seeking the opportunity of work, are the newest migration into the Río Grande. In a way, they continue the stream of migration that has always moved north and south along our border region, and a new time of transformation and change awaits them. As they renew elements of our Mexicano past they play a positive role in our culture.

Today, reflecting on seventy-five years of statehood provides us an excellent vantage point. It is time to reflect.

Without that reflection the pace of life and its tensions will increase, and it is a pity and a loss to move forward without knowing whence we came.

Each of us changes in relationship to others. We grow and explore the world and experience love and joy and tragedy. Cultures are that way, always growing and changing. The Hispanos of Nuevo Mexico have changed in response to their relationship to the Anglo culture, and to other cultural groups of the Río Grande region. The relationship to the Indian Pueblos of the Rio Grande not only changed the culture centuries ago, it helped give it definition. The process of growth is constant and, yes, often painful.

For the Hispano community, the process of growth and change has been painful. But the turbulence of the surface change can be met if the values of the ancestors remain rooted to our memory, if our language, values, and ceremonies don't die. The surface is like the surface of the muddy waters of the Río Grande, sometimes turbulent, sometimes peaceful. But beneath lie the elements of water and earth, and the old principal elements of faith. To those we can always pledge our allegiance.

Hispano: In New Mexico the Spanish-speaking Mexican-American community uses this term for identification.
compadres: godfather, or a very close friend
comadres: godmothers
patrón: a landowner, political boss
viejitos: old people, elders

Mythical Dimensions/
Political Reality

Many of us who live in the Southwest have developed a mythical dimension that enables us to relate to the land and its people. This dimension keeps us close to the land and its history. We value the indigenous myths that have evolved on this continent. Now the tremendous economic changes that came with the Sunbelt boom that began in the 1960s have not only altered the landscape, they have altered the way people relate to the land and each other, and there is a danger of losing this dimension. Many of us are asking what happens when we lose our mythic relationship to the earth and allow only the political and economic forces to guide our way of life.

I take much of my identity from the values and tribal ways of the old Nuevo Mexicanos, from their legends and myths and from the earth which they held sacred, and so I am concerned about the process of world politics and economics that is altering the Southwest so radically. The development of the Southwest has altered our perception of our landscapes: the personal, the environmental, and the mythic. The old communities, the tribes of this region, have been scattered, and they have lost much of their power. If we do not take action now, that creative force of the people which has nourished us for centuries may be swept aside.

Our future is at stake. We who value the earth as a creative force must renew our faith in the values of the old communities, the ceremonies of relationship, the dances and fiestas, the harmony in our way of life, and the mythic force we can tap to create beauty and peace. We must speak out clearly against the political and economic processes whose only goal is material gain.

It is the individual's relationship to the tribe and one's response to the elements of the earth and the cosmos that give shape to our inner consciousness. These relationships create meaning. They have shaped the Indian and Hispano Southwest, just as they have shaped part of the Anglo reality and myth.* But the old communal relationships are changing as the new urban environments change our land. In New Mexico, the diaspora from the villages that began in the 1940s has continued, the once-stable villages and pueblos are emptied to create a marginalized people in the ghettos of the new urban centers.

Many of us no longer live in the landscape our parents knew. We no longer enjoy that direct relationship with nature which nurtured them. The Southwest has slowly changed, becoming an urban environment. We no longer live in the basic harmony that can exist between humanity and the earth. A new and materialistic order has become paramount in the land, and we have little control over this intrusion. The land that nurtured us is by and large now in the hands of world markets and politics.

True, some of our neighbors survive in mountain villages and pueblos, on ranches and reservations. These folk remain a historic link to our mythic dimension. They keep

---

*I use "Hispano" to mean the Spanish-speaking community of New Mexico. I could just as well use "Mexicano" or "Nuevo Mexicano," the Mexican-American community.

alive the values and communal relationships of our grandparents, and they struggle against the destructive overdevel-
opment that characterizes the present.

Urban Sunbelt population growth; renewed attention to
the oil, gas, and mining industries; the construction of air
bases and weapons laboratories; and a high-tech boom
with its dream of a new economy are some of the elements
of the politicizing process that our generation has seen
become reality in the Southwest. The full force of that
change has been felt in our generation as the New York and
world money markets gained control over and exploited the
resources of this land.

The signs of the web of the political world are all around
us. Visit any of the large cities of the Southwest and you
see unchecked growth, a plundering of land and water,
and a lack of attention to the old traditional communities.
Immense social disparity has been created overnight. We
have lost control over our land. The crucial questions for
us are: Have we let go of our old values? Have we been
defeated?

Because I write and understand the power of literature,
I have to ask what this means to writers from the Southwest.
For some it means a retreat into formula: the cowboy-and-
Indian story is still being churned out. Some writers armed
with computers simply make that formula longer and more
ponderous to read. For others the retreat means moving
out of the city to the suburbs or if possible to the villages
or the mountains. The Indian and Chicano way of life is
idealized as the refusal to deal with the new, engulfing
economic and political reality grows. Some draw closer to
the Indian and Hispano communities, to the old tribes of
the land, seeking spiritual warmth from, and reconciliation
with, these earth people. Others create new tribal centers:
Zen centers, mosques, monasteries in the desert, and hippie
communes. Some writers just drink and quarrel more, sub-
consciously surrendering to the old Western movie plot in
their withdrawal.

In my lifetime I have seen this tremendous change come over the land. Most of my contemporaries and I have left our Hispano communities and became urban dwellers. The people, the earth, the water of the river and of the acequias, and the spiritual views of the tribal communities that once nurtured me are almost gone. The ball game has changed, and it is appropriate to use the ball game metaphor, because the original game of la pelota in Mesoamerican history has a spiritual orientation, a deep meaning for the tribe. Now the ball game is played for profit. In our most common ceremonies and rituals we see the change, we see the new view of the West.

Politicizing the Southwest has meant corralling people in the city. Reckless developers take the land for the false promise of the easy life where homogenized goods and services can be delivered. Work in one's cornfield has become work for wages, wages that can never keep up with ever-spiraling taxation. The pueblo plaza or village post office, where the community once gathered to conduct both business and ceremony, is being engulfed by chaotic urban sprawl. The center is being lost.

What does this mean to me? I who have now lived longer in the city than in the rural landscape of my grandparents, I who have seen this drastic change come over the land?

When I was writing *Bless Me, Ultima* in the early 1960s, I was still tied to the people and the earth of the Pecos River Valley, the small town of Santa Rosa, the villages of Puerto de Luna and Pastura. The mythic element infuses that novel because it is a reflection of the world I knew. Now the West has lost its natural state, and development after development sprawls across once-empty desert. Growth and change are inevitable, but that which is guided only by a material goal is a corrosive element that has insidiously spread its influence over the land and the people. How can I write and not reflect this process?

Who has taken charge of our lives? We are now informed by television, the daily dose of news, the homogeneous school system, and other communication media that are in the hands of the power manipulators. Many ancient ceremonies and dances are still intact along the Río Grande, but even the people who sustain these ceremonies are affected by the bingo parlors and quick cash. My city is hostage to those who control the flow of the river, and the quality of that water will continue to be affected by the chemical and nuclear waste it washes away. This reality must affect our writings.

The Chicanos, Indians, and old Anglos who worked the land are now a labor force to serve the industries that the world economic and political system imposes on us. The time is disharmonious; no wonder we gather together to discuss the changing landscape, and the changing humanscape. We know we have been manipulated, and in the resulting change we feel we have lost something important.

Our people have been lulled into believing that every person can get a piece of the action. We set up bingo games as we pray for rain, and we train our children to take care of tourists even as they forget to care for the old ones. We begin to see the elemental landscape as a resource to be bought and sold. We do not dream the old dreams, we do not contemplate the gods, and less and less do we stand in front of the cosmos in humility. We begin to believe that we can change the very nature of things, and so we leave old connections behind, we forget the sacred places and become part of the new reality—a world reality tied to nerve centers in New York, Tokyo, London, and Hong Kong.

The old patterns of daily life are forgotten. The cyclical sense of time that once provided historical continuity and spiritual harmony is replaced by atomic beeps. The clock on the wall now marks the ceremonies we attend, ceremonies that have to do with the order of world politics. It is no wonder we feel we are being watched, our responses recorded. We are being used, and eventually we will be discarded.

But there is hope. The sensitive writer can still create meaningful forms that can be shared with the reader who is hungry for a mythic sensibility. We still have the materials and beliefs of our grandparents to work into poetry and fiction. Reflection in our writings need not become mired in paranoia. The old relationships of the mythic West need not be reduced to a formula. Technology may serve people; it need not be the new god. If we flee to the old communities in search of contact with the elemental landscape and a more harmonious view of things, we can return from that visit more committed to engaging the political process. We can still use the old myths of this hemisphere to shed light on our contemporary problems.

We, the writers, can still salvage elements of beauty for the future. We can help preserve the legends and myths of our land to rekindle the spirit of the old relationships. We can encourage the power of creativity that takes its strength from the elemental and mythic landscapes. The problems we face are not new; prior generations of Mesoamerica dealt with many of the same problems.

In exploring the legend of Quetzalcóatl while writing *The Lord of the Dawn*, I was astounded at the close parallels between the world of the ancient Toltecs of Tula and our own time. Then, as now, men of peace and understanding struggled against the militaristic and materialistic instincts of the society. Both the historical king and the deity known as Quetzalcóatl came to the Toltecs to bring learning in the arts, agriculture, and spiritual thought. Under the benign rule of Quetzalcóatl, the Toltecs prospered. But much of their prosperity was taken by the warrior class to conduct war on the neighboring tribes. Toltec civilization rose to its classic apex, then fell.

In the end, Quetzalcóatl was banished from Tula. The materialists of the society, who waged war and conducted business only for profit, had their way. The deity who brought art, wisdom, and learning was banished, and the Toltec civilization fell. The influence of Quetzalcóatl was later felt in the civilizations of the Aztecs and Mayas, for every society seeks truth and the correct way to live.

Even now, the story of the Toltecs and Quetzalcóatl speaks to us across the centuries, warning us to respect our deep and fragile communal relationships within and among nations, and our meaningful relationships to the earth.

The past is not dead; it lives in our hearts, as myth lives in our hearts. We need those most human qualities of the world myths to help guide us on our road today.

My novel *Alburquerque* addresses some of these questions. The city where I live, like any other city in the Southwest, reflects the political processes that have permeated our land. The novel is about change, the change that has come during our lifetime. In it, some of the principal characters are driven by the desire to conquer the landscape, to control the land and the water of the Río Grande. Others, members of the old tribes, take refuge in withdrawal in order to survive urban poverty. They withdraw to their circles of belief to wait out the storm.

We, the writers, cannot wait out the storm; we have to confront it. For us, the bedrock of beliefs of the old cultures provides our connection, our relationship. From that stance we must keep informing the public about the change that has come upon our land.

The battle is of epic proportions. We are in the midst of one of those times from which will emerge a new consciousness. The environment seems to reflect this struggle between evil and good; it cries out to us. We see it scarred and polluted. The people of the old tribes cry out; we see them displaced and suffering. Even the elements of nature reflect the change: acid and toxic chemicals pollute the water, nuclear waste is buried in the bowels of the earth. These are the same signs the Toltecs saw hundreds of years ago as their society faced destruction.

We, too, face a measure of destruction. The goal of material acquisition and a homogeneous political process supporting that goal have taken hold, driving us deeper into the complex nature of materialism. Is it any wonder we look back to legend and myth for direction?

We are poised at the edge of a new time. We have the opportunity to look again into the nature of our hemisphere. We can see that the struggle for illumination is not easy. It was not easy for the Toltecs, and we know now that as they gave up their old knowledge and turned to militarism and material gain, they destroyed their society.

Will we preserve our old values or let them die? Will we rediscover our relationship to the earth? What of the communal relationships that are so fractured and split in our land? Is there time to bring peace and harmony to our tribal groups?

The first step in answering these questions is to realize that we have turned away from our inner nature and from our connection to the earth and old historical relationships. We have allowed a political and economic world order to impose itself on us and take control of our lives. How we engage this moment in history not only describes us but also will inform future generations of our values. Our writings will say where we stood when this drama of opposing forces came to be played out on our land.

The New World Man

My wife and I first traveled to Spain in the fall of 1980. We took an overnight train from Paris to Barcelona, journeyed through Andalusia and then on to Madrid. We returned home with wonderful memories of the Alhambra, Toledo, Madrid, El Escorial, and many other places we visited. At the famous El Prado museum I fell under the spell of the genius of Goya, and the images of his prophetic vision are still with me. In 1988 when we returned to Spain, my trip was in part a pilgrimage to meditate again in the presence of Goya's work and to visit and contemplate the genius of Gaudi's inspiring church, La Sagrada Familia, in Barcelona.

That return was made possible by my invitation to Barcelona to discuss my work at the Third International Conference on Hispanic Cultures of the United States; after that conference I attended a small gathering of Spanish scholars and professors from the University of New Mexico at La Fundación Xavier de Salas in Trujillo.

Spain was preparing for the celebration of its 1492–1992 quincentennial, and the conference was the beginning of a series intended to review the relationship of Spain with

Hispanic America. We Nuevo Mexicanos are part of that history: we speak the Spanish language. I prefer the term "Nuevo Mexicano" to describe my cultural heritage. My parents and my grandparents of the Puerto de Luna Valley of New Mexico spoke only Spanish, and as I honor my ancestors, I keep up their language and folkways. "Hispano" to me means using the Spanish language of my ancestors. The term, like "Latino," also connects me to other Spanish-speaking groups in this country and in Latin America.

The great majority of the Mexicanos of the Southwest are Indo-Hispanos, part of La Raza of the New World, the fruit of the Spanish father and the Indian mother. We take pride in our Hispanic heritage; that is, we know the history of the Spanish father, his language, and his character. We also know that in this country it has been more seductive to identify with one's white, European ancestry. But the identification with that which is Spanish has often caused us to neglect our indigenous Native American roots, and thus we have not known and honored the heritage of our mother, the Indian mothers of Mexico and the Southwest.

In world mythology there are few archetypal searches for the mother, perhaps because the mother is always evident, she is always there; in early religions she was the goddess of the earth, the provider. We forget that it is the mother who cultivates and in many ways creates our nature, both in an individual and in a communal sense.

For the Mexicanos of the Southwest the mother is Malinche, the Mexican woman who was the first Indian woman of Mexico to bear children fathered by a Spaniard. But the mother figure is more real than the symbolic Malinche; our mothers embody the archetype of the indigenous Indian mother of the Americas. If we are to truly know ourselves, it is her nature we must know. Why have we neglected her? In other words, why have we neglected that part of our history that was shaped by indigenous America?

I was born and raised in New Mexico, heir to the land

of my Nuevo Mexicano ancestors, son of those Spanish and Mexicano colonists who settled the fertile Río Grande Valley of New Mexico. My ancestors settled in the Atrisco land grant, across the river from present-day Alburquerque. I trace my family back a few generations because the land grant has created a sense of communal belonging for the Anayas. But how do we relate to that Hispanic legacy that left the Peninsula in 1492 to implant itself in the New World? How do we relate to the peninsular consciousness of the people who crossed the Atlantic five hundred years ago to deposit their seed on the earth of the New World?

Located at the heart of what is now the Southwest United States, the people of Nuevo México have retained the essence of what it means to be Hispano, having preserved the Spanish language, the Catholic religion, and the folktales and folkways that came from Spain. Our ancestors imbued the history of Nuevo México with their particular worldview. For more than four centuries our Mexicano ancestors have lived in the isolated frontier of northernmost New Spain. But they did not survive and multiply in a vacuum; they survived and evolved because they intermarried and adopted many of the ways of the Pueblos. The Spanish character underwent change as it encountered the Native Americans of the Southwest, and from that interaction and intermarriage a unique American mestizo was born.

We need to describe the totality of the worldview that was formed in what we now call the Southwest, understanding that we are heirs not only of the Spanish character but of our Native American nature as well. The Spanish character may be the aggressive, conquest-oriented part of our identity; the Native American nature is the more harmonious, earth-oriented side. We need to know both sides of our identity in order to know ourselves. We need to know the unique characteristics that have evolved from this union. To pay attention only to one side of our nature is to be less knowledgeable of self. If we are to fulfill our

potential, it is important that we know the indigenous side
of our history.

As I review my writings, I understand that it is the indigenous American perspective, or New World view, that is at
the core of my search. I have explored the nature of my
mother, not only the symbolic Indian mother but the real
Indian mothers of the Americas. The blood that whispers
my feelings about the essence of the earth and people of
the Americas is the soul of my mother; it reveals the symbols
and mythology of the New World, and that comprises the
substratum of my writings.

During the Columbus quincentennial, a discourse will
take place between Spain and its former colonies in the
Americas. I wish to add a definition of my New World
view to that discourse, hoping not only to share some
of the findings of my personal literary quest but also to
encourage my community of raza to pay more attention
to our multicultural and multiethnic history. We must know
more of the synthesis of our Spanish and Indian nature,
and know more of the multiple heritages of the Americas.

The Americas represent a wonderful experiment in the
synthesis of divergent worldviews, and each one of us is a
representative of that process. The illuminations of self that
are revealed as we explore and understand our true natures
can be one of the most rewarding experiences of our lives,
for so much of the sensitive part of life is a search and
understanding of the inner self. To define ourselves as we
really are and not as others wish us to be allows us to
become authentic, and that definition carries with it the
potential of our humanism.

In the mid-sixteenth century, our Hispano and Mexicano
ancestors begin to settle along the Río Grande of Nuevo
México, bringing to the land a new language. They gave
names to the land and its features. It is in the naming that
one engages in the sacred; that is, by naming, one creates
a *sacred sense of time*, a historic sense of time. By engaging
in naming, our ancestors imposed themselves on history

and gave definition to history. The language used in that naming ceremony is our birthright.

I live in Alburquerque, a name that invokes some of the history of the Iberian Peninsula. In Spain, I spoke my Nuevo Mexicano Spanish, a language preserved and evolved by my ancestors in the mountains and valleys of New Mexico. But language changes with the passage of time and the vicissitudes of survival, and so I returned to Spain more proficient in English than in Spanish. All my novels and stories are written in English. While my parents' generation still communicated only in Spanish, my generation converses almost completely in English, a function of survival in the Anglo-American society. We struggle to retain the Spanish language, not only because it was the language of our ancestors but because it connects us to our brethren in Mexico and Latin America.

I returned to Spain to share with Spaniards the nature of my New World consciousness. At times I felt uncomfortable, believing I had to conform to the Spanish character, but the truth is that we who return to Spain no longer need to feel constrained to conform to the Spanish character. My generation of Hispanos, or Mexican-Americans, liberated ourselves from that constraint by naming ourselves Chicanos. For us, using the word "Chicano" was our declaration of independence, the first step toward our true identity. By creating a Chicano consciousness we created a process by which we rediscovered our history.

By naming ourselves Chicanos we stamped an era with our communal identity; we reaffirmed our humanity by exploring and understanding the nature of our mothers, the indigenous American women. We took the word "Chicano" from "Mexicano," dropping the first syllable and keeping the "xicano." We are proud of that heritage even though we are not Mexican citizens, and although we are citizens of the United States we are not Anglo-Americans. We have our own history rooted in this land. The word "Chicano" defined our *space in time*, that is, our history and our identity. "Chicano" embraced our Native American heritage, an important element of our history.

Our first declaration of independence was from Anglo-America; that is, we insisted on the right to our Indo-Hispano heritage. Now I believe the declaration has to go further. We have to insist on being the *señores of our own time*, to borrow a phrase from Miguel León-Portilla. To be the *sēnores and señoras of our own time* is to continue to create our definition and sense of destiny; it is a process of synthesis that embraces the many roots of La Raza.

This essay is a declaration of independence from a narrow view which has defined us *only* as Hispanos with only a Spanish heritage. The definition of our identity must be a New World definition. Such a definition should encompass the multiple roots and histories of the Americas; it should encompass the nature of the mothers whose soul provides the unique aesthetic and humanistic sensibility that defines us.

Language is at the essence of a culture, and we must remember that in Nuevo México, as in the rest of the New World, there existed pre-Columbian languages. The indigenous Indians had named their tribes, the rivers, mountains, and the flora and fauna. They were the *señores of their own time*. The New World did not live in silence, awaiting the sound of European languages; thousands of years before 1492 it had its languages and it had participated in the sacred ceremony of naming. This is a fact that we must accept when we discuss our ethnicity, for not only was the Mexico of our indigenous ancestors peopled with Indians, the Río Grande Valley, which became the home of our Hispano/Mexicano ancestors, also was thriving with many great Indian pueblos.

Language follows the urge of the blood: it moves with the adventurer to take root and be nourished by the colonist who tills the new soil. Languages mix, as does the blood, and so my gene pool is both Indian and peninsular. In reality, it has deeper and more interesting roots; roots I will never know. Knowing this allows me to honor las madres de las Américas. My journey has been that of a writer, and in my first novel it was the curandera Ultima, the indigenous woman who came to speak to me and share her secrets. She reflects the nature of La Virgen de Guadalupe, the indigenous mother born of the synthesis of Spanish virgin and Indian goddess. It is through Ultima that I began to discover myself. In my writings I have sought the true nature of the New World man, that person who is authentic to the New World view. I had only myself to encounter in the journey; I am the New World man I sought. I am an indigenous man taking his essence and perspective from the earth and people of the New World, from the earth that is my mother.

One of the most interesting questions we ask ourselves as human beings is that of identity. Who am I? We seek to know our roots, to know ourselves. When we encounter the taproots of our history we feel authentic and able to identify self, family, and community. Finding self should also mean finding humanity; declaring personal independence also means declaring that independence for all individuals.

How did I begin this journey of self-knowledge? I listened to the cuentos of the old people, the stories of their history, and in retelling those stories and starting my own odyssey, I had to turn within. I had to know myself. Everyone does. The spiritual beliefs and mysticism of the Catholic Church and the love of the earth were elements of my childhood, so I used those sources in my stories. The folkways of my community became the web of the fictions I create, for the elements of drama exist within the stories of the folk. Even today, when I feel I have outgrown some of the themes I explored as a young writer, I know my best writing still comes when I return to the essence of my Nuevo Mexicano culture.

But in all writing the depth of the universal element is that which allows us to communicate across national or

ethnic boundaries, and so for me the most meaningful and
revealing area to enter in search of the New World person
was mythology. It is in myth that we find the truth in the
heart, the truth of "our place in time." Everyone can enter
and explore his or her memory, and to discover there the
symbols that speak to the personal and collective history.
It is in this search that I found the legend of the golden
carp and the other mythological symbols that permeate
Bless Me, Ultima and my later work. I found universal
archetypal symbols, but these symbols were colored with
a Native American hue. The earth, the elements, the sacred
directions, the tree, the owl of the old curandera Ultima,
the golden carp, the shaman as mentor or guide—all of
these elements spoke to me of my New World nature. And
it was Ultima, my Native American mother, who led the
way and taught me to see.

My search continued. In Heart of Aztlán I reworked the
myth of Aztlán, a legend that describes the place of origin
of the Aztecs. I attempted to make that legend meaningful
in a contemporary context by exploring its possibilities as
a Chicano homeland. In Tortuga I continued the search
into the earth and totem animals, the search into the healing
process of water and earth as well as the art of writing
itself. The writer may well be the new shaman for the old,
displaced tribes of the Americas. In the novel Tortuga I
returned to the important revelations available to us in the
nature of the mother, whether the mother was viewed as
earth goddess or the feminine presence of the young girl
who loves Tortuga.

I understand that many of my manitos, my Nuevo Mexicanos, often praise our Hispanic identity and shun the
indigenous roots that have also nurtured our history. The
young Chicano artists have changed part of that, and now I
declare my independence of consciousness from the Iberian
Peninsula. I have found that the symbolic content that best
describes my nature comes from the people and earth of
the Americas. So I declare, as an important step in the

process of knowing myself, my independence. I see myself as a New World man, and I feel that definition is liberating and full of potential.

During this time of the Columbus quincentennial, it is important to look at the evolution of the consciousness of the Americas and to discern the unique worldviews that that evolution created. It is important for us and for Spain to look at the Americas and find, not an image of the Spanish character, but an image of our unique New World nature.

When I first traveled in Spain in 1980 I went into Andalusia. There in those wide expanses and mountains, which reminded me of New Mexico, I felt at home. But a person needs more than the landscape to feel connected; we need the deeper connection to the communal body.

The broad, political history of the independence of the Spanish colonies in the Americas is well known; now we must turn to an exploration of our personal and communal identity. That is what Chicano writers and artists have been doing since the cultural movement of the 1960s. The definition of Chicano culture must come from a multicultural perspective. Many streams of history define us and will continue to define us, for we are the synthesis that is the Americas.

Christ and Quetzalcóatl are not opposing spiritual figures; they fulfill the humanistic yearning toward harmonious resolution. Harmony within, harmony with neighbors, harmony with the cosmos. The Virgin of Spanish Catholicism and the Aztec Tonantzin culminate in the powerful and all-loving Virgen de Guadalupe. And los santos of the Catholic Church, and those more personal saints of my mother's altar, merge with and share the sacred space of the kachinas of the Indian pueblos.

This metaphor, "Los santos son las kachinas," the saints are the kachinas, has become a guiding metaphor of synthesis for me. The Old World and the New World have become one in me. Perhaps it is this syncretic sensibility of harmony that is the ideal of New World character. The New World cultures accepted the spiritual manifestations of Catholicism; Christ and the saints entered the religious cosmology of Indian America. A new age of cultural and spiritual blending came to unite humanity's course in the Americas. It was an age born in suffering, but the very act of birth created the children who were heirs to a new worldview.

The New World view is syncretic and encompassing. It is one of the most humanistic views in the world, and yet it is a view not well known in the world. The pressure of political realities and negative views of the mestizo populations of the Americas have constrained the flowering of our nature. Still, that view of self-knowledge and harmony is carried in the heart of the New World person.

What is important to me as a writer is to find the words by which to describe myself and my relationship to others. I can now speak of my history, and posit myself at the center of that history. I stand poised at the center of power, the knowing of myself, the heart and soul of the New World man alive in me.

This is a time of reflection for those of us who are the mestizos of the New World, and I believe the reflections in my writings and my attention to the myths and legends of Mesoamerica and the Río Grande help expand the definition of our Indo-Hispano heritage.

From Spain I brought back memories of the Alhambra where I felt my soul stir to Moorish rhythm, and in the paintings of Goya's dark period I saw his apocryphal vision of an era ending. At La Sagrada Familia of Gaudi I bowed to genius, in the Valle de los Caidos I reflected on the Civil War . . . and on the wide expanses of Andalusia I thought of home. In all these places my memory stirred, and still I yearned for my home in Nuevo México, the mountains I know, the sacred places of my way of life. In that yearning the message whispered its secret, it was time for me to declare my independence, time to center myself in the consciousness of the New World.

I was the New World man I had sought, with one foot in the glorious mestisaje of Mexico and the other in the earth of the Indo-Hispanos of Nuevo México; my dreams are woven of New World earth and history. I could walk anywhere in the world and feel I was a citizen of the world, but it was Nuevo México that centered me; it was the indigenous soul of the Americas that held my secret.

It is important to know that the search for identity is not an esoteric search and not a divisive process. It is a way to reaffirm our humanity. We are all on this search, we all advocate justice, basic human rights, and the right of all to declare their independence of consciousness. We hope the spirit generated in Spain during the 1992 celebration addresses and encourages these basic rights.

History and the collective memory are vast. One delves into these powerful forces and finds that one is part of every other human being. I am proud of my New World heritage, but I know the tree of mankind is one, and I share my roots with every other person. It seems appropriate to end on the archetype of the tree. The tree, or the tree of life, is also a dominant symbol of the Americas, and its syncretic image combines the tree of Quetzalcóatl and the cross of Christ. My ancestors nourished the tree of life; now it is up to me to care for all it symbolizes.

Aztlán

The ceremony of naming, or self-definition, is one of the most important acts a community performs. To particularize the group with a name is a fundamental step of awareness in the evolution of tribes as well as nations. The naming coalesces the history and values of the group, provides an identification necessary for its relationship to other groups or nations, and most important, the naming ceremony restores pride and infuses renewed energy which manifests itself in creative ways.

I have reflected often during the last fifteen years on the naming ceremony that took place in the southwestern United States when the Chicano community named Aztlán as its homeland in the late 1960s. This communal event and the new consciousness and consequent creative activity which was generated within the Chicano community during this period marked an important historical time for our people.

The naming ceremony creates a real sense of nation, for it fuses the spiritual and political aspirations of a group and provides a vision of the group's role in history. These aspirations are voiced by the artists who recreate the language and symbols that are used in the naming ceremony. The politicians of the group may describe political relationships and symbols, but it is the artist who gives deeper and long-lasting expression to a people's sense of nation and destiny. The artists, like the priests and shamans of other tribes, express spiritual awareness and potential, and it is the "expression" of the group's history, identity, and purpose that I label the "naming ceremony." In the ancient world this expression of identity and purpose was contained in the epic; thus, we read Homer to understand the character of the Greeks.

Various circumstances create the need for national or tribal definition and unity. The group may acquire cohesion and a feeling of nationhood in times of threat, whether the threat be physical (war or exploitation) or a perceived loss of tribal unity. Group existence may also be threatened by assimilationist tendencies, which were a real threat experienced by the Chicano community in the 1960s. A time of adventure and conquest or the alliance of political interests may also bring nations to self-definition. Most notably, times of heightened spiritual awareness of the group's relationship to the gods create this sense of purpose and destiny in the community. Usually these times are marked by a renaissance in the arts, because the artists provide the symbols and metaphors that describe the spiritual relationship.

So it was for La Raza, the Mexican-American community of this country in the 1960s. This cultural group underwent an important change in their awareness of self and that change brought about the need for self-definition. The naming ceremony not only helped to bond the group, it created a new vision of the group's potential.

Where did the Chicanos turn for the content needed in the naming ceremony? Quite naturally the community turned to its history and found many of its heroes in the recent epoch of the Mexican Revolution. Some of us explored the deeper stratum of Mexican history, "myth" and "legend." It was in the mythology of the Aztecs that the Chicano cultural nationalists found the myth of Aztlán. How did the content of that myth become part of the new consciousness of our community? That is the question that our philosophers have tackled from various perspectives, and it has been part of my preoccupation.

The naming ceremony, or redefinition of the group, occurred within the ranks of the Indo-Hispanos of the Southwest in the 1960s. Leaders within the Hispanic community—educators, poets, writers, artists, activists—rose up against the majority presence of Anglo-America to defend the right of the Hispanic community to exist as a national entity within the United States. Two crucial decisions were made during this period by these guardians of the culture: one was the naming of the Chicano community and the second was the declaration of Aztlán as the ancestral homeland. "Somos Chicanos," we are Chicanos, declared the leaders of the nationalistic movement, and thus christened the Mexican-American community with a name that had archaic roots. By using this term the Chicano community consciously and publicly acknowledged its Native American heritage, and thus opened new avenues of exploration by which we could more clearly define the mestizo who is the synthesis of European and Indian ancestry.

"Aztlán is our homeland" was the second declaration, and this assertion defined the "national" status for the group. Aztlán was the place of origin of the Aztecs of Mesoamerica, the place of the seven caves recorded in their legends. The Chicanos had returned to Native American legend to find the psychological and spiritual birthplace of their ancestors.

These declarations were of momentous, historical significance. An identity and a homeland were designated once again on the northern borders of Hispanic America. The naming of Aztlán was a spontaneous act which took place throughout the Southwest, and the feat was given authenticity in a meeting that was held in Denver in 1969 to draft

El Plan Espiritual de Aztlán. The naming of the homeland created a Chicano spiritual awareness which reverberated throughout the Southwest, and the naming ceremony was reenacted wherever Chicanos met to discuss their common destiny. I believe that no other activity of the Chicano Movement was as important as this declaration. It is now time to explore why such an event took place, and to examine closely the possibilities that were inherent in that event.

The threat to the Chicano community was most often defined by the leaders of the Chicano Movement of the 1960s as a political and economic threat, an exploitation of the Mexican-American population. Finding solutions to economic and political exploitation was of paramount importance, but within the movement were also heard the voices of cultural nationalists who insisted that the definition of the homeland, Aztlán, and the reconstitution of the old tribal history and heritage were just as vital for the Chicano community. In fact, the two issues went hand in hand, and in retrospect we can see that the leaders of the two factions of the movement should have worked closer together. The cultural nationalists created the symbol of national unity for the community; the political activists should have seen its potential and used the symbol to provide access into the mainstream political structure. The two areas of endeavor should have combined efforts, but often that was not the case.

The context of the Chicano Movement was broad, and the struggles for definition of goals and leadership within the movement still need more historical analysis. I leave that review of the broader picture of the movement to other disciplines; my focus is the naming of Aztlán. What indeed took place when the Chicanos defined their homeland? How did the momentous act serve the Chicanos then and today? Why had we returned to Aztec legend to name the homeland, and how did that return to legend create "rights (to homeland) by legend"? Would this "right by legend" be as powerful a binding force for Chicanos as "right by treaty"? We knew we could turn to the Treaty of Guadalupe Hidalgo, a historical treaty between nations, to define ourselves as Mexicans with certain rights within the borders of the United States, but that political definition had never been enough. A group not only defines itself politically but also defines its character, that is, its soul. To define ourselves we turned to Native American legend, and there we found a meaningful part of our ethos.

My thoughts lead me to believe that the tribes of our species arrive at new stages of communal awareness as they evolve. During these historical moments of illumination, the group creates the context of its destiny in time, and so the group becomes master of its own time, or as Miguel León-Portilla, the renowned Mexican philosopher, would say, the group becomes the "señores of their own time." Did we indeed become the "señores of our own time" during the 1960s? Did we take charge of the time and create the epic literature that would define us?

Let us review the historical setting for the Indo-Hispanos of the Southwest when we celebrated the naming ceremony. It was a time when we saw our community assaulted by poverty and oppression; the denigrating effects of racism ate away at our pride and stamina. Assimilation, on the other hand, only raised false hopes for our people, so it was a time of crisis, a time that begged for the "señores of the communal time" to once again insist on our right to our values and history. If this didn't happen our community was doomed to existence as a tourist commodity, admired for its quaint folkways but not taken seriously by the world of nations.

For too long the Indo-Hispano community had projected only its Spanish history and heritage, for that projection suited the powers that dealt with this community as a tourist commodity and as a community that could do service work for the society in power. That identity left out the reality of our mestizo heritage. Part of the Movement's work was to revive our connection with our Indian past, and to seek a truer definition of that past. This meant reviving the history, myths, spiritual thought, legends, and symbols from Native America which were part of the Chicano's collective history. The search found the umbilical cord that led to Indian Mesoamerica and the Pueblos of the Río Grande; that is, in the act of declaring our identity and nationality, we acknowledged our Indian-American parentage.

It was in Mesoamerica that we rediscovered the legend of Aztlán, a story of mythic proportions, rooted as it was in the tribal memory of the Aztecs. Why was the legend not readily available to us, say in the legends of the Pueblos of the Río Grande? Perhaps it was, but by the middle of the twentieth century we as "Hispanos" were separated from the Pueblo Indian world of our ancestors. A color consciousness which has been such a negative element in the history of the Americas affected our own people, and, falling prey to the pressure, the large mestizo population moved to identify with that which was Hispanic. Indian thought, once accessible to our ancestors, was withdrawn to the inner circle of the pueblo, and the myths of the Americas were revealed only to those of us who delved into the symbolic meanings in the collective memory.

In 1848 there was the continued sense of separation when the United States annexed what is now the Southwest from Mexico. Separation from roots created vulnerability because our worldview was centered in community and its relationship to the earth. Even in the endeavor of education where democracy promised equality and access, we felt denied. Thus our search for Chicano roots led to Mesoamerica and Aztec legend, and there we found Aztlán; put another way, Aztlán was waiting for us.

In Aztlán, the legend said, the seven tribes emerged from the seven caves of a mountain, a descriptive and archetypal metaphor which expresses the coming into a new age of consciousness from a prior time. They left Aztlán because they had received the prophecy to migrate south in search of Tenochtitlán, there to establish their new civilization. How may we interpret this? Was this archetypal expulsion from the place of origin (Aztlán) like an expulsion from the Garden of Eden, the motif of an archetype in myth repeating itself? Or was leaving the place of origin a challenge to humanity, a challenge of evolution?

The ancestors of the Aztecs named their homeland Aztlán, and legend placed it north of Mexico. Aztlán was the place of origin, the sipapu, the Eden of those tribes. There they came to a new relationship with their god of war, Huitzilopochtli, and he promised to lead them in their migration out of Aztlán. This was spiritual yearning and evolution working hand in hand. They figuratively and literally emerged into the present world, their present time, and they became the "señores of their own time." More literal interpretations have suggested the seven tribes were seven clans who broke the covenant of Aztlán and were expelled; I choose to interpret the legend in the context of world mythology. Leaving the caves of Aztlán was paramount to being born, and with birth came suffering and the migration out of Aztlán to the land promised by their war god. Spiritual aspiration had moved them to form a new covenant with Huitzilopochtli which would sustain them during the long years of migration southward, eventually to found the civilization of Tenochtitlán, present-day Mexico City.

The migration and quest of the original inhabitants of Aztlán can be viewed in the context of world mythology: like the Jews migrating from Egypt in the time of their Exodus to settle in the promised land, the Aztecs migrated south to establish the new nation of Tenochtitlán. These elements of the saga are the stuff of great drama and tragedy. In 1521 Cortés and his Spaniards were to lay siege to the Aztec kingdom and destroy it. But good drama and tragedy rise from the archetypal content of myth, and the time of myth is continuous. For me, the most interesting element in that history is the often-hidden fact that it was those Mesoamerican Indians who later journeyed up the Rio Grande with the Spanish conquistadores; they were returning to their original homeland.

Chicano writers interested in the old legends that revealed our Native American past were drawn to the legend of Aztlán and its meaning. In it we saw a definition of our homeland from a Native American point of view, and we explored that area of history. What and where was the mythic Aztlán? Could the old legends of indigenous America serve a useful purpose in the Chicano Movement? Why did this legend of the indigenous homeland have such an influence on our thinking? We knew that the absorption of the Chicano into the mainstream American culture was occurring so quickly that unless we reestablished the covenants of our ancestors our culture was threatened with extinction. In fact, some suggested that the Chicano community should assimilate into the Anglo-American mainstream and forget its history and language. The concept of a bilingual, bicultural group within the United States was seen as a threat, and in many quarters that view is still held today. The time of crisis for our community demanded a new definition of national unity.

For me, part of the answer lies in an interpretation of human nature and its relationship to myth. Myth is our umbilical connection to the past, to the shared collective memory. After long years spent in the realm of imagination and creativity, I came to understand that many of the symbols that welled up from my subconscious were not learned, they were part of my ethos, symbols from the archetypal memory residing in the blood. Another question intrigued me: our communal relationship with time. The ancestors of the Aztecs had lived through a period of heightened awareness. Were we the Chicanos living through a similar period of time in the 1960s?

I believe the essence of the Chicano Movement was the naming ceremony I have described, and the creation of a cultural nationalist consciousness which brought together our community. This coming together in the naming ceremony duplicated the earlier time in the history of our ancestors. Yes, there was a real Aztlán, but there was also the spiritual Aztlán, the place of the covenant with the gods, the psychological center of our Indian history. During the period of awareness, the collective soul of the group renewed itself through myth; it is what the tribes of humankind have done throughout history.

The communal activity was crucial to the scenario, for myth is a communal response to spiritual crisis. The new consciousness created in the 1960s was a psychological centering, and the possibility of being in touch with our real history was available to each individual. We had become the "señores and the señoras of our own time" in the ceremony of naming, and it is important to stress the role of the Chicana, for the women of our community played a pivotal role in creating the Movement. One only has to look at the literature of the period to read the celebration of Aztlán that we created.

We took a new look at the history of the Indo-Hispano community in the Southwest, a group whose traditions dated back to the sixteenth century and the entry of the Hispanos and Mexicanos into the pueblos of the Río Grande. A unique Indo-Hispano culture had evolved along the northern Río Grande, a product of the process of synthesis which was already at work in Mexico as the Old World and the New World met and merged. The most interesting development of that process was the evolution of the "New World person," the person in touch with the mythology of the Americas which I have explored in my writing.

The same synthesis would not take place when the Anglo-American came to the Southwest in the mid-nineteenth century. The Hispano and Anglo worlds remained apart, meeting to conduct business in an ethnic mosaic, but seldom creating a personal commingling. The genetic pools have not mixed in a significant way, and only in a small way is it occurring in contemporary times. Still, the issue of ethnicity is not static and it is one we need to face creatively.

The established Indo-Hispano culture was based in the villages, but by the 1960s the community was largely an urban group, and so to reconstitute our history during this time of crisis some returned to the villages to look for origins. Another meaningful return was into the history of the Americas where we examined our Indian roots, the soul of the Americas. There we found not only indigenous historical time but mythical time, which is continuous; that discovery was to have a tremendous impact on the healing of our social fabric. In Mesoamerica we encountered the pre-Columbian thought of Mexico. That return to the legends and myths of the New World led the Chicano to Aztlán. In the process of returning to our myths and legends we were not shortsighted idealists that thought the oppression our community suffered would disappear. We knew better, but our search was spiritual in nature, and our community desperately needed the reaffirmation. We had faith that by bringing to light our history, even the esoteric history of myth and legend, we could bring to fruition a cultural renaissance and create a new time of hermandad. That new era of brotherhood would not only unify us, it would unleash the creative potential of the Chicano community.

In the 1960s the same spiritual yearnings and crisis that had concerned the original inhabitants of Aztlán now concerned the Chicanos. A cycle of Chicano history was repeating itself. Our poets and writers became the leaders of the Chicano Movement, and as they brought to focus the aspirations of the people, they took upon themselves a role common to our culture, the role of older, wiser leaders, or ancianos, the role of those señores and señoras who dare to be aware of the burden of time and act to alleviate the burden for the communal good of the people. Needless to say, those same leaders would be criticized when the ambitious goals of the Movement were not fully realized.

A new question arose: Would the promise of continuity and self-actualization inherent in our myths and legends bring with it the fruition of potential and freedom? Could we save our history and community from obliteration within the confines of Anglo-America by reincorporating the old legends into our worldview? Some said no. Myth was ephemeral, it had no substance, it distorted reality. What the Chicanos needed was direct political mobilization, perhaps revolution. They did not need to arm themselves with ancient stories.

Those of us who saw the potential of myth as truth, or myth as self-knowledge, argued that it was indigenous America that held the taproot of our history; its mythology was the mirror by which to know ourselves. Chicanos had to experience a new awareness of self, just as our Native American ancestors had come to that new plane of consciousness eight centuries before in Aztlán, and coming to this knowledge of our historical continuity was a means toward community action.

Aztlán is real because myth is real, we argued. Aztlán was potential because it was a place of prophecy. Migrating groups of Asians, in the process of becoming indigenous Americans, had settled in Aztlán. There they evolved new levels of spiritual orientation to cosmos, earth, and community. Isn't this the process of spiritual and psychological evolution? Isn't this how our human potential evolves? So it happened to these tribes of Native Americans. Somewhere in the deserts and mountains of what we now call the Southwest, they created a covenant with their gods and from there they moved south to Mexico to complete the prophecy.

Of course they did not arrive at full potential, no one ever does. They were still heir to human failure, but we know their later artistic achievements were of a grand scale. Even their warring society would incorporate the religion of peace of Quetzalcóatl. All of Mesoamerica and the tributaries as far north as Chaco and Mesa Verde were, I suspect, renewed during that era. A new age of spiritual illumination had come to the Americas, and the journey from Aztlán to Mexico was part of that tremendous change. From the Pueblos of the Río Grande to Mesoamerica and neighboring tribes, the people of the Americas were evolving into new realms of consciousness.

The need for a homeland is inherent in the collective memory of any group, it is a covenant with the tribal gods. The spiritual yearning for homeland is encompassing, but because the geography of the earth is limited, homelands rub against each other and create friction. We have not yet moved to a new consciousness where the earth truly becomes the homeland of everyone. Perhaps that is our next step in evolution, and perhaps there are already signs that this is happening. Do we as heirs and inhabitants of Aztlán dare to take this next step and consider our homeland without boundaries? Do we dare to reach out and encompass the true spiritual relationship inherent in homeland with every other group who dreams of homeland?

The Indo-Hispano of the Southwest was influenced by the spirituality of the Pueblos of the Río Grande, even though the Catholic faith was imposed on the indigenous faith. There were elements of brutality in the Spanish conquest, this is documented, but the synthesis that was taking place in Mexico between the Old World and the New World was accelerated in Aztlán after the 1680 Pueblo Revolt. The Indo-Hispano religious sensibility was influenced by the Pueblos, and so respect for the earth became an important ingredient in the unique worldview being formed in Aztlán. The recognition of the earth as mother (la sagrada tierra) permeated the spiritual life of the Hispanic villages, and the process of synthesis fused Spanish Catholicism with Native American thought. The clearest symbol of this process of syncretism was the merging of the Virgin Mary with the Indian goddess (Tonantzin) to give form to the brown Madonna of Mexico, La Virgen de Guadalupe.

Truly, an original blend of American spirituality was evolving.

What did all this mean to the real world of politics which the Chicano struggled to enter and influence in the 1960s? Unfortunately, the historical assessment made thus far weighs heavily on a materialistic interpretation. I am convinced that a history of that era and of our culture must take both the sacred and the profane into account. To understand our culture only through a materialistic account will not provide a true picture of the nature of our community. For me, the Chicano Movement succeeded because it changed part of our social and political role within the society, and also because it created a cultural renaissance in the Chicano community. The release of creative energy in which the artists defined self and community was the hallmark of the Movement. The spiritual energy that once filled the consciousness of the original inhabitants of Aztlán and propelled them south to Mexico to fulfill their destiny led us to proclaim our existence and found our nation.

A spirit of liberation swept over our people, releasing a chain reaction of new energy, initiative, and originality. The Movement gave birth to the term "Chicano," the bold new image born of Hispanic and Indian synthesis. To some extent that image penetrated the Anglo-American consciousness, and to some degree it moved onto a world stage. But the image was really for our community, the naming was to renew identity and awareness of our history. The changes wrought in the psyche of the Hispanos of the Southwest by the use of the word "Chicano" were enormous. True, some in our community resisted the naming and to this day do not identify with Chicano, but one cannot deny the positive benefits of reinvigorated pride, especially in artistic creativity, which swept across the land.

The true guardians of Aztlán have been the Rio Grande Pueblo people, and the knowledge and love for their homeland has kept their spiritual thought alive in the face of overwhelming odds. They have kept themselves centered with the earth, and that has provided their communities a spiritual and psychological center. The Chicano, the new raza of the Americas, is heir to the same earth and a legacy of spiritual thought which can help center the individual. In a world so in need of ecological and spiritual awareness which would allow us to save the earth and practice democratic principles of love and sharing, these ties to the earth and the care we must give to this area we call Aztlán still provide hope for our community. We have within us the inner resources to become new guardians of the earth and of peace.

We have seen the blossoming of this potential in our generation. Chicano art, music, and literature have gained a foothold and are shaping new perceptions. Within the arts lie reflections of our values, not only the cultural trappings of the day-to-day world but the old values which spring from our mythologies. Respect for the earth of Aztlán is one of these values, and if we are truly living in an era of a new consciousness, we must reach further into our human potential and consider Aztlán a homeland without boundaries.

This is a most difficult proposal, the idea that we can move beyond our ethnocentric boundaries, that we can envision the limitations of ethnicity even as we extol our self-pride. The argument of survival in our modern world seems to urge us toward the common center of our humanity. When we established our rights to the homeland of Aztlán, we understood that that right belongs to every group or nation, and we understood how we share in all the homelands of world mythology. The children of Aztlán are citizens of the world. We must move beyond the limitations of ethnicity to create a world without borders. Each community rising to its new level of awareness creates respect for self and for others, and we are in need of this awareness before we destroy the earth and each other.

An idealistic, utopian thought? Perhaps, but one we need

to dare to consider. Those who deal in competition and the selfishness of the modern nation-state are in control, and they have falsely named competition and material gain as the true values of the world. Perhaps it's time to think of unity. Aztlán can become the nation that mediates between Anglo-America and Latin America. We can be the leaders who propose human answers to the human problems of the Americas. The real problem of border regions when addressed from a world perspective should be dealt with in human terms, in terms of families and neighbors, not terms of profit or ideology. Unity and human potential should guide us, not market values and the gross national product. This, after all, is the challenge of our generation, to create a consciousness that fosters the flowering of the human spirit, not its exploitation. We need healing in our world community; it can start here.

This is the legacy of Aztlán: it is a place where seven tribes of humankind came to a new awareness of their potential, a new sensitivity in their relationship to earth and cosmos. Here those first inhabitants of Aztlán took their destiny into their own hands, they were born into a new prophecy, and they moved to complete it. Can we do less?

That illumination and leap of faith for those people did not make for perfection. History moves us toward perfection through small epiphanies. The tribes moved out of Aztlán as Adam and Eve moved out of Eden, to challenge the future and to fulfill their potential. Our nature moves us forward, groping for illumination, yearning for a truer knowledge of our spiritual and human relationships. We know within that we can create a more fulfilling and harmonious future. For me, this is the promise of Aztlán.

Take the Tortillas
out of Your Poetry

In a recent lecture, "Is Nothing Sacred?," Salman Rushdie, one of the most censored authors of our time, talked about the importance of books. He grew up in a household in India where books were as sacred as bread. If anyone in the household dropped a piece of bread or a book, the person not only picked up the piece of bread or the book but also kissed the object by way of apologizing for clumsy disrespect.

He goes on to say that he had kissed many books before he had kissed a girl. Bread and books were for his household, and for many like his, food for the body and the soul. This image of the kissing of the book one has accidentally dropped made an impression on me. It speaks to the love and respect many people have for books.

I grew up in a small town in New Mexico, and we had very few books in our household. The first book I remember reading was my catechism book. Before I went to school to learn English, my mother taught me catechism in Spanish. I remember the questions and the answers I had to learn, and I remember the well-thumbed, frayed book that was sacred to me.

Growing up with few books in the house created in me a desire and need for books. When I started school, I remember visiting the one-room library of our town and standing in front of the dusty shelves lined with books. In reality, there were only a few shelves and not over a thousand books, but I wanted to read them all. There was food for my soul in the books, that much I realized.

As a child I listened to the stories of the people, the cuentos the old ones told. Those stories were my first contact with the magic of storytelling. Those stories fed my imagination, and later, when I wrote books, I found the same sense of magic and mystery in writing.

In *Bless Me, Ultima*, my first novel, Antonio, my main character, who has just started to school, sees in books the power of the written word. He calls books the "magic of words."

For me, reading has always been a path toward liberation and fulfillment. To learn to read is to start down the road of liberation. It is a road that should be accessible to everyone. No one has the right to keep you from reading, and yet that is what is happening in many areas in this country today. There are those who think they know best what we should read. These censors are at work in all areas of our daily lives.

Censorship has affected me directly, and I have formed some ideas on this insidious activity, but first, I want to give an example of censorship which recently affected a friend of mine. My friend is a Chicano poet and scholar, one of the finest I know. For some time I have been encouraging Chicano writers to apply for the National Endowment for the Arts literary fellowships. A number of poets who use Spanish and English in their poetry applied but did not receive fellowships; they were so discouraged they did not reapply. This happened to my friend. He is an excellent poet, mature, intelligent, and he has an impressive academic background. He knew that when you apply for a fellowship you take your chances, so he did not give up after being turned down twice. He also knew, we all knew, that many of the panels that judged the manuscripts did not have readers who could read Spanish or bilingual manuscripts. In other words, the judges could not read the poetic language that expresses our reality. My friend rightfully deduced that his poetry was not receiving a fair reading.

"You know," he told me, "if they can't read my bilingual poetry, next time I apply I'm sending them only poems I write in English. My best poetry is bilingual, it reflects our reality, it's the way we speak, the way we are. But if I stand a better chance at getting a fellowship in English, I'll send that. But the poems I write only in English are really not my best work. It's just not me."

I was dismayed by my friend's conclusion. How he coped with the problem has tremendous cultural implications. It has implications that we may call self-imposed censorship. My friend was censoring his creativity in order to fit the imposed criteria. He sent in his poorer work because that was the work the panelists could read, and therefore consider for reward.

My friend had concluded that if he took his language and culture out of his poetry, he stood a better chance at receiving a fellowship. He took out his native language, the poetic patois of our reality, the rich mixture of Spanish, English, pachuco and street talk which we know so well. In other words, he took the tortillas out of his poetry, which is to say he took the soul out of his poetry. He still has not received a fellowship, and many of those other poets and writers I have encouraged to apply for the fellowships have quit trying. The national norm simply does not want to bother reading us.

I do not believe we should have to leave out the crucial elements of our language and culture to contribute to American literature, but, unfortunately, this is a conclusion I am forced to reach. I have been writing for a quarter century, and have been a published author for eighteen years. As a writer, I was part of the Chicano Movement which created a new literature in this country. We struggled to change the way the world looks at Mexican-Americans by reflecting our reality in literature, and many eagerly sought our works, but the iron curtain of censorship was still there.

Where does censorship begin? What are the methods of commission or omission that censorship employs? I analyze my own experiences for answers. Many of my generation still recall and recount the incidents of censorship on the playgrounds of the schools when we were told to speak only English. Cultural censorship has been with us for a long time, and my friend's story suggests it is with us today.

If we leave out our tortillas—and by that I mean the language, history, cultural values and themes out of our literature—the very culture we're portraying will die. Publishing has often forced us to do just that. Trade publishers who control publishing in this country continue to have a very narrow view of the literature of this country. At a time when multicultural diversity is challenging the literary canon of this country, the major publishers still are barely now responding to the literary output of Chicano writers. After twenty-five years of contemporary Chicano writings, there are still only a few Chicano writers who publish with the big trade publishers. Thankfully, there appears to be a change in the air.

The alternative presses of the 1960s were created to contest the status quo. The views of ethnic writers, gay and lesbian writers, and women writers had been consistently censored out of the literary canon. Most of us grew up without ever seeing our identity reflected in the books we read; we knew that had to change.

Twenty years ago when Chicano writers began to create poetry and stories that reflected our contemporary reality, we were met with immediate hostility. The arbiters of literary acceptance immediately branded our works as too political. They complained it wasn't written in English.

Does it speak to the universal reader? they continually asked. Of course the works of the Chicano and Chicana writers were universal, because their subject was the human condition. The problem was that in the view of the keepers of the canon, the human condition portrayed in our literature was Chicano and the keepers knew nothing about us.

And, yes, it was political. All literature, especially poetry and fiction, challenges the status quo. Our literature introduced our history and heritage to American literature. There was a new rhythm, music, and cultural experience in our works, and a view of an ethnic working class that performed the daily work but that was invisible to those in power. Yes, there was a political challenge in the work, it could be no other way. The country had to change, we insisted.

Many refused to listen. Censorship is fear clothed in the guise of misguided righteousness. Censorship is a tool of the powerful who don't want to share their power. Of course, our poetry and literature reflected to our communities our history and our right to exist as a distinct culture. Look at the plays of Luis Valdez and the changes they brought about in the agricultural fields of California. Look at the generation moved to pride and activism by "I am Jaoquin." Even my "nonpolitical" novel, *Bless Me, Ultima*, has moved people to explore the roots of their agrarian, Mexicano way of life. And the healing work of Ultima, a curandera, illustrated to my generation some of our holistic, Native American inheritance.

Free at last! each of our works proclaimed. Every Chicano poem or story carried within it the cry of a desire for freedom and equality. That is what literature should do: liberate. But the status quo does not like liberation. It uses censorship as a tool. As I have suggested, in some cases, it is a thinly veiled censorship. Let me provide another example.

A few years ago, the editor of a major publishing firm asked me to submit a story for a middle school reader.

Those readers have the power to shape how thousands of children think about Mexican-Americans. The criteria were: "It can't have religion in it, it can't be mystical, it can't have Spanish in it." Everything that was in *Bless Me, Ultima* was rejected out of hand before the publisher would look at a manuscript. Needless to say, I didn't submit a story. Like my friend applying for the fellowship, I was censored before I got to first base.

In other cases, the censoring has been direct and brutal. On February 28, 1981, the Alburquerque morning newspaper carried a story about the burning of my novel *Bless Me, Ultima*. The book was banned from high school classes in Bloomfield, New Mexico, and a school board member was quoted as saying: "We took the books out and personally saw that they were burned."

Obviously, my novel did not meet the criteria of the status quo. Using a technique censors often use, they zoomed in on one detail of the novel, the so-called bad words in Spanish, and they used that excuse. Had they read the novel they would have discovered that it is not about profanity. That was never the novel's intent. The novel was a reflection of my childhood, a view into the Nuevo Mexicano culture of a small town. I looked at values, I looked at folkways, I created heroic characters out of poor farmers. I wrote about old healing remedies used by the folk to cure physiological and psychological illness. I elevated what I found in my childhood because that's the way I had experienced my childhood. Poverty and suffering did not overwhelm us, they made us stronger. My novel was my view of the human condition, and it reflected the Mexicanos of New Mexico because that was the community I knew.

What was its threat? I've asked myself over the years. Why did the censors burn *Bless Me, Ultima*? I concluded that those in power in the schools did not want a reflection of my way of life in the school. The country had not yet committed itself to cultural diversity. Fifteen million Chicanos were clamoring at the door, insisting that the schools also belonged to us, that we had a right to our literature in the schools, and the conservative opposition in power fought back by burning our books. Those narrow-minded reactionaries are still fighting us.

The burning of my novel wasn't an isolated example. Every Chicano community in this country has a story of murals being attacked or erased, poets banned from schools, books being inaccessible to our students because they are systematically kept out of the "accepted" textbook lists. We know there are well-organized, well-funded groups in this country that threaten publishers if the editors publish the work of multicultural writers. The threat is simple but often persuasive. Books such groups don't like will not be adopted by the school district where they hold power.

The 1990 attack on the NEA by fundamentalist censors has created a national furor and discussion. Those of us who believe in the freedom of expression have spoken out against this infringement on our right to know. But as Chicanos who belong to a culture still existing on the margin of the mainstream society, and as a community that has struggled to be heard in this country, censorship is not new to us. We have lived with this vicious attack on our freedoms all our lives.

For us, take your tortillas out of your poetry means take your history and way of life out of the poems and stories you create. That is what the censors who burned *Bless Me, Ultima* were telling me. Your literature is a threat to us, we will take it out of the classroom and burn it. We'll say it's the profanity we don't like, but what we really fear is the greater picture. Your view is a multicultural view of this country, and the status quo doesn't like that. We will not share our power.

The threat to keep us subservient did not abate. The English-only movement continued the old censorship we had felt on the school playgrounds, but now the game had moved into the state legislatures. This threat continues to be used against our language, art, and literature.

The struggle for liberation continues. This summer a magazine from New York advertised for subscriptions. Here are quotes from their letter: "There is only one magazine that tells you what is right and what is wrong with our cultural life today." The next quote: "Do you sometimes have the impression that our culture has fallen into the hands of the barbarians?" And, finally, "Are you apprehensive about what the politics of 'multiculturalism' is going to mean to the future of civilization?"

The editor is telling us that he knows what is right or wrong with our cultural life, then goes on to call those that do not fit in his definition barbarians. He then identifies the barbarians as those of us who come from the multicultural communities of this country. We are supposed to have no culture, and so they assign themselves the right to censor. This dangerous and misguided attack of the status quo on our creativity continues.

This type of censorship was focused against the National Endowment for the Arts in the Halls of Congress in 1990. The censors of the far right attacked two or three funded projects because they objected to the content of the works. The censors assumed the right to keep these creative works away from all of us. Censors, I have concluded, are afraid of our liberation. Censorship is un-American, but the censor keeps telling you it's the American way.

Let me return to the theme of bread and books. Tortillas and poetry. They go hand in hand. Books nourish the spirit, bread nourishes our bodies. Our distinct cultures nourish each one of us, and as we know more and more about the art and literature of the different cultures, we become freer and freer. Art is a very human endeavor, and it contains within its process and the objects it produces a road to liberation. The liberation is significant not only to the individual artist, it is a revelation for the community. It is not we who are the barbarians, it is those who have one narrow view which they are convinced is the only right view. Multi-culturalism is a reality in this country, and we will get beyond fear and censorship only when we know more about each other, not when we know less.

I don't know anyone who doesn't like to sample different ethnic foods, just as many of us enjoy sampling (eating) books from different areas of the world. I travel to foreign countries, and I know more about myself as I learn more about my fellow human beings. Censorship imposes itself in my path of knowledge, and that activity can be justified by no one.

On the Education of
Hispanic Children

Hispanics in the United States are well aware that attaining a good education is crucial to the future of our children. In the Southwest, where large communities of Mexican-Americans make their home, the debate is not over how much education we want for our children, since every parent wants the best-quality education available; the question is what form that education should take.

We know the public schools in our country are failing in offering a top-notch educational curriculum to a high percentage of students, especially the Mexican-American youth. Recent reports document an atrocious dropout rate, and reports on the quality of our schools indicate students graduating with little or no reading skills. Many of us continue to ask if there is something in the environment of the school that turns off the Mexican-American child. Why have our children become the objects of these alarming dropout statistics?

We know not only that our future as a cultural group is threatened if our children are not educated but that our role in the future of this country is threatened. The education of our children should be the concern of all of us.

As a lifelong educator, I have argued for years that education must take into account the culture of the individual child. No one can develop his full potential in an uncomfortable environment; one only learns to escape from an uncomfortable environment as quickly as possible.

The first task of the school is to make the child feel secure and safe in the learning environment. This means that the language and cultural background that the child brings to the school should be reflected in the school curriculum and setting. Children should not have to give up their history to partake in a solid education that will prepare them for the future. It is important for parents and grandparents who speak only Spanish to be welcomed to the school so the children can take pride in their affiliation with that school. These parents, who may not yet be as pragmatic as their Anglo-American counterparts, and who possess their own inherent cultural values, are as hopeful as other parents that their children will succeed in school.

My generation was often made to feel ashamed of our language, food, and other cultural values because those values were not reflected in the schoolroom or curriculum. Many still tell me stories of the torment school became for them as recently as the 1950s. That is one reason so many of my generation dropped out. We felt we didn't belong in the school, and I believe that feeling of *not* belonging affects many of our children today.

The educational system has never committed itself to a curriculum that puts an emphasis on learning foreign languages. (Many of us remember being reprimanded for speaking Spanish on the school grounds.) This country has, in a very narrow way, insisted on the monolingual approach in creating its national identity. It has refused to see the value of being multilingual. Students whose native tongue is not English are still told that the monolingual way is best, and that they must give up their native tongue in order to succeed. The English-only movement is a direct result of an effort that encourages children to discount the language of their parents.

We must reverse that narrow and damaging perception of language. Languages are the core of identity and creativity, and they are tools to better world understanding. If we build on the native language the child brings to school, we can not only educate the child in English but sustain the mother language. It is simply better to create multilingual students than monolingual. We must commit our schools to the importance of language study. Every other country in the world does this.

Those who fear diversity in education, and fear that the canon of Western civilization is under attack, continue to belittle efforts to include different languages and histories in the school curriculum. Hispanic/Latino efforts to participate in the school systems have been demeaned, and it is our children who have suffered. Children know when they're not respected, and when they feel they have lost self-respect they leave the schools.

In our Spanish-speaking culture to lose one's respect is to be "sin vergüenza."* Many of my generation were made to feel shame or vergüenza in school because we were different. The burden of feeling shame is very heavy; it makes the individual feel worthless. The schools must respect the cultural background of the children, for otherwise they create a climate of shame which drives the child away.

We want our children to learn English and study Western civilization, but we also see the value in learning many languages and our own history. As Mexican-Americans, we are heirs to those many languages and worldviews that

---

*"Sin vergüenza," literally, is *a person without shame*. To be a person without shame is a negative value in our culture. As children we are told, "Ten vergüenza," have a little shame. That is, don't do anything to ruin the respect of the family name. Put in its positive aspect, the concept teaches the child to be proud of the family name. Be proud, excercise good manners, have respect for the elders, and be polite or you might be labeled sin vergüenza.

connect us not only to Western civilization but to the civilizations of the Americas.

We must not allow our children to feel shame simply because of their cultural background. It is not shameful to be different; rather it is part of the beauty of the cultural diversity of this country. We must insist that quality education for our children in this country include a reflection of their language and history.

I have taught and lectured at many schools and universities. I know children love to learn, and when they feel secure in the learning environment, there are no limits. We know this, and yet Mexican-Americans continue to leave schools at alarming rates; our community cannot afford another generation of dropouts.

We are now engaged in a struggle of immense importance to our future and to the future of the country. Each one of us must make a commitment to that struggle. We understand the power inherent in the educational process, and we know that fulfillment is the birthright of our children. Those who understand that every individual is worthy of fulfilling his or her potential will join us. Ours is a battle of liberation against old oppressions.

We ask educators and parents to join us in this struggle of the 1990s. We will educate our children; that is our commitment. Everyone must be actively engaged in the educational process, as surely as everyone will be affected by the consequences if we continue to allow the horrendous dropout rate of our children.

I now understand why I felt shame for so many years of my life while I was in school. I was told too many times that I didn't belong. I was made to feel (and bigotry works as much in subtle ways as through direct confrontation) that my language and my parents didn't belong. Even as a graduate student, I was still feeling shame because I was constantly reminded I was not like the other students, I did not come to school with an Anglo-American background.

I had to battle that feeling of vergüenza every step of the

way. My family helped me in my struggle, and writing novels and stories reflecting my cultural ways helped me find the pride I needed to continue my education. I knew many of our traditions were beautiful, and that my history was as important as any other. Finally, I realized that shame was not something I was born with, it was a negative feeling put on me by those with prejudice.

Education is liberation. For Hispanics in this country, the 1990s must be a decade of educational enchancement and advancement. We must open the doors to the schools, and insist that not only the resources be made available to our children, but that the sense of shame they are made to feel should be expunged. Discrimination against ethnic groups, that insidious discrimination that creates shame in the child, must be eradicated forever.

We need our language and our history taught in the schools, and we need important role models with which the children can identify. We need more parents involved in the schools. We know our literature, language, and history will enrich the curriculum and help provide a positive environment in which learning can take place.

The Censorship
of Neglect

The theme of the 1991 NCTE convention in Seattle was the freedom to teach and to learn. In a country that is finally acknowledging its multicultural nature, the idea proved engaging. I want to examine this theme from my point of view as a Mexican-American educator and writer.

I have taught English language and literature for twenty-five years in this country, and I know that we have not been free to teach. The literary history of this country has been shaped by forces far beyond the control of the classroom teacher. Our curriculum has been controlled by groups with a parochial view of what the curriculum should and should not include. These groups include teachers who hold narrow views of what literature should be, publishers who control what is printed, and politicians who defend their particular social and political interests. These groups represent the status quo and call themselves "universalists." For a long time these groups have told us they know what is universal in literature, and this has translated into a course of action that has kept the ethnic literatures of this country out of the curriculum.

The time for that narrow view to be exposed is now, and the time for us to take charge and implement into the curriculum the many literatures of this country is today.

For generations, freedom to learn has meant reading only the very narrow spectrum of literature proposed to us by the universalists. Most of us know there is no literature with a capital L. There are many literatures, and our country is rich with them. And yet most of us have succumbed to the pressures brought to bear by those in power.

Folk wisdom says, you can lead a horse to water, but you can't make it drink. You can lead students to books, but if the content doesn't engage them, they lose interest and soon become dropouts. My experience, and the experience of many teachers I know, have taught me that part of the cause for our alarming dropout statistics is this narrow, circumscribed curriculum in language and literature. To reverse these deplorable dropout statistics and to help create a positive self-image in our students, I firmly believe we need to present the literatures that reflect our true diversity.

The literature of the barrio, of the neighborhood, of the region, of the ethnic group, can be a useful tool of engagement, a way to put students in touch with their social reality. What is pertinent to our personal background is pertinent to our process of learning. And so, if students are going to be truly free to learn, they must be exposed to stories that portray their history and image in a positive manner. They must be given the opportunity to read the literatures of the many different cultures of our own country.

That we are free to teach is a myth. We know every nation has a vested interest in perpetuating the myth of national unity and coherence. We know there is a social and political intent behind the concept of national unity. Those who hold political power in this country have used it to try to create a homogenous, monolithic curriculum. That intent betrays the many communities that compose this country because it denies their histories.

This country cannot continue on this limited path and serve its people. Those in power can no longer be allowed to believe they are the sole possessors of the truth. I believe I represent, as a Chicano writer, part of that truth. Every educator represents part of that truth. We are tired of being told that we do not understand the needs of our youth because we belong to a particular ethnic group. We are told that because we are Mexican, Native, black, or Asian-American—or women—somebody else has the right literature and language to describe our reality. Each of our communities has much to teach this country. Each barrio, each neighborhood, each region, men and women, all have a vested interest in education, and it's time we made that interest known.

We have not been free to teach. We have accepted the literature that is presented to us by publishers, those producers of books who have a direct link and a vested interest in the status quo. Big publishers have neglected or refused to publish the literature of minority communities of our country; their lack of social responsibility has created a narrow and paternalistic perspective of our society. The true picture of this country is not narrow: it is multidimensional; it reflects many communities, attitudes, languages, beliefs, and needs. Our fault, as teachers, is that we have accepted the view of those in charge: teacher-training programs, publishers, politicians, and sectarian interests.

And yet we know better. We know one approach is not best for all; we know we have to incorporate the many voices of literature into the curriculum.

It is time to ask ourselves some tough questions. Exactly what literature are we teaching in classrooms? Who writes it? What social reality does it portray? Who packaged it for us? How much choice do we really have as teachers to step outside this mainstream packaging and choose books? Who provides the budget? Who calls the shots?

I raise this issue and try to analyze and understand it from my experience. I am a native son of the Mexican-

American community of New Mexico, a member of the broader Hispanic population of the country. When I published my first novel in the early seventies, I was part of the Chicano literary movement. We asked ourselves then the same questions we are still asking today.

We knew then that the desire to form a monolithic social reality that served those in power was very costly in human terms. We knew the oral and written literature of Native Americans had been neglected. It was never in the curriculum I studied. Even the better known African-American writings have not been a consistent part of our undergraduate education. Chicano literature, in a country that has over fifteen million Mexican-Americans, is still virtually unknown in the classroom.

Our community stretches from California to Texas, and into the Northwest and Midwest. But not one iota of our social reality, much less our aesthetic reality, is represented in the literature read in the schools.

Where is our freedom to teach? Who trained us, or brainwashed us, to the point that we cannot see fifteen million people? The teachers of this country cannot see, I mean that literally, the children of fifteen million people. That is how strong the censorship of neglect has been. That is why I say we have not been free to teach.

Living within the confines of a mainstream culture has caused me to look at this idea of cultural and self-identity. You have to ask yourselves the same question: How do your students create their self-image? Specifically, what role do the school and the curriculum play in the formation of identity? Literature is one of the most humanistic endeavors used to reflect back to readers their own images. And yet until very recently the image, and therefore the history, of the Mexican-American was missing from the spectrum of literature. Most teacher-training programs and departments of English still refuse to admit the presence of the ethnic literatures of this country. Much of that training never teaches the diverse stories of the country, and so the teachers who go into the classroom are never really "free to teach."

Reading is the key to a liberated life. We must take action to wrest our freedom to teach from those forces that still don't acknowledge the existence of the multidimensional and multicultural realities of our country. We must infuse into the study of language and literature the stories of the many communities that compose our country.

The cost of having denied these many voices their rightful role in the study of language and literature has been enormous. The ethnic communities of this country have suffered the loss in human terms for many generations. We see the loss each day, and it hurts us. Now the loss is being felt in monetary terms by business and government agencies, and perhaps this is what will wake up this country. Our children who go into the world unprepared to deal with real-life experiences, our children lost to dope and prisons and those who suffer from poor images of themselves, are all a costly burden. Our ideal to be free to teach is based on our desire to enlighten humanity, our desire to contribute to a better world. Now, belatedly, those in power are waking up and seeing the devastation their universalist, colonialist approach has caused. Now they awaken and produce token changes in education, not because they are interested in freedom for the individual, but because they understand that an uneducated populace is not good for the business of the country.

Our diverse communities are rightfully demanding to be included in the curriculum of language and literature courses. This is perceived as a threat to those who want to keep the status quo, those who want to stay in power. There is a very strong element among writers and educators who insist that the ethnic writers of this country are not writing according to universalist guidelines that have been established. We, the people of the multiple communities of this country, no longer trust, nor do we believe, those who hold that view. We will no longer be demeaned and lose our students to that view. Our challenge is to incorporate into the curriculum all the voices of our country. Old worldviews have been crumbling since the advent of the twentieth century. Change and new views of reality must be acknowledged. And yet educators have resisted the formation of the new multidimensional world. Why?

Have we become the problem itself? Have we become the defenders of the status quo? Is it really we who have refused to see the reality of the African-American experience, the Chicano world, the Asian-American struggle, the woman's search for her own self-representation? Are we free to teach when we fear the social and aesthetic reality of other groups?

If you are teaching in a Mexican-American community, it is your social responsibility to refuse to use the textbook that doesn't contain stories by Mexican-American authors. If you teach Asian-American children, refuse the textbook that doesn't portray their history and social reality. This kind of activism will free you to teach. If you don't refuse, you are part of the problem. But you don't have to be teaching in a Mexican-American barrio to insist that the stories and social reality of that group be represented in your textbook. You shortchange your students and you misrepresent the true nature of their country if you don't introduce them to all the communities who have composed the history of this country. To deny your students a view into these different worlds is to deny them tools for the future.

The future is only going to get more complex. We need better and more educated answers to a plethora of issues that face us. The old, one-dimensional, narrow view of the world hasn't worked and will not work. It was kept in place by power that sacrificed human potential. We cannot applaud the liberation the eastern European countries have recently achieved and still espouse a colonial mentality when it comes to teaching in this country. We cannot applaud the democratization of the Soviet Union if we still believe a monolithic, iron fist must rule our curriculum. Wake up, America. We are a diverse country, let us be free to teach that diversity.

La Llorona,
El Kookoóee,
and Sexuality

In *Bless Me, Ultima*, my first novel, I looked at my childhood through the eyes of a novelist. In the process of writing the novel, I explored childhood experiences, dreams, folklore, mythology, and communal relationships that shaped me in my formative years. Writing became a process of self-exploration.

Why is childhood so important? During childhood one undergoes primal experiences, and one responds to experience directly and intuitively. The child occupies the space of first awareness, and thus the child is closer in spirit to the historical dawning of first awareness of humankind on earth. The child is a storyteller who assigns roles; the child is a mythmaker.

I grew up on the banks of the Pecos River in eastern New Mexico, and as a child I spent a great deal of my free time along the river, and in the hills and lakes that surrounded the small town of Santa Rosa. In the 1940s the town was going through wrenching changes brought on by World War II, but it was still, in many ways, immersed in an ambience created by the first settlers of the valley generations before. For the Nuevo Mexicanos of the valley, the heritage was the Spanish language, the Catholic religion, and the old folkways preserved by the farmers from villages like Puerto de Luna, where my grandfather lived.

I am grateful for the cultural and natural environment in which I lived as a child, because the ambience provided me with a set of values that have served me all my life. Growing up along the river taught me that nature is indeed imbued with a spirit. One of my first awarenesses of this was the wailing cry I heard one afternoon along the river. My mother told me it was the spirit of La Llorona, the wailing woman of legend who wandered the river in search of her lost children. This fearful figure of our folktales was the first ghost in the bush that I encountered as a child.

Later, as I grew and expanded my territory, I made the journey with my boyhood friends to the Hidden Lakes. In the hills of the llano I felt the spirit of nature throb with life; I heard the voices on the wide plain and in the darker solitude of the lakes and river. Some of the ghosts were communal figures that were part of the Hispanic and Native American folktales. These characters from the folktales had names and personalities; they lived in the oral tradition. Others were more personal spirits which we as children created when we told stories; they were our ghosts, our childhood entry into mythmaking.

Because I grew up in a Catholic household, I was taught that life had a meaning. Later in life I began to understand that as we mature we question meaning, and we learn to construct new answers to the questions of life. Growing up in a Catholic family meant I spent a lot of time trying to understand the nature of God. The traditions of my ancestors and the church helped shape my knowledge as I grew into young manhood.

One of the most important rites of passage that children experience is the awareness of their sexuality. We are sexual creatures, and much of our identity is tied up with our sexuality. Sexuality was not discussed in our home or school, and in the religious arena it was only associated with sin. As I grew into young manhood there was no one to explain the new realm of sexual awareness. Many years later I realized that there were characters in the cultural stories that had a direct relation to sexuality. These folk characters were there to teach sexual taboos. To understand that important time in my life, I returned to childhood and analyzed the role of two such folk figures whose stories seem intricately tied to sexuality.

I hope to shed some light on childhood sexuality by looking at these two figures from our Nuevo Mexicano folklore, a folklore that is part of the wider Hispanic culture of Las Américas. We know that if repressed or made a fearful thing by narrow rules, sexual awareness can be stifled. If the rites of passage into one's sexuality are understood, that understanding can enhance one's positive sense of identity.

Everything in the universe is related; we are all connected; from stardust to human flesh, we vibrate with the same elements of the universe. The web of life is infused by spirit, and each one of us has the power to use that creative energy to manifest our potential. This light that shines within can extend itself to others, and thus we very early learn about love and caring, kindness and joy, and we also learn that using this energy we have within, we can overcome the negative obstacles in our path.

In life we move from one level of awareness to the next, one identity to the next. Growing into the new levels of awareness in our journey is not just a function of aging, it also means growing in understanding. When there is a crisis of self-identity, we attempt to shed light on the passage. That struggle to know one's self is the crux of life.

The stories of the folk tradition helped me in that search, but I know now that my time to learn the truth embedded in the stories that dealt with sexuality was interrupted. With time the figures in the stories would have made sense, but at age seven I entered the Anglo-American school system and began to lose touch with the folk material of my culture. Long after, as a grown man, I had to return to the stories to understand what they had to teach me.

Some of the stories of the folk tradition told of the monsters that existed in the bush, and because I was to spend so much time in the hills, lakes, and river of my native town, I listened closely. It is in the bush that we encounter the darkness that assails our spirit. In the bush exist the monsters of our legends and myths, the ghosts of the communal stories. The spirits and monsters of the bush are creations of our minds, both the communal psyche and the personal. Awareness and coming to a new consciousness are steps toward maturity, and the stories can serve as guideposts.

For us Nuevo Mexicanos growing up in the Spanish-speaking villages, the cuentos of the folk tradition related the adventures of heroes who overcame the monsters, and through these stories it was possible to understand the role of the ghosts in the stories.

The historical role of the storyteller has been to characterize these monsters. We all have monsters to conquer, ghosts to confront in the bush. Today the bush has become the dangerous urban streets, the corporate boardroom, or the bedroom, but the folk stories have such a strong hold on the psyche that they serve us even in these new settings. When we understand the monsters within, we know ourselves better.

My childhood environment was a primal setting; it was the river and its bosque. There, under the canopy of the gigantic cottonwood, Russian olive, and tamarisk trees I met my ghosts. I traveled deeper and deeper into the river darkness, always full of fear, because the presence of the monsters was palpable. My ghosts were real. The cry of the doves became the moan of La Llorona; the breeze shifting shadows in the dark paths where I walked could be the monstrous figure of El Coco, the bogeyman of our stories.

In the oral tradition of my folklore, La Llorona and El

Coco, or Cucúi (Kookoóee, as I spell the name to fit the sound), were well known. I heard many stories about these two monsters, sitting by the warm stove of my mother in her safe kitchen when family or visitors told stories. And at the end of the stories the warning for us children was always the same: "Be good, be careful, or La Llorona will get you. Don't stay out late at night or El Coco will get you." These two figures put fear in our hearts; the folk were warning us about something. Was it only about staying out late at night? Or was there a deeper meaning in the stories of these two figures?

Sometimes in the warm summer nights the gang of boys I grew up with stayed out late, in the hills or by the river, and we would build a fire and tell stories. We began to talk about women, or the young girls we knew at school, and we bragged about our newfound sexual powers. We told stories about witches and monsters, and the two favorite stories were about the well-known figures La Llorona and El Cucúi.

When we left the warmth and safety of the fire, we had to walk home in the dark, which was full of sounds and shapes and lurking figures. Then someone would shout that he saw something move in the dark; any shadow could become one of the dreaded ghosts. "¡La Llorona!" was a cry of terror which turned our blood to ice. Oh, how we ran. I was safe only after I entered my home, the sanctuary that held the proper Christian fetishes to ward off the evil spirits of the night.

Sometimes I found myself alone in the dusk along the river when I had to go down to the river to cut wild alfalfa for our milk cow. I would work fast and hard; I didn't want to be there when darkness engulfed the river. At that haunting time, the presence of the river came alive. The ghosts of the bush walked in the shadows. I felt fear, dread—real emotions which I had to understand and conquer. I had been warned: Hurry home or La Llorona will get you!

I did meet La Llorona, and I did meet El Kookoóee. There in the darkness of the bushes of my river, I met them more than once. The ghosts of the bush are real, whether we explain them as projections of our psyche or a creation of communal oral tradition; when you meet them in the dark and you are a child, you know they are real!

La Llorona, according to legend, had killed her children and drowned them in the river. There are hundreds of variations on the story, but the point is she gave birth to illegitimate children. She broke a rule of the tribe. She was jilted or cast away by the man who fathered her children, and in her rage at being used she killed the children. Her penance was to wander the banks of the river looking for the children she drowned.

El Kookoóee was a masculine ghost, more nebulous, larger and more powerful, but as frightful as La Llorona. He was the father figure who warned the male child of the dangers inherent in sexual awareness and practices. A friend told me that when he was a child he was told to hurry back from the outhouse. "The Cucúi will get you," was the warning. He was being warned not to take time to play with himself.

One ghost is feminine, the other masculine; both are there to warn the child not to indulge in sexual practices. I didn't know that then, I only knew I was aware of, and fascinated by, my new sexual world. Unfortunately, there was no one with whom to discuss my new feelings. Sex was sin, the priest at the church said. I sensed there was something in the story of La Llorona that would help me understand my change. I was drawn to La Llorona; I felt I had something to learn from her. She was, after all, a mother. Was I her child? How? What secret did she have to reveal to me?

Was she a product of the fear of sexuality of the elders of the tribe? Was she created to keep me from the sexual desires and fantasies that began to fill my world? They had made a monster out of her and banished her to the river, where I spent my time with my friends. After we swam we rested naked on the warm sandbars and spun myth after sexual myth.

In the evenings when we played hide-and-seek with the neighborhood girls, the awareness of sexuality was overwhelming. We ran to hide with the girls, to be close for a moment and to touch them. The girls whispered, "You're not supposed to touch, or that might make babies." Even kissing might make babies in that mysterious world of sex about which we knew so little. As the evening grew darker our parents called us in. "Cuidao. La Llorona anda cerca." La Llorona lurks nearby.

Now I know that those old men who condemned sexuality and insisted that we fear that natural part of our lives created the spirit of La Llorona. As a child I was on the brink of awareness that would shed light on my entry into young manhood. La Llorona and El Kookoóee were playing a part in my passage into sexual identity.

El Kookoóee was the father ghost, the old abuelo who rose up from the shadows. He was so powerful, I knew he could eat me alive, tear at my flesh, devour me. He sought my unquestioning obedience, he was a deity who allowed no transgressions. He was a reflection of the fathers of the village who warned me of sexual taboos. Perhaps it was more than masturbation the elders feared; the taboo of incest was also hidden in the warning.

Both folklore figures had a proper role to play, which were to teach me sexual taboos. Did they have to be so fearful? My guess is that most figures in the legends and mythology that are used to teach sexual taboos are fearful creatures. Their role is to frighten the young and to keep them within the fold of family, community, and religious dogma.

At each stage of life we enter different awarenesses of our sexuality, and that sexuality is so closely tied to the energy that connects us to others that it is crucial to understand those new awakenings of body and soul. Understanding is liberation, and when I finally understood the meaning of those childhood ghosts I understood myself better. But understanding did not come in one epiphany, it came over many years of searching—a search not yet done.

My childhood was shaped by a worldview that has a long history in the valleys of New Mexico, but at age seven when I first attended school I discovered a new universe. The society of the school knew nothing about my world, it knew nothing about La Llorona and El Kookoóee. They taught me about a gnome who lived under a bridge, a monster who would devour the Billy Goats Gruff if they dared to cross the bridge to greener meadows. (The figure of the goat is appropriate. It has come to be a symbol of sexuality or lust.) Of course I knew it was really La Llorona who lived under the bridge that I crossed every day on my way from my home on the hill into town. I heard the older kids whisper as we crossed the bridge. Lovers had spent a few moments under the bridge, by the banks of the river. The evidence of the night's passion for high school students was there. They dared, I thought, to enter the world of sex in the very home of La Llorona and El Kookoóee. Weren't they afraid? Sex was supposed to be fearful.

Awakening into the world of sexuality was not easy; it was a fearful journey. The ghosts of the bush were there to warn us of our indiscretions, and the strict rules of the church were there to punish us. It was, after all, the patriarchal church that ostracized La Llorona for her sin.

In school I read the story of the Headless Horseman which Ichabod Crane met one fearful night. This Headless Horseman was like my Kookoóee, but the headless wonder was tame compared to El Coco. I knew about El Kookoóee, and what Ichabod experienced in one night I had already experienced many times. In my time of awakening sexuality, in that crucial time which was a crisis of identity, I had already met the taboo ghosts of my culture.

On the feminine side, the two characters I remember

from school storybooks are Snow White and Cinderella. Both young girls were feared by the older, uglier stepmothers. Both young heroines are enslaved by the taboos of the older women. Both will eventually free themselves, and the stories have a happy ending. There is no happy ending to the story of La Llorona. She comes from a Catholic world, and breaking the taboo has finality to it. She is condemned to search for her children forever.

Was I, the boy coming into the awareness of my expanding sexual world, to be part of her condemnation? If I did not heed the warnings of my group, would I also become an outcast? The writer I was to become would question everything, and I would eventually break with some of the narrow ways of my community. I was destined to leave the strict, dogmatic teachings of the church.

My first sin was insignificant and natural; I broke a taboo in the youthful epiphany of masturbation. I became a confidant of La Llorona, and like her, I had no one in whom to confide. We were both sinners, doomed to wander outside the proscribed rules.

During my elementary schooling I realized the school was unaware of the centuries of oral tradition of my New Mexican culture. The school system didn't acknowledge the ghosts of the bush which I knew so well. The stories of La Llorona and El Kookoóee were never told in the classroom; there was no guide to lead us through our folktales. I was not helped to understand the meaning of my own world.

The schools did not deem important my oral tradition and the stories of my ancestors that came from that tradition. I worked my way through a graduate degree, and never did I hear the stories of my culture in the curriculum. The school was telling me that my folkways and stories were not important enough to be in the classroom. A very important part of my identity was never acknowledged.

Some will say there is no great loss at losing the stories

of these ghosts in the bush I have described, but I insist they are crucial in the maintenance of culture. As these folk figures of the culture disappear, the culture that created them also is lost. And because El Kookoóee and La Llorona deal directly with the world of sexuality, they are not mere stories to frighten children, they are archetypal characters which speak forcefully about self-awareness and growth.

We bring the mythic characters of our folktales to the classroom. We need wise teachers to help the children understand their growth during their critical years. After all, the stories were created to teach values. The story of La Llorona and El Kookoóee have much to teach us. In the reading circle a good teacher can lead the children into illuminating revelations about the role of these figures. Teaching can be an open process of revelation, not one that fears the intimate areas of growth. An open, accepting process is far better than one that favors fear and whispered interpretations.

We should learn the oral traditions of many tribes, of many places of the world. It was important for me to learn about the gnome and the Headless Horseman and Snow White and Cinderella, because the stories were a window into the culture that created the stories. The more stories I learned, the closer to the truth I got, the more liberated I became, the more I realized the common problems that beset all of us.

I understand that culture often disappears in small pieces. When the children no longer know La Llorona or El Kookoóee stories, a very important ingredient of our culture is lost, and we will be forced to look for those ingredients in foreign cultures. Part of my role as a writer is to rescue from anonymity those familiar figures of my tradition. I wrote a book, *The Legend of La Llorona*, a novella that describes, from my point of view, the trials and tribulations of the New World wailing woman, the Malinche of Mexico. In this love story I not only looked into the motives of the lovers, Cortés and Malinche, but I also analyzed the political and cultural impact of the Old World conquest on the New World.*

But what of the Kookoóee? Were the children learning about this bogeyman of our culture? Was one more element of our folk culture about to disappear? Was the old bogeyman already gone?

In the summer of 1990 I gathered together a group of Chicano artists in Albuquerque. I proposed to them that we build an effigy of El Kookoóee and burn it at a public fiesta. The artists responded to the idea enthusiastically. No one knew what El Kookoóee looked like, but given our creativity, we came up with sketches and began to build the sixteen-foot-high effigy. He had rooster's feet, some said, so that's what we put on him, and long arms with huge hands, and his head was big and round with red eyes and a green chile nose. His teeth were sharp, his fangs yellow and long. Matted hair full of weeds fell to his shoulders. He carried a large bag, so we decided to have each child write his or her fear on a piece of paper and put it in the bag. When the effigy was burned those fears would go up in smoke. The same cleansing effect stories have was duplicated in the burning of the effigy.

We drew together as a community to re-create one of our ghosts of the bush, the bogeyman of our childhood. We re-created El Kookoóee, told stories about him as we worked, and made sure the children understood the effigy and the stories of the old bogeyman. We re-created a cultural figure many thought was insignificant, and in so doing we understood the role of El Kookoóee better. A deep feeling of community evolved; we were no longer alienated artists working alone, we were a group with common roots.

When we burned the effigy one evening in October at a community festival in the South Valley of Albuquerque,

---

*Malinche was a very intelligent Native American woman from the east coast of Mexico. She spoke native Mexican languages and Spanish, and thus became the consort of Cortés, the conqueror of Mexico. In *The Legend of La Llorona* I suggest that she is the first llorona of the New World.

over five hundred people attended. People gathered to look at the effigy, and they remembered stories they had heard as children. They began to tell the stories to their children.

The children were the winners. Unlike my generation's experience at school, they saw that the stories from their culture were worthy of artistic attention. As the sun set and the Kookoóee went up in flames, we realized that we had created a truly moving, communal experience. We had taken one character out of the stories of our childhood and rescued him from anonymity.

After the burning of the effigy, I began to look closer at the role of this ghost of the bush in my childhood. El Kookoóee and La Llorona are not only connected to the awareness of sexuality; they resonate with many other deeper meanings. But to understand those meanings we have to pass on the stories, we have to re-create the characters in our time, and we have to make the schools aware of their importance. For us, building and burning the effigy of El Kookoóee helped validate an element of our cultural ways. Nothing is too insignificant to revive and return to the community if we are to save our culture. We can rescue ourselves.

We still have much to teach this country, for we have a long history and many stories to tell. The stories from our tradition have much to tell us about the knowledge we need in our journey. We need to get our stories into the schools, as we need the stories of many different ways of life. We need to be more truthful and more sensitive with each other as we learn about the complexity that comes with growth. It is futile and wasteful to depend on only one set of stories to learn the truth. There are many stories, many paths, and they are available to us in our own land.

Bendíceme, América

May the spirit of our ancestors watch over us as we enter the new century. May we walk in the path of beauty. Now it is our turn as poets and writers to take the breath of life, these words that are our gift, and bless the earth and people of the Americas. In the midst of the pain and the atrocities we commit on one another, in the enslavement of the worst oppression, we must remember the blessing. As long as we can draw breath to bless one another, we are still human.

Bendíceme, América. We ask the blessing of the earth, in return. O ravaged earth, O Eden we have trampled, O paradise we have filled with greed and hate and murder, bless us. Forests we have burned and llanos we have plowed, bless us. O sky we have polluted, bless us with your rain and kind breezes. It is the earth that nurtures us. Our mother, Las Américas, bless us.

Let us resolve with this blessing that we will commit our hearts and souls to the earth and the people of these continents. To the guardian spirit of the Americas, to the grandfather and all the deities of our people, to the sacred directions, we turn and ask for blessing. Center us in joy, in harmony, so we may act with purpose this day and during the difficult years ahead.

The history of the Americas tells us many things. We know that in 1492, the Old World met the New. And at once began the exploitation and colonization of these lands, which became a battleground for the souls and bodies of the Native Americans. We know, too, that the Eurocentric view has always been challenged by the indigenous cultures on which it was imposed—as it is being challenged today. And by those who have not had a voice in shaping their own destinies, the quincentennial is being celebrated as five hundred years of resistance. We, the many communities of the Americas, are the heirs of that long legacy. Today we must raise our voices to proclaim our various identities. We must demand an active role in determining the direction this hemisphere will take in our generation and in the future.

What should the quincentennial mean to us? There are fundamental issues facing the citizens of the Americas today: We must protect basic human rights. We must help formulate the hemisphere's economic policies. And we must champion the cause of democracy. We need to take part, as well, in the new age of technology and information, and understand how this new age affects our children. And yet we need to protect the resources of the earth.

In this sector of the globe, a very small percentage of the population consumes the majority of the products, while many suffer in poverty. This year can be a time of activism during which all groups work at better understanding one another. The walls of separation must come down. The hermandad of the Americas must be proclaimed. Let us seek to establish fellowship and peace. Let us help instill a new pride in our children so they can face the coming millennium with confidence.

For five hundred years, another people's way of seeing the world became the dominant interpretation of history throughout North and South America. Indigenous histories were destroyed, and educational systems were remodeled on those of Europe. That Eurocentric view failed to portray the essence of our diverse civilizations. Now is the time for us to acknowledge and proclaim the true multicultural nature of the Americas. To listen to the many voices of the Americas.

Eduardo Galeano, in *The Book of Embraces*, reminds us of an African proverb: until lions have their own historians, histories of the hunt will glorify the hunter. The hunters who wrote the histories of the Americas have glorified the European perspective. And in the meantime, the chronicles of our peoples have been neglected, lost, even systematically obliterated. Now we must be the lions who rediscover right and redress the balance. Now we must restore and take pride in our own histories.

Each cultural group of the Americas must tell and write its stories and inform the world of its many accomplishments. One often hears that those who do not know their history are doomed to repeat it. Lest we subject our children to the oppression endured by their ancestors, we must teach them to be lions who are familiar with their past and who can wisely chart a course through the decades ahead.

Such knowledge will help foster a spirit of liberation. All of our communities have played a role in building the Americas, yet the efforts of many have not been acknowledged. When people recount their achievements, they create and inspire pride. That is why our children need to hear our voices. That is why our histories need to be read in the schools. Only in this way will our offspring be empowered to introduce a new vision of the Americas—one that transcends the offenses of the past.

At a gathering of writers in Managua, Nicaragua, during the summer of 1989, I heard Eduardo Galeano tell a story. A child is being born on an isolated ranch. By the time the doctor arrives, the mother is near death. It is a breech delivery, and the baby's body lies twisted in its mother's womb. The doctor does not think the child is alive, until its hand reaches out and grabs his fingers. The baby wants to live. And so the doctor goes to work and completes the delivery.

This, Galeano tells us, represents the birth of the Americas, a birth that took place in the midst of the cataclysm of 1492. Born into the exploitation, poverty, and pain of workers, that child nevertheless showed a tenacity for life. Against all odds, the Americas were born, survived, and became the mother we know.

From Tierra del Fuego to the Arctic Circle, our mother is known by many names, and she has herself given birth to many nations. Our mother, the Americas, has a history—or rather, many histories, which we are obliged to celebrate. And I am not speaking only of the past five hundred years, but also of the time before Columbus's crossing. For the roots of our own histories lie in those of the indigenous people of the Americas. Each one of us can help write a new and complete account of our past. And the more we learn from one another, the more encompassing our vision of the future will become.

This willingness to learn the multicultural story of our land and cultures will help us deal with the real issues of life. As we know ourselves, we recognize our beauty. The old class and color distinctions must be eradicated. We cannot liberate one another if we do not first liberate ourselves.

Many of the voices of the Americas have been repressed. But there is change in the air. New songs are being sung, new stories told. New battles for human decency are daily being fought. During our own time, writers from many oppressed nations have spoken out. Mothers have marched in the streets against unjust governments. They are the lions, pointing the way for us to follow. Together, then, let us take command of our destinies and make our voices heard.

PLAYS
AND
POEMS

Who Killed Don José?

Who Killed Don José? opened on July 24, 1987, at the Menaul School in Albuquerque, produced by La Compañía de Teatro de Alburquerque, Irene Oliver-Lewis, Producer/ Artistic Director, and Daniel Ortega, Executive Director. The premiere was directed by Dr. Jorge Huerta, scenic design by José García, lighting design by Sergio Palermo, costume design by Leslie Wood, sound design by Vicente Silva and Maria Villaverde of COMUN, stage-managed by José Medina. The cast, in order of appearance:

TONY	Gene Ornelas
MARÍA	Yvonne C. Orona
DON JOSÉ	Michael David Blum
DOÑA SOFÍA	Angie Torres
DIEGO	Pete García
ANA	Elena Citlali Parres
RAMÓN	Joseph Andrade
SHERIFF	Durand García

Rudolfo A. Anaya and
Who Killed Don José?

We are the New World.
—LUIS VALDEZ

In the summer of 1980, during a sight-seeing trip to London, Rudolfo and Patricia Anaya attended Agatha Christie's famously long-running dramatic mystery *The Mousetrap*. Walking from the theatre into the West End's busy streets, Anaya turned to his wife and said, "I could write a Chicano *Mousetrap*!" A half decade later, he began *Who Killed Don José?*, a "whodunit" in which the title character, shot at the first act curtain, returned at the play's end to expose his enemies and marry his mistress. After several years of revisions and roundtable arguments over its plot, theme, characters, and ending, *Who Killed Don José?* was produced by La Compañía de Teatro de Alburquerque and directed by Jorge Huerta, a historian and director of Chicano theatre from the University of California, San Diego. The play's premiere production had only a limited artistic success, but it ran for three weeks to good houses in the summer of 1987.

Even as Anaya gained a national reputation as a Chicano novelist during the 1970s, he frequently alluded to a youthful desire to write for the stage. The artistic director of La Compañía de Teatro de Alburquerque, José Rodríguez, reawakened that desire in 1979 by commissioning *The Legend of La Llorona* as part of *A New Mexican Trilogy*.

Soon thereafter, Anaya wrote *Rosa Linda*, a full-length tragedy of blood and sex on the llano which was developed into a film script under a grant from the Public Broadcasting Service in 1982. (It remains unproduced in any form.) Then Anaya wrote a one-act play, *Death of a Writer*, which probed the controversies and contradictions of today's Chicano culture. Since *Don José*, he has continued to write for the stage: La Compañía presented his Christmas story, *The Farolitos of Christmas*, in a dramatic adaptation for the 1987 holiday season, and during 1988, a new play entitled *Matachines* made the rounds of his friendly readers. He has written no piece for the theatre as hilarious as the Christmas play sequence of his first novel, *Bless Me, Ultima*, but Anaya has been writing drama uninterruptedly for the past decade.

His scriptwriting has been part of a determined effort to stretch himself as an artist during the 1980s. After finishing his trilogy of novels—*Bless Me, Ultima* (1972), *Heart of Aztlán* (1976), and *Tortuga* (1979)—he embarked on one surprise after another. "I tend to get tagged as a person who should be writing more about the folklore of New Mexico," he told an interviewer at the time of *Don José*'s premiere. "But I've always tried new genres. I did the epic poem in 'The Adventures of Juan Chicaspatas' . . . I did a journal, *A Chicano in China*, that's a completely different form in a completely different country. And then the logical conclusion of toying with the theatre and TV is this play." Such diversity reflects Anaya's personal independence, his ornery resistance to political and cultural consensus. "I get a kick out of doing things that I know people will respond to, especially critics," he says.

But his experimenting is also part of the increasing sophistication of Chicano literary culture, which has traveled a great distance since its urgent political beginnings in the fields and barrios of the mid-1960s. Jorge Huerta, who has chronicled the entire development of Chicano drama, found *Who Killed Don José?* intriguing because "I've never seen

a Chicano play about a wealthy Hispanic." The artistic
director of La Compañía, Irene Oliver-Lewis, produced the
play for similar reasons: "I wanted to break stereotypic
images of what New Mexicans are. We live in the eighties.
We're dealing with different social and economic structures.
And why not have a Chicano mystery?" Those few Chicano
spectators who faulted Anaya for not treating the subjects
of earlier Chicano literature—injustice, oppression, poverty, or the border—sounded like aging lefties who had
never outgrown the 1960s.

Who Killed Don José? is about bridging the traditions
and the futures of Chicano culture. The title character re-
calls the "ricos" of the late nineteenth century, men like
José Leandro Peréa of Bernalillo and Mariano Yrisarrí of
Los Ranchos de Alburquerque who earned fortunes from
herding and freighting sheep. While rehearsing, Huerta
called Don José "an aristocrat" and contrasted New Mexico, with its deeply traditional culture, and his home state:
"I do not know of an aristocracy in California. Sure, we
have multi-millionaires, but they're basically nouveau-
riche." Anaya, who was amused at the idea of a Chicano
"aristocracy," is nonetheless an artist who has always
stressed the past—its importance, its vitality, its present-
ness. He has repeatedly declared his need to resuscitate
ancient myth and to revere "the land" as "a whole historic
essence that lives within me." He deliberately describes his
culture as "Chicano" to remind readers that his tradition
is not metaphysically "Hispanic" but indigenously and his-
torically New Mexican:

My roots have always been firmly anchored to the soil
of the Southwest, and I have always been fiercely proud
of this region I share with my people. My roots were
planted here four hundred years ago when the Spaniard
first came to the Southwest, and before that they were
nourished by the pre-Columbian thought and cultures
of the indigenous people, the Native Americans.

Don José is both the keeper of the traditional flame and the prophet leading his people from an agrarian and small-town past into a high-tech future. Anaya's life has traced just such a journey: from farm and llano (his mother's people were farmers, his father a vaquero) to a small town (Santa Rosa, New Mexico, where he lived until the eighth grade) to a large city, Alburquerque. There he began in the barrio but moved, via three university degrees and years of writing, to a professorship, a suburban home with a terrific view, and all the cultural trophies available to a New Mexican. Anaya describes Chicanos generally as undergoing a similar change: from a pastoral period before World War II, "when the only things that affected us happened within our family or our village," through intense changes—"new and positive things," "some threats," and "a lot of decisions to make, pretty quick"—to a forward-looking belief that the community must "create our own future." The idea that *Who Killed Don José?* portrays a community in transition was shared by director Huerta: "It deals with what happens to people and communities if they don't adapt and change—they get left behind. . . . If we don't control the information of tomorrow we will always be tradition-bound . . . [and] that also means poverty."

In Anaya's play, as in his trilogy of novels, a young character goes through a rite of passage and learns to master la tristeza de la vida with insight gained from the older generation. But *Who Killed Don José?* ends on several provocative ironies. First, the wisdom of the past appears here in very odd dress, ironically implanted in a computer which serves to unlock both the immediate mysteries of chicanery and murder and the deeper mystery of the people's future. Second, the Chicano future turns out to be Chicana. The character who learns from the past and represents hope for the community is, for the first time in one of Anaya's major works, female. María, "la patrona," returns from UCLA and Anglo-America to el rancho and la gente in a way that recapitulates Anaya's direction as a mature writer. "I have come back to a communal universe," he says in a recent interview. "I grew up in that tradition, I left it in some of my wanderings, and I returned to it; and what the tradition of the community has to teach us is . . . respect, love for the family and for the village that is the community."

Connection with "the community" may sound like cheap literary talk, but I saw it illustrated in the starkest light one August night in 1987. As with most of its productions during the 1980s, La Compañía followed its three-week commercial run of *Who Killed Don José?* with a free performance at the South Broadway Cultural Center in one of Albuquerque's poorest neighborhoods. The overheated Center was jammed with its usual collection of neighborhood children, poor people, bohemians, and winos, and these people laughed and laughed at the simple-minded Sheriff, the drunken Diego, the haughty Ana, and the other characters. Line after line about the future of Chicano New Mexico zinged into the bull's-eye of this audience's attention. As with its earlier performances at Menaul School, La Compañía held a contest at intermission encouraging the audience to guess who killed Don José, and this audience participated most avidly. Then they watched with intensifying wonder as the piece moved past the simple question of "Whodunit?" to the thought-provoking conclusion. Out in the big world, I had been hearing too much from sophisticates, both Anglo and Hispanic, about the problems or contradictions of Anaya's play, but now I stood at the rear of the Center watching that audience as they watched that second act. I was particularly drawn to a Chicano in his sixties who sat nearby. His faded blue jeans and work shirt covered a short, robust body that seemed to have been molded by life on horseback. His face was deeply lined and bronzed, a mestizo face produced by centuries of cross-breeding, and it crinkled when he laughed, lit up when he wondered. Beside him a young girl—his granddaughter?—

sat up on her knees to see the actors, and she too was completely absorbed by the play. These people, I decided, were the living reasons I needed to include *Who Killed Don José?* in this anthology.

So here is Anaya's tale of the folk, especially for them.

David Richard Jones

CHARACTERS

DON JOSÉ	The patrón
MARÍA	His daughter
ANA	Lady friend of Don José
TONY	A car dealer
RAMÓN	The computer man
DOÑA SOFÍA	The housekeeper
DIEGO	Her son
THE SHERIFF	The law of Santa Fe County

ACT ONE

It is a cold and windy October night in Santa Fe County. The time is the present. The scene is the spacious living room of Don José's ranch. The room is decorated in old, territorial New Mexico style. There is a large fireplace, brick floor, Indian rugs on the walls, a table with wine and other drinks, comfortable sofa and chairs, all covered with well-worn Chimayo rugs. There is no one in the room. Outside the wind moans, dogs bark, and the distinct bleating of sheep can be heard.

Someone tries to open the door. When it does not open, there is a knock. Again the knock. Then MARÍA *enters from the left and opens the door.* TONY, *about thirty-five, a car dealer in Santa Fe, enters. He wears a three-piece suit and is slick and confident. When* MARÍA *opens the door, he is holding a werewolf mask to his face. He leaps forward and frightens her.*

TONY: Trick or treat!
MARÍA: Tony! You scared me!
TONY: Who were you expecting? Dracula? (*He embraces her, tries to kiss her.*) How about a treat? (MARÍA *allows a peck to the cheek.*)

MARÍA: Hey, Señor Werewolf . . . What's this?

TONY: My trusty .38.

MARÍA: A gun?

TONY: Yeah, a gun. Come on, get your dancing shoes on! We're going dancing!

MARÍA (*pulls back*): I didn't know you carried a gun.

TONY: I've sold a lot of used cars—a man needs protection. Hey, if it'll make you feel any better, I'll leave it in the car. (TONY *takes the pistol from under his jacket.*) It's a beauty, huh. Pearl handle. Got it from a guy who had to leave town in a hurry.

DON JOSÉ (*offstage*): María! Did you get the door?

MARÍA: Father! He doesn't allow guns in the house!

TONY: No guns. Why?

MARÍA: Since his father was shot. It's a rule.

TONY: Yeah.

MARÍA: Here. (*She takes the gun, looks around.*)

TONY: Hey, what are you doing?

MARÍA: Getting rid of this. (*She goes to the telephone table. She opens a drawer, takes out the telephone directory, and puts the pistol in the drawer.*)

TONY: That's a joke. Don José afraid of guns. Ha!

MARÍA: He's not afraid of anything. He just won't allow them in the house. (*Offstage*, DON JOSÉ *singing "Rancho Grande."*)

TONY: But my—

MARÍA: Shh.

(DON JOSÉ *appears from door to left. He is fifty, silver-haired, handsome. He has made a good living raising sheep. He is wealthy, traditional, well-mannered and sophisticated. He wears an elegant smoking jacket.*)

DON JOSÉ: Oh, Tony. I thought it was somebody important.

TONY: Don José, anytime you need a job as a salesman, let me know. You always have a joke.

DON JOSÉ: It wasn't a joke. What brings you out on a night like tonight?

TONY: This beautiful daughter of yours. She's swept me off my feet.

DON JOSÉ: Qué lástima.

TONY: We're invited to an important party, lots of wealthy people. They're important people to know.

MARÍA: I didn't know you were coming by, Tony. I had planned to stay home with Father . . .

DON JOSÉ: Don't worry about me, mi'jita. But you've been dancing every night for a week. Wouldn't you like a change of pace . . . and partner?

MARÍA: There really isn't much to do here.

TONY: She's the best dance partner I've ever had.

DON JOSÉ: Life is just a dance, huh, Tony?

MARÍA: He's a killer on the dance floor.

TONY: If a man wants to keep ahead in this town, he needs to know the score.

DON JOSÉ: María, hurry and decide on that car you said you needed. I don't know if I can live through this.

MARÍA: Father, offer Tony a drink.

TONY: Treat me right and I can get it for you wholesale.

DON JOSÉ (*weakly*): Drink, Tony?

TONY: Double scotch, si voo play? For example, I see María in a Seville. And for you, Don José, I have just the thing. A gold El Dorado just came in. It's got style. A man like you should drive an expensive car.

DON JOSÉ: No, gracias, my old truck runs just fine.

MARÍA: Maybe you should treat yourself to a new car, Dad. You've been working too hard.

DON JOSÉ: Yes, you're right. Since you got home I've hardly seen you. We need to take time, just the two of us! To ride on the rancho like we used to . . . This new plan has taken all my time.

TONY: Maybe your father can't afford a new car, María. I can get you credit, Don José.

DON JOSÉ: That'll be the day!

MARÍA: Dad!

TONY: What's the matter, don't you trust me?

MARÍA: Of course he does.

TONY: My father trusted you, Don José. Remember?

DON JOSÉ (*grows pensive*): Don Estevan, que descanse en paz.

TONY: Hey, that's the past. Come on, let's go dancing!

MARÍA: Will you be all right?

DON JOSÉ: Sí. Sí. I was just thinking.

MARÍA: You seem to have something on your mind.

DON JOSÉ: Didn't I tell you? Ramón's delivering my computer tonight.

TONY: A computer?

MARÍA: He's going to put the whole ranch on a computer program—even the sheep.

TONY: I don't believe it.

MARÍA: When most people are planning to retire, he's starting a new project. I tell him to sell the ranch and move to Santa Fe, or Albuquerque, but no, the ranch is too important.

DON JOSÉ: Retire? Leave the rancho? My friends? My workers? No, impossible!

MARÍA: You can't be responsible for them all your life.

DON JOSÉ: ¿Por qué no? Our family has been on this land for many generations. Your grandfather taught me to love the land and take care of the workers. He was a real patrón.

MARÍA: But times have changed.

DON JOSÉ: So we change with them. Use computers.

TONY: Let me get this straight. The computer's going to take care of your sheep?

DON JOSÉ: Every single borreguito. I'm moving into the future.

TONY: Just be careful you don't move too fast, Don José.

DON JOSÉ: The computer age is here whether we like it or not. If we don't change now, we get left behind.

TONY: But nobody's making money in sheep anymore. You should get into politics. That's how you make money.

MARÍA: You could get elected. Or appointed to a position.

TONY (*chuckling*): Yeah, Goodwill Ambassador to Australia. They have sheep there!

DON JOSÉ: Appointed? No. It's men like me who put governors in office in this state. I still deliver a large part of the vote in this county. Politicians come to me for votes and advice, I don't go to them. And after they're elected they are surrounded by the sheep they appoint. At least here on the rancho my sheep are honest.

TONY: Can't argue there.

DON JOSÉ: My work is here. New opportunities are coming to this state: technology, bullet trains, new investments . . .

TONY: A man can still get rich, if he's in the right place, at the right time.

DON JOSÉ: We have to create our own future. That's why I need you here.

MARÍA: I'm not sure how a degree in music can help.

DON JOSÉ: Just being here is enough. One day you will take over the rancho.

MARÍA: Someday. Right now I want to travel, see Europe, maybe study there—

DON JOSÉ: There's time for that, too. Just as soon as my plan is in place, we can take a trip together. Vas a ver.

MARÍA: I'd like that.

TONY: Anything beats raising sheep.

DON JOSÉ: You know what your grandfather used to say.

MARÍA: ¿Cada borrega es un mundo?

DON JOSÉ: Be serious, mi'jita. It is our sacred duty to protect this land. Now, excuse me. Ramón will be here soon . . . and maybe other guests. (*He kisses María on the forehead and goes out, whistling "Mary Had a Little Lamb."*)

TONY: I think your father's getting senile.

MARÍA: No, he's just set in his ways.

TONY: He could get a real deal for this ranch. Especially now—

MARÍA: Father won't sell. This land is his life. It can be confining and slow, but it's home. I've been out riding every morning since I've been back. I had forgotten how beautiful it is.

TONY: You can't bank beauty, honey. You gotta have money to buy the good things in life.

MARÍA: I do want to travel, but right now all this excitement's rubbing off on me.

TONY: I wish I were the one rubbing off on you.

MARÍA: It's been fun, Tony. But there's more to life than dancing.

TONY: Hey, we're meant for each other. I've always had my eyes on you. I remember the first time I saw you. I made up my mind then, someday we would be together.

MARÍA: You never said anything.

TONY: You were the daughter of the great Don José. I was a poor man's son. I could just watch you from a distance. Now I know better.

MARÍA (*teasing*): I bet you do. Tony, the lady's man.

TONY: Don't believe Santa Fe gossip. I'm on one track, and that's you. (*They are interrupted by* DIEGO *singing in the kitchen: "Yo no soy borreguero, soy capitán, soy capitán . . ."*) Who's that?

MARÍA: Diego. He's been drinking—

TONY: Is he still around?

MARÍA: He's part of the family. He'll always be around. Anyway, if we're going dancing I'd better change. Be a few minutes.

TONY: Don't keep me waiting.

MARÍA: I bought Los Lobos' new album. It's in the library down the hall. I'll be there in a few minutes.

TONY: Great! (MARÍA *goes out.* TONY *finishes his drink.*) I could get used to this. Don Tony. Ha, ha . . . (TONY *exits, chuckling. There is only a pause, then the voices in the kitchen grow louder.* DOÑA SOFÍA *and*

DIEGO, *her son, enter. Doña Sofía is bent, in her late sixties. They carry a small computer table which she places in the middle of the room. Diego is drunk. He is a typical ranch hand, dressed in Levi's, boots, work shirt, leather vest. Offstage we hear salsa music.*)

DOÑA SOFÍA (*scolding*): ¡Malcriado! ¡Sinvergüenza! How many times do I tell you, ¡no tengo dinero! If you want to waste your life drinking, use your own money, borracho! Ay, qué martirio es ser madre.

DIEGO: I ain't drunk, jefa, I just had a few beers.

DOÑA SOFÍA: Sí, a few beers. I know. Drinking con esos sin oficio—

DIEGO: They're my friends, jefa.

DOÑA SOFÍA: ¡Andale! ¡Ayúdame con la mesa!

DIEGO: What is the table for?

DOÑA SOFÍA: For la computadora—

DIEGO: What's that? A high-priced woman? (*He laughs to himself*).

DOÑA SOFÍA: No, it's a machine. A Japanese machine Don José bought. He said it can do anything. I hope it can wash the floors.

DIEGO: Come on, jefita, just lend me a few pesos. I'll pay you next week.

DOÑA SOFÍA: You already spent your paycheck?

DIEGO: ¡Qué paycheck, ni que nada! Don José pays me cacahuates! The foremen of the other ranchos make good money, but they got cattle. And me? Stuck with these borregas of Don José. I'm sick of them!

DOÑA SOFÍA: Sí, sick enough to take one every week?

DIEGO: The coyotes take the sheep, not me.

DOÑA SOFÍA: Then get poison for the coyotes.

DIEGO: I bought some today. (*He lifts a bottle of whiskey at the bar and stares at it.*) When I put the poison, olvídate!

DOÑA SOFÍA: I know you take good care of the sheep, mijo, pero no importa. Someday soon this machine is going to replace you. You won't have work.

DIEGO: No work? What are you saying, jefa?

DOÑA SOFÍA: The machine, it takes care of the sheep—

DIEGO: ¡Chale! No pinche máquina can take care of sheep! You crazy?

DOÑA SOFÍA (*pensive*): Máquinas del diablo, that's what they are, Japanese machines to do our work. Con razón que hay tanta gente sin trabajo.

DIEGO: I got a job!

DOÑA SOFÍA: You? You're a pendejo who can't even take care of your money. You have to give Don José credit, he takes good care of his sheep. ¿Y por qué no? They made his family rich. (*She goes to the fireplace to stir the fire.*)

DIEGO: Yeah, but they don't make me money! I know a man who's selling a ranchito, jefa. If I only had some lana I could buy it. Raise cattle up in Mora, get out of this pinche rancho!

DOÑA SOFÍA: A rancho in the mountains. Sí, that would be nice.

DIEGO: But I need the money!

DOÑA SOFÍA: You'll get the money.

DIEGO: From where? From you? Ha! If Don José is as tight as a coffin, then you're as tight as the grave!

DOÑA SOFÍA: ¡Malcriado!

DIEGO: So I take a couple of sheep a month, sell them to buy beer. Como dicen los políticos, those are my fringe benefits! (*He laughs.*)

DOÑA SOFÍA: ¡Cállate! Estas paredes tienen orejas.

DIEGO: Ah, nobody's listening. So, tell me how can I get some lana. Did you find a treasure?

DOÑA SOFÍA: No te importa—

DIEGO (*grabs her arm*): Anda, ¿qué sabes?

DOÑA SOFÍA: I shouldn't tell you anything.

DIEGO: Come on, jefa, what are you hiding?

DOÑA SOFÍA: Shh! Last week I was cleaning Don José's room. He had all his papers out of the safe.

DIEGO: Yeah?

DOÑA SOFÍA: I found a very important paper.

DIEGO: What?

DOÑA SOFÍA: Don José's will.

DIEGO: His will?

DOÑA SOFÍA: Sí. His will. That's where he puts down what he gives to people when he dies.

DIEGO: I know what a will is, jefa. But why should I care? The old bastard wouldn't put me in his will if it killed him. Ha, you get it? If it killed him!

DOÑA SOFÍA: He's tough, like an old ram. Like his father, Don Andrés. They shot him, or he would still be alive.

DIEGO: Yeah, he's like an old coyote.

DOÑA SOFÍA: But a kind man. In his own way. He put you in his will.

DIEGO: Me? In the will?

DOÑA SOFÍA: Sí! When Don José dies, you get a share of money. Enough to buy that rancho you want.

DIEGO: Are you sure?

DOÑA SOFÍA: I can read! That's what it says in the will!

DIEGO: Damn! That's good news! So that old sonofabitch is gonna cut me in. I don't believe it.

DOÑA SOFÍA: It's true.

DIEGO: I can buy a rancho! Be my own boss.

DOÑA SOFÍA: No seas loco. You don't get a penny until Don José dies.

DIEGO: Yeah. The will. He has to die . . .

DOÑA SOFÍA: That's the way it is. (*She sees the telephone book and goes to place it in the drawer. She sees the pistol. She nervously picks up the pistol, stuffs it in her apron pocket, places the telephone book in the drawer.*) Don José is as healthy as a goat. He's going to live a long life—

DIEGO: Unless he has an accident in his truck.

DOÑA SOFÍA: What do you mean?

DIEGO: Or somebody puts coyote poison in his drink—

DOÑA SOFÍA: ¡No digas eso! The devil will hear. It can come true.

DIEGO: Yeah, he could choke on his drink!

DOÑA SOFÍA: Don't be crazy. If Don José dies, it has to be a natural death.

DIEGO (*puts his arm around her*): Pero que truchas, jefita. You're not so dumb. You go sniffing around and you find the will. Qué suave. I gotta think about this. I need a beer.

DOÑA SOFÍA: No more beer.

DIEGO: Enough money to buy my own rancho. (*They exit. The telephone rings in the empty room.*)

DON JOSÉ (*offstage*): Doña Sofía, answer the phone! María, the telephone! (*He walks in.*) Women! When you need them, they're never around. (*He picks up the phone.*) Hello. Sheriff? Yes. Yes. Oh, I understand. But I have nothing to say to you. No, no deal! Tell that to your friends. I don't care what you say, there's nothing to talk about. ¡Buenas noches! (*He slams the phone down. There is a knock at the door.*) Ramón? (DON JOSÉ *opens the door.* ANA *enters. She is forty-five, a very attractive woman, well groomed. She wears a fur jacket. The small bell hung on the door tinkles when it is opened and shut.*) Ana! Come in. It's good to see you.

ANA: Why haven't you called? (*They kiss. He takes her coat.*)

DON JOSÉ: You know I've been busy.

ANA: Have you heard the news from Santa Fe?

DON JOSÉ: Yes!

ANA: As of today, your land is worth millions.

DON JOSÉ: Just as I planned.

ANA: And the land the Santa Fe gang bought is worthless.

DON JOSÉ: Serves them right. The gang of crooks. They stole the foundation money and bought the wrong piece of real estate. Instead of going through their land, the bullet train is going through my ranch. And you know the Attorney General is already investigating.

ANA: Then it's true, you have information from the foundation files!

DON JOSÉ: How did you know?

ANA: A very important file is missing. They know you
have it, and they want it back. They're ready to murder
for it.

DON JOSÉ: Murder? I don't think they'll do anything as
long as I have this. (*He takes a floppy disk from his
jacket pocket.*)

ANA: Is that it?

DON JOSÉ: Yes. This little disk is what they want. As
soon as I get my computer, I'll be able to read it, then
I'll know who in the gang is involved. In the meantime
it's my insurance.

ANA: While you have it, they won't touch you?

DON JOSÉ: They can't. It's this file they want, not me.
As long as I have it, I'm safe.

ANA: What's in it?

DON JOSÉ: Bookkeeping entries and other information
they don't want exposed.

ANA: How did you get it?

DON JOSÉ: By accident. Somebody left the file in the
general information files. When I saw what was in it, I
knew it was dynamite. So I "borrowed" it.

ANA: You stole it?

DON JOSÉ: Let's say in the interest of research I checked
it out.

ANA: But it can only mean trouble, José.

DON JOSÉ: Yes, I know. And that's why I won't turn
my back on this. They stole from the people of this state.
It's not right, every new investor that lands here takes a
piece of our pie! Only the crumbs are left for the people.
The foundation was set up for the good of the entire
state, not just for the políticos who have their fingers in
the pie!

ANA (*sighs*): I agree. But I'm worried. Don't say I didn't
warn you . . .

DON JOSÉ: Thank you, Ana, but I'm safe, as long as I have this . . . (*He slips the disk into his pocket.*)

ANA: You're being too complacent.

DON JOSÉ: Me, complacent? Never, my dear. I know New Mexican politics too well.

ANA: Did you know they've talked about hiring somebody to kill you?

DON JOSÉ: I don't believe it.

ANA: It's true! I was there!

DON JOSÉ: Where?

ANA: At the Bull Ring in Santa Fe. Everybody was there, even the Governor. They were all waiting for the foundation board vote. When it was announced and they knew they had lost, they got together in a back room to decide what to do.

DON JOSÉ: And?

ANA: As Vicente Silva used to say, your life ain't worth a plugged nickel.

DON JOSÉ: I need a drink. How about you?

ANA: Yes. Por favor.

DON JOSÉ (*goes to the bar*): You're serious, aren't you?

ANA: Dead serious.

DON JOSÉ: Who was there?

ANA: You know the group, the people you call the High Tech Mafia.

DON JOSÉ: So you think they would do it?

ANA: Of course they would. They not only lost their money, but like you said, the Attorney General is asking questions.

DON JOSÉ: Damn!

ANA (*offering a toast*): To Don José. You are a genius.

DON JOSÉ: There was never any doubt. I just don't plan to be a dead genius. But who would they get to do their dirty work?

ANA: You're worried, huh? The great Don José is afraid. I never thought I'd see the day.

DON JOSÉ: Don't play games, Ana. This is serious. Do you know?

ANA (*challenging him*): It could be me!

DON JOSÉ: You?

ANA: Why not? You know I can shoot the head off a rattlesnake at fifty feet. (*She pulls a pistol from her purse.*)

DON JOSÉ: Ana, be careful!

ANA: You know I always carry a gun. What if it's me? It could be my revenge.

DON JOSÉ: Revenge for what?

ANA: For all those years you kept me waiting!

DON JOSÉ: Don't tease me, Ana. Tell me who they hired.

ANA: On one condition!

DON JOSÉ: What?

ANA: Marry me.

DON JOSÉ: You're impossible!

ANA: I don't think so. You're in trouble, and I'm the only person who can help you. I'm simply collecting for all the years I've waited. (DON JOSÉ *smiles*, *holds her*, *kisses her. She responds.*)

DON JOSÉ: Tell me.

ANA: Marry me.

DON JOSÉ: My dear Ana, you drive a hard bargain. Let's see if I understand your proposal. My future in a coffin, or my future in marriage. I'll have to think about it.

ANA: ¡Cabrón! I'm crazy to love you.

DON JOSÉ: I'm irresistible.

ANA: You're egotistical!

DON JOSÉ: Ana, we've been good friends, good lovers all these years. Let's not spoil it.

ANA: It may already be spoiled.

DON JOSÉ: What do you mean?

ANA: You're a dead man!

DON JOSÉ: Come now, Ana, don't be so melodramatic. I admit, there's a few things that I hadn't planned on. I need your help.

ANA: Uh-huh. The only time you show affection is when you need my help.

DON JOSÉ: I haven't told María anything about the foundation vote or my plans for the ranch. I was going to tell her tonight, until Tony showed up.

ANA: So tell her.

DON JOSÉ: It's not that simple. The sheriff just called me.

ANA: Ah-ha . . .

DON JOSÉ: I think he's going to drop by tonight. I know the sheriff is involved with that bunch of crooks, but how deep is he? Enough to murder? No, I don't think so. But I can't be sure.

ANA: You can't be sure of anybody. You've made enemies.

DON JOSÉ: All great men make enemies. Especially in this state. You make a name for yourself, and the zopilotes are there, pecking at you.

ANA: That's politics—(*They hear the sound of laughter offstage.*) Who's that?

DON JOSÉ: María, and Tony Montoya.

ANA: Tony Montoya, from Tony's Cadillacs. I thought your daughter had better taste.

DON JOSÉ: She does, but you know those California universities. Anyway, she's buying a car from him.

ANA: I bought a car from him, and it was a lemon! And he wouldn't fix it. I don't like that man.

DON JOSÉ: But I have to talk to María, now.

ANA: I'll wait in the kitchen.

DON JOSÉ: Thank you, Ana. (*He takes* ANA *to the door, kisses her, then calls:*) María! (*Enter* MARÍA *and* TONY.)

MARÍA: Tony was showing me a new step. What's up?

TONY: We're going to be *the* couple at the party tonight.

DON JOSÉ: Wouldn't it be less painful if you just bought the damned car?

MARÍA: Papa, be nice. What do you want?

DON JOSÉ: Look, I have something to tell you. I wanted to wait until tomorrow, but I think you should hear it now. Stay. Have a drink. Tony?

TONY: Why not? Double scotch, si voo play.

DON JOSÉ: Good. Sit down, sit down. I'll get us a drink.

MARÍA: No, you sit, I'll get the drinks.

DON JOSÉ: A lot has happened today. I have very good news!

TONY: The price of mutton just went up?

DON JOSÉ: Much better!

TONY: The price of wool went up?

DON JOSÉ: How about . . . Don José, the millionaire.

TONY: That would impress me.

MARÍA: What's the joke, Father?

DON JOSÉ: It's no joke, María.

TONY: You struck oil!

MARÍA: Daddy, quit teasing. What's the secret?

DON JOSÉ: I want to relish the story. Where do I begin?

MARÍA: Just get to the point.

DON JOSÉ: Bueno. As you know, there are plans to build a bullet train to run from Los Alamos to Sandia Labs in Albuquerque.

TONY: That's all Santa Fe is talking about. If you ask me, this bullet train idea doesn't look too good for the car business.

DON JOSÉ: Good or not, it's here. And I just found out that the right-of-way for the corridor is going right through my rancho. This has just become the most valuable land in the state.

MARIA: That's wonderful!

DON JOSÉ: Now I have the money I need to carry out my plan.

MARÍA: What plan?

DON JOSÉ: Your grandfather, que descanse en paz, always said: Hold on to the land. It's our salvation.

TONY: Hey, who cares about salvation. You scored, right where it matters: making money!

MARÍA: Is that all that matters to you?

TONY: Hey, baby. Your daddy can write his own ticket. This is better than winning a Las Vegas jackpot. It's the big time! This really calls for a Fleetwood 60 Special!

DON JOSÉ: Not now, Tony. (*He turns to María.*) I wanted to be the one to tell you the news. I didn't want you to hear about this in Santa Fe.

MARÍA: I understand. And I'm happy. But you look worried.

DON JOSÉ: No, not worried. But I have to be careful. A lot of people wanted . . . (*They are interrupted by a loud knock at the door.*) Ramón . . . I hope.

(DON JOSÉ *goes to the door.* RAMÓN, *the computer man, enters. He is a handsome, young man of twenty-five. He rolls in a computer on a small dolly.*)

RAMÓN: Buenas noches, Don José.

DON JOSÉ: Ramón. Entra, entra.

RAMÓN: Sorry I'm late.

TONY: What the hell—

MARÍA: Ramón!

RAMÓN: María! I didn't know you were home.

MARÍA: I've only been here a week.

RAMÓN: And you didn't call?

DON JOSÉ: She's been too busy buying a car.

RAMÓN: I see.

MARÍA: Can I help?

TONY: Watch out, it might bite.

RAMÓN: Speaking of bites, how's the car business, Tony?

TONY: We have the best in town. Remember that when you think of getting rid of that junk heap you drive.

DON JOSÉ: Get her up there. Careful, careful. Ah, what a beauty!

TONY: I see you're still selling video games.

RAMÓN: Not video games. Computers. You know, information systems.

DON JOSÉ: And he who controls information, controls power.

RAMÓN: There you are, Don José. Turn it on!

DON JOSÉ: The program disk?

RAMÓN: Right here.

DON JOSÉ: Ah, this is what I need.

RAMÓN: So, how are things?

MARÍA: Fine. I finished my degree.

RAMÓN: Congratulations. The last time we talked you said you might go to Europe.

MARÍA: Someday. I want to study more. And you?

RAMÓN: I keep busy. The computer business is booming. I'm expanding every day.

MARÍA: I remember we agreed that computers and music were compatible.

TONY: How cute.

RAMÓN: This one does everything but play the piano.

DON JOSÉ: Don't mention music, he's liable to take you dancing.

TONY: María's the only dance partner I need.

DON JOSÉ: Look at that, it works like a charm. It's already asking me what I want to do.

TONY: What do you know? It works!

MARÍA: It's the fanciest computer I've ever seen.

DON JOSÉ: This is not just any computer, this is a Mitsubishi 2000. The latest Japanese model.

RAMÓN: State-of-the-art!

DON JOSÉ: Yes sir, state-of-the-art.

RAMÓN: Hot off the boat from Japan.

DON JOSÉ: But those boats won't be sailing for much longer. As soon as I build my factory, we'll be making these computers right here on the ranch!

MARÍA: Factory? Here?

DON JOSÉ: That's the plan. To build the biggest and best computer plant in the Southwest! Right here! El Patrón Monolithic Systems! It's going to revolutionize this state!

TONY: Are you serious?

MARÍA: So that's it! It wasn't just for the sheep.

DON JOSÉ: That's only the first step. We're going to build computers.

RAMÓN: The El Patrón ATM 1000!

DON JOSÉ: I want to train my workers here! I want my

plant to become a model factory! This state is ready for it, and we're right in the middle of the whole chingadera!

MARÍA: Daddy!

DON JOSÉ: Excuse my language, but I get excited when I think of what can be done here. Don't you see the possibilities?

MARÍA: Yes, yes I do. I can't believe you learned to run this thing. I'm impressed.

DON JOSÉ: Nothing to it. It was harder learning to speak English when I was a kid.

RAMÓN: He's a whiz. He was computer literate in a few weeks.

TONY: Computer literate? Don't make me laugh.

RAMÓN: You need brains to run this machine, Tony.

TONY: Be careful, Ramón.

RAMÓN: Sorry, Tony, but you wouldn't understand Don José's plan, you're only interested in selling Cadillacs and making money.

TONY: So, I make a good living. I like to deal with people who can afford nothing but the best—nothing wrong with that. This whole thing sounds like a pipe dream.

DON JOSÉ: A dream that can become a reality. I will build the factory, train my workers, and help some become engineers.

MARÍA: It's about time we had Chicano engineers and technicians.

RAMÓN: Yeah, if Los Alamos won't do it, we'll have to do it ourselves.

TONY: Train cowboys and Indians to build computers?

DON JOSÉ: Why not? To survive we have to adapt. And in today's world that means build a better computer.

RAMÓN: The El Patrón model is going to make IBM look like second class. What we have here is pure Chicano ingenuity!

TONY: What are you going to build them with, baling wire? (*He laughs.*)

RAMÓN: No, Mr. Repo Man. We build them with the best know-how we have!

MARÍA: I think it's a great idea.

DON JOSÉ: It is. Ramón has a program which can inventory every borrega on the ranch. Instead of the borreguero, we now have the computer!

RAMÓN: A small transistor is implanted in each sheep. The computer records their location, their pulse, whether or not they need food or water. Maybe we can get it to tell the ewe and the ram the precise time for mating.

DON JOSÉ: Imagine the wear and tear it will save on my prize rams.

TONY: Sounds like you've been watching too many science fiction movies. You really think you can train people who have been sheepherders all their lives to build computers?

DON JOSÉ: We can start.

MARÍA: Sounds like the future has come to New Mexico.

RAMÓN: Our job is to make it user friendly.

TONY: Hey, I like that. Tony's Cadillacs, User Friendly.

DON JOSÉ: Ramón has some very interesting theories.

TONY: I bet.

MARÍA: I want to know more.

DON JOSÉ: We can always use a partner.

MARÍA: We?

DON JOSÉ: Ramón knows what I want to do. If anything happens to me, the project keeps going.

MARÍA: What could happen to you?

DON JOSÉ: Believe it or not, mi'jita, I am mortal.

MARÍA: You're going to live to be a hundred.

DON JOSÉ: I hope. But a man never knows. I want to make sure what I start continues.

TONY: Sounds like you need professionals for the job, not amateurs.

DON JOSÉ: Ramón knows the business.

TONY: So, he's a real Chicano success story. But can he handle it? What if it goes to his head?

RAMÓN: What do you mean, Tony?

TONY: You know the old saying, power corrupts.

DON JOSÉ: Power only corrupts the corruptible.

TONY: The idea's crazy. A Silicon Valley here. There's only coyotes and sheep. It'll never fly.

DON JOSÉ: Oh, it will. We're going to put a computer in every kitchen and every classroom!

RAMÓN: Not cowchips, microchips!

DON JOSÉ: It means a revolution; work, education and opportunity for everybody!

MARÍA: It's what you always wanted, Father. Count me in.

DON JOSÉ: As your grandfather used to say: ¡Sí, se puede!

RAMÓN: Right on!

TONY: I think you all have computer fever.

RAMÓN: Why not? We can make them work for us. Hey, I have one more delivery to make. May I use your phone?

DON JOSÉ: Help yourself. It's on the table. (RAMÓN *goes to the phone.*)

MARÍA: The phone!

RAMÓN: Yes, the phone. I have to call in. Do you mind?

MARÍA: No, of course not . . .

RAMÓN (*picks up the phone*): That's strange, the line is dead.

DON JOSÉ: What?

RAMÓN: The line is dead.

TONY: Maybe the wind knocked it down.

RAMÓN: But you have lights.

DON JOSÉ: Maybe I should check it out.

MARÍA: Dad, it's just the wind.

RAMÓN: Yeah, no telling where the problem is. Well, I'll just head on back.

MARÍA: So soon?

RAMÓN: I'm done here. How's the computer working, Don José?

DON JOSÉ: Like a '57 Chevy.

MARÍA: Won't you stay and have dinner with us?

TONY: Hey, I thought we were going dancing?

MARÍA: That can wait. I want to hear more about this project.

DON JOSÉ: ¡Eso es!

RAMÓN: I have another delivery to make tonight, but I could be back in an hour if that's okay?

MARÍA: Perfect. We'll wait.

RAMÓN: By the way, did you call the sheriff?

DON JOSÉ: The sheriff? Why?

RAMÓN: He passed me on the way out here.

MARÍA: He didn't come here.

RAMÓN: But you're the only ones out here. If he had turned back I would have seen him.

MARÍA: That's strange.

DON JOSÉ: Maybe not.

RAMÓN: Well, I gotta go. See you later.

MARÍA: We'll wait for dinner.

RAMÓN: Thanks. It's good to see you, María. You're looking great.

MARÍA: You too, Ramón.

RAMÓN (*turns to Don José*): Any questions, Don José?

DON JOSÉ: No, todo está bien.

RAMÓN: Bueno, may your monitor glow brightly.

DON JOSÉ: May the force be with you. Keep your floppy disk dry.

MARÍA: I'll see you out.

RAMÓN: My pleasure, señorita.

TONY: I'll go with you.

RAMÓN: Tony, three's a crowd.

TONY: I know, but I have to protect my business interest.

MARÍA: What do you mean?

TONY: I wanna look at that wreck Ramón is driving. Maybe I can do something for him.

RAMÓN: Always looking for a sale, huh?

TONY: Business is business.

RAMÓN: Buenas noches, Don José.

DON JOSÉ: ¡Buenas noches! Drive carefully. The sheriff may be on the road. (*They go out.* DON JOSÉ *looks around suspiciously. He goes to the fireplace, takes the disk from his pocket and stuffs it into the toy lamb on the mantel. He is interrupted by* DOÑA SOFÍA *and* DIEGO.)

DOÑA SOFÍA: Diego, ¡Escúchame! Ay, ¡hijito!

DIEGO: No more lectures, jefa! I want my lana.

DOÑA SOFÍA: Don José, please don't listen to him. He's been working too hard.

DON JOSÉ: Uh-huh. Working at a six-pack.

DIEGO: No, taking care of your pinche borregas!

DON JOSÉ: An obvious case of sheep stress syndrome.

DOÑA SOFÍA: Maybe he had one drink . . . no más uno.

DON JOSÉ: Un barril—

DIEGO: I ain't drunk!

DON JOSÉ: Okay, you're not drunk. ¿Qué quieres, Diego?

DIEGO: ¡Mi dinero! That's what I want!

DOÑA SOFÍA: Diego, por el amor de dios—

DON JOSÉ: ¿Dinero? It's not payday?

DIEGO: Don't act dumb, patrón. I want my share!

DON JOSÉ: Here, sit here.

DIEGO: I don't want to sit! I want my share of the money! Then I quit!

DON JOSÉ: What money? Quit? Not take care of the flock?

DIEGO: To hell with your flock!

DOÑA SOFÍA: Don José, he doesn't mean that. When he drinks, the devil makes him say things.

DON JOSÉ: I understand. But I'm disappointed. A good shepherd never leaves his flock. Abel didn't leave his sheep—

DIEGO: Yeah, and he got killed!

DOÑA SOFÍA: Diego, por favor.

DON JOSÉ: Yes, Cain killed Abel.

DIEGO: Yeah, Cain was smart. He got what he wanted. Now I want my part—

DON JOSÉ: Part of my sheep?

DIEGO: No! Screw your sheep! I want my part of the will!

DOÑA SOFÍA: Diego!

DON JOSÉ: What do you know about the will, Diego?

DIEGO: I know you have one.

DON JOSÉ: So, I see . . . I see your mamacita is watching out for you.

DOÑA SOFÍA: Patrón, discúlpeme. It was an accident.

DON JOSÉ: Don't apologize, Doña Sofía. Diego, that will won't be changed. You'll get your share—when I die.

DIEGO: Sí, when you die. You may be the patrón, Don José, but la muerte don't give a damn about that. (DIEGO *advances toward Don José but is interrupted by* MARÍA *coming in the front door.*)

DON JOSÉ: María. Just in time.

MARÍA: It's cold out there.

DON JOSÉ: Where's Tony?

MARÍA: He said he was going to check the telephone line. What's going on?

DOÑA SOFÍA: Señorita. It's nothing. Diego's not feeling well. He works too hard. (DON JOSÉ *makes a sign, tipping a bottle.*)

MARÍA: Oh, I see. Saturday night, huh?

DIEGO (*turns meek*): Ah, María, I just had a couple of beers. I ain't drunk.

DON JOSÉ: No, he ain't drunk. Just abusive. Do me a favor, get some coffee in him.

MARÍA: Come on, Diego, let's drink some hot coffee and talk. Okay?

DIEGO: Don't forget, Don José, I get what's mine.

DON JOSÉ: I won't forget, Diego.

DOÑA SOFÍA: I'll put lots of sugar in it, Diego. Just like you like it.

DIEGO: Okay, jefita.

MARÍA: Sure. Just like old times.

DON JOSÉ: Just like old times.

(*All exit to the kitchen. ANA enters but sees the* SHERIFF *in the window. ANA hides in the closet as the* SHERIFF *stealthily enters and goes to the computer.*)

SHERIFF: Program disk. There's got to be another. (*The* SHERIFF *puts the disk in his pocket and is searching the table when* DON JOSÉ *enters.*)

DON JOSÉ: Sheriff!

SHERIFF: Don José! Sonamagon, you almost gave me a heart attack!

DON JOSÉ: What are you doing here? Who let you in?

SHERIFF: I knocked . . .

DON JOSÉ: We were in the kitchen.

SHERIFF: I thought maybe because of the wind you couldn't hear me.

DON JOSÉ: So you made yourself at home.

SHERIFF: Pues, like your people always say, mi casa es su casa.

DON JOSÉ: I think that rule of hospitality should be: mi casa es *mi* casa! But being the good caballeros that we are, we even treat our enemies with courtesy.

SHERIFF: Don't think of me as your enemy, Don José. Think of me as a collector.

DON JOSÉ: I see. All in friendship, huh?

SHERIFF: Sure.

DON JOSÉ: In that case I should offer you a drink.

SHERIFF: You know I don't drink on duty. But it is cold out there. A shot of whiskey, por favor.

DON JOSÉ: So you came to collect . . . some information.

SHERIFF: You're a smart man.

DON JOSÉ: And if I don't have it?

SHERIFF: Let's not play games. Look, some of your old friends are very angry. But we're friends, right? They asked me to talk to you. Man to man. I don't want to see you hurt, Don José. Hell, we've known each other too long. We went to school together. My father knew your father. I'm not the kind of man who wants to see an old friend get hurt. Not if I can help it.

DON JOSÉ: And it can be helped if I turn the information I'm supposed to have over to you . . .

SHERIFF: Yes.

DON JOSÉ: Instead of the Attorney General?

SHERIFF (*grimaces*): Please, Don José. Don't mention the Attorney General. He's like the others, he just wants to get in the papers so he can run for governor. No, Don José, we got to keep this to ourselves— (DIEGO *shouts in the kitchen*.) Who's that?

DON JOSÉ: Diego.

SHERIFF: Diego. He was in Santa Fe this afternoon. Drinking. Telling everybody that one of these days he was going to give you a dose of coyote poison.

DON JOSÉ: It's been a bad night for the patrón.

SHERIFF: Diego could be a suspect.

DON JOSÉ: A suspect? To what?

SHERIFF: To your murder, Don José. Those old friends of yours would like to see your hide hanging in the Santa Fe plaza.

DON JOSÉ: That would be quite a sight. I'd find out who my friends really are. They'd come to the rosary. Imagine all the beautiful women crying by the side of my coffin.

SHERIFF: I didn't come to talk about your funeral, Don José. I came to get the evidence.

DON JOSÉ: But what you call evidence is my insurance policy. As long as I have it, I'm safe.

SHERIFF: Insurance? Wait a minute. Could it be that Don José is going to practice a little blackmail?

DON JOSÉ: Let's just say I know Santa Fe politics. My father always said, if you want to live to a ripe old age in New Mexico, never turn your back on a rattle-snake . . . or a politician.

SHERIFF: A wise man, your father. As I remember, he died in Doña Carmela's bed. Shot by her husband.

DON JOSÉ: Don't believe Santa Fe gossip, Sheriff. You

know in Santa Fe the mitote is about two things: love and politics.

SHERIFF: And money.

DON JOSÉ: No wonder the women in Santa Fe are lonely.

SHERIFF: God save us from the politicians, Don José.

DON JOSÉ: My father didn't trust sheriffs either.

SHERIFF: What? Enough jokes. Now— (MARÍA *calls for Don José.*) Who's that?

DON JOSÉ: María. I don't want her to know you're here.

SHERIFF: You mean, you don't want her involved.

DON JOSÉ: She doesn't know anything. I don't want her hurt.

SHERIFF: I can understand that. But she'll be fine if I get what I came for, the foundation file.

DON JOSÉ: You'll get it. But leave, now!

SHERIFF: No, I won't leave, but I'll be waiting outside. Get rid of her so we can talk.

DON JOSÉ: Yes.

SHERIFF: I'll be watching. (*The* SHERIFF *goes out the front door.* MARÍA *enters from the kitchen.*)

MARÍA: Dad! Come quickly! Diego has a gun!

DON JOSÉ: A gun?

MARÍA: There was a gun! He grabbed it and ran. We've got to find him!

DON JOSÉ: Yes, yes, I'm coming! (MARÍA *goes out.* DON JOSÉ *starts to follow her but stops. He looks at the computer.*) The program disk? It's missing. What in the devil did I do with it . . . (*He sits and rummages at the desk. At the same time the lights go off.*) Damn! The lights! (DON JOSÉ's *outline appears in the glare of the monitor screen. He senses someone in the room.*) Sheriff? Is that you?

(*There is a gunshot, a flash of fire, a moan as* DON JOSÉ *falls to the floor. A woman screams. A figure runs across the monitor screen, footsteps sound, the woman screams again. A moment later the lights come on.* MARÍA *appears at the door. She sees* ANA *standing over the crum-*

pled body of Don José. ANA *is holding the pistol in her hand. The* SHERIFF *rushes in.* MARÍA *screams, runs to her father.* DOÑA SOFÍA *runs in from the door to the kitchen.* TONY *follows her. He stops, slowly removes his gloves.*)

MARÍA: He's dead! Oh my God, he's dead!

TONY: Dead?

DOÑA SOFÍA: ¡Dios mío! ¡Dios mío!

MARÍA: You killed him.

ANA: No. I didn't.

SHERIFF: Don't nobody move!

TONY: Listen! (*All pause and turn to the voice which comes from the computer. The screen is flashing wildly. A computerized voice begins to sing.*)

COMPUTER VOICE: "Mary had a little lamb . . . little lamb . . . little lamb . . . Mary had a little lamb . . . whose fleece was white as snow . . ."

Blackout

ACT TWO

The living room. It is dark and somber. ANA *sits with a drink.* MARÍA *paces slowly.* MARÍA *goes to the window, looks out.*

MARÍA: Such a dark and lonely place . . .

ANA: Sí, the llano is lonely at night.

MARÍA: This morning I rode out on horseback, as far as the mesa. The sun was coming up. There is nothing more beautiful than morning on the llano. There are autumn colors everywhere. I thought, how beautiful life is on the rancho, how peaceful. (MARÍA *sobs.* ANA *reaches out.*) And now . . .

ANA: María . . .

MARÍA: I just can't believe he's dead. This morning, at

breakfast, he was full of life, giving the men orders about bringing the sheep down from the mountains. And he was singing, the song he sang every day: "Allá en el Rancho Grande."

ANA: He was always singing that silly song. I think the rancherita he was singing about was you. He loved you. He missed you when you were gone.

MARÍA: And I was gone too long. I think now of the time I could have spent with him . . . here.

ANA: This land was his blood. Soy puro Nuevo Mexicano, he used to say. He could taste the earth . . . taste the rain, the wind . . .

MARÍA: Now he's gone. I feel so empty. The ranch is empty.

ANA: And I . . .

MARÍA: I had a premonition this morning. I saw him walking outside, and I felt a shiver. I felt something was going to happen. For a moment there was a shadow. Now I see only darkness and emptiness.

ANA: You have to give yourself time.

MARÍA: This morning there was meaning and promise, now there's nothing.

ANA: I know how you feel, but you're alive. You'll have to think of the future. We have to find out who did this.

MARÍA: Father would want me to be strong . . .

ANA: Of course he would. He would want you to continue his plans.

MARÍA: Yes, you're right. Ana, I know you didn't—

ANA: Kill him? No, of course not. I loved your father.

MARÍA: But the sheriff . . .

ANA: The sheriff has his own motives. He wants to settle this in a hurry, so right now I'm his suspect. But I'm not worried.

MARÍA: What was really going on? Why was Father so secretive and worried?

ANA: I can tell you the little I know. It seems that for

months a group of men have been taking money, illegally, from the foundation. Your father found a file that showed these entries. It may also have named names.

MARÍA: So they killed him?

ANA: They were desperate. Millions are missing. You see, if the foundation had bought that group's land, they would have replaced the money, and no one would have been the wiser. They would have made a fortune, using the foundation money, and they would be clean. It didn't turn out that way. Now they're trying to cover their tracks, but it's too late.

MARÍA: Father knew. Others may know.

ANA: Maybe. Anyway, it goes all the way to the top.

MARÍA: To the Governor?

ANA: I don't know. The information is in the file. In fact, it may even point to the murderer.

MARÍA: Where is the file?

ANA: It's missing. Whoever came in and shot José must have taken it.

MARÍA: We have to find it!

ANA: Both the program and the foundation diskettes are missing. I've looked—they're not here.

MARÍA: Are you sure?

ANA: Yes, someone took them. (*The* SHERIFF *and* TONY *enter from the kitchen. The* SHERIFF *carries Ana's pistol in a plastic bag.*)

TONY: I brought you some coffee.

MARÍA: Thanks. What happens now?

SHERIFF: As soon as the coroner comes I'm taking Ana in and booking her. Murder one.

ANA: What's my motive, Sheriff? Or do you need a motive?

SHERIFF: I know your motive, Ana, but I don't need it. When I came in and flipped on the lights, you were standing over the body, with this pistol in your hand. I got you where I want you.

TONY: You couldn't get her the last time, Sheriff.

MARÍA: What last time?

TONY: When Ana's husband was killed, five years ago. He was found dead. Shot. A lot of people thought you did it for the insurance money.

ANA: You lie! It was suicide and you know it!

SHERIFF: I still think it was murder, but I couldn't pin it on you. This time the evidence is clear. We saw you right over the body, holding this.

TONY: Her husband had lost everything in a deal with Don José. So there is a motive, Ana, since you ask. Revenge.

ANA: You're crazy! ¡Estás loco!

MARÍA: Revenge? Now?

SHERIFF: Why not? I know Ana. I know what she's capable of.

TONY: Yes you do, don't you, Sheriff? Isn't it true, Ana, that the sheriff was in love with you, but you wouldn't have him?

SHERIFF: Shut up, Tony!

ANA: That's ridiculous.

TONY: Sheriff, everybody knows she turned you down. Why so sensitive?

SHERIFF: I said shut up!

MARÍA: And now you're trying to get even . . . is that it?

SHERIFF: I'm not interested in the past. I'm interested in what happened here tonight. Ana shot Don José.

ANA: I didn't kill him.

TONY: I think you're right about that, Sheriff.

MARÍA: Well, I don't believe it.

SHERIFF: What?

MARÍA: I don't believe she shot my father.

SHERIFF: God almighty! The woman was standing over the body when the lights went on, and you can't believe it? You're still in shock. The evidence is all there!

MARÍA: No, that's not true.

SHERIFF: What's missing? You came in here and saw her over the body. The pistol in her hand. Right?

MARÍA: Yes.

SHERIFF: Go on. What did you see?

MARÍA: Blood . . . It was horrible.

SHERIFF: What did you say?

MARÍA: I said, "You killed him."

SHERIFF: There you have it.

MARÍA: Then there was the eerie song from the computer. He was trying to tell me something.

SHERIFF: Nothing to that. I don't know much about these things, but this one has an audio component. See. A tape player with a timer, that's all it is. It can be set to play at any time.

TONY: Voices from the dead, María?

ANA: José had a reason for everything he did—

TONY: Come on, Ana! Quit putting crazy ideas in her head! You did it! Quit the games!

ANA: I'm not admitting anything. (*She turns to the sheriff.*) And I'm not afraid of you. I know about you and your little group in Santa Fe. You want to blame me to cover up your tracks.

SHERIFF: You don't know what you're talking about! This time I got you! I'm going to see that justice is done!

ANA: Justice? Don't make me laugh. You tell us what you were doing here tonight.

SHERIFF: What? Oh, I was just driving by, doing my rounds. Lucky I decided to stop.

ANA: Lucky? I saw you sneak into the house. I was in the closet. I heard you arguing with José.

MARÍA: Why were you hiding?

ANA: I came to warn him. I went for coffee, then to the library, and when I came in here I saw the sheriff at the window. I knew José didn't trust him, so I hid.

SHERIFF: Don't believe a word she says. She murdered him, and now she's making up stories. Just like when she shot her husband.

MARÍA: Why hadn't you told us why you were here?

SHERIFF: I came because your father called me. He knew he was in trouble. When he heard Diego shouting, he asked me to stay and keep an eye on things.

MARÍA: But you made it look as if you had just gotten here.

SHERIFF: I had to, but don't go getting crazy ideas in your head. I was here for a reason. Don José needed help. He had received a threat, because of the information he had from the foundation.

MARÍA: You certainly weren't much help. Why would he have told you about the information he had?

SHERIFF: Everybody in Santa Fe knew your father had won the right-of-way. That's why he called me. I had just gotten here when we heard the commotion in the kitchen. He asked me to step outside. How was I to know the murder was about to take place?

ANA: That's a lie. He didn't ask you for protection. I heard what you said. You were desperate for that information!

SHERIFF: Believe what you want, it's my word against yours. A sheriff with a very good reputation, and a woman who's been at the scene of two murders.

TONY: It's a tie.

MARÍA: I believe Ana. When you came in, what did you see?

SHERIFF: Nothing. The lights went out, then I heard the shot. I opened the door, flipped on the lights, there was Ana.

ANA: And you.

SHERIFF: You're the only suspect, Ana. Know why? Because ballistics is going to show that the bullet came from your gun, not mine. And mine will be tested, don't worry. I'm going to be very careful about this.

MARÍA: Ana?

ANA: My pistol wasn't fired. That's easy to check.

MARÍA: Sheriff? She's right. Just smelling it will tell us.

ANA: Go ahead.

MARÍA: Sheriff?

SHERIFF: This is evidence. I'm not going to allow any tampering—

MARÍA: Sheriff, I insist!

TONY: Let it go, María.

ANA: Go on, Sheriff, what are you afraid of?

SHERIFF (*angrily removes the pistol from the plastic bag, smells it*): No powder smell . . . Damn! It's fully loaded.

TONY: It can't be!

ANA: I told you!

SHERIFF: I don't like this.

TONY: Maybe she used another pistol . . . and hid it.

MARÍA: Where? How? There wasn't time.

TONY: All she needed was a few seconds.

MARÍA: Why would she have two pistols? She didn't kill my father, I'm sure. Somebody else did.

TONY: She had the gun, she was standing right over him when he came in. What more do you want?

SHERIFF: I want a gun that's just been fired, that's what. Are there any other guns in the house?

MARÍA: Yes. Tony's!

SHERIFF: Tony?

TONY: I carry a pistol, Sheriff. I have a license.

SHERIFF: I'm going to have to ask you to hand it over, Tony.

TONY: I don't have it on me.

SHERIFF: Where is it?

TONY: When I got here, María took it.

SHERIFF: Took it? Why?

MARÍA: Father never allowed guns in the house. So I put Tony's pistol in the telephone table.

SHERIFF: Mind getting it for me?

TONY: Remember, Sheriff, I haven't had it on me since I walked in that door.

MARÍA: Here . . . No, it's gone.

TONY: Gone?

SHERIFF: Let me see . . . Nothing here. Are you sure you put it in here?

MARÍA: I'm positive! Dear God, could it have been the pistol used to—

TONY: Somehow Ana got ahold of it.

SHERIFF: Yeah. No telling how long you were in that closet. No telling what you heard. Come on, Ana, I'm gonna take you in. You have a lot of questions to answer.

ANA: I'm not going anywhere with you! (DOÑA SOFÍA *enters holding a pistol.*)

DOÑA SOFÍA: Is this what you're looking for, Señor Sheriff?

SHERIFF: Doña Sofía! Be careful, that thing can go off.

DOÑA SOFÍA: I know it can go off. I know how to use a pistol. (*She advances on the sheriff.*) I've lived on a ranch all my life.

MARÍA: Doña Sofía, don't—

SHERIFF: I'm warning you, I'm a law officer.

DOÑA SOFÍA: Law officer? You're a crook! Don José knew about you! Maybe you killed the patrón, and now you want to blame my son Diego!

SHERIFF: Diego—

DOÑA SOFÍA: You leave him alone! He didn't do anything! Don José promised him the money.

SHERIFF: What money?

DOÑA SOFÍA: The money in his will. Now that Don José is dead, Diego can get his money. That's all he wanted.

SHERIFF: Put the pistol down, Doña Sofía. We have to talk about this.

DOÑA SOFÍA: No.

MARÍA: Doña Sofía, don't make any trouble for yourself.

DOÑA SOFÍA: There's already trouble. Your father is dead, but I'm not going to let him hurt Diego.

SHERIFF: I won't hurt him. I just want to talk to him— There's Diego! (DOÑA SOFÍA *turns. The* SHERIFF *grabs the pistol.*)

DOÑA SOFÍA: ¡Hijo del diablo!

TONY: Good trick, Sheriff.

SHERIFF: Don't move! Stay where you are. This pistol has been fired. Is this yours?

TONY: No. My gun has a fancy pearl handle.

SHERIFF: Do you recognize this?

MARÍA: No. It's not Tony's.

SHERIFF: So where the hell did this come from?

DOÑA SOFÍA: I took it.

SHERIFF: I have to warn you, anything you say may be used against you.

DOÑA SOFÍA: Used against me? ¡Qué me importa! I will do anything to protect my son.

SHERIFF: Including murder?

DOÑA SOFÍA: All my life I've take care of Don José. ¿Y qué gané? My son is in trouble. With the money from the will, we could have bought a ranchito, away from this máquina del diablo who is taking away our work.

ANA: What will, Doña Sofía?

SHERIFF: Don José's will?

DOÑA SOFÍA: Sí. Don José put Diego in his will.

MARÍA: How do you know?

DOÑA SOFÍA: I read it, that's how I know!

ANA: You read his will?

DOÑA SOFÍA: Sí. I found it by accident.

TONY: I bet.

DOÑA SOFÍA: I was cleaning his oficina . . . There were all his papers. And his will.

SHERIFF: And Diego is mentioned in the will?

DOÑA SOFÍA: Sí.

SHERIFF: Did Diego know he was mentioned in the will?

DOÑA SOFÍA: Sí. I told him.

MARÍA: Oh no.

TONY: Sounds like she's handing you a new suspect on a platter.

MARÍA: You don't have to say anything to the sheriff—

DOÑA SOFÍA: Ay, hijita, I have nothing to hide. I only

want to protect my son. I know he drinks, but he works hard. You know he works hard.

MARÍA: Yes.

DOÑA SOFÍA: And he's always wanted his ranchito . . . up in the mountains . . . Oh, dear God, but this is not the time to think about that. The patrón is dead. Pobrecita mi'jita. (*She embraces María.*) Así es la vida . . . un momento estamos aquí, y el otro adiós. Doña Sebastiana viene por todos.

MARÍA: Sí, así es la vida . . .

SHERIFF: This is a whole new ball game.

TONY: And how.

SHERIFF: You knew Diego would get some money when Don José died?

DOÑA SOFÍA: Sí.

SHERIFF: Did you kill Don José?

DOÑA SOFÍA (*softly*): No.

SHERIFF: Did Diego?

DOÑA SOFÍA: No! I'm telling you, no! He wouldn't kill the patrón.

SHERIFF: Go on.

DOÑA SOFÍA: It was all my fault. I saw the gun there, I put it in my apron. Maybe it was the devil who told me to take the pistol. Sí, fue el diablo.

MARÍA: Don't blame yourself. I put the gun there in the first place.

DOÑA SOFÍA: You? But why?

MARÍA: It was a mistake, a terrible mistake.

SHERIFF: Did you take the pistol into the kitchen?

DOÑA SOFÍA: Yes.

SHERIFF: I'd like to know exactly what happened in there.

MARÍA: I took Diego in there. He had been drinking.

SHERIFF: Then?

MARÍA: When he saw the pistol he grabbed it and ran out.

SHERIFF: Where was it?

DOÑA SOFÍA: On the table, where I put it.

MARÍA: I ran in here to get Daddy, then back into the kitchen and out the back door. I called Diego, but he was gone. Then I heard the shot . . .

SHERIFF: He grabbed the pistol, came in here and shot Don José. Open-and-shut case!

TONY: It makes sense.

ANA: Wait a minute. If he used that pistol, how did it get back in the kitchen?

TONY: He came back and dumped it there, hoping somebody else would get blamed.

SHERIFF: Possible . . .

ANA: Something's not right . . . Doña Sofía, did you take the pistol with the pearl handle?

DOÑA SOFÍA: Sí. That was the gun.

ANA: That was your pistol?

TONY: Yes.

ANA: But that isn't it. Where is your gun?

TONY: Diego has it.

SHERIFF: Quit meddling in this, Ana. I'll do the questioning. I've got a gun that's been fired recently and a new suspect who has a hell of a lot of questions to answer. You ought to be glad. This might let you off the hook.

ANA: I'm not on a hook, Sheriff!

DOÑA SOFÍA: Yo tengo la culpa, toda la culpa.

MARÍA: Don't say that, Doña Sofía. We'll find out who murdered Father.

DOÑA SOFÍA: It was the devil—

SHERIFF: The devil doesn't kill people, Doña Sofía, guns do. I can't arrest the devil, but I'm going to have to arrest Diego.

DOÑA SOFÍA: Arrest me! I'm to blame. Don't hurt my son.

SHERIFF: You may be an accomplice, Doña Sofía, but right now it's Diego I want.

TONY: He's probably halfway to Juárez by now.

SHERIFF: I don't think so. I'm going to look around. I don't want anybody to leave this house. Comprende?

ANA: We comprende, Sheriff. (*The* SHERIFF *goes out the front door.*)

DOÑA SOFÍA: Ay, Dios, what a terrible thing has happened. This ranch has always been so peaceful. And now this. These máquinas coming. Look what it has done to Diego. My son who was never greedy, who was always happy, and now he's accused of murder.

ANA: No se apene, Doña Sofía. Things will work out. A while ago the sheriff was blaming me for the murder.

DOÑA SOFÍA: You? Why you? You two were friends.

ANA: Yes, we were.

DOÑA SOFÍA: More than friends.

MARÍA: The sheriff needs a suspect.

DOÑA SOFÍA: Ay, the sheriff can blame you and my son, but who blames the sheriff? Listen. Don't trust him. I have good ears. I heard somebody out there. Like a coyote, sniffing around. It was him, it was the sheriff!

TONY: She's got a point. I did some snooping around outside. The sheriff parked his car down the road, where it couldn't be seen. Another thing. I checked the telephone wire. It's been cut.

MARÍA: Are you sure?

TONY: Positive. And there's a clear set of prints out there. Boot prints. The sheriff wears boots . . .

MARÍA: And Diego. And Ramón . . .

DOÑA SOFÍA: Don't trust the sheriff, that's all I can say. The sheriff used to be a good man, but now he works for those bad políticos in Santa Fe . . . I think I'll make some coffee. (*She exits.*)

MARÍA: I feel sorry for her. She's always had problems with Diego, but he never threatened Father.

TONY: He did tonight, and it looks like he killed him.

ANA: We don't know, there are too many unanswered questions.

MARÍA: I'm not going to rest till I find out who murdered Father.

ANA: If we could only find the disk with the information.

MARÍA: The disk. The answer has to be on the disk. The song?

ANA: "Mary had a little lamb . . ." What does it mean?

MARÍA: That's what he used to sing to me. Except he would say, "María had a little lamb." (*She goes to the fireplace.*) He gave it to me. It was my favorite toy, my security blanket. It could have something to do with . . . What's this?

TONY: What?

MARÍA: A disk? Here . . .

ANA (*takes the diskette*): This is it! The foundation file!

MARÍA: Are you sure?

ANA: Yes. He showed it to me.

MARÍA: Can we play it?

ANA: We need the program disk.

MARÍA: Ramón!

ANA: Call him!

TONY: You can't. The phone's dead, remember?

MARÍA: I'm sure some of the answers are on it. Why would he hide it?

ANA: He knew there was going to be trouble. The answers are in here!

TONY: I can take it into town, get somebody I trust to play it. I could be back in an hour. (*He reaches for the disk.*)

ANA: I wouldn't let this out of my sight.

TONY: Would you rather the sheriff got hold of it?

MARÍA: I'll take it. When this is put in a computer I'm going to be right there to read it.

TONY: Hey, I'm just trying to help. I got an attorney in town who can do anything. I don't blame you for being cautious, but you're getting carried away, aren't you?

MARÍA: You think so?

TONY: Diego, the sheriff, or . . . you don't have to look any further, but I'm not getting mixed up in this. Right now all I want is some fresh coffee. (*He goes out.*)

ANA: I bet he's a Scorpio.

MARÍA: What do you mean?

ANA: Capable of murder if you get on his bad side.

MARÍA: And you?

ANA: I'm a Scorpio . . . and I know I'm capable of murder. I admit it, I have to get what I want.

MARÍA: Like Father?

ANA: Sooner or later, I'd have gotten him. Now it's too late. Let me be truthful: I've always loved your father, but our lives took different paths. The past few years, seeing him, they were the best years of my life. Oh, he could get on my nerves, with that bossy way of his. But inside he was a kind, considerate man.

MARÍA: You loved him.

ANA: Yes. (*There is a pause, a moment of understanding.*) And you, what's with you and Tony?

MARÍA: Nothing. I've been dating him, that's all.

ANA: He's gotten serious. Now a lot of people are going to get serious about you. Now you have the money and power.

MARÍA: Yes . . . that's probably true. I really haven't had time to think about my new responsibilities.

ANA: People are going to be wanting things from you . . . favors. And you could be in danger.

MARÍA: You mean, there may be more than one person involved?

ANA: Yes.

MARÍA: So I can't trust anyone. (*They are interrupted by the* SHERIFF *entering, leading* DIEGO.)

SHERIFF: You can breathe easy, Ana. I got my man. He confessed.

MARÍA: Diego?

SHERIFF: Found him hiding in the barn. Didn't even put up a fight. Came right out and said he killed Don José.

MARÍA: He couldn't have. Diego, tell me what happened?

DIEGO: I don't remember . . .

SHERIFF: Tell 'em what you told me.

DIEGO: The sheriff said Don José is dead.

MARÍA: Yes.

DIEGO: That was the shot I heard. Chingao, I knew it was a bad thing when I heard it.

MARÍA: Tell us what happened.

DIEGO: I ran out of the kitchen, then I heard a shot, very close. I got scared, so I hid in the barn.

SHERIFF: There you have it.

ANA: You don't know if you fired it or not?

DIEGO: I don't remember . . .

SHERIFF: Don't confuse him! A few minutes ago he told me he did it. That's good enough for me.

ANA: You want to wrap up everything in a hurry, don't you, Sheriff? Any suspect will do, as long as you get the credit, and stop the questions.

SHERIFF: You're not out of this yet, Ana. How do I know you two aren't in this together? Diego's got problems, but you're not free yet.

MARÍA: Diego, where's the pistol you took from the kitchen? (DIEGO *shrugs, then reaches in his pocket, takes out the pistol and points it at the* SHERIFF.)

DIEGO: 'Hora sí, cabrón!

SHERIFF: I forgot—

MARÍA: That's it! That's Tony's gun!

SHERIFF: Stand back, you two. Come on, Diego, hand it over.

DIEGO: No! Don't move! I ain't drunk now! You try to take it and I'll shoot!

SHERIFF: You did shoot Don José, didn't you?

DIEGO: No!

SHERIFF: You're in a lot of trouble, boy. This only makes it worse. Now give me the gun.

DIEGO: No! I'm getting out of here.

MARÍA: Diego, don't make things worse. We can talk about it.

ANA: Listen to her, Diego.

DIEGO: It wasn't me, María. I didn't kill the patrón. I was drinking, I got crazy, I heard the shot, but I didn't

kill him. I'm not going to prison. Don't move, Sheriff,
I'll shoot—

(TONY *enters from the kitchen.*)

TONY: You found Diego, huh? (DIEGO *turns and, while
he is distracted, the* SHERIFF *grabs the gun from him.*)

SHERIFF: Hold it!

TONY: What the hell?

SHERIFF: Thanks, Tony. I've got him.

TONY: That's my pistol.

SHERIFF: You sure?

TONY: Yes, I'm sure. The pearl handle . . .

MARÍA: Yes.

SHERIFF: This is the one Doña Sofía took into the kitchen.
He picked it up, came around and shot Don José. I'm
taking you in on a homicide charge, Diego. Anything
you say may be used against you . . . (*The* SHERIFF
*reaches for his handcuffs. As he draws them out, a floppy
disk falls to the floor.*)

MARÍA: What's this?

SHERIFF: Here, give me that! You stay put! Don't move!
(*He handcuffs Diego.*)

ANA: The program disk.

MARÍA: Are you sure?

ANA: Positive! It's marked—

SHERIFF: I said give it to me.

ANA: How did you get it, Sheriff?

SHERIFF: Evidence, that's how. Now hand it over!

MARÍA: Father wouldn't have given it to you.

ANA: No he wouldn't. With this we can play the foundation disk!

MARÍA: Can you?

ANA: I think so (*She goes to the computer.*)

SHERIFF: Hold it! You can't do that!

MARÍA: Why?

SHERIFF: You're tampering with evidence—

MARÍA: But it could reveal the murderer.

TONY: Listen to the sheriff.

SHERIFF: That's right, listen to me. Things are getting out of hand. I can't let you play around with evidence. Hand it over.

MARÍA: Don't give it to him, Ana! We don't trust you, Sheriff. If you want it, you're going to have to arrest us all!

TONY: Hey, I don't want any part of this. Give him the damn thing.

SHERIFF: You don't trust me? I'm the sheriff. The law in this county. Your father trusted me.

MARÍA: And he's dead.

SHERIFF: You're not suggesting that I—

ANA: Listen!

VOICE OF DON JOSÉ (*on the computer*): María, listen carefully. I have recorded everything you need to know on this disk. If anything happens to me, go ahead with my plans. We must use this opportunity to provide work and education for our people. There are men in this state who only want to exploit the people. They must be stopped. You must not trust— (*The* SHERIFF *flips off the computer.*)

SHERIFF: That's enough!

MARÍA: Sheriff!

SHERIFF: This has gone far enough.

DIEGO: Don't hurt her!

SHERIFF: You stay where you are!

ANA: What are you afraid of, Sheriff? That we will find out it was you who came to kill José?

SHERIFF: You're crazy! I'm going to take all of you in.

ANA: And arrange an accident for us? Would you go that far?

SHERIFF: I have enough evidence on you and Diego.

MARÍA: We have a bit of evidence on you, Sheriff.

SHERIFF: Evidence?

MARÍA: Why did you hide your car when you came to-night?

SHERIFF: Hide my car? I told you, Don José suspected something. He told me not to let anybody see me.

MARÍA: Did he tell you to cut the telephone line?

SHERIFF: You think I cut the wire?

MARÍA: There are boot prints there. Tony found them. You're wearing boots.

SHERIFF: Tony? You believe Tony?

MARÍA: Why not?

SHERIFF: Your father didn't trust him.

TONY: Of course he trusted me. Why wouldn't he?

SHERIFF: Because of the past . . . a past he thought you couldn't forget.

MARÍA: What about the past?

TONY: Don't listen to him, María, he's going to dream up wild stories. I had nothing against your father.

SHERIFF: She doesn't have to believe me. You tell her, Ana, about Tony's dad.

MARÍA: What is it?

ANA: Yes, maybe you have reason to hate Don José, because of your father—

TONY: Hey, you know the sheriff, he wants to involve everyone he can. Don't you see what he's doing? He needs one of us as a suspect to save his neck! What are you saying, Sheriff, all of us pulled the trigger? We all killed Don José? Ana, Diego, me? It makes me laugh.

MARÍA: Tell me what happened.

ANA: Years ago, Tony's dad and Don José were partners in a business deal. For whatever reasons, the deal went sour. Tony's dad lost everything. He was sued by his creditors, and he died within the year. Some people say he had put a curse on Don José.

MARÍA: Are you saying Tony has wanted revenge . . . all these years?

TONY: I told you it was a crazy story. Look, if I had wanted revenge I would have taken it years ago. Why tonight?

ANA: No, it doesn't make sense . . . unless . . .

MARÍA: Unless you're part of the group that wanted the information.

SHERIFF: It's possible, isn't it, Tony?

TONY (*laughs*): You're making quite a story out of this. But what kind of evidence do you have?

MARÍA: There's one way to find out. Switch the computer back on. Let's see what Father found in his file.

ANA: He thought it might name names.

SHERIFF: Now I'm curious. Why not? Let's see whose names comes up. (*The* SHERIFF *turns to the computer.* TONY *grabs the pistol in the sheriff's holster. The* SHERIFF *whirls, still holding the pearl-handled pistol. For a moment they face each other.* TONY *laughs.*)

TONY: There are no bullets in that pistol, Sheriff. (*The* SHERIFF *fires. There is a click.*)

SHERIFF: Damn! So you're the one!

TONY: Don't you think that's a good touch, Sheriff, to bring my pistol empty.

MARÍA: Tony. You . . .

TONY: Don José caused my father's death, and I've never forgotten that. He was always meddling, always sticking his nose in. This time he went too far.

MARÍA: You planned it, you brought in your pistol, clean and empty.

ANA: And he had a second pistol in his car.

SHERIFF: And a pair of boots he put on to cut the wire.

ANA: And when you came in, after the shot, you came in the kitchen door.

MARÍA: It was all fitting into place, wasn't it? You came in here and shot him, then you went through the kitchen and left the gun there. Without any prints on it. You almost had a perfect alibi.

TONY (*takes the disk*): Yes, you've got it all figured out, haven't you? Now I'll take this . . . and the score is even.

MARÍA: Daddy didn't kill your father.

TONY: I vowed at my father's deathbed to kill Don José. Now it's done.

SHERIFF: But it wasn't just for revenge, was it, Tony? Your name is on that disk, isn't it? You're part of that group that stole the foundation money.

TONY: Part of the group? That shows how little you know. I am the brains of the group. Taking the money from the foundation was my idea. A brilliant idea, until today when the decision was made to use Don José's land. We lost everything. And to top it off, he found the file.

MARÍA: You'll never get away with this.

DIEGO: You killed the patrón! (DIEGO *lunges forward.* TONY *hits him with the pistol.* DIEGO *falls.*)

TONY: No heroics! Okay! I'm going to get out of here, and anybody who gets in the way gets shot!

ANA: What are you going to do? Murder all of us?

SHERIFF: Tony, you could stop now, take your chances with the law. Don't make it worse on yourself.

TONY: Worse? No, it's going to be beautiful. I have plenty of money to get out of the country. Enough to live like a king in Mexico. Let the others answer to the D.A., I'll be long gone. (TONY *grabs María.*) And I'm taking you with me! In case anybody tries to stop me.

MARÍA: No! Let me go!

ANA: María!

SHERIFF: Don't do it, Tony!

MARÍA (*struggles*): No! No! (TONY *forces María to the door. As he opens it,* RAMÓN *rushes in and grabs* TONY. *The gun goes off. The* SHERIFF *helps Ramón. The* SHERIFF *takes the gun.*)

SHERIFF: Hold it!

MARÍA: Ramón!

RAMÓN: What the hell's going on here? Why the gun?

MARÍA: He murdered Father.

RAMÓN: What? Tony?

MARÍA: Yes, he killed him. Shot him. He was trying to get away.

SHERIFF: I need the handcuffs. (*He throws keys to* ANA, *who uncuffs Diego.*)

RAMÓN: I knew he was a big talker, but murder!

SHERIFF: Yes, murder. And he gave himself away. You were smart, Tony, but not smart enough.

MARÍA: Diego, are you okay?

DIEGO: Yeah, I'm okay, it's just a scratch. I'd like to see him try that when I'm not handcuffed.

SHERIFF (*snaps handcuffs on* TONY): He won't have a chance. I'm taking him in. Come on, Tony, let's go. Remember, anything you say can be used against you . . . (*The* SHERIFF *and* TONY *exit.* DOÑA SOFÍA *appears at the arched doorway.*)

DOÑA SOFÍA: Dios mío, ¿qué paso? Diego, you're bleeding.

DIEGO: It's nothing, jefa.

MARÍA: He's all right, Doña Sofía. He needs a bandage.

DOÑA SOFÍA: Ven, ven . . . I'll take care of that.

DIEGO: I'm okay, jefa. I could have gotten that cabrón. (DOÑA SOFÍA *and* DIEGO *exit.*)

RAMÓN: Somebody tell me what happened?

MARÍA: Father had information that involved Tony in the foundation robbery.

RAMÓN: And he killed him?

ANA: Apparently the file names the group who took the money.

MARÍA: Tony was the head of the group. He stole the foundation money.

RAMÓN: And Don José found out about it. María, I'm sorry about Don José. How can I help?

MARÍA: You did. If you hadn't gotten here when you did, I hate to think of what he would have done.

RAMÓN: Don José was a great man. I can't believe he's dead. What can I say? I'm sorry.

MARÍA: Daddy wasn't perfect. He was impatient and set in his ways, but he did want to help the people.

ANA: He was an honorable man . . . a good man.

RAMÓN: Yes, he was. María, can I get you anything?

MARÍA: Yes, something to drink.

RAMÓN: Water?

MARÍA: No. I think at a time like this, Daddy would have said a brandy.

RAMÓN: Brandy? Sure.

ANA: Make that two. (RAMÓN *goes to the bar.*)

MARÍA: I have a lot to do. Father would have wanted me to continue with his plans.

RAMÓN: You're right.

MARÍA: What was your arrangement with him?

RAMÓN: I was helping him on the computer end, you know, doing research, finding the best experts to bring on board.

MARÍA: Do you want to continue?

RAMÓN: Of course. This is an important project. But it's up to you. You're in charge now.

MARÍA: I would appreciate your help.

ANA: Then let's toast the success of Don José's project.

RAMÓN: And la patrona.

Blackout

Billy the Kid

CHARACTERS

BILLY	MORTON
PAT GARRETT	FRED
ASH	TOM
PACO	BELL
DON PEDRO MAXWELL	OLINGER
JOSEFINA	LA MUERTE
ROSA	GOVERNOR WALLACE
DON JESÚS	SQUIRE WILSON
CATHERINE	JOE GRANT
DOÑA ANA	MANUELITO
JOE	CAHILL and CAHILL'S
LILY	FRIEND
TUNSTALL	SHERIFF ROMERO
McSWEEN	DEPUTY POE

ACT ONE

July 14, 1881, the night of the death of Billy. It is just before midnight at the home of Pedro Maxwell in Fort Sumner, New Mexico. The stage is dark, the outlines of the room may be suggested by curtains. Sitting on a stool fore and left of stage is ASH, observing the events while he writes in a notebook. Next to him rests a small pile of books.

BILLY lies on a bed, reading a land contract, his boots on the floor nearby. Billy is twenty-one, curly-haired, a fine face with an always ready smile. The only light is a lantern near the dresser where ROSA is combing her hair. Rosa is eighteen, dark and lovely. She is dressed in a chemise, her long black hair flowing. She and Billy are sweethearts. He sees her when he visits Fort Sumner. Both are clearly happy.

BILLY: Time to settle down . . . give up being a vagamundo.

ROSA: Siempre lo prometes . . .

(BILLY *rises, paper in hand, goes to* ROSA, *holds her.*)

BILLY: Esta vez lo voy hacer. Mira. A hundred acres, enough land to run a small herd. You should see it, Rosa. There's good grazing, plenty of water, and the beauty of the mountains. It's what I always wanted—

ROSA: Es un sueño, Billy.

BILLY: Tu eres mi sueño, amor . . .

(*They start to kiss, he turns away.* ROSA *reaches after him.*)

ROSA: Billy. (*She holds him.*)

BILLY: ¿Te vas conmigo?

ROSA: Mi padre no lo permite.

BILLY: Yo hablo con el. Vas a ver. Voy a cambiar . . .

(*He returns to the bed, lies down, studies the contract.*)

ROSA: Porque te gusta tanto ese maldado condado de Lincoln? Quedate aquí.

BILLY: Me gustan las montañas, y la gente.

ROSA: Pero los tejanos no te quieren.

BILLY: Qué importa. Anda, casate conmigo. Quiero hijos . . .

ROSA: ¿Seria posible?

BILLY: Sí, es posible. Ven. (*He slaps the bed beside him.*) Imagina. El Bilito, con hijos. Let the papers write about that. Y despues, I'll be a grandfather.

(BILLY *laughs gayly.* ROSA *smiles, starts toward him when there is a knock on the door. She stops.*)

BILLY: ¿Quién es?

ROSA: ¿Sera don Pedro?

(BILLY *rises, pulls a hunting knife from his belt, starts toward the door.*)

BILLY: ¿Quién es?

(*The door swings open and* PAT GARRETT *rushes in, pistol in hand. He fires a shot,* BILLY *falls back on the bed.* ROSA *screams,* PAT GARRETT *fires a second shot.*)

ROSA: Billy!

(ROSA *flings herself on* BILLY, *protecting him, holding him in her arms. There is shouting offstage, people running to the scene.* DON PEDRO MAXWELL *and his daughter* JOSEFINA *are among the first to enter, followed by* PACO *and other Nuevo Mexicanos who work for don Pedro.* JOSEFINA *pauses to look at* PAT GARRETT, *who turns aside.*)

DON PEDRO: ¿Qué pasa?

ROSA (*cries*): ¡Mato a Billy! ¡Mato a Billy!

PAT GARRETT: He was armed. I had no choice . . .
(*A visibly shaken* PAT GARRETT *turns away.* PACO *picks up the knife Billy had drawn.*)

PACO: A hunting knife!

PAT GARRETT: I thought it was a pistol—(*He winces as if in pain.*)

PACO: ¡Cobarde! (*An angry* PACO *cocks his pistol and aims at Pat Garrett.*)

PAT GARRETT: It was him or me . . .
(*The men pull* PACO *away before he can shoot Garrett.*)

FIRST MAN: Vente, Paco. No lo vayas a matar.

SECOND MAN: No vale la bala . . .

PACO: ¡Cobarde! You're the sharife, Mr. Garrett, but you're going to pay for this.
(*The men pull* PACO *away. They cover Billy with a sheet, then slowly raise the bed and carry it out as if carrying a coffin.* ROSA *follows, the other women comforting her.* PACO *remains.* ASH *rises from his stool and looks at the audience.*)

THE ACTORS *sing "El Corrido de Billy the Kid":*
Una noche oscura y maldita
En el pueblo de Fort Sumner
El Sharife Pat Garrett
a'Billy the Kid mato, a'Billy the Kid mato . . .

Mil ochocientos ochenta y uno
Presente lo tengo yo
En la casa de don Pedro Maxwell
No mas dos balas le dio, No mas dos balas le dio . . .

Vuela, vuela palomita
A los pueblos de Río Pecos

Y cuentale a las morenitas
Que ya su Billy murio, Que ya su Billy murio . . .

Hay que cobarde el Pat Garrett
Ni chansa a Billy le dio
En los brazos de su amada
Ahi mismo lo mato, Ahi mismo lo mato . . .

Hay que tristeza me da
De ver a Rosita llorando
Y el pobre del Billy sangrando
No mas un suspiro le dio, No mas un suspiro le dio . . .

Vuela, vuela palomita
A los pueblos del Río Pecos
Y cuenta le a las morenitas
Que ya su Billy murio, Que ya su Billy murio . . .
      (*The corrido fades, Billy is carried out.* PACO *remains,*
      glaring at Ash. ASH *turns to address the audience.*)
ASH: My, my, isn't that sweet. They even composed a
      corrido for him. Sure, he liked the Mexican señoritas,
      but he didn't die in the arms of Rosita. The way I heard
      it, Billy had just walked into don Pedro's room, and Pat
      Garrett was waiting for him. Challenged him and shot
      him dead.
      (PACO *jumps forward to rebut Ash.*)
PACO: Billy wasn't armed!
ASH: Who the hell are you?
PACO: Paco Anaya. I was in Fort Sumner that night! Pat
      Garrett never gave Billy a chance!
ASH: How would you know?
PACO: I was there!
ASH: My, my, everybody's got a story to tell. Since that
      fateful night of July 14, 1881, I've heard the stories of
      a hundred men—each one claims he was there. That
      bedroom must have been a crowded place. (*He chuckles.*)
PACO: I was there, cabrón! I helped bury the kid! I wrote
      it in my book! (*He pulls a crumpled book from his back*

pocket.) ¡Mira! ¡Aquí sta! Billy's story! Just like he told me. And what I saw that night!

(ASH *takes the book, looks at it, smirks.*)

ASH: A little vanity press publication. Don't you know there's been a hundred dime novels written about Billy's death, and each one claims to know the truth. (*He turns to the audience.*) This doesn't look like a very literary work.

PACO: I was there! You weren't!

ASH: True, I wasn't there. But I got the real story from Pat Garrett. I helped him write the true account, I was the "ghost writer." (*He reaches for his book.*) See here, *The Authentic Life of Billy the Kid*, as told to me by Pat Garrett.

PACO: ¡Mierda! That's what I call your truth! You didn't know the kid the way *we* knew him.

ASH: You Mexicans. Yes, you had a soft spot in your heart for Billy. He spoke Spanish like a native . . .

PACO: He treated us como hombres! ¡Mexicano o gringo, todos eranos iguales!

ASH: ¿Iguales? Sure, if you carried a Colt and a Winchester you were iguales. That was the problem. Violence was a way of life! Live by the sword, die by the sword. As Billy lived, he died.

(PACO *turns away, covers his face.*)

PACO: A good man died . . . Just when he was ready to—

ASH: To settle down? With the señorita. No, Billy couldn't settle down. Don't you see, he had the seed of violence in him. (*Turns to audience.*) You might say he was a product of his time. The New Mexico territory after the Civil War was a violent place. Everyone was armed, and human life was cheap. Southern soldiers whose own land had been devastated, and Texans looking to make a quick buck rustling cattle were rushing into Lincoln County. The only law was the quick gun. Shoot first, ask questions later. That same violence was bred into Billy. I saw him turn from an innocent kid into a cold-

blooded killer. You want to know the real story? I'll tell
you.

PACO: The real story? You call what Pat Garrett told you
la verdad? I should have shot that sanamabiche!

ASH: I'll tell the truth as I know it . . . We newspapermen
are trained to tell the truth—

PACO: Ha!

ASH: I have no reason to lie. I never took sides in the
Lincoln County Wars. I just reported what happened.
Told it like it is—

PACO: You believed Garrett!

ASH: Tell you what. I'll make a deal with you. I'll tell my
story as I know it, you tell yours.

(PACO *is suspicious at first.*)

PACO: You promise to tell the truth?

ASH: As near as I know it.

(PACO *nods. He goes to right and sits.*)

PACO: Okay. But tell the truth. (*He pats his pistol.*)

ASH: That's right, you just sit there. No need for violence.
After all, this is just storytelling . . . (*He turns to audience.*) Marshal Ashum Upson, at your service. You may
be asking what qualifies me to tell the story of Billy the
Kid. Well, friends, I helped Pat Garrett write the true
life of Billy. You might say I got the story straight from
the horse's mouth. (*Goes to his chair and picks up notebook.*) Now I'm writing a new book. I want to know
more than the events, I want to know what made Billy
tick. I want to know why this boy became a cold-blooded
killer.

PACO: Because that sanamabiche Dolan gang killed Tunstall. That's why!

ASH: Well, you're partly right. Tunstall had become like
a father to Billy. And Billy never knew his father . . .
(PACO *nods.*)

Where was I? Well, I arrived in New Mexico during the
Civil War. Worked in newspapers from Alburquerque to
Mesilla. I was postmaster in Roswell for a while, and a

JP in Lincoln County. I met the kid on various occasions. First time I met Billy was March 1, 1873, in Santa Fe. His mother, Catherine McCarty, was marrying William Antrim. Marriage took place in the La Fonda Hotel. I hear the hotel's still there. Billy was fourteen. His older brother, Joe, was there. Joe didn't say a word that day, but keep this in mind, he's going to be important to the story.

(CATHERINE McCARTY, *dressed in wedding gown, and* WILLIAM ANTRIM *enter to the tune of a wedding march. Catherine is thin, pale, she has tuberculosis. She turns aside to talk to Billy and Joe.*)

CATHERINE: William is a fine man.

(*Both boys nod.*)

He wants to move to Silver City. Get away from the politics of Santa Fe, the violence. Make a fresh start.

JOE: Yes, ma'm.

CATHERINE: He'll make a fine father . . .

BILLY: Yes, ma'm.

(CATHERINE *draws* BILLY *to her and holds him.*)

CATHERINE: Oh, Billy, I want you to be happy for me—

BILLY: I am happy, Mother.

CATHERINE: I do worry for you. Joe's older, he can take care of himself, but I do fear for you. My orphan son. It hasn't been easy growing up without a father. But it's going to change. We don't have to keep moving anymore.

(*She coughs, lets go of Billy, and turns away.*)

BILLY: Mother.

CATHERINE: I'm better. Really, I am. (*She turns back to Billy.*) Billy, I'm afraid.

(BILLY *embraces her, they hold onto each other.*)

BILLY: Don't be afraid, Mother. I'll take care of you.

CATHERINE: Oh, this world is too much with us. So much violence, the men drinking and fighting, and everyone carries a gun. Promise me, Billy, promise me you won't carry a gun.

BILLY: I promise . . .

CATHERINE: Promise me you'll never drink, Billy.

BILLY: I won't, Mother.

CATHERINE: Promise me you'll always be a gentleman.

BILLY: I promise . . .

CATHERINE: Men just don't know how much women suffer. Do you understand, Billy? Men don't know how much women suffer . . . (*She coughs again, turns away.*) I'm afraid . . . afraid of the dark germs eating away at my lungs. I thought coming out here from New York would help. The desert air, the doctor said. But once the germ starts eating away . . . There's no cure, Billy, no cure . . .

BILLY: Silver City will be good, Ma. High mountain air, plenty of sunshine. You'll get better, you'll see.

CATHERINE: Oh, you're such a fine son. Yes, we'll move south. Clean mountain air and plenty of hot chile. I've heard the Mexicans say the chile burns away the germs. (*She pauses, looks at Billy. BILLY coughs.*)
I'm afraid for you, Billy. Afraid of this curse I carry—

BILLY: I'm all right, Mother, I am. I'm strong, and I got Joe.

JOE: I'll take care of him, Ma, really I will.

CATHERINE: You're brave boys. Yes, Joe will watch over you. So let's be happy. This is my wedding day. Dance with me, Billy.
(BILLY *and* CATHERINE *dance to* "Turkey in the Straw," *showing off* BILLY's *skills as an excellent dancer. Lights dim as scene fades.* ASH *turns to the audience.*)

ASH: She was consumptive, you know. TB. No cure. It was a slow and sure death in those days. That's why they left New York, wandering through the Midwest to Denver, Santa Fe, and finally Silver City. Where she died just eighteen months after her wedding day . . .
(CATHERINE *pauses and coughs. She slumps in pain, then she looks up and raises her arms.*)

CATHERINE: I see them coming, Billy.

BILLY: Who, Ma?

CATHERINE: A horde of angels, Billy. A horde of angels
coming to take my soul to rest ... (*She raises her arms
in ecstasy, then looks at Billy.*) Be good, Billy. Be good.
Oh, my orphan son. Now you are truly alone ...
(CATHERINE *falls into* BILLY'S *arms. Six of the men
on the dance floor reach for her, put her on a coffin-like
litter, and carry her across the stage to where Billy's bed
rests. The music turns to dirge.* BILLY *follows and kneels
before the coffin.*)

BILLY: I love you, Mother. I'll be good. I promise.
(BILLY *rises, coughs. A chorus of "Amazing Grace"
ends the scene.*)

ASH: Billy never married. Oh, he had a way with women.
They flocked to him. He didn't drink or smoke, and he
loved to sing and dance ... but he never married.
(ASH *looks at* PACO, *who nods.*)

PACO: Estaba tisico. He had TB, just like his mother. Oh,
he could hide it real good, but we knew. This old Mexican
curandero he met in Sonora gave him a weed to chew
for the cough.

ASH: Who was that old man?

PACO: Manuelito. Billy met him in Mexico right after he
killed Cahill. The old man taught him Spanish, came
back with him. He was always trying to help Billy.

ASH: So that's the old man always hovering around the
kid?

PACO: Billy would chew on that weed and never cough.
But even the old curandero couldn't get rid of the TB.
One night we were out at my campo where I took care
of sheep. Billy told me. "It's a curse," he said, "and not
even don Manuelito can get rid of it."

ASH: And Rosita?

PACO: She loved him. She wasn't afraid.

ASH: So now Billy is an orphan. The mother had taught
him song and dance, and for a while he joins a minstrel
show. Think of it, folks, a cold-blooded killer who as a

child loved to sing and dance. What if someone with compassion had taken him in? Encouraged his abilities. Instead he fell in with Sombrero Jack, took to reading the *Police Gazette*, and petty thievery . . .

PACO: But he wasn't a cold-blooded killer!

ASH: He killed Cahill.

PACO: Cahill had it coming.

ASH: Well, maybe Cahill was a bully. But dammit, Billy was hanging out with Sombrero Jack. They were up to no good.

PACO: That's not the way I see it. (*He opens his book.*) April 17, 1877. Billy was over in Arizona, hanging around the army camps . . .

(*Scene of a bar, music, army soldiers, bar women. WINDY CAHILL stands at the bar with a FRIEND. BILLY, his friend SOMBRERO JACK, and Billy's brother JOE enter the bar. JACK and JOE order a drink. LILY, one of the young bar girls, goes to Billy and puts her arm through his. Two of the other girls gather; Billy is obviously a favorite.*)

LILY: Come dance with me, Billy.

BILLY: Whoa, give me a chance to clear the dust from my throat.

CAHILL: That's right, bartender, give the squirt a glass of lemonade.

(CAHILL *and* FRIEND *laugh.* BILLY *whirls but* LILY *pulls him away.*)

LILY: Pay no attention, Billy. Sing us a song.

BILLY: If the piano man can play a decent melody.

(*The* PIANO MAN *smiles, plays,* BILLY *sings, the women gather around him.*)

BILLY: *When Irish eyes are crying*
          And the boys are off to war
          Then I'll raise my cup in parting
          And kiss the tears away
          Then I'll raise my cup in parting
          And kiss the tears away.

(*The bar women clap.*)

LILY: That's beautiful, Billy.

BILLY: My mother taught me the song. She was my bonny lass—

LILY: And you're our bonny boy, Billy.

BILLY: Hey, I like that. Bill Bonny.

CAHILL: My, my, isn't that sweet.

CAHILL'S FRIEND: A bit too sweet . . .

CAHILL: Sweet as a pimp bird.

(BILLY *whirls and faces Cahill. The bar goes silent.*)

BILLY: You have a loud mouth, Cahill. Put up or shut up!

(CAHILL *reaches for his pistol, hesitates.*)

CAHILL: I got no quarrel with you, Billy boy. It's your brother who turned me into the law.

(JOE *steps up next to Billy.*)

JOE: You deserved what you got, Cahill. So make something of it.

(CAHILL *sees the odds, curses, turns back to the bar.*)

BILLY: Come on, Joe, the bully don't have it in him. (*He turns to Lily and the piano man.*)

BILLY: Play another tune, piano man.

(CAHILL *glares at Joe, whispers through clenched teeth.*)

CAHILL: There's two of you little bastards, otherwise I'd whip your ass.

JOE: There's just one of me. Let's step outside and see whose ass gets whipped.

(JOE *starts toward the door. CAHILL follows then draws his pistol and shoots Joe in the back. CAHILL turns and aims at Billy, but Billy is too quick. BILLY fires and kills CAHILL. Everyone takes cover as BILLY rushes to Joe.*)

BILLY: Joe! Joe!

JOE: He got me, Billy. Oh, Lord, it burns . . .

BILLY: We'll get you to the doctor! Jack! Give me a hand!

JOE: No, Billy, don't move me. I'm dying . . .

BILLY: Jack! Get the doc!

JOE: Don't turn your back on any man . . . Listen.

BILLY: What is it?
(*The strains of the old spiritual "I Looked over Jordan"
sound far away.*)
JOE: It's Mother. I see her . . .
(CATHERINE appears in white.)
CATHERINE: My son, my son, the violence has come to
claim you.
BILLY: Where, Joe? Where? (*He looks around anxiously.*)
JOE: Mother . . . (*He reaches out.*) I'm dying, Billy. You
gotta run. The sheriff is friend to Cahill! Run, Billy,
run . . .
(JOE *coughs, dies.* BILLY *holds him and rocks him, and
begins to cry.*)
BILLY: Don't die, Joe. You're all I got. You're all I
got . . .
(*One chorus of "I Looked over Jordan" as the light
fades.* BILLY *rises and goes out. He moves to a Mexican
sheep camp, where don* MANUELITO *sits at the fire.*)
MANUELITO: ¿Cómo te llamas?
BILLY: Billy.
MANUELITO: Bilito, eh. Sientate. Come . . . (*He offers
Billy a plate of food, coffee.*) You are running from the
law.
(BILLY *nods, coughs.*)
BILLY: Thanks for the food, don . . .
MANUELITO: Manuelito.
BILLY: Gracias, don Manuelito.
MANUELITO: How long do you have the toz?
BILLY: Cough? It's nothing.
MANUELITO: How long?
BILLY: 'Bout a year . . .
MANUELITO: Maybe your father or mother also had the
toz?
BILLY (*nods*): It killed my mother . . .
MANUELITO: Sí. It grows in the lungs, makes you spit
blood, then it kills you. It is a germ that has no cure. I

have some medicine, a plant we Indios use. It takes away the cough, but not the toz.

BILLY: Nothing I can do, huh?

MANUELITO: Stay in the desert, in the sun, in the air, eat the goat cheese, and you will live. Return to el norte, and you will die.

BILLY (*laughs*): I'll stay with you, old man. You give me some of that medicine and you teach me Spanish, and I'll herd sheep for you.

(*They both laugh in agreement. Fade.*)

ASH: Is that what you think happened?

PACO (*nods*): He stayed with the old man a year, and when he came north don Manuelito came with him.

ASH: Nobody mentions the old man in their writings.

PACO: Nobody mentions the Mexicans in their writing. Why would they write about the old man?

ASH (*uncomfortable*): Ah-hem, you got a point there.

PACO: Don Manuelito could see into Billy's destiny. He could see the soul. He knew the violence would kill the kid . . .

ASH: Well, one more story to add to the myth of Billy the Kid.

PACO: El Bilito.

ASH: You really did have a soft place for him?

PACO: He was a boy. I was just a few years older, but I could tell, in his heart he was just a kid . . .

ASH: You're right. In a manner of speaking. At that point, he still could have been saved. *If* he shot Cahill in self-defense. But, Lord, the times were just too violent for a kid to make it on his own.

PACO: He needed a familia . . . That's what he was looking for. The Mexicanos always made a place at the table and accepted him as one of the familia. They understood the bad breaks he had with the law.

ASH: So Billy was looking for love, huh? He picked a strange place to find it. Lincoln County. Lord, if there was a lawless place in the New Mexico territory, it was Lincoln County. The Texans were coming in and grabbing up the land, rustling . . . There were fortunes to be made supplying the army with beef. So Billy came up from Mexico and began to call himself William Bonney. Took up with the Jesse Evans gang . . . Met John Tunstall . . . And thus began the last three violent years of his short life . . .

(*Shift to* JOHN TUNSTALL'S *ranch.* ALEXANDER McSWEEN, *Tunstall's attorney, is there.* BILLY *and* FRED WAITE *enter.*)

TUNSTALL: Billy, good to see you. Howdy, Fred.

FRED: Mr. Tunstall.

(TUNSTALL *embraces* BILLY. *Both are glad to see each other.*)

BILLY: Sorry we're late, Mr. Tunstall. Fred and me were over on the Peñasco . . .

TUNSTALL: What's this I hear 'bout you buying a place?

BILLY: Yeah. Fred and me, we figure we can run forty, maybe fifty head up there . . .

TUNSTALL: Billy, Billy. You know I need you here . . .

BILLY: Yes, sir.

(TUNSTALL *turns to McSween.*)

TUNSTALL: Billy's the best vaquero I've had since I came here. He can ride, shoot, and he knows no fear.

McSWEEN: And he's a good dancer. Sue says he's the only cowboy in Lincoln County who can carry a tune. So how you been, Billy?

BILLY: Been fine, thank you.

(TUNSTALL *puts his arm around Billy's shoulder.*)

TUNSTALL: You know a small place ain't gonna make it, Billy. U.S. Army wants beef to feed the black soldiers at Fort Stanton. Fifty head is a drop in the bucket. You gotta think big, Billy.

McSWEEN: They need the kind of Texas dogies John Chisum is rustling up.

(McSWEEN *and* TUNSTALL *laugh.*)

TUNSTALL: Chisum's a good man. Sonofabitch I can't stand is Dolan. You know what that cocksucker's gone and done?

BILLY: We heard. That's why we came right away.

TUNSTALL: Sonofabitch began by getting Sheriff Brady to confiscate Mac's office, now the sheriff's taken over my store! My store, Billy! My merchandise! Dolan wants to be número uno, and he's got that no-good sheriff doing his dirty work! I won't stand for it!

BILLY: Yes, sir.

TUNSTALL: What do you think about that, Billy?

BILLY: Well, sir . . .

TUNSTALL: You've been like a son to me, Billy. You're part of the family.

BILLY: Yes, sir. I appreciate everything you've done, sir. I—I never knew my father. I mean, it was just Mom and Joe . . .

TUNSTALL: And they're dead.

BILLY: Yes, sir.

TUNSTALL: It hasn't been easy for you, Billy. But you've found a home here.

BILLY: Yes, sir. I feel I belong.

McSWEEN: But they've got a warrant out for you in Arizona . . . They ain't never gonna let you forget the Cahill killing.

TUNSTALL: The law can be for you or against you, Billy. If the sheriff don't like you, he sure as hell is going to make it hard on you. Just like Dolan has Sheriff Brady on my back.

McSWEEN: Dolan charged me with embezzling a life insurance policy, and he got one of the heirs of the policy to sue me! That no-good judge Bristol over in Mesilla has attached my property! And John's too!

TUNSTALL: It's war! Dolan wants war, and I know I can depend on you. (*He puts his arm around Billy.*)

BILLY: I'll do what you need done, Mr. Tunstall.
(TUNSTALL *smiles.*)

TUNSTALL: You see, Mac. He's a good boy. I can depend on Billy. (*He slaps Billy on the back.*) We're gonna fight back! Show Dolan and Sheriff Brady we got the best vaqueros in Lincoln County. What do ya say, Fred?

FRED: I stick with Billy. Where he goes, I go.

TUNSTALL: You see, Billy, you've got friends here. You go up to the Peñasco on your own, and men like Dolan will burn your place down.

McSWEEN: And use the law to cover their tracks.

TUNSTALL: The law's rotten in Lincoln County! It's law-abiding citizens like us who have to be the law! You understand?

BILLY: Yes, sir. I do.

TUNSTALL: I knew you would.

BILLY: Just tell me what you need done, I'll do it.

TUNSTALL: Dolan's got a posse. Forty-three men. They stole my cattle from the Feliz. I say we start out at first light and teach them a lesson. Meet them head-on! Get my cattle back!

BILLY: We'll be ready.

TUNSTALL: Good. And remember, we're doing the right thing. We've got the law on our side.

BILLY: Yes, sir.

(BILLY *and* FRED *start for the door.*)

TUNSTALL: Billy.

BILLY: Yes, sir.

TUNSTALL: Thanks for your loyalty. It's loyalty that makes a man. I know I can depend on you, son.

BILLY: You just stay close to me and Fred, Mr. Tunstall. We'll take care of you . . .

(*They go out, the light fades. Two opposing groups of cowboys enter the stage. The spotlights are on TUN-STALL facing BILLY MORTON, JESSE EVANS, and TOM HILL.*)

MORTON: There's Tunstall, alone. If he resists, shoot 'im!

BILLY (*offstage*): Mr. Tunstall? Where are you, Mr. Tunstall?

TUNSTALL: Over here, Billy! Over here!

MORTON: Hold up, John Tunstall! We've been deputized by Sheriff Brady to bring you in.

TUNSTALL: You're not deputies! You're crooks! (*He turns and shouts.*) Billy!
(*The three men open fire and* TUNSTALL *falls, mortally wounded. The three escape as* BILLY *enters and finds Tunstall on the ground.* BILLY *rushes forward and holds Tunstall in his arms.*)

BILLY: Mr. Tunstall . . . Oh, God . . .
(McSWEEN *rushes in.*)

McSWEEN: He's dead . . .

BILLY: I came too late . . . We got separated in the thicket . . .

McSWEEN: They murdered him, Billy.

BILLY: Oh, God, I promised him, I promised him . . .

McSWEEN: Cold-blooded! They ambushed him in cold blood!

BILLY: I swear I'll get them, Mr. Tunstall, I swear . . .
(*Light fades,* BILLY *holding Tunstall in his arms.*)

ASH: The murder of John Tunstall was the spark which ignited the Lincoln County War. For Billy, the only man who ever treated him like a father had just been murdered. Think of it. Those he loved were now gone: his mother, his brother Joe, now Tunstall. Open warfare had come to Lincoln County. Vigilantes riding at night and firing on innocent people, one gang of cowboys against the other . . .

PACO: And we were in the middle . . .

ASH: The Mexicans? But you were armed too.

PACO: We had to protect ourselves! We didn't make the war! We were herding sheep and raising beans and corn along the Pecos! There was enough land for everyone to make a living, but people like Dolan and the others wanted too much! The posses came and went! The innocent suffered.

ASH: Ain't that the way with war. Each side thinks it's in the right. Dolan's side had warrants out to arrest McSween and his vaqueros, and McSween got a J.P. to issue warrants to arrest Sheriff Brady. So McSween, crazy as he was, sends Billy and Fred Waite to arrest Brady. He sends two young boys right into Dolan's store. Like sending lambs into the lion's cave.

(BILLY *and* FRED WAITE *enter the store.* SHERIFF BRADY *is backed by a posse.*)

BILLY: Sheriff Brady, we got a warrant for your arrest—

BRADY (*laughs*): Sonofabitch if the kid don't have balls! Did I hear right? You're here to *arrest me?*

BILLY: We've got a warrant from Constable Martinez. States you committed larceny on the Tunstall store. And we got a warrant for members of your posse for the murder of John Tunstall—

BRADY: You little sonofabitch! You can't arrest me! I'm the sheriff!

(BRADY *approaches Billy and Fred. His posse surrounds them.*)

BILLY: If you come peacefully, we assure you safe conduct—

(*The posse overpowers Billy and Fred, takes their pistols and holds them.*)

BRADY: That McSween must be loco if he thinks he can arrest me! (*He strikes Billy across the face.*) Next time you pull a pistol on me, kid, you better be prepared to use it!

(BRADY *strikes Billy again.* BILLY *struggles but the men hold him.*)

You little squirt! Go back and tell McSween to send a man to do his dirty business! Not a kid!

(BRADY *pushes Billy and Fred out the door. The men laugh.*)

FRED: Sonofabitch was waiting for us. You okay, Billy?

BILLY: Nobody pushes me . . .
(McSWEEN *appears*.)
McSWEEN: Did you get Brady?
BILLY: He's got too many men.
McSWEEN: You let that stop you? I thought you were fast—
(BILLY *draws his pistol and points at McSween*.)
BILLY: I am, Mac. But no sense in dying when you don't have to!
McSWEEN: All right, Billy, all right. I've got another plan. Dolan's taken the law in his hands, so I'm going to form a posse. Call ourselves the Regulators . . .
FRED: What do you mean?
McSWEEN: I mean we're the only law in Lincoln County! And the first sonofabitch we'll get is Brady. He's sitting on my property and acting like a king! I aim to put a reward on his head! Bring him in dead or alive!
(McSWEEN *laughs crazily as he exits. Other cowboys come in to join Billy and Fred*.)
BILLY: Mac just put a bounty on Sheriff Brady . . .
FRED: We've got a warrant for his arrest. Nothing worse than a bully with a badge.
BILLY: He killed Tunstall . . . the only man who ever treated me like a son. Ain't it right for a son to want revenge on those who killed his father?
(*The other cowboys nod*.)
FRED: We're with you, Billy!
(*Don* MANUELITO *has kept to the background but now steps forward*.)
MANUELITO: No, Billy! If you seek revenge, it never stops. You kill them, they come to kill you. Let the law take care of this.
BILLY: Brady is the law, and he's a cold-blooded murderer! I'm sorry, don Manuelito, but I've got to settle this my way.
MANUELITO: Revenge will start a war you cannot end . . .

FRED: We are the law, Billy. We been deputized!

BILLY: And I say we get the sonofabitch! He didn't give Mr. Tunstall a chance. Gunned him down in cold blood. He deserves the same!

MANUELITO: No, Billy . . .

(*The cowboys shout their approval. BILLY, FRED, and friends run to hide. SHERIFF BRADY and two deputies walk down the street. BILLY and friends open fire. BRADY goes down. BILLY runs to him and takes the pistol from Brady's belt.*)

BILLY: An eye for an eye, Sheriff Brady! We're even!

(*BILLY and friends exit. The frightened and subdued townspeople come out to stand over the sheriff's body.*)

ASH: Now there was no turning back . . . Governor Axtell had declared Sheriff Brady the law of Lincoln County, and now he's been assassinated. On April 29 the Battle of Lincoln begins. Dolan's boys against McSween's Regulators. A warrant is served on Billy . . . On July 15 there is an open battle on the streets of Lincoln. Colonel Dudley, who's in charge over at Fort Stanton, marches in with his black soldiers, but that only makes things worse. For five days the battle wages back and forth, until McSween's house is burned down and he's killed. Billy escapes. (*He looks at Paco.*)

PACO: He, his friend Tom O'Falliard, and don Manuelito rode north on the Río Pecos. That's where I met him. I was just a boy, herding sheep outside Fort Sumner. They showed up at my camp over by Ojo Hiedondo. I took them to my home . . .

(*BILLY, TOM, and don MANUELITO enter Paco's home, meet DON JESÚS and DOÑA ANA, his father and mother, and ROSA.*)

PACO: Mamá, papá. Estos son amigos . . .

DON JESÚS: Pasen, pasen.

BILLY: Muchas gracias, señor. (*He looks at ROSA. They smile at each other.*)

DON JESÚS: ¿Cómo te llamas?

BILLY: Bill Bonney, a sus ordenes.

PACO: Es el Billy the Kid.

DON JESÚS: Oh, el Bilito. Te anda buscando la ley.

BILLY: Alla en el condado de Lincoln no hay ley, señor.
Solo la pistola es la ley. (*He pats his pistol.*)

DON JESÚS: Asi es el tiempo, muy violente. Los sharifes
son un bola de sinvergüenzas. Yo soy hombre de paz.
No quiero violencia en mi casa.
(BILLY *looks at* ROSA, *then unbuckles his pistol belt
and hangs it on a hook on the door.*)

BILLY: En su casa, también yo soy hombre de paz.

DON JESÚS: Entonces, bienvenido. Sientense. Oye, vieja,
dales de comer a estos jovenes.

PACO: This is my sister, Rosa.
(ASH *looks surprised.*)

BILLY: A pleasure to meet you, señorita . . .
(BILLY *holds her hand. They look at each other with
deep attraction.* ROSA *blushes.*)

ROSA: So you're the famous Billy the Kid? You look like
a plain, and dusty, vaquero.
(BILLY *smiles, turns to* PACO.)

BILLY: I am dusty. Been riding hard from Lincoln County.
Where can I clean up?

PACO: There's a cajete outside. Ven.
(ROSA *steps in front of him.*)

ROSA: I'll show him. He needs lots of hot water, and
soap.
(PACO *looks at* BILLY *and shrugs.* BILLY *laughs.*)

BILLY: Gracias.
(ROSA *lifts a kettle with hot water from the stove and
leads* BILLY *outside. She pours the water in the washtub
and he strips his shirt to wash.*)

BILLY: I hear there's a baile tonight in Fort Sumner.

ROSA: Yes. Don Pedro Maxwell is having a fiesta. You
know don Pedro?

BILLY: Yes, I know him. We brought some cattle up to
him a year ago. I only wish I had met you then.

ROSA: So, are you going to the baile?

BILLY: Only if the girl of my dreams will accompany me.

ROSA: She must be very brave.

BILLY: Why?

ROSA: Because you're a bandido.

(BILLY *laughs, reaches for the towel she hands him.*)

BILLY: Bandido? I only draw my pistol when I have to protect myself.

ROSA: We hear about the killings.

BILLY: And about me?

ROSA: Yes. They say el Bilito killed Sheriff Brady.

BILLY: Brady killed John Tunstall. I was just settling the score.

ROSA: We don't want the violence of Lincoln to come here. We want to live in peace—

BILLY: Yeah, I can understand that. Live and let live . . . But down the Pecos the Dolan vaqueros don't think like that.

ROSA: And you?

BILLY: Some of those vaqueros want my hide . . . so I keep my pistol handy.

ROSA: A person can change.

BILLY: I've thought about that. Thought about getting myself a place, minding my business, running a few head of cattle. Pero no es posible.

ROSA: ¿Por qué?

BILLY (*shrugs*): The territory changed after the war. All those Texans and southern soldiers returning home found nothing but ruin. They spent four years killing each other, living day to day with death. And when the war ended they found the South was in ruins. Devastation all around. They came west, and they were armed. So this has become the new battlefield, and the man who isn't armed gets pushed out.

ROSA: My father isn't armed.

BILLY: Yeah, but the Mexicanos down in Lincoln County are armed. Look, when it comes to war you need to protect your place. Protect your family. (*He puts on his shirt.*)

ROSA: You have a familia?

BILLY: No.

ROSA: No one?

BILLY: They killed my brother, and they killed the only man who ever treated me like a son. Now I trust only my pistola.

ROSA: That's sad.

BILLY: You said a person could change . . .

ROSA: Any man can change.

BILLY (*moves toward her*): Become a sheepherder on the llano?

ROSA: We are happy, we are content. We have our families, the vecinos who help, the fiestas of the church . . .

BILLY: I'm afraid if I came here—

ROSA: What?

BILLY: The vaqueros would follow me. There's a U.S. warrant for my arrest. Somebody would come looking for me, and one day I'd be standing behind a plow, and—

ROSA: Is your destino to live by the gun?

(BILLY *turns and looks at don* MANUELITO.)

BILLY: An old friend told me that revenge only makes for more killing, but every time I try to change, someone starts a new fight. (*He stops, ties his bandana around his neck, smiles.*) There. How do I look?

ROSA: Muy guapo.

BILLY: Now I'm going to ask the most beautiful señorita of Fort Sumner to the dance.

ROSA: Oh, and who is that?

BILLY: You.

ROSA: You are a flirt.

BILLY: I mean it.

ROSA: I will go with you, if my father permits it.

BILLY: Let's ask him.

(BILLY *takes her hand and they walk into the house. The scene changes to the dance. A wild polka is playing;*

everyone, including BILLY *and* ROSA, *is dancing. Rosa's father and mother sit and watch. They nod approval.*)

DON JESÚS: Es buen muchacho. No toma como los otros.

DOÑA ANA: Tiene mucha cortesía. Y habla bien nuestra idioma.

DON JESÚS: Es simpático . . .

(DON PEDRO MAXWELL *enters with his daughter* JOSEFINA. *Don Pedro is middle-aged, silver hair, dressed in the fine suit of a rico. Josefina is tall, slender, black hair tied back, and dressed in a very expensive gown for the period. The music stops and men step forward to greet him.* DON JESÚS *and his wife stand to greet Don Pedro.*)

DON JESÚS: Bienvenido, don Pedro, Josefina . . .

DON PEDRO: Don Jesús, doña Ana. ¿Cómo 'stan?

DON JESÚS: Todo pacífico, gracias a Dios.

DON PEDRO: ¿Y estos jovenes?

DON JESÚS: El Bilito y su amigo—

DON PEDRO: ¿Bilito? ¿Pero que haces aquí?(*He warmly embraces Billy.*) Josefina, mira quien anda aquí. Billy.

BILLY: ¿Cómo le va, don Pedro, Josefina?

(JOSEFINA *smiles, greets Billy warmly.*)

JOSEFINA: Billy, it's been a long time. Shame on you for not telling us you were here.

BILLY: I came in a hurry . . .

DON PEDRO: No excuse. Sabes que aquí tienes tu casa. ¿Cuánto hace?

JOSEFINA: It's been a year since he stayed with us. And you didn't write as you promised. I should be angry.

DON PEDRO: But you forgive him.

JOSEFINA: Yes, I forgive him, if he will dance with me. (BILLY *fidgets, introduces Rosa.*)

BILLY: This is Rosa . . .

DON PEDRO: Of course I know Rosa. Rosa is my god-child. ¿Cómo estás, Rosa? (*He embraces Rosa.*)

ROSA: Bien, padrino.

JOSEFINA: How are you, Rosa?

ROSA: ¿Bien, gracias, y tu, Josefina?

(JOSEFINA *straightens Rosa's collar.*)

JOSEFINA: I am fine, but look at you. You're wearing the same gown you wore last year. Come by the house and we will take up one of mine. It will fit perfectly.

(ROSA *lowers her head.*)

DON PEDRO (*to Billy*): And you come home with us tonight. I want you to tell me what's happening in Lincoln County.

(BILLY *looks at Rosa.*)

BILLY: I—

JOSEFINA: No argument. The guest bedroom is always ready for you.

(*The music strikes up a waltz.*)

Now dance with me. I, too, want to hear of your adventures.

(BILLY *looks at* ROSA, *who dashes out. He takes* JOSEFINA's *hand and dances.*)

JOSEFINA: I should be angry with you.

BILLY: ¿Por qué?

JOSEFINA: Not coming to see me.

BILLY: I just rode in. Met Paco, and he—

JOSEFINA: Billy! You surprise me.

BILLY: ¿Por qué?

JOSEFINA: Being in the company of sheepherders? Tch, tch.

BILLY: Many a sheepherder has saved my life out in the llano. Son buena gente.

JOSEFINA: Pero no tiene mañas.

BILLY: Me gusta la gente humilde.

JOSEFINA: Y yo. ¿Ya no te gusto?

BILLY: Sabes que sí . . .

JOSEFINA: You promised to write, and you didn't.

BILLY: I've been too busy.

JOSEFINA: Did our night of love mean so little to you?

BILLY: Things changed when I got back to Lincoln.

JOSEFINA: And now the law has offered a reward for you. I worry for you.

BILLY: Why?

JOSEFINA: Because I care for you. And Papá cares. He can help you.

BILLY: ¿Cómo?

JOSEFINA: Come tonight and talk to Father. He knows the governor. Maybe he can get you a pardon.

BILLY: A pardon? Me, a free man?

JOSEFINA: Yes, it's possible. Come and stay with us. We can help you. Unless you're still friendly with John Chisum's niece Sallie? Is that why you didn't write?

BILLY: Oye, news travels fast on the Río Pecos.

JOSEFINA: There are no secrets. Father's sheepherders and vaqueros move up and down the river. They hear everything . . .

BILLY: My life is a book.

JOSEFINA: Yes, what you do is known to all. The Mexicanos think you're Robin Hood. They say you rob from the rich, give to the poor.

BILLY: The poor need help—

JOSEFINA: I am rich, Billy, and you robbed me.

BILLY: ¿Qué dices?

JOSEFINA: You stole my heart.

BILLY: What would your father say?

JOSEFINA: He likes you. He wants to help you.
(BILLY *looks toward the door.*)
Come tonight. I've waited a year . . .
(*The waltz ends.*)

BILLY: I'll come. I promised don Pedro.
(BILLY *goes out the door where* ROSA *stands alone. She has been crying. He goes to her.*)
¿Rosa? ¿Qué pasa?

ROSA: Nada.

BILLY: Why did you leave?

ROSA: It's warm inside.

BILLY: Nice and cool out here. Stars look like the milk of heaven. Peaceful. A man could—

ROSA: Change?

BILLY: I never thought the shooting down in Lincoln County would stop, but now—

ROSA: Yes.

BILLY: Just meeting you makes me think there's a chance.

ROSA: A man has to decide, Billy.

BILLY: I know, and I've been thinking. There's a new governor in Santa Fe. Lew Wallace. He's granted a pardon to those who fought in Lincoln County. I won't surrender to Dolan's posse, but I might turn myself in to the army, or to the governor.

ROSA: The governor would protect you!

BILLY: Yes. If the pardon's good, I could leave Lincoln, come up here—(*He pauses, holds her at arm's length.*) Maybe I'm putting the wagon before the horse.

ROSA: What would it take to make you change your ways?

BILLY: If I knew the beautiful woman I've met tonight would wait for me while I go down to Lincoln and settle things.

ROSA: You mean Josefina?

(BILLY *laughs, draws her into his arms.*)

BILLY: You know who I mean.

ROSA: Do you make these promises so easily?

BILLY: I never have, not to a single woman.

ROSA (*cynically*): Can I believe your sweet words?

BILLY: I never felt like I feel toward you.

ROSA (*turns serious*): ¿Qué sientes?

BILLY: Un amor . . . (*He holds her close.*)

ROSA: I was jealous when you danced with Josefina. I have never felt that before.

BILLY: I never said "I love you" to a woman till tonight . . .

(*They are about to kiss when* BILLY *turns away.*)

ROSA: Billy? ¿Qué pasa? What did I say?

BILLY: It's not you.

ROSA: ¿Pero qué?

BILLY: I can't.

ROSA: Why, Billy?

BILLY: A curse, Rosa. A curse I carry . . .

ROSA: I don't understand,

BILLY: My mother's curse . . . (*He coughs.*)

ROSA: There is no curse between us. Not if we love—

BILLY: I do love you. (*He takes her hands in his.*)

ROSA: Do you want to kiss me?

BILLY: Yes. I want to kiss you, and hold you, and love you. But I can't!
(ROSA *holds him.*)

ROSA: Our love can be stronger than any curse.
(BILLY *looks at her, believes.*)

BILLY: ¿Seria posible?

ROSA: Con amor, todo es posible.
(BILLY *gathers Rosa in his arms in a warm embrace as* TOM *comes running out the dance hall door.*)

TOM: Billy! It's a posse!

BILLY: Go inside, Rosa!
(BILLY *pushes Rosa toward the door as a group of heavily armed men appear in the shadows. They are tall, big, and stocky, armed to the teeth with belts of cartridges, pistols, Winchesters.*)

BILLY: Make a run, Tom!

TOM: I'm stickin' with you, Billy!
(*The man in charge of the posse is Sheriff Desidero Romero. He calls out.*)

ROMERO: Billy!

BILLY: ¿Quién es?

ROMERO: Soy Desidero Romero, Sharife del condao de San Miguel!
(*There is a tense moment as* BILLY *and* TOM *get ready to draw their pistols.*)

BILLY: ¿Qué quieres?

ROMERO: Oímos que vas al rumbo de Las Vegas.

BILLY: It's a free country, Sheriff.

ROMERO: No queremos plaito en Las Vegas. Marchate pa Lincoln.

BILLY: Me marcho a donde quiero. No sharife is going to tell me where to go!

ROMERO: I'm warning you, Bilito!

BILLY: Consider I've been warned.

TOM: Billy, there's too many of them . . .

(*There is a tense moment as the men place their hands on their pistols ready to draw.*)

BILLY (*whispers*): Yeah. Armed to the teeth . . . Come to think of it, Sheriff, we were really headed for Puerto de Luna.

ROMERO: We just don't want no trouble with you.

BILLY: I promised don Jesús not to make trouble here. Why don't you and your boys come in and have a drink? (*There is a break in the tension.*)

ROMERO (*nods*): I sure could use one. We've been riding all day . . . (*He steps forward.*)

BILLY: Who told you I was headed for Las Vegas?

ROMERO: Some sheepherder.

BILLY: ¡Esos borregeros saben todo!
(*The posse laughs.*)

ROMERO: We got some good gambling in Las Vegas, and a few people thought you might be coming up.

BILLY: I earn my living at cards, Sheriff, and one of these days I'll come up north—
(ROMERO *frowns, places his hand on his pistol.*)
But not tonight, Sheriff, not tonight!
(*They all laugh and go into the dance hall.*)

ASH: All's well that ends well.

PACO: Not so well . . .

ASH: Why the reservation? Sheriff Romero and his Las Vegas posse had their drink and headed home. There was no shoot-out.

PACO: I wasn't thinking of Romero.

ASH: Ah, Josefina.

PACO: She lured him home that night. Promising her father could get a pardon from Governor Wallace. Hell, the warrant on Billy was a federal warrant! Nothing the governor could do!

ASH: She wanted him—

PACO: In her bed.

(ASH *turns to audience*.)

ASH: Now I swear, folks, I don't know anything about this. I never got into Billy's love life. Oh, everyone knew the women loved him. He didn't drink, didn't smoke, could sing and dance. He was quite a ladies' man. But this thing with Josefina is part of the myth, part of the many stories people were to tell about the Kid. Take it with a grain of salt is all I've got to say.

PACO: Someone knows.

ASH: Who?

PACO: Rosa.

ASH: She found out?

PACO: A woman knows those things in her heart. Don Pedro's house was very near our house. A short walk. Billy spent some time talking to Don Pedro, then he was put in the guest bedroom.

ASH: The same room in which Pat Garrett later gets him?

PACO (*nods*): The guest room is right next to don Pedro's bedroom . . .

(BILLY *enters the dark room. There is a candle burning on the dresser. He takes off his shirt and lies down. JOSEFINA appears at the door, dressed in a nightgown.*)

JOSEFINA: Billy?

BILLY: ¿Quién es?

(JOSEFINA *enters, goes to him.*)

You shouldn't be here.

JOSEFINA: The last time you were here you told me you loved me. (*She goes to his bed and sits by his side.*)

BILLY: Josefina. I was here a few days. I—

JOSEFINA: I've dreamed of you day and night. I want you. I want you more than anything.

BILLY: Your father—

JOSEFINA: Father knows how I feel. I love you, Billy . . .
(JOSEFINA *lets the nightgown slip from her shoulders
and reaches to snuff out the candle. The stage goes dark.*)

PACO: Ay, ¡qué mujer! She would do anything to keep
Billy!

ASH: An aggressive woman. And you think Rosa knew . . .
(PACO *nods.*)
Lord, ain't life complex. What dark webs we weave when
first we practice to deceive . . . (*He turns to audience.*)
The plot begins to thicken, as the theatre people are wont
to say. I suggest we take a short intermission. ¿Qué dices,
Paco?

PACO: Bueno. I need a drink.

ASH: Yes, and I'm sure some of our friends want to wet
their whiskers and stretch their legs while they try to
sort out what's fact and what's fiction. This story ain't
done yet. What I've learned so far makes me worry for
Billy.

PACO: Now you know Billy wasn't all bad. He deserved
a better life, he deserved to settle down in his ranchito
with Rosa, but things worked against him.

ASH: They were star-crossed lovers?

PACO: Las estrellas o el destino, ¿quién sabe? Some men
have a destiny they can't fight. Billy tried, but he couldn't
change his destino.

ASH: Is this destino some of that Mexican fatalism we
hear about?

PACO: Ash, for an educated man you disappoint me. Destino is a way to explain life. Time repeats itself; life
repeats itself . . .

ASH: You got a point. I've seen men, and women, so
trapped by circumstances that they die. Just wither away,
or die violently. So Billy was destined to be in that room
when Pat Garrett shot him.
(PACO *shrugs.* ASH *turns to audience.*)
That question has plagued me, and Pat Garrett never
answered it for me. How did the sheriff know what room

in Pedro Maxwell's house Billy was going to be in? No, it wasn't a one-room house, it was the big house of a rico. Richest man in Fort Sumner, to be exact.

PACO: I know.

ASH: You telling?

PACO: Read my book. (*He laughs.*)

ASH: Let's go get that drink.

(ASH *and* PACO *walk offstage.*)

End of Act One

ACT TWO

BILLY *lies in a plain cot. He is asleep. On a nearby trastero a short candle burns next to a small, plain cross. There is a small table nearby. There is a cough in the shadows. BILLY awakens, sits up, and reaches for the pistol at his bedside.*

BILLY: ¿Quién es?

(CATHERINE, *Billy's mother, appears from the shadows. She is ghost-like, dressed in her faded wedding dress.*)

CATHERINE: It's me, Billy, your mother.

BILLY: Mother?

CATHERINE: It's such a warm night . . . I couldn't sleep. Did I disturb you?

BILLY: No, Mother. (*He puts aside the pistol.*)

CATHERINE: You have a gun? Oh, Billy, I warned you about guns.

BILLY: It's for self-defense, Ma. I need it.

CATHERINE: I don't care for guns. They frighten me. I was afraid that the "law of the West," as the men are apt to call it, would catch up with you. Get rid of it, Billy. Guns only bring trouble.

BILLY: I can't, Ma.

CATHERINE: You're disobeying me?

(BILLY *gets up, goes to her, starts to embrace her then pulls away.*)

BILLY: I never disobeyed you, Ma.

CATHERINE: No, you didn't. But you know, he who lives by the sword will perish by the sword.

BILLY: Ma, if a man don't carry a pistol he's nobody. He gets stepped on.

CATHERINE: And if he carries one—You know what happened to Joe.

BILLY (*nods*): Cahill shot him.

CATHERINE: Now I'm afraid for you.

BILLY: Cahill was a bully, Ma. But I got him!

CATHERINE: But the law, Billy—

BILLY: There is no law! Every man takes care of himself.

CATHERINE: And you had to avenge Joe's death?

BILLY: Yes.

CATHERINE: Vengeance is for the Lord, Billy, not for us mortals. Don't you see, once you take up arms and put the law aside, you might as well live in the jungle. There is no end to vengeance.

BILLY (*cries out emotionally*): I tried, Ma, I tried! But everyone I ever loved was taken from me . . .

(CATHERINE *reaches for Billy but does not touch him.*)

CATHERINE: My son, my poor orphaned son . . .

BILLY: I ride with a few of the boys . . .

CATHERINE: But you are alone . . .

BILLY: Yeah. Most of the time. Out there the only mother I know is the llano, and the only father the Pecos River. At night I sleep under the stars . . . I cover myself with that glittering blanket . . .

CATHERINE: Alone . . .

(BILLY *nods.*)

If you found a woman . . .

BILLY: There is one.

CATHERINE: That makes me happy. A woman can help a man. Who is she, son?

BILLY: Rosa. She's as beautiful as her name. I've known

a lot of women, but never one like Rosa. (*He grows animated.*) She lives up on the Pecos. She comes from a good family, Ma. And I love her. I know in my heart I love her!

CATHERINE: You don't know how happy that makes me. Go to her, Billy. Put away the gun and make a life with her. Make a life of peace, or the violence will consume you. (*She coughs.*)

BILLY: And take the curse to her?

CATHERINE: If she loves you, Billy, she'll understand.

BILLY (*shakes his head*): I can't infect her with this germ I carry—this germ I have to hide from everyone. Don Manuelito has tried everything he knows, but there's no cure, Ma. There's no cure!

(CATHERINE *yearningly reaches for Billy but does not touch him.*)

CATHERINE: Her love, Billy! Her love will make you strong! Don't you see, we have lived with this scourge forever. And we have conquered it!

BILLY (*surprised*): It killed you, Ma!

CATHERINE: Is that what you think? Oh no, Billy. The tuberculosis didn't kill me . . . (*With great effort and love she finally can take Billy in her arms and embrace him like a child.*) I died of a broken heart, my son. I died because it hurt me to see the violent world you would inherit . . . There was nothing I could do, Billy. Perhaps I was too meek, too sensitive, but you're strong! You and Rosa can be strong together! (*She holds Billy away from her.*) Go to Rosa. Go to her, son! There is salvation in her love. I know that now! (*She turns and disappears into the shadows.*) Goodbye, Billy.

BILLY: Ma! Ma! Don't leave me, Ma! Don't leave me . . . (BILLY *falls to his knees, sobbing softly. The light fades.* ASH *and* PACO *appear from the left. They carry a bottle of tequila, two tin cups. They have been drinking.*)

ASH: You got it wrong, Paco! It was February 18, 1879, when Billy and Dolan met to declare a truce.

PACO: You want every pinche date to be correct! What the hell are you, a historian?

ASH: Well, yes, in a manner of speaking—

PACO: What about the man? What about the spirito inside? Don't that count?

ASH: Yeah, it counts. I guess it matters to St. Peter. (*He laughs and fills their cups.*) Get it, it matters to St. Peter! (*He laughs loudly.*) St. Peter cares about your soul, in Lincoln County they cared how fast you could draw your pistol!

PACO: I think Lew Wallace was a no-good sanavabiche!

ASH: There you go again, demeaning the good governor. You just can't go around saying bad things about those you don't agree with.

PACO: He was only interested in writing that book—

ASH: *Ben-Hur*.

PACO: Yeah. He didn't give a plug of tobacco for Billy!

ASH: Governor Wallace was a righteous man. He gave Billy a chance.

PACO: But he wanted Billy to put the finger on Dolan!

ASH: No, not put the finger on, not snitch, testify! He wanted Billy to testify!

PACO: ¡Poner dedo! It's the worst thing a man can do.

ASH: How else you gonna put the crooks in jail?
(PACO *shrugs, both sit to enjoy a drink.* GOVERNOR WALLACE *and* SQUIRE WILSON *enter and sit at the small table.*)

WALLACE: A cold night for March.

WILSON: These "northers" have no respect for spring. The land starts to warm up, lambs are born, and a storm can come down and freeze everything.

WALLACE: Yes. I find the New Mexico territory to be an enchanting land, but with spring winds and winter storms to match its beauty. There's a deep history. But there's also violence in the land.

WILSON: Men make violence, Governor. The land abides, the land will nurture. It's men that make the violence.

WALLACE: It's gotten out of hand. The newspapers back east are calling us savages. We're not savages, we're Christians! By the will of God, I intend to bring a modicum of civilization to this land. (*He pauses.*) Do you think he'll come?

WILSON: If Billy gives his word, he keeps it.

WALLACE: You have faith in the Kid?

WILSON: Lot of people 'round here do. The Mexicans treat him like a hero. For them he's a Robin Hood. He watches out for them and they watch for him.

WALLACE: They think we're too harsh, don't they?

WILSON (*shrugs*): It's our destiny . . .

WALLACE: The white man's destiny? It is a heavy load . . . (*He stands and muses.*) I've been studying these people since I came to Santa Fe. They are good workers, no doubt. Consistent, except when one of their saints' fiestas comes along. Then they spend their time at church, hauling the images of their saints back and forth. They seem to have a good time at their religion, dancing and drinking after the praying is done. Spending all day with their families . . .

WILSON: Sounds pretty civilized to me—

WALLACE: Humph. God knows we could never get along without the work they do. They build our houses, clean our streets, prepare our food, bring wood down from the mountain to heat our homes, and at end of day they leave. I often muse on where they go. What do they say about us in the privacy of their homes? I've been observing them, but it seems I don't know them. (*He straightens his shoulders, voice rises.*) But they're God's children, and they are under the protection of the United States government. I was sent to institute law and order over them, and I intend to keep my pledge.

WILSON: Not so much them that need law and order . . .

WALLACE: Yes, you're quite right. In general, they are quiet, law-abiding citizens. I agree, it is our own kind that has created this mess in Lincoln county . . .

(*There is a knock at the door.* WILSON *looks at his watch.*)

WILSON: Right on time.

WALLACE: Enter!

(BILLY *enters, pistol in one hand and Winchester in the other. He looks around, holsters his pistol, and steps forward.*)

BILLY: Governor Wallace?

WALLACE: Billy Bonney. Pleased to make your acquaintance.

(THEY *shake hands.*)

You know Squire Wilson.

BILLY (*nods*): Howdy, Squire.

WALLACE: Please, sit.

(BILLY *places his rifle on the table and sits.*)

I'm glad you came. I received your letter and I am very encouraged that you will testify in this matter. As you know, I am eager to put an end to this lawlessness which has gripped the territory.

BILLY: Whoa, Governor. Go slow. I already made a truce with Dolan's gang. I don't bother them and they don't bother me.

WALLACE: A truce among gang members isn't worth the paper it's written on. I need convictions! I need to show them I mean business!

BILLY: What do you want me to do?

WALLACE: Testify! Come into the courtroom and testify against them!

BILLY: You mean snitch? Tell what I know about Dolan's gang?

WALLACE: In a courtroom. All nice and proper—

BILLY: If I testify, they'll kill me.

WALLACE: Thou shalt not testify against your fellow gang member, is that the code of the West?

BILLY: Something like that.

(WALLACE *sits across the table from Billy and looks at him intently.*)

WALLACE: I can offer you protection.

BILLY: Protection? The law out here can't be trusted. Sheriff Peppin is a Dolan man. It was Peppin who attacked us for no good reason.

WALLACE: I will use the full extent of my office . . .

(BILLY *studies* WALLACE *closely*.)

BILLY: Out here, a man's life depends on trust . . .

WALLACE: I understand that. I may be new to the New Mexico territory, but I understand law and justice. I understand the law and the prophets, Billy, and we can trust in that.

BILLY: What's the prophets got to do with Dolan's boys?

WALLACE: I've studied the Bible, Billy. I know it inside out. This land looks exactly like the Israel of the prophets. Dry deserts and high mountains, the wind moaning across the landscape like the word of God. Jew and Muslim struggling to live side by side, to raise their sheep and crops! There is a seed of mistrust between the two. God has planted the seed of enmity!

BILLY: Am I the Jew or the Muslim, Governor?

WALLACE: You're a Christian, Billy. I've read a few of the dime novels written about you. Your mother brought you up a Christian. Don't you see, we the Christians are the soldiers that strike away enmity! That is our role in these occupied territories! We have come to deliver the citizens of these harsh climates to a better future!

WILSON: The white man's destiny . . .

WALLACE: Yes! Let us recognize our role and be proud of it! It is our manifest destiny to Christianize these lands! Join me, Billy, and together we can bring forth a new millennium of peace!

BILLY: All I have to do is rat on Dolan.

WALLACE: Testify, Billy. Testify. We have to start somewhere.

(BILLY *stands, looks hard at Wallace*.)

BILLY: I have no love for Dolan and Jesse Evans and Billy

Campbell. And I'm not interested in Christianizing the folks here. Most of them do well by what they got. I have my own honor, and I'm going to tell you what I know because I trust you. And because I truly want this peace you promise.

WALLACE: You won't regret it, Billy. Your name will be writ in history as a peacemaker. (*He puts his arms around Billy's shoulders.*)

BILLY: I hope so, Governor, 'cause what I'm doing ain't easy.

WALLACE: This is a historic moment! Squire? Call the photographer!

BILLY: Photographer? (*He reaches for his Winchester.*)

WALLACE: I knew you would see things my way. I came prepared to record this moment. A photograph, Billy. An image I can send to Washington. I've brought peace to the territory, Billy! I want it recorded for posterity! (WILSON *lets in the photographer with camera. He sets up.*)

One of you and me, Billy. Shaking hands. I give you your warrant and you agree to testify against Dolan! (BILLY *reluctantly shakes hands with the governor. The flash explodes.*)

Excellent! Now one of Billy alone. For the newspapers! Without your guns, Billy. Without your guns!

BILLY: With all due respect, Governor. You can take my picture till hell freezes over, but you can't take my pistol or my rifle till Dolan signs the peace.

(*The flash explodes. The classic picture of Billy standing with his Winchester appears on the screen in the background.*)

WALLACE: Dolan will sign. The days of gang warfare in Lincoln County are over! Now sit here, Billy. The squire will take down all the names and events exactly as you state them. This is the beginning of a new time, Billy, and it's going to mean a pardon for you.

(BILLY *and* WILSON *sit, and as* BILLY talks, WILSON writes. WALLACE *rubs his hands in accomplishment. Light fades.*)

ASH: A week later Billy was arrested in San Patricio.

PACO: And Governor Wallace was there to enjoy it.

ASH: I admit, he was a bit condescending . . .

PACO: Just like all the others. They come here from the East and look down their noses at the paisanos.

ASH: Not all of us . . .

PACO: You're no different!

ASH: I am! I've gotten to know your people. A lot of those prejudices I had early on . . .

PACO: Like Christianizing the territory . . .

ASH: All right, all right! So the governor was a sonofabitch! He really believed his mission was to Christianize the New Mexico territory.

PACO: Not much has changed in a hundred years. Every time we get a new expert in here, he thinks he knows what's best for us.

ASH: Hey, amigo, give me some credit. I'm learning . . .

PACO: Mucha suerte. We might all be gone and forgotten by the time you finish your lesson. ¡Pasa la botella!

(*ASH passes the bottle.*)

ASH: They jailed Billy in Juan Patrón's house—

PACO: And Governor Wallace was staying next door. That night he learned just how much la gente loved Billy. They came to the window and serenaded him.

(BILLY, *behind bars, smiles at the group which has gathered to sing a quickly composed corrido to the tune of "Las Mañanitas."*)

CHORUS OF PEOPLE: Buenos días, Bilito. We came to sing you a song.

(BILLY *laughs gaily and waves.*)

BILLY: I hope it tells how the governor double-crossed me.

CHORUS:
          Buenos días, Bilito Bonney
          Hoy te vengo a celebrar
          Hoy por ser día de tu santo
          Te venimos a cantar!

          La semana antepasada
          Nos llego el governador
          Hoy te encuéntras en la carcel
          Lamentando la traición!

          El Wallace nos trae mas "taxes"
          Y promesas de Santa Fe
          Y el pelado que no se cuida
          Hasta la camisa va perder!

          Despierta, Bilito Bonney
          Mira que ya amanecio
          Y tu como pajarillo cantas
          En la jaula que's tu carcel!

(*The* CHORUS *roars with laughter,* BILLY *applauds.*)

ASH: There was a flurry of action after that.

PACO: Old Judge Bristol got busy . . .

ASH: Yeah. The grand jury over in Mesilla handed out two hundred indictments. Billy testified and identified Dolan and Campbell as the men who killed Chapman.

PACO: And not a man went to jail.

ASH: The law works in mysterious ways . . . Any of that hootch left?

(PACO *passes him the bottle.*)

PACO: So Billy kept his promise to Wallace, but got no pardon. He went up to Fort Summer to see Rosita . . .

ASH (*clears his throat*): And other women?

PACO: There were a lot of women in love with the Kid. But after he met Rosa he was interested only in her.

ASH: He felt betrayed by Governor Wallace.

PACO: If the governor had kept his word, the Kid

would've settled down. Instead he started rustling cattle to sell down at White Oaks and Tularosa . . .

ASH: What could Wallace do? January 10, 1880, Billy kills Joe Grant in a Fort Sumner saloon.

PACO: Joe Grant was a bully!

ASH: I know that, and you know that, but you can't kill people just 'cause they're bullies!

PACO: Joe Grant drew on him!

ASH: And Billy was faster.

(*Bob Hargrove's saloon.* BILLY *and* TOM *are at a monte table playing,* JOE GRANT *is at the bar drunk.*)

JOE GRANT: I hear you're fast, Billy Bonney.

(BILLY *stands, faces Joe Grant.*)

BILLY: Fast enough to stay alive. But I'll tell you, I'd rather be smart than fast.

JOE GRANT: Hear you got it in for John Chisum.

BILLY: Sonofabitch owes me some money.

JOE GRANT: He's standing right there. If you're man enough, take your money now.

BILLY: That's not John. That's his brother Jim. I got no quarrel with him . . .

(BILLY *turns to sit.* JOE GRANT *draws his pistol.*)

JOE GRANT: You're yellow, that's why!

(JOE GRANT *shoots but his pistol misfires.* BILLY *whirls and shoots him dead. As* BILLY *holsters his pistol* ROSA *rushes in.*)

ROSA: Billy!

BILLY: You shouldn't be in here.

(BILLY *takes her arm and walks her outside. Manuelito is standing in the background.*)

The cantina's no place for a woman.

ROSA: You killed him . . .

BILLY: He fired first. I knew the hammer would fall on an empty cylinder.

ROSA: You knew?

BILLY: I placed it there earlier in the evening. Like I told him, sometimes a man stays alive just being smart.

ROSA: And you shot him . . .

BILLY: It was him or me. Let me take you home—
  (ROSA *tears away*.)

ROSA: No!

BILLY: This is no place for you!

ROSA: And it is for you?

BILLY: I can't help it.

ROSA: Why, Billy, why?

BILLY: It's the only thing I know.

ROSA: How can you promise me love?

BILLY: What I do for a living has nothing to do with us!

ROSA: Yes it does! That's what you can't see!

BILLY: I earn my living playing cards—

ROSA: And rustling cattle.

BILLY: Nothing wrong with that. You see a loose steer
  and you take it.

ROSA: Take what's not yours?

BILLY: Everybody rustles. Chisum, Dolan, the Santa Fe
  Ring at the capital. Everybody rustles!

ROSA: My father doesn't!

BILLY: He's the only honest man in the territory.

ROSA: No. There are many honest men.

BILLY: I guess I just haven't been riding with them.

ROSA: It's not too late to ride with honest men.

BILLY: What do you mean?

ROSA: My father is delivering sheep to Mexico. I'm going
  with him.

BILLY: I thought we—

ROSA: Come with us.

BILLY: Saddle up and leave?

ROSA: What do you have here?

BILLY: Only you.

ROSA: Then come with me. Leave this behind you.
  (BILLY *goes to her, embraces her. He looks at* MANU-
  ELITO.)

BILLY: That's what my friend has been telling me—¿Qué
  dice, don Manuelito? ¿Nos vamos a México?

MANUELITO: Vámonos!

ROSA: We can start a new life. You can leave your gang. But *you* have to decide.

BILLY: I decided the day I met you. Wherever you go, I'll go.

(ROSA *and* BILLY *embrace tightly.*)

ROSA: Oh Billy, you'll see, together we can make a new life!

BILLY: Forget the past . . .

ROSA: Make a new future. For our children . . .

(BILLY *looks at her.*)

BILLY: It's what I wanted. Una familia, un ranchito . . . not the shootings . . .

(ROSA *pulls him.*)

ROSA: Let's tell Father.

BILLY: You go on. I'll be right there. There's a few accounts I have to settle.

(ROSA *kisses him lightly.*)

ROSA: Don't be long.

(ROSA *goes out. A smiling* BILLY *looks after her.* JOSEFINA *enters.*)

JOSEFINA: Bilito?

(BILLY *turns.*)

BILLY: Josefina. ¿Cómo estás?

JOSEFINA: I've been looking for you. Was that Rosa?

BILLY: Yes.

JOSEFINA: You promised to come. Father is waiting.

BILLY: I was on my way—

JOSEFINA: Before you met Rosa.

BILLY: We're going to Mexico!

JOSEFINA: You and Rosa?

BILLY: I'm sorry, Josefina.

JOSEFINA: Sorry? Don't you dare feel sorry for me!

BILLY: I meant—

JOSEFINA: Tell me it's not true!

BILLY: It is true, Josefina. I'm going with Rosa.

JOSEFINA: You made love to me!

BILLY: I made no promises—

JOSEFINA: You used me!

BILLY: I never meant to hurt you.

(*JOSEFINA clutches at him.*)

JOSEFINA: I won't let you go! I love you, Billy! Only you! (*She falls to her knees.*) Father is going to talk to the governor! You can stay here, Billy! Stay with me!

BILLY: It's no good—

JOSEFINA: You can't leave! I won't let you. I love you, Billy, I love you!

(*She sobs. BILLY tears away.*)

BILLY: I'm sorry . . .

JOSEFINA (*sobbing*): I won't let you go, Billy!

(*BILLY goes out, leaving JOSEFINA crying on the floor. PACO has been watching the action. ASH is scribbling in his notebook.*)

ASH: A tearful scene . . . but I don't like what you're getting at.

PACO: No, you don't like it, because you listened only to Pat Garrett! You wrote what he told you! You didn't know what was going on in Fort Sumner!

ASH: I never claimed to know a woman's heart . . . I looked for facts. (*He reads from his notes.*) November 2, 1880, Pat Garrett is elected sheriff of Lincoln County . . .

PACO: There you go with all your pinche dates again!

ASH: Just trying to keep the record straight. I mean, it is Pat Garrett that's going to kill the Kid. You know, after Billy and his amigos shot Carlyle at Coyote Springs, he lost a lot of friends.

PACO: Not us.

ASH: No, not the Mexicans, but the ranchers and Governor Wallace turned against him. Wallace even put a $500 reward on the Kid's head. And the New York papers wrote him up. Called him the bandido número uno of the territory.

PACO: You can't believe the goddamn papers! (*He spits.*)

ASH: We tell the truth!

PACO: What is the truth? You made up half that book you wrote!

ASH: I embellished a little . . . but so did you.

(PACO *jerks as if slapped.*)

PACO: I was an old man when I wrote my book. I had forgotten a few things . . .

ASH: So you stuck in this and that—

PACO: I told the truth!

ASH: It's mostly myth when it comes to Billy's story. People believe what they want.

PACO: So what are we doing here?

ASH: Well, amigo, we came to tell stories, and to have a drink.

(ASH *laughs, then* PACO *laughs.*)

PACO: ¿Por qué no? Let's have a drink!

ASH: ¿Solamente una copita?

PACO: ¡Una, nada mas! We have nothing else to do. We're two writers out of work! Just making up stories!

(*They laugh loudly.*)

ASH: A couple of sinvergüenzas!

(*A roaring laughter.*)

Making up stories!

PACO: Making up the truth!

ASH: A little of this, a little of that!

(PACO *gets serious. Looks at the audience.*)

PACO: And them?

ASH: They're fools if they believe the musings of two drunks.

PACO: ¡Pendejos!

ASH: Leave them alone. They paid their money.

PACO: Well, maybe they're finding out what *really* happened to Billy the Kid.

ASH: At least your point of view. Now where were we?

(PACO *sits, takes a drink.*)

PACO: Garrett killed Tom O'Folliard, then he followed Billy and his compañeros to the old Rock House near

Fort Sumner. There he killed Bowdre and took Billy prisoner.

ASH: He took him to Las Vegas, where Billy met old Sheriff Romero again. Slept in his jail. Then down to Mesilla, where on April 13, 1881, Judge Bristol sentenced Billy to hang for the murder of Sheriff Brady.

PACO: And Governor Wallace washed his hands . . . like Pontius Pilate.

ASH: Except Billy wasn't no Christ.

PACO: Billy was the scapegoat! Wallace wanted to show the New York papers that he had brought law and order to New Mexico. It was politics! They played politics with the Kid's life! Wallace left the state for a new appointment and left Billy to hang! What kind of justice is that?

(ASH *shrugs.* GARRETT *enters, leading a shackled* BILLY. *Two deputies,* BELL *and* OLINGER, *follow with shotguns.*)

GARRETT: Well, Billy, this is your new home for a month.

(BILLY *is cheerful. He looks around.*)

BILLY: Dolan's old store.

GARRETT: County can't afford a courthouse, so we're using this.

(GARRETT *goes to the window, looks out. Sound of hammer banging on wood.*)

They're building the scaffold, Billy.

(BILLY *sits at the table.*)

BILLY: We covered our tracks when we headed up to the Rock House. How'd you find me?

GARRETT: Let's say I had a tip. (GARRETT *sits, takes a pack of cards from his pocket and tosses it at Billy.*) Might as well make ourselves comfortable till hanging day . . .

BILLY: I ain't gonna hang.

GARRETT: Court said to hang you come May 13, and I intend to follow the orders of the court.

BILLY: And I got a trip to Mexico planned. Hey, I can play better if you take these bracelets off . . .

(BILLY *holds up his hands and* BELL *starts forward with a key.*)

GARRETT: No! You give Billy Bonney a break and it'll cost you your life.

(BILLY *smiles. The two deputies back off as* GARRETT *and* BILLY *play monte.*)

BILLY: Sure makes it hard to deal . . .

GARRETT: I'll deal.

BILLY: How long we known each other, Pat?

GARRETT: First met in the autumn of '78, up in Fort Sumner.

BILLY: You were rustling cattle . . .

(GARRETT *looks uncomfortable. Glances at the deputies.*)

GARRETT: Some things in life a man'd rather forget.

BILLY: And now you're sheriff of Lincoln County.

GARRETT: That's fate.

BILLY: The Mexicans call it el destino. Forces that shape our life . . .

GARRETT: You are what you do, Billy. Don't go blaming anything or anyone.

BILLY: Oh, I'm not blaming anyone. I just remember don Manuelito telling me I was going to die at the hands of someone I helped . . . My destiny was to be betrayed by a friend.

(GARRETT *stares at Billy, again uncomfortable.*)

GARRETT: Our friendship was over long ago . . .

BILLY: Yeah, I guess. You know, I thought I was doing the right thing when I joined Tunstall and McSween.

GARRETT: Maybe so, but that gave you no right to kill Sheriff Brady.

BILLY: He killed Tunstall!

GARRETT: Tunstall treated you right, didn't he?

BILLY: Closest thing to a father I ever had . . .

GARRETT: I see . . .

BILLY: Back in '78, when we first met, I admired you, Pat. I still do.

GARRETT: They were good times. I haven't forgotten you saved my ass.

BILLY: Salazar and his boys were going to shoot you for rustling their cattle.

GARRETT: I was just trying to set up a meat store . . . (*They both laugh.*) I needed a few sides of beef to start. (*They laugh louder.*)

BILLY: You owe me one.

GARRETT: Yeah, I guess I do.

BILLY (*leans across the table*): You know it ain't right I should be the only one to pay for a gang war I didn't start. (GARRETT *nods.*) Turn me loose, Pat. Let me walk out of here and I'll get my woman and head for Mexico. I swear you'll never see me again.

GARRETT (*hesitates, then shakes his head*): I can't.

BILLY: I never begged, Pat. You know that. But you got me tied up like a monkey in a cage. (*He holds up his shackles.*) This ain't right, Pat! I'm a man! If I ain't free I'll die. (GARRETT *stands.*)

GARRETT: You should've thought of that when you took up the gun! Took up with your gang!

BILLY: Damnit, Pat! Bowdre and Tom and me were only protecting ourselves! You want to know where the real gang hangs out? Up in Santa Fe! The politicos of the Santa Fe Ring are the real gang! Catron and his business buddies make the money and we small fry got caught! Turn me loose, Pat! I'm begging you . . . (*He pleads, looks up at Garrett.*)

GARRETT: I'm sorry, Billy . . .

BILLY: I'm not going to hang, Pat.

(GARRETT, *shaken, turns to the two deputies.*)

GARRETT: I've got to ride up to White Oaks. You two watch Billy real close.

(OLINGER *approaches with shotgun in hand.*)

OLINGER: Why don't we just shoot him right now! Shoot him cold like he shot Beckwith! (*He strikes Billy with the rifle butt.*)

GARRETT: Back off, Bob! The Kid's a prisoner! He's in irons! (*He helps Billy to his feet.*)

BILLY: Pecos Bob likes to hit unarmed men. I've met bullies like you . . .

(BILLY'S *glare frightens* OLINGER.)

OLINGER: Let me kill 'im, Garrett! Kill 'im and be done!

GARRETT: The law will do that. You just watch him. (*He turns to Billy.*) Dammit, Billy! I wish there was something I could do.

(GARRETT *turns quickly. As he goes out* OLINGER *warns him.*)

OLINGER: Hurry back from White Oaks, Sheriff! You might not have a live prisoner when you return. (*He turns and points his shotgun at Billy.*) I'd just as soon shoot you now!

BELL: Hold on, Bob! You got no call.

OLINGER: I'm gonna dance the day you hang, Billy.

BILLY: I made a promise, Bob. I ain't gonna to hang.

OLINGER (*laughs*): I'd like to hear those words when I put the noose around your neck.

BELL: Give the Kid a break.

OLINGER: Okay, okay. Let 'im think about the noose. Let him squirm a little. You watch 'im, I'm goin' for a drink. (*He places his shotgun by the door and goes out.*)

BILLY: Play a little monte?

(BELL *is nervous.*)

BELL: No.

(BILLY *sits at the table, slips out of one handcuff.*)

BILLY: Just thought we'd pass the time.

BELL: I never played monte. I got my orders, I do them, and that's it.

BILLY: Then how about letting me go to the outhouse? It's been a long day.

(BELL *turns to open the door.* BILLY *jumps up, strikes Bell over the head, and takes his gun in the scuffle.*)

BILLY: Don't make me kill you!

(*A frightened* BELL *turns and runs.* BILLY *shoots him. Somebody shouts: "He shot Bell! He shot Bell!"* (BILLY *reaches for Olinger's shotgun.* OLINGER *rushes in.*)

BILLY: Greetings, Deputy.

(OLINGER *draws his pistol but realizes he has no chance.*)

OLINGER: Ah, God, he's killed me too.

BILLY: Rot in hell! (*He fires and kills Olinger, then goes to the window and spies the blacksmith.*) Gus! Bring up an axe and cut my irons! (BILLY *speaks to the gathering crowd.*)

You folks out there know I won't hurt you. I'm sorry I had to kill Bell, but he ran. Olinger was a rattlesnake who deserved killing. I'm gonna ride out of Lincoln, and I ain't ever coming back.

Sheriff Garrett wanted to hang Billy Bonney to teach you a lesson! You just remember, I didn't start the Lincoln County War! Big rancheros with a lot of greed in their hearts started the shooting. And they've got friends up in Santa Fe! That whole Santa Fe Ring wants to take your land and cattle and everything you got.

Dolan killed my friend Tunstall, and I evened the score. A hundred men took part in the fighting, and many a good one died. But it's not right only Billy Bonney be sentenced to death. Is it?

(*Someone shouts: "Head for Mexico, Billy! They won't find you there!"*)

BILLY: Thanks for the advice.

(GUS *enters with axe and cuts Billy's leg irons and shackles.* BILLY *shouts a cry of freedom and rushes out.*)

PACO (*whispers*): Head for Mexico, Billy . . .

ASH: He didn't.

PACO (*nods*): He went for Rosa . . .

ASH: Ah, I see what you mean about destino. Fate is about

to catch up with Billy. Garrett recruited John Poe and Tip McKinney to go up to Fort Summer to arrest Billy. On the night of July 14, by sheer coincidence, Garrett entered the bedroom of Pedro Maxwell, and is asking him if he's seen Billy, when Billy backs into the room . . .

PACO: You don't believe that, do you!

ASH: It's what Garrett told me.

PACO: He lied!

ASH: Pat Garrett was an honest man! There was no reason for him to lie!

PACO: Then you tell me! Why would Garrett go into don Pedro's bedroom in the middle of the night?

ASH: I've thought of that . . .

PACO: And if Billy ran into Poe outside, why didn't Poe shoot? Why did Billy enter don Pedro's bedroom right at that moment?

ASH (*shakes his head*): I don't know . . .

PACO: I'll tell you why . . .

(GARRETT *waits under a light in the dark on left side. At the right there is a bed with don Pedro in it. A lantern appears.*)

GARRETT: ¿Quién es?

JOSEFINA: Yo.

GARRETT: Josefina?

JOSEFINA: Buenas noches, Sheriff Garrett.

GARRETT: Buenas noches. You're up late.

JOSEFINA: I can't sleep, Sheriff. I walk the lonely streets at night . . . the people call me La Llorona. In my heart I am crying . . .

GARRETT: I'm looking for Billy.

JOSEFINA (*bitterly*): He's here. Walking the streets of Fort Sumner like a free man.

GARRETT: Where is he now?

JOSEFINA: With his querida.

GARRETT: I've got a warrant for his arrest. If you help me—

JOSEFINA: Billy won't be taken alive.

GARRETT: I've got two deputies with me. I aim to take him, dead or alive.

(JOSEFINA *shudders, moans softly.*)

JOSEFINA: If I cannot have him . . .

GARRETT: Do you know where he is?

JOSEFINA: Yes. Go to my father's bedroom. Wait there. Billy will come to you . . .

(JOSEFINA *goes out.* GARRETT *moves across the stage to the bed of don* PEDRO MAXWELL.)

GARRETT: Don Pedro?

DON PEDRO: ¿Quién es?

GARRETT: Sheriff Garrett.

DON PEDRO: Sit down, Pat. Don't make any noise . . .

(*A light shines,* BILLY *and* ROSA *enter. He holds her.*)

BILLY: Espera aquí.

ROSA: No. Voy contigo.

(BILLY *laughs.*)

BILLY: We have plenty of time to be together, querida. Tomorrow we leave for Mexico.

ROSA: A new life . . .

BILLY: Don Pedro wants to see me.

ROSA: Why so late?

BILLY: He owes me some money. Josefina said he's ready to pay.

ROSA: Josefina? No, Billy, don't go!

BILLY: Why are you trembling?

ROSA: There's no light in his room . . .

BILLY: The old cheapskate doesn't like to burn his oil. Wait.

ROSA: Billy.

BILLY: ¿Qué?

ROSA: I love you.

BILLY: Y yo te amo a ti . . .

(THEY *embrace warmly. Deputy* POE *appears.*)

ROSA: ¿Quién es?

(BILLY *pulls out his knife.* POE *backs away.*)

BILLY (*whispers*): Just one of don Pedro's vaqueros. Espera aquí. (*He leaves Rosa and softly enters don Pedro's bedroom.*)

BILLY: Don Pedro. Who is the man outside—
(GARRETT *stands. Billy faces him.*)
¿Quién es? ¿Quién es?

DON PEDRO: That's him!

BILLY: Garrett?

GARRETT: Soy yo.
(GARRETT *fires once,* BILLY *grabs at his gut in pain, steps forward, reaching for Garrett. The figure of death,* LA MUERTE, *appears.* CATHERINE *also appears, but* LA MUERTE *pushes her aside and goes to stand by Billy.*)

BILLY: Pat . . . You got me cold-blooded, Pat . . .
(GARRETT *fires again.* BILLY *winces, stumbles.*)

GARRETT (*in a trembling voice*): Die, Billy!

BILLY: Oh God, Pat . . . an old friend would kill me . . .
(BILLY *falls. The figure of* LA MUERTE *stands over him. There is a scream and* ROSA *rushes in to gather Billy in her arms.* POE *enters.* GARRETT *lights a candle.*)

POE: Did you get him?

GARRETT: I got him . . . (*He holds the candle over Billy and a sobbing Rosa.*)

ROSA: Billy! Billy! Oh, Bilito . . .

BILLY: I love you, Rosa . . .

ROSA: Amor, amor . . .
(BILLY *dies.* PACO *and three other men rush in. They look at Billy.*)

PACO: Billy!

ROSA: He's dead . . . Amor, amor . . . (*She holds and rocks Billy in her arms.*)

GARRETT: I had to shoot. He was armed.
(PACO *kicks the knife Billy dropped.*)

PACO: Armed? It's only a knife! (*He draws his pistol and aims at Garrett.*) ¡Cobarde!

GARRETT (*wincing*): I had to shoot . . .

(*The men pull PACO away.*)

1ST MAN: No, Paco!

2ND MAN: He's not worth killing.

(*PACO lowers his pistol; his head sinks.*)

PACO: Cobarde . . . Cobarde . . .

(*The men lift Billy and lay him on the bed. ROSA kneels at the bedside. Women carrying lighted candles appear. They place the candles around Billy's bed and kneel to pray.*)

WOMEN: Santa María, madre de Dios, ruega por nosotros pecadores hora y en la hora de nuestra muerte, amen. Ave María, llena eres de gracia, el Señor es contigo, bendita tú eres entre todas las mujeres, y bendito es El Fruto de tu vientre, Jesús . . .

(*The prayer decreases in volume. CATHERINE, Billy's mother, rises and walks slowly toward the bed. She is dressed in her wedding gown, appears pale and ghostly. LA MUERTE backs away into the shadows.*)

CATHERINE: Billy?

(*BILLY sits up.*)

BILLY: Mother?

CATHERINE: Yes, Billy, it's me.

BILLY: It's so dark, Mother. I can barely see you.

CATHERINE: It's always dark in this land of death. One never gets used to it. And the wind blows, the cries are the cries of lost souls . . . But I've found you, Billy. Thank God, I found you. It's time to go . . .

(*CATHERINE reaches out. BILLY draws back.*)

BILLY: But I was goin' to Mexico. Rosa and me—

CATHERINE: Hush, son. That dream is done. Come with me . . .

(*BILLY reaches for Rosa but cannot touch her.*)

BILLY: Tell her, Rosa! Tell her we're goin' to Mexico! We're gonna start a new life. Get married, raise kids, start a ranch! Just like we planned!

(BILLY *reaches frantically for Rosa but cannot hold her.*)

CATHERINE: She can't hear you, son. She's full of grief. Maybe with time she'll hear your voice, or dream you are near her. But now the violence of life is ended. Come with me.

(CATHERINE *holds out her hand.* BILLY *looks longingly at Rosa, then takes his mother's hand and walks away with her.* LA MUERTE *follows them quietly. The women continue to pray softly as the men sing the corrido.*)

CORRIDO:

Escuchen paisanos, Nuevo Mexicanos,
Voy a cantarles un corrido muy triste
De un joven valiente que murio traisionado
Alla en Fort Sumner esta enterado

Era valiente y muy aresgado
Le gustaba cantar y baile pero suave
Sabia jugar la barajas y jugar el amor
Pero con pistola muy lista y muy brava.

No piensen que fue solo una mujer
Que le puso el dedo y lo traisiono!
Es que en este mundo, cada hombre es prisionero
De un destine que a la muerte lo lleva.

Cuenta la gente del Río Pecos
Que ya le tocaba, y por eso murio
Fue balaciado por el sharife de Lincoln
Que le traiva las ganas, y dos balas le dio!

Y aquellos políticos del Santa Fe Ring
Se reien y se pagan con oro
El governor Wallace a otras tierras se fue
Dejando a los pobres sufriendo.

Hay, Rosita, Rosita, que tristeza me da
De verte llorando y llorando

Y madres de mundo, aconsejen sus hijos
Que no acaben su vida, como el Bilito querido.
(*The corrido ends, the women continue to pray softly
around the bed. All are frozen onstage, except PACO,
who approaches* ASH.)

ASH: You don't believe that don Pedro and his daughter—

PACO: How else did Garrett know Billy was going to show up in don Pedro's room?

ASH (*shrugs*): A question that has remained unanswered—

PACO: Until now.

ASH: But it's conjecture, nothing more—

PACO: Hey! You made up what you wrote in that little pinche book!

ASH: But I—

PACO: I know! You had Pat Garrett telling you the story. Big deal, ese! Everybody tells the story to suit himself! (ASH *hands* PACO *the bottle. He empties it.*)

PACO: We need a new bottle.

ASH: There's a cantina down the street . . . (ASH *places his arm around* PACO *and they go off the stage, down one of the aisles, arguing.*)

ASH: What do you think, amigo? Is there any truth to history?

PACO: There is if you put it in! (PACO *laughs.* ASH *pauses.*)

ASH: Or is history a myth we write to please ourselves . . .

PACO: El Bilito is a myth. He had good and bad in him, just like every man. I saw the good, el sharife Garrett saw the bad.

ASH: So you were prejudiced when you wrote about him?

PACO: Sure, I loved the kid.

ASH: Your love becomes a new element in the myth . . .

PACO: Why not? Those were violent times. You needed a little love to keep you going.

ASH: It's sad to see a kid die that young . . . For a moment he had Rosa's love . . .

PACO: That's all he had, amigo. That's all he had.
   (PACO *places his arm around* ASH's *shoulders and they*
   go out.)

   The End

"Walt Whitman Strides the Llano of New Mexico"

I met Walt, kind old father, on the llano,
    that expanse of land of eagle and cactus
Where the Mexicano met the Indio, and both
    met the tejano, along the Río Pecos, our
    River of blood, River of Billy the Kid,
    River of Fort Sumner where the Diné suffered,
    River of the Golden Carp, god of my gods.

He came striding across the open plain,
    There where the owl calls me to
        the shrine of my birth,
    There where Ultima buried my soul-cord, the
        blood, the afterbirth, my destiny.

His beard, coarse, scraggly, warm, filled with sunlight,
    like llano grass filled with grasshoppers, grillos,
    protection for lizards and jackrabbits,
    rattlesnakes, coyotes, and childhood fears.

"Buenos días, don Walt!" I called. "I have been
 waiting for you. I knew you would one day leap
  across the Mississippi!
 Leap from Mannahatta! Leap over Brooklyn Bridge!
   Leap over slavery!
 Leap over the technocrats!
  Leap over atomic waste!
 Leap over the violence! Madonna!
   Dead end rappers!
    Peter Jennings and ungodly nightly news!
 Leap over your own sex! Leap to embrace la gente
  de Nuevo México! Leap to miracles!"

I always knew that. I dreamed that.

I knew you would one day find the Mexicanos of my land,
 the Nuevo Mexicanos who kicked ass with our
 Indian ancestors, kicked ass with the tejanos,
 And finally got their ass kicked by politicians!
 I knew you would find us Chicanos, en la pobreza,
 Always needing change for a ride or a pint,
 Pero ricos en el alma! Ricos en nuestra cultura!
 Ricos con sueños y memoria!

I kept the faith, don Walt, because I always knew
 You could leap continents! Leap over the squalor!
 Leap over pain and suffering, and the ash heap we
 Make of our Earth! Leap into my arms.

Let me nestle in your bigote, don Walt, as I once
 nestled in my abuelo's bigote, don Liborio,
 Patriarch of the Mares clan, padre de mi mamá,
 Farmer from Puerto de Luna, mestizo de España y
 México, Católico y Judío, Moro y indio, francés
 Y mountain man, hombre de la tierra!

Let me nestle in your bigote, don Walt, like I once
   nestled in the grass of the llano, on summer days,
   a child lost in the wide expanse, brother to lagarto,
   jackrabbit, rattlesnake, vulture and hawk.
   I lay sleeping in the grama grass, feeling
   the groan of the Earth beneath me, tierra sagrada!
   Around me, grasshoppers chuffing, mocking bird calling,
   meadowlark singing, owl warning, rabbit humping,
   flies buzzing, worms turning, vulture and hawk
   riding air currents, brujo spirits moving across
   my back and raising the hair of my neck,
   golden fish of my ponds tempting me to believe
   in the gods of the earth, water, air and fire.
   Oriente, poniente, norte, sur, y yo!
   Dark earth groaning beneath me, sperm flowing,
   sky turning orange and red, nighthawks dart, bats
   flitter, the mourning call of La Llorona filling the
   night wind as the *presence of the river* stirred, called my
   name: "Hijo! Hiiiii-jo!"

And I fled, fled for the safety of my mother's arms.

You know the locura of childhood, don Walt—
   That's why I welcome you to the llano, my llano,
   My Nuevo México! Tierra sagrada! Tierra sangrada!

Hold me in the safety of your arms, wise poet, old poet,
   Abuelo de todos. Your fingers stir my memory.

The high school teachers didn't believe in the magic
   of the Chicano heart. They fed me palabras sin sabor
   when it was your flesh I yearned for. Your soul.
   They teased us with "O Capitan, My Capitan!"
   Read silently so as to arouse no passion, no tears,
   no erections, no bubbling love for poetry.

Qué desgracia! What a disgrace! To give my soul only
   one poem in four years when you were a universe!

Qué desgracia! To give us only your name, when you were
   Cosmos, and our brown faces yearned for
   the safety of your bigote, your arms!

Qué desgracia! That you have to leap from your grave,
   Now, in this begetting time, to kick ass with
   this country which is so slow to learn that
   we are the magic in the soul! We are the dream
   of Aztlán!

Qué desgracia! That my parents didn't even know your name!
   Didn't know that in your *Leaves of Grass* there was
   salvation for the child.
   I hear my mother's lament: "They gave me no education!"
   I understand my father's stupor: "They took *mi honor, mi
   orgullo, mi palabra.*"

Pobreza de mi gente! I strike back now! I bring you
   don Walt to help gird our loins!
   Este viejo es guerrillero por la gente!
   Guerrillero por los pobres! Los de abajo!

Save our children now! I shout. Put *Leaves of Grass* in their
   lunch boxes! In the tacos and tamales!
   Let them call him Abuelo! As I call him Abuelo!

Chicano poets of the revolution! Let him fly with you
   As your squadrons of words fill the air over
   Aztlán! Mujeres chicanas! Pull his bigote as you
   Would tug at a friendly abuelo! His manhood is ours!
   Together we are One!

Pobreza! Child wandering the streets of Alburqué! Broken
   by the splash of water, elm seed ghost, lost and by winds

of spring mourned, by La Llorona of the Río Grande
    mourned, outcast, soul-seed, blasted by the wind
        of the universe, soul-wind, scorched by the
    Grandfather Sun, Lady Luna, insanity, grubs scratching
        at broken limbs, fragmented soul.

I died and was buried and years later I awoke from
    the dead and limped up the hill where your
        Leaves of Grass lay buried in library stacks.

"Chicano Child Enters University!" the papers cried.
    Miracle child! Strange child! Dark Child!
        Speaks Spanish Child! Has Accent Child!
    Needs Lots of Help Child! Has No Money Child!
        Needs A Job Child! Barrio Child!
    Poor People's Child! Gente Child! Drop Out Child!

"I'll show you," I sobbed, entering the labyrinth of loneliness,
    dark shadows of library, cold white classrooms.

You saved me, don Walt, you and my familia which held
    Me up, like a crutch holding the one-leg Man,
        Like Amor holding the lover,
            Like kiss holding the flame of Love.

You spoke to me of your Mannahatta, working men and women,
    miracle of democracy, freedom of the soul, the suffering
    of the Great War, the death of Lincoln, the lilacs' last
    bloom, the pantheism of the Cosmos, the miracle of Word.

Your words caressed my soul, soul meeting soul,
    You opened my mouth and forced me to speak!
    Like a cricket placed on dumb tongue,
    Like the curandera's healing herbs and
    Touch which taught me to see beauty,
    Your fingers poked and found my words!

You drew my stories out.
You believed in the Child of the Llano.

I fell asleep on *Leaves of Grass*, covering myself with
your bigote, dreaming my ancestors, my healers,
the cuentos of their past, dreams and memories.

I fell asleep in your love, and woke to my mother's
tortillas on the comal, my father's cough, my
familia's way to work, the vast love which was
an ocean in a small house.

I woke to write my *Leaves of Llano Grass*, the cuentos
of the llano, tierra sagrada! I thank the wise
teacher who said, "Dark Child, read this book!
You are grass and to grass you shall return."

"Gracias, don Walt! Enjoy your stay. Come again. Come
Every day. Our niños need you, as they need
Our own poets. Maybe you'll write a poem in Spanish,
I'll write one in Chinese. All of poetry is One."